WITH EACH NEW DAWN

This extraordinary story classically captures the mindset of the 1940s. Addie and her friend Kate reflect the voices women hear as they face confusing dilemmas 75 years later—my first read kept me up into the wee hours. I will refer my readers to *In Times Like These*!

Patricia Evans, author of
The Verbally Abusive Relationship

Wartime brings out the best and the worst in people. I loved the way Addie and Kate, each in her own way, dug down inside to become more than either had ever dreamed. *With Each New Dawn* will inspire you toward resilience and personal growth even as it keeps you riveted with each page turn.

Sonia C. Solomonson, freelance writer and life coach
Way2Grow Coaching

I*n Times Like These* clearly portrays the difficulties for women during WW2. First, there are the challenges of raising food, preserving it, making money stretch, wisely using ration cards and just plain living in fear of the war. But then the overlay of Addie's controlling husband made me instantly empathize with the main character. His verbally abusive and cold treatment of Addie unfortunately is not just a problem from another era. God's provision for her was intriguing. The value of faith, friendship and compassion are evident in this book. I personally enjoyed the food tips and recipes, as well as vivid descriptions of farm life. This may be my favorite book by Gail Kittleson. It is the first in the mini-series, *Women of the Heartland*. Be sure to read the books in order.

Cleo Lampos, co-author of
A World War 2 Holiday Scrapbook
The Food That Held the World Together

Gail Kittleson introduces us to a small town community, under the strains of World War II. The everyday lives of the town folks unfolding their thoughts and concern for the husbands and brothers fighting for their country. The family and friends dynamics in this story keeps the reader wanting to turn page after page. The author knows how to keep the reader engaged. Looking forward to Ms. Kittleson's next book.

K Currie

Kittleson's writing style fosters instant empathy as her quiet heroine, Addie, struggles through daily living in Iowa during WW2. Readers are introduced to Addie through patriotism, friendship, and self-realization. "I've spent my whole life in fear instead of living each day," highlights Addie's growth in overcoming an emotionally abusive husband. Highest recommendation.

Carolyn Cobb

…the pages almost turned themselves. Great period piece exploring family dynamics and interpersonal relationships as well as the growth of self-esteem and the importance of friendship.

Lisa Lickel

Kittleson deftly writes strong female characters facing heartbreaking tragedies. *Until Then* features two: Marian, caught in the Blitz, and Dorothy, a surgical nurse whose work with the 11th Evacuation Hospital has taken her to North Africa, through Sicily and into France. Their stories intertwine in a narrative that touches then heals the soul. Highly, highly recommended!

Literary Soirée

Land that I Love compares to the best of all literature from throughout the ages … an enriching and enchanting experience.

D.A. Featherling, author of
Fear Not

Also by Gail Kittleson

Women of the Heartland Series
In Times Like These
With Each New Dawn
A Purpose True
All for the Cause
Until Then
Kiss Me Once Again

and

In This Together
Catching Up With Daylight
Secondhand Sunsets
Land That I Love

with Cleo Lampos
The Food that Held the World Together
A World War II Holiday Scrapbook

with Billy Rae Stewart
Country Music's Hidden Gem

Women of the Heartland, Volume 2

With Each New Dawn

a novel

GAIL KITTLESON

WordCrafts

To the women who fought their own battles on the home front.

Chapter One

Moist clay stuck to Kate's two-toned Sylvia heels as she turned past a demolished block toward Mrs. Tenney's house. Cement powder rode the air even in the heavy May mist, a reminder of the Luftwaffe reducing great hunks of London to dust during the Blitz.

On Kate's left, a displaced occupant sifted through the remains of his home every afternoon. The hunch-shouldered, white-haired phantom never even looked up when she passed. Mrs. Tenney said his hair had bleached overnight as he failed to grasp the reality of losing his family—for two years now, he'd faithfully searched the rubble.

Shattered bricks dotted the surrounding area like limestone rocks in an Iowa pasture. The image roused a wave of homesickness and brought Kate's best friend Addie to mind.

"Oh, Addie, I miss you so much. We thought my trip would last months at most, but fate had other ideas."

A few blocks from home, a short-legged, barrel-chested fellow approached. His low-slung beret slanted like an awning over his eyes and his upturned collar buttressed him against the drizzle. Built low enough to the earth that his trench coat grazed the sidewalk, his girth made up for his height.

She'd noticed him a few times before, but today, he came near enough to waft the smell of old wool, strong coffee, and a hint of stale tobacco. Kate stiffened. Maybe, like the man going through his house, the war had *tipped* him.

With two blocks to go and not another soul in sight, he halted before her and removed his beret, standing his thick dark hair on end. Three deep, leathery creases tunneled above a prominent nose set between dark, fiery eyes that seemed oddly familiar. His deep resonant tone sent a chill through Kate.

"Marguerite Dumont."

"Pardon me?"

"*Aussi vrai que je respire. Vous êtes la fille du Madame Dumont.*"

His smooth statement rang with certainty, and ignited Kate's childhood French. *As I live and breathe, you are the daughter of Madame Dumont.* His resonant voice jolted something deep inside her, almost as if she'd heard this exact intonation before. A fitting response sat on her tongue, but she'd better resort to English, to keep him wondering.

"As you live and breathe? Sir, I cannot be Marguerite Dumont's child, for that name is unfamiliar."

A brown stained forefinger waggled. "I knew your mother." Caressing the English with slow deliberation, his breath wafted onion and a mysterious spice. His full lips twitched under a vagabond mustache, but his eyes held no malice.

"No, Monsieur, that is not possible. I am American."

The fire in his eyes flared higher. "*Oui*, you come from Iowa." His imperfect pronunciation of the *i* like an *e* tightened Kate's throat. How could he possibly know that? A trickster breeze tickled her ankles and she shivered again.

"Iowa—"

"Without question, you are Madame Dumont's daughter."

The trill of truth skittered her spine. "Monsieur, I'm afraid you mistake me for someone else."

Sharp heels clicked, and the peak of Mrs. Tenney's shiny black umbrella appeared over a slight rise. Her version of Veronica Lake's perfect victory roll upheld a tawny velvet hat, and sunlight emblazoned the Women's Auxiliary pin on her jaunty red plaid wool jacket.

Always the lady, she paused a reasonable distance away, but

held out a courteous gloved hand with a verbena scent. Although grateful that Mrs. T allowed her to share her home when her son Charles hired her at his office, Kate sometimes resisted her caretaking. But this time, relief flooded her.

"I had begun to worry about you, Kathryn. Is anything wrong?" She returned Kate's grasp and, eyes narrowed, faced the stranger. "Good day, Sir."

"*Bonsoir, Madame.*"

"This man says he knew my mother. I told him he's mistaken, but nothing shakes him." Mrs. Tenney towered over the Frenchman while questions deluged Kate, along with a weight in the pit of her stomach. Someone who knew her mother, right here on the streets of London—how could this be?

"Do you speak English, Monsieur, and what is your name?"

He shrugged and took a long breath. "A leettle. I am Monsieur Le Blanc."

"You say you know this young woman's mother?"

"*Oui,* from France."

"When?"

"She worked as an *Allô Fille* at the Front." His profuse eyebrows formed a fuzzy caterpillar between his temples. "In ze Great War. Beleef me. Ees true."

Kate's scalp went cold. Her mother did work overseas, though Aunt Alvina never mentioned her being a Bell Telephone Hello Girl. After Kate moved from the East Coast to Halberton when her parents died, Aunt Alvina offered only sparse information. The "Hello Girl" scenario seemed plausible enough. Still, she'd never pictured her mother tending a switchboard at the front in the Great War.

A lump blocked Kate's throat, for a peculiar security came in knowing few specifics about the past. That way, she could hold it at bay, free to imagine whatever she pleased. But at the same time, an old, tenacious hunger gripped her at the word *mother* and the backs of her eyes burned.

Mrs. Tenney tightened her hold on Kate's hand. "What documentation do you offer?"

"I haf photographs of Madame Dumont. I know her husband, also."

Nameless, ragged desire inundated Kate. She wanted to shout, "Prove it to me," as she had a few months back when officials notified her of her husband Alexandre's death. After all the wild ups and downs of searching for him, finding him, and then having him crash again, she'd been loathe to believe the worst.

But when the RAF messengers quietly held out a parcel containing Alexandre's dog tags and personal effects, she had no choice. She'd been working at starting life anew without him, but now this stranger was asking her to open another painful wound from long ago.

Mrs. Tenney propelled her sharp nose forward like a goose, directly into the Frenchman's line of vision. "This girl has already lost her husband in the war. If you are serious, be at that little park down the way at precisely seven thirty tonight."

She gestured with her umbrella. "My son, Mr. Charles Tenney, a lawyer and government official, will be present."

Variegated brown and yellow teeth peeked between Monsieur's lips. "I will be there, Madame. *Au revoir.*" He saluted and turned on his heel.

Mrs. Tenney steered toward home, but halfway there, Kate pulled on her elbow. "I can't help but wonder how he happened to come this way just when I was walking home. I've seen him before, though, and usually about this time of day."

"Quite the coincidence, eh? War can play such peculiar tricks on a person."

"Did you say Charles is a lawyer?"

Mrs. Tenney sputtered, "Not *technically*, Dear, but he's equal to one. I wanted to show that chap what sort of people he's dealing with. You never know these days, Kathryn. Deceivers pull all kinds of stunts, and we must beware." She turned to Kate. "Do you think that man's story could possibly be true?"

"I don't know—that would've been before I was born, and my aunt told me very little."

Back home, Mrs. Tenney called Charles, who said he'd stop by for Kate. Dinner was leftover meat pie and a biscuit sweetened by a jar of jam Addie had sent a few weeks before.

"Do tell your friend when you write again how much we enjoy this bit of sweetness, Kathryn. Just think how dry our biscuits would be without it. Do you think she made it herself?"

"She did. Addie can cook almost anything."

"And she's so generous to share with us. Have you heard? Those American P-38s did indeed kill Admiral Yamamoto last month. Your folks back home must be celebrating."

"I'm sure they are."

"We've taken Tunisia's Longstop Hill, and soon, allied troops will command Tunis. Thank Heavens for your fighter squadrons and the Palm Sunday Massacre—I'm so grateful you Americans came to our aid."

Mrs. Tenney seemed bent on discussing recent war events, but Kate had all she could do to concentrate on the conversation. A rising riptide of curiosity swelled inside her with every bite she took. That very night, in just a little over an hour, she might learn something about the puzzle that had haunted her sleep all through her youth.

Charles rang at seven fifteen, and at seven thirty, true to his word, the Frenchman awaited them on a bench. His coat collar was bunched up around his chin, and a thickening haze added to his intrigue.

Kate clasped her throat beneath a heavy scarf Mrs. Tenney had wrapped around her neck before she and Charles left the house.

Solid as steel, he tightened his elbow to secure Kate's fingers against his coat. Monsieur stood, and her mouth went dry. She croaked to Charles, "You do the talking."

"If you wish."

Mr. Tenney held out his hand. "Monsieur?"

"Le Blanc. And you are Meester Tenney?"

"Yes, Kate's employer, and er—" He hesitated. "My mother says you have some photographs to show her?"

Monsieur Le Blanc sprawled across the bench and fumbled with the latches of a black leather attaché case. He pulled out a yellowed envelope with his stumpy fingers.

This moment will change your life forever. Suddenly faint, Kate let go of Charles' arm and sank beside the Frenchman. Charles stepped back to hold the umbrella over her as Monsieur le Blanc twisted her way.

"Madame Dumont liked to speak of Iowa, land of corn and cows. Her sister, her name ees—Alveera?"

A precise knot cinched Kate's stomach, but she held her piece. *Alvira—definitely close enough to Aunt Alvina's name.*

He wiggled out a black and white photograph showing a young woman at the end of a long wooden telephone switchboard. Behind her, a cord battened back a tent flap.

Fine black hairs above Monsieur's fingernails hovered over that blond Hello Girl's long black dress. A tremor traced Kate's backbone. The young worker's profile could not have borne more resemblance to her mother's portrait on Aunt Alvina's bookshelf.

Mr. Tenney touched Kate's arm, his eyes reflecting concern. She straightened her shoulders as he addressed the stranger.

"You have more?"

At another photo with an even more vivid rendering of Madame Dumont's face, Kate hugged her arms, helpless in the draw of those sparkling eyes.

Once again, Charles took up her cause. "This afternoon you made a rash pronouncement that profoundly unsettled my employee. What else do you know about this Madame Dumont?"

"That ees not my intent. I would not speak so eef eet were not true." The Frenchman slipped out a third photograph, a close-up that snatched Kate's breath.

"But ees true."

His wide palm balanced her mother's graduation likeness, a copy of the very one that hung above Aunt Alvina's mantel. Sometimes, when no one was looking, Kate used to sit before the fireplace, simply staring at her mother's likeness. She would know that expression anywhere.

"Where did you get this—?"

He answered in melodic French phrases. "Madame Dumont stood out as a leader among the operators. Once, she refused an evacuation order and rallied the others." Monsieur Le Blanc spoke quickly, then he closed his eyes and tipped his head as if calling up memories. Perhaps because of Mr. Tenney's throat clearing, he broke into English.

"Ah, sorry—ees difficult to say in English."

But Kate understood every word.

"Madame Dumont, she say, 'We shall continue to do our job. We came here to work—we'll show zem what women are—how you say—made of.'"

He gave Kate a broad smile. "Your mother ees very strong, Mademoiselle."

You're just like your mother. That was Aunt Alvina's consistent comment when Kate's headstrong nature reared in defiance of Halberton, Iowa's outdated traditions. The correlation brought Kate's breath up short.

Mr. Tenney leaned toward her. "Have you seen enough?"

Enough? She hesitated. How could she ever see enough? Perhaps the envelope contained more photographs. Monsieur might know how her parents met, or even what led to their deaths. What if he held more clues to unravel all of her troubling questions? Monsieur's eyes never left her face, and she saw that he read her longing.

He reopened the envelope. "You desire to see more?" The next photograph featured a large group, including three men. "The one in the shadows on the right ees your father—*le Renard Intrepid.*"

His rolled *r* dipped right into Kate's heart, and a broken sigh parted her lips. She almost cried out, "My father?"

Monsieur held up his palms. "All ze *allo* girls—how you

say?— *swooned* over him, but your mother, she won ze prize." His sigh accompanied a faraway look. "You would like to keep zese?"

"Oh, yes. Thank you." Kate's thoughts churned. What was Monsieur le Blanc doing with this photograph?

"I stay perhaps one more month at this address." He scrawled something on a piece of paper and handed it to her. She was experiencing an almost irresistible urge to move closer, to hold onto this encounter, to learn as much as possible about her father.

At the same time, something told her this mysterious stranger knew that she did. She'd never met him until today, but had the sensation that he saw into her soul. That intuition in his eyes caused her to sidestep closer to Mr. Tenney, who offered her his arm.

"*Merci, Monsieur.* Good evening to you, then."

They started to walk away, but with each step, Kate's incessant curiosity swelled. She'd always denied her insatiable questions as unanswerable, yet now—Perhaps she could ask just one more thing. But when she turned to look back, her heart fell. Monsieur Le Blanc had already vanished in the ever-thickening haze.

Charles saw her to the back door, and Kate hurried upstairs to prop the photographs on her bureau. Alone with her scant memories and still wearing her coat and scarf, a groan rose from her inmost being.

"Mother—who are you? Who were you?"

Reading what Monsieur added below his address on the paper scrap only heightened her interest. "Your eyes reveal your mother's courage. Many suffer now and need your help."

He seemed to know her better than she knew herself—he reminded her of a fortune-teller passing through Halberton one summer in a gypsy caravan.

A sharp kick in the abdomen reminded Kate of her unborn child, the last remnant of the love she and Alexandre shared, the fruit of his twenty-four hour Christmas pass. She sloughed off her wraps and smoothed her bulging midriff.

"But this stranger had no idea—my coat hid our baby." The

realization brought her some comfort as she put on her warm nightgown and stacked pillows against her headboard.

Maybe reading a book would calm her mind. But her mother's determined brows and that set-to-conquer-the-world look in her eyes laid claim to Kate. What must it have been like in earshot of the terrible fighting on the Front? And the journey across the Atlantic—undoubtedly much more arduous than her own a year and a half ago.

A knock on the door forced Kate back to the present. "Come on in."

"Are you feeling all right?"

"Yes, fine. Thank you for asking."

Mrs. Tenney followed Kate's glance. "Is this your mother, then? She's beautiful, and your facial features replicate hers. Your dark eyes must come from your father's side?"

"My father's side—maybe so. Until today, I knew nothing about him. "Kate's voice forsook her, so Mrs. Tenney continued.

"What a day it has been for you, Kathryn. Who would have guessed such a treasure would come to you in this extraordinary way?"

"Yes. I–I don't know quite what to think. Maybe it's just the war. Otherwise, Monsieur Le Blanc might not even be in London."

"Indeed. And neither would you. That reminds me, have I mentioned lately how glad I am that you came?"

Mrs. Tenney crossed the room and eased her forefinger over the photograph. "She truly is lovely. Those eyes, so dauntless and daring—she left her home for such a dangerous task. I would think your Aunt would have regaled you with stories about her—"

"No, Aunt Alvina never mentioned her unless I asked. And then, she always seemed abrupt. I've often wondered why."

"Hmm. Families can be so complicated. Perhaps she hesitated to open old wounds. Perhaps she loved your mother dearly, but couldn't bear having her taken from this life so young."

"I'll never know." Once again, Kate connected with her mother's eyes in the photograph. "But it's nothing new, really. My whole life, I've hungered to know about my parents, and finally learned to set my questions aside. I guess I can do it again, can't I?"

"At least now you know what your father looked like, and what they called him. He must have been quite famous." Mrs. Tenney turned to Kate with thought lines deep in her brow. "In the States, do you ever use our old saying, 'Let sleeping dogs lie?'"

She paused and Kate recalled her kindness on those winter days when nausea forced her home from work. Often, Mrs. Tenney produced dry toast and precious rationed tea, and sometimes even an egg in the middle of the day. When asked how she managed with such severe shortages, she skirted the question.

"I have my methods—never underestimate a determined British woman."

But now, Mrs. Tenney stepped back as if dismissed. "Good night, then. Do let me know if you need anything." Her footsteps continued down the hall, and from her bedside table drawer, Kate pulled out a picture Aunt Alvina took years ago, of her and Addie dressed up like Barbara Stanwyk and Myrna Loy.

"We can always talk mysteries through, Addie, and you often see things I don't. Your ship must be leaving soon. Believe me, I have a million questions for you when you get here, and we'll make up for lost time."

Kate padded to her bureau for a magnifying glass and turned over the switchboard photograph. On the back, black ink faded into the pale blue cardboard.

"*Bon courage. Marguerite.*" The crackled backing showed another muted inscription: "*Au Renard Intrepid.*"

"To the Intrepid Fox. Why, my mother gave this to him, wishing him good luck! But if the Intrepid Fox really is my father, how did Monsieur Le Blanc get these photos?"

She propped the picture above her bedside table and shut off the light. When she opened the blackout drape, faint moonshine danced through the curtains and played with the sparkles in her mother's eyes. The sight piqued a vast ache under Kate's ribs.

Your mother's courage—many suffer now and need your help. For sleepless hours, Monsieur's note troubled her. Why should she meet him now, when she needed help herself? Another kick from her baby reminded her that Addie crossed a dangerous ocean right now for that very purpose.

"If only I knew what he meant about your courage, Mother."

But the silent photograph lent her no favors. *Let sleeping dogs lie.* Maybe Aunt Alvina had good reason not to detail the past—in every other way, she'd provided for Kate's needs.

But those sleeping dogs barked all night long, and in the half-light before dawn, Kate sat up in bed and punched her pillow. Her mother's smile seemed to chastise her now. What good did all of her conjecturing do? She gave herself a fierce talking-to.

"You must forget all this, Kate Isaacs, be the best mother possible, and honor Alexandre's memory. The last thing this world needs is another orphaned child."

But that thought led to more queries. Had her mother considered her when she went off on her last trip, years after her stint for Bell Telephone? What if she'd been given a post-war espionage assignment, and she couldn't say no? Or, had the thrill of adventure called more strongly than her own daughter? And what had caused Aunt Alvina's steadfast silence about the woman Monsieur Le Blanc called courageous?

Kate swallowed a spike of bitterness, though she knew speculating about her mother's frame of mind would do no good. No matter what, she wanted to turn the tables and be there completely for her own child. Nothing was worth risking that all-important responsibility. She buried her head in her pillow and tried to catch a little sleep before her alarm called her into the new day.

But that scrap of paper Monsieur slipped into her hand appeared before her mind's eye—*perhaps one more month at this address—* She grappled with the final searching expression in his eyes until daybreak.

Chapter Two

Late winter 1943, the Department of Lot, Southern France

A captive ewe bleated in early morning sunshine while Domingo combed its fleece for insects. Finally, *La Résistance* had left him alone for a few days, so he fell into shepherding, as Basque shepherds were born to do. In the unforced rhythm of night following day and the utter reliability of Maman's rich porridge, he regained his balance.

Yesterday afternoon, unseasonable warmth and a gentle breeze wooed him to sleep, and he might well succumb again today. With the dependable family sheepdog at hand to alert him of trouble, he enjoyed this uncommon leisure.

He loosed the ewe from his grasp and without a sound, his mother, no taller than his shoulder, stood near him. She clasped her ever-present shawl in one hand and a lunch basket in the other. "Hard thoughts fill your head, my son."

Domingo chuckled. "You are so stealthy, *Maman*. If you were the Germans, I would be dead."

Her visible tremble caused him regret, but her next utterance challenged him. "Will they reach our land?"

"I have heard nothing for a few days."

"But you know."

"No one has yet seen troops cross the border into Lot, and the sentries are watching, believe me. Remember, we live more than three hundred kilometres from Vichy, and Paris is almost six hundred kilometres north of here."

Her worry lines gave way a bit.

"After this war, Maman, I only want to care for sheep. To never leave these hills again will be my delight." Domingo feasted his eyes on gentle slopes nestling the back pasture and the farmyard into a pleasant circle.

"But Jean-Luc Edorta says Général Petain will not protect us. The new capitol, up on the banks of the Allier, turns to the enemy now. Your father would not believe such of the Général, but even Jean-Luc says it is true."

"People only repeat what they hear. We hope the fighting will not range south of Vichy, but rest assured, the Ségala heights teem with men to defend us if necessary."

Maman fixed her eyes northward to the high plateau that grew the best rye in the land. These days, doomsayers multiplied like the chestnut groves peppering the border between the Departments of the Cantal and the Lot. Predictions of Nazi tank battalions rolling through these quiet hills en route from their winter fittings at Toulouse shook Domingo, too.

Where once life revolved around flock and family, the evil order that stalked Basqueland commandeered everyone's attention. And yes, he'd heard the rumors. How could peasants stand against iron monsters with swastikas emblazoned on their sides? But why frighten Maman?

"Aitaita's father won this land at great price. Would that we had a proper Basque house with hay in the top story for insulation and animals below to lend us their warmth in winter, but I have grown to love this place." She glanced around the homestead, which Domingo's great-grandfather, Ager Ibarra, earned through many years' labor for a childless French couple.

Thickness swelled Domingo's throat at her reference to his grandfather. For, always, Aitaita lingered close to his heart. Maman nurtured ancient traditions as she did her growing boys. Now, she left the basket near Domingo and shrank back toward their homestead.

"No, those detested Nazis must not come here. Such a thing must not be." Domingo formed a fist and held it high against the Reich. Every pilot he saw to safety over the Pyrénées, every parachute drop he met on starlit meadows made a difference for France, but in his solitary moments, uncertainty niggled him. Would these efforts be enough?

He moved sheep to fresh pasture, cleansed an infected eye, and checked an ewe showing abnormal signs of bloat. He couldn't expect his brother Gabirel to recognize such subtle issues—after all, he was only fourteen and should still be in school.

At midmorning, two scruffy *Maquisards* appeared over a ridge, gesturing east. "A downed plane, toward the mountains."

They vanished as quickly as they had come, but their message changed Domingo's plans. As suddenly as a fly lands on a sheep's ear, he inherited another mission.

Gabirel, eight years younger, but strong and capable, responded to Domingo's whistle. His profile reflected Aitaita's, but Domingo refrained from ruffling the lad's thick black hair in brotherly affection. Because of this war, Gabirel had passed into manhood far too young.

"I'll be back. Take care." The explanation Domingo might have given a year or two ago had become unnecessary—Maquisards, men of the brush, the backbone of the La Résistance, stood waiting, and Gabirel was no stranger to them stopping with an urgent task for Domingo. Gabirel headed toward the sheepfold, and Domingo raced to the house, where Maman had already filled his knapsack.

Her delicate frame, slender as a twig in his embrace, made him gulp. Once outside, he waited until Gabirel turned his back. Better not to know the direction he took, in case of interrogation, for deceiving well was a learned art. Domingo, once unschooled in lying, now misled the gray-coated authorities without a pang of conscience.

Miracle enough, considering the retribution he and his older brother Ander suffered for playing childhood tricks. Ander's idea of fun often led to trouble, and once to a very sick pig. In that case, hard labor had assuaged their neighbor Jean-Luc Edorta's wrath.

The messengers pointed down the path a distance, and Domingo's next guidance came in the form of another partisan devoted to helping the Allies. They exchanged greetings, and Domingo adopted the man's fast pace toward the waiting pilots. On the way, he revisited that experience with Jean-Luc's pig.

Ander must have been twelve, two years older than Domingo, so when he proposed a plan, Domingo never thought to question. They were cutting weeds for Jean-Luc in the stifling summer heat, and at one point, Ander wiped his dripping brow.

"It is so miserable today—*bero-bero*." True enough—not just hot, but *hot-hot*. "We need some fun. Let's throw some rotted garlic in the slop and watch what the pigs do." A pleasant, temporary diversion from pitching hay—besides, Jean-Luc had gone to Figeac for the day.

In blessed shade, they watched the greediest animal, Edorta's prize pig, down their offering in one enormous swallow. But some time later, back at their work, Ander poked Domingo.

"Look. Over there."

In the corner farthest from the slop, the pig hunched its back, and its hair stood on end like a porcupine's. "His hind legs are far under its body—that garlic must've constipated him."

Ander's grave tone alerted Domingo. "What can we do?"

By the time Edorta came home, conscience had its way. Ander alerted their neighbor to his sick pig, now digging at the ground with its hooves.

Jean-Luc Edorta came running and checked for any droppings around the pig. "His insides have tightened."

His face contorted. A prize pig was no small matter. He raced to the house, returned with some applesauce, and between pitching forkfuls of hay, Ander and Domingo watched him coax spoonfuls of sauce down the pig's throat. They flitted between laughter and terror.

Before sunset, when they needed to go home, the pig's droppings showed that the applesauce had worked, and Jean-Luc wiped his forehead with relief. Still, he maintained vigil, though his treasured animal guzzled swill as usual.

It was a mystery how Jean-Luc ascertained their guilt—perhaps one of his daughters observed the entire scenario. But two sweltering afternoons of digging out the drainage ditch sufficed to teach Domingo wariness toward Ander's next brilliant idea.

The memory brought a chuckle as he followed the Maquisard. But back then, the sting of Papa's switch had added to their shame. Years would pass before either of them could say the word *garlic*. As time passed, hearing it sent the two of them into laughter—if only he could see dear Ander once more.

The trail steepened, and ten minutes later, Domingo waited as his Maquisard guide unearthed two fresh-faced young flyers in RAF uniforms from a farmer's outbuilding. They leaned in for instructions, but before they set off, Domingo's comrade pulled him aside, made the sign of the Cross over him, and issued a warning.

"Be careful, the Gestapo tightens the noose around the Jews. The enemy chose Vichy for its hotels built for thermal bath visitors and its up-to-date telephone lines, the better to spread Nazi propaganda. Yet now, the Gestapo moves farther south because of all the cargo heading toward the Massif Central. But take heart—telephones cannot squelch our efforts."

By *cargo*, he meant displaced people flocking to the hospitable Vivarais-Lignon Plateau to the east, instructors and munitions for the growing *Résistance*, and downed pilots seeking to return to England. Dozens of guides risked all in the effort. Lately, Domingo heard some women had volunteered to become partisans, too.

His beloved Sancha longed to help, also, so Domingo sent a plea heavenward.

"Keep her content in her father's house. That is all I ask."

The two downed pilots wordlessly followed Domingo down familiar paths toward the west, ever closer to the border with Spain. Best make time while the sun shone. They halted only for water from clear springs along the way, and hours later, as dusk enveloped the land, a work-worn peasant offered them a full water bladder.

Heavy cheese and peasants' bread, brown and textured with

grain, accompanied milk still warm from his cow. The man insisted they sit at his table to eat, and Domingo expressed his gratitude. The peasant, with his wife close behind him, shrugged as if to say, "This is our small part for the cause."

The man's beret shaded his sharp blue eyes as he bid them godspeed. Domingo sighed at their generosity and led the way through waning daylight. Under cover of darkness, they would pass through Sare, where Austrian sentries fulfilled their duties at the same hour every day.

A hundred times, other trusted guides reassured him. "If we can slip through anywhere, it will be there."

On his first trip, Domingo doubted, but a few successful journeys quieted his trepidation. The Almighty allowed great suffering on earth, yet in the midst of it, made ways for His people.

At dawn, Domingo slanted down a slope north of Orthez and slid the last yards, almost into a stone shed's door. There, the pilots gobbled warm goat's milk, bread, *des oeufs* with golden yolks like wildflowers in morning light, and fell into the leisure of straw beds until the moon rose.

In sleep's helplessness, the pilots' fingers splayed on rough barn boards. The men bore chain bracelets on their wrists with name and serial number, and metal dog tags slumped from their necks. Domingo peered close enough to read *Lunde, Soren. Lutheran.* The fair-skinned soldier looked to be from the far north, where Aitaita said light sometimes lasted all night long.

Domingo dozed, but heard the wind shifting and cows munching in their sleep. A few hours later, before dawn, they skulked through St. Pee, the Gestapo headquarters. The place made Domingo's pulse race, but soon they passed into verdant forest pastures where horses peppered the land.

The Navarra's wide forested bumps held winter's cold and reflected indigo in dawn's light. Domingo twisted toward the men and proclaimed their longed-for hope. "Espagne."

The flash of understanding in their eyes sent fulfillment through him as he led them to the designated stone shed where a haggard-faced peasant waited. The pilots shook his hand and retreated after their host.

Back on the trail, Domingo's feet flew as if he played a game of pelota in the schoolyard with his youthful comrades once again. His commitment to these missons strengthened with each fruitful rendezvous—so many foreigners now safe in Spain, and some of them God's Chosen, *les Juifs*. True, they might all have been captured and met a terrible fate—but they hadn't, and now these two pilots could return to England and fly again.

Domingo retraced the same trails, but with each step, wondered how long England and Amerika could send men falling from the sky. Did they not have land and animals to tend? Sunlight blazed as he topped an incline, and he decided to continue through Mont-de-Marsan to see Sancha for a moment.

Crossing the opposite way last night, a flare showed near there. Remembering that sight, a possible warning signal, worked at Domingo like a rat chewing on old wood.

When someone fell in behind him on the path, he scrambled into a thicket. Whoever shadowed him halted not two feet away and greeted the brush.

"Brother, I know you not, and yet have faith we could travel together." The stranger's Euskara, the language of his birth, touched Domingo like balm, so he emerged from his hiding place. The man's features and espadrilles, shoes of woven fabric tied with twine at the ankles, reflected the clan just west of Aitaita's land.

"I have come from the Plateau Vivarais-Lignon."

"You travel so far?"

"For the children, for the persecuted, like our ancestors of old. Now, Protestant and Catholic alike, the Swiss, Swedes, Quakers from Amerika, and others unite to save God's Chosen."

Morning brightened wildflower swatches along a shallow stream. Content in the stillness, Domingo aimed toward Sancha's family homestead, but his comrade took up the conversation.

"Those from Le Chambon-sur-Lignon guide the Jews on the same route to Switzerland our ancestors followed. Different oppressors, but all the same."

Yes, Aitaita spoke of Spanish persecution and night flights over the mountains to safety, but always highlighted the Basque staying power.

"Did you hear our *Résistance* destroyed three hundred tons of tires at the Michelin Company in Clermont-Ferrand. That should set the Nazis back a bit."

Domingo squashed his curiosity—better not to know details, in case he were caught and interrogated. A hill away from Sancha's village, the journeyer stopped. "Here I leave you. Godspeed."

A few minutes later, Domingo reversed his belief that safety lay in little information, for Sancha gave no response to their secret whistle. In the haughty sibilance of a raucous crow perched on a high branch, he hesitated. A shiver took him as a French phrase lanced his consciousness. *Un assassiner des corbeaux*—perhaps the term *a murder of crows* was no coincidence.

That harsh birdcall unsettled him.

Domingo attempted in vain to dislodge the fearful sensation in his chest. He whistled a second time, then waited before searching out Sancha's father. In the barn's recesses, he held his beret, watching her Papa lace leather with crooked fingers. Never before had he hesitated to meet Domingo's eyes.

At last, when Domingo's knees quivered with suspense, her Papa spoke. "She has gone."

A peculiar scraping started low in Domingo's gut. "Gone?"

"They need strong young women to guide *les Juifs*. Two others from our village went with Sancha, to the plateau."

Gone to guide the Jews—Domingo's insides twisted at the image of lovely Sancha, out there somewhere, traipsing through storm and danger.

His inquiry grated like charred wood. "Who was this man?"

"Tall, with hair the color of lavender stalks after a wet harvest."

"When?" A suffocating sensation threatened to cut off Domingo's air.

"Seven—no, eight days ago."

By now, they would have trod the Plateau Vivarais-Lignon, maybe even left the refuge village, Chambon-sur-Lignon, with a helpless gaggle of God's Chosen. He could see Sancha and the children, like unsuspecting prey in that vast, high wilderness. Domingo backed out the door.

"God go with you, son." Sancha's father had never called him that. How he must have ached to let his firstborn daughter go. Yet Sancha, so hearty and quick-witted, had wanted to help, and begged Domingo to teach her the routes.

He refused, but now cursed his shortsightedness—far better to have her with him. He could barely think of her out where those vile French traitor-police, the *Milice*, stalked. He tore off toward his own hills, Aitaita's land, across a valley outrageous in beauty.

But he noticed nothing, and in the dense hours before dawn, burrowed in a haymow. He dreamed he fought through brambles to a fence bordering Sancha's home, and once there, whistled their surreptitious tune.

She flew to him with the clean scent of tomatoes on her hands, touched his palms and whispered, "I give you my promise." He swore the same. They had, indeed, made that vow two years ago.

Domingo woke and stumbled home. He must hold her up to the Almighty, but worry taunted him. Then the Maquisards appeared, needing him to "meet a parcel."

All the way to the appointed landing spot, he contemplated. This terrible time would end one day, and he would ask for Sancha's hand. They would build a proper Basque home on the land Aitaita had presented to him before he died. Aitaita's eyes flashed pride, grandfather to grandson, and the tremor of his weakening pulse lived in Domingo still.

"You, Domingo, will carry the family name and prosper here."

When he arrived, he hunkered down in some brush until the

moon rose enough. Sometimes the airplanes landed, sometimes they simply dropped their precious cargo.

One by one, other helpers took their places and settled in to wait in silence. Domingo's inner gaze moved from Aitaita's eyes to Sancha's, limpid as a cave's far reaches. But they altered into a different set of black eyes, much younger and utterly innocent.

Those eyes he'd witnessed soon after the Nazis took Paris were always with him. How could he forget that day, June 14, 1940? As Papa and Aitaita had always done, he'd guided sheep to the market in Figeac, below the Church of Notre-Dame-du-Puy on the city's high point. But on his way home, his life was altered.

Scuffling feet and sharp heels resonated on street stone, so Domingo scaled the nearest tree. Several woebegone youngsters, unaware of his presence, huddled under him. He hadn't meant to see that young girl peering up to the heavens.

Fueled by fresh Nazi orders concerning Jews, the Milice brought her to the earth. Her cry scathed the heathery branches, and rough laughter spewed as they forced the other children to watch.

No match for three *Miliciens*, Domingo grappled in his pocket for the sharpened pebbles he kept to strike predators.

Below him, the swint reared his head and bawled, "Ihre ganze Rennen zu uns, Madchen beugen!" Domingo understood only partially—something like *your whole race bows to us, girl.*

Fading sunlight highlighted the perpetrator's temple, and as the miscreant worked himself into feverish pleasure, Domingo brushed his gold cross, aimed, and struck the offender's glinting right eye. A howl erupted, shrill and bone chilling.

The drunken soldiers surrounded their wounded companion, thrust the girl aside and carried him away. The children scattered.

Certain every leaf on the tree quaked with him, Domingo gave thanks they never thought to consider the origin of the stone, and adjusted to an inward alteration. No longer could he simply care for the family's sheep. En route home, he put words to his determination. "I will terrorize these beasts as they do to the helpless."

In his small village, he stopped to seek his parish priest, Père Gaspard. Often away on an errand for *La Résistance française,* this time he scraped mud from his boots.

"I have wounded a fellow human being." Domingo rehearsed the grim details and Père Gaspard took forever to respond. But Domingo knew his wait would be rewarded.

"Not all wounding offends heaven. The Almighty hates evil, and used you to protect His Chosen. Remember Saint Theodosia, toppling a soldier's ladder when he defaced a symbol of our faith in ancient Constantinople."

Domingo's destiny rolled before him. For all those dark eyes, he would join the Maquisards. And so he had, without telling even Maman. But she knew by his absences. Now, he awaited a telltale drone, for helping these pilots ultimately aided God's innocents. Once, he might have chafed at the long wait, but he'd learned acceptance, and merged with the earth, since the Gestapo might also hear the motor and rush to the scene.

A faint hum increased, and Domingo prayed for the parcels—radios, guns, food, supplies, francs, or a new fighter—to land safely.

Finally, silver wings reflected moonlight, and local greeters bearing lanterns formed a lighted L on the flat landing area. Then, one by one, four chutes opened.

The first drop fell hard and fast—supplies. Others ran to release the crates from their chutes. Good. The second parachute drifted west, but the third garnered Domingo's attention. Near a fourth fluttering chute, a man executed a perfect fall.

The celestial trespasser pointed to the other parcel, once he broke free from his silk web and heard Domingo whisper the password, *Build Up.* Foreign sounds, but Domingo practiced a new set for each drop.

He liberated a weighty package and hefted the heavy packet—munitions. Ah, this must be the long-awaited weapons instructor bound for the Ségala. The instructor followed him down a path Domingo knew like his confirmation pledge.

Chapter Three

Big Ben struck the hour, proving it had survived the bombing of Britain. Though the clock tower suffered a strike, on this sunny June day, the timepiece reminded Londoners that afternoon waned, and regardless of the miserable war, life went on.

A few minutes after three, Mr. Tenney stopped at Kate's desk. "Would you please take a dictation in my office, Mrs.Isaacs?"

Discomfort from her expanding midsection increased daily, so Kate welcomed the chance to flee her chair. She grabbed her notepad and poised in the polished mahogany chair opposite Mr. Tenney's desk. But he only shuffled papers, rubbed his temple, and tossed his pen in the air.

He never paused before a dictation and certainly never juggled his pen. She tried to read his grin, as bent as his nose from youthful Rugby games. His eyes harbored a unique twinkle, and creases divided his forehead like a national highway.

Kate studied her notepad, her shoes, and the floor's lovely walnut grain. Finally, she could stand the suspense no longer.

"You wish me to take a dictation, Sir?"

"Oh, not really." He scratched his freckled cheekbone and flicked back a swatch of dark hair trailing his brows.

"Should I—would you like me to go back to my desk, then?"

"Actually, Mrs.Isaacs, I should like to take you for a drive."

"Surely, if I can be of service."

"This is not about being of service."

A finger of doubt crept up her backbone. But for his battle injury,

Mr. Tenney would still be piloting a Spitfire. He had no time for anything but work, and certainly no time for—

She hoped he missed the hot flush flooding her cheeks.

But his goofy half-smile reminded her of Richy, the Wonder Boy in the *Captain Flag Comics*—or was it Rang-A-Tang, the Wonder Dog? She smoothed her dress as he held out a small envelope.

A telegram. Trepidation joined the pinch of her garter belt. Fifteen years ago, her governess stood with one in her hand. Her grandmotherly face twisted, and Kate never forgot the look in her eyes.

After that, black-garbed people gathered. At her parents' graveside, her new black dress itched horribly. When she scratched, the matron hissed, "Stop that!"

A trumpeter played a mournful tune, and a uniformed man handed her a heavy, folded flag. A few months ago, when Alexandre's plane was downed, a telegraph heralded the news, too. Nothing good came from telegrams. And yet, Mr. Tenney's bright blue eyes calmed her. She forced herself to concentrate.

> *Expected package docks June 26 Stop*
> *Evening train Liverpool Street Station Stop*
> *Love you Stop Addie*

"Why, that's today." Kate's heart skipped a beat.

"Indeed."

"Oh, Mr. Tenney, you do possess a cruel streak."

"I fear my gaming ability is lost on you, Mrs. Isaacs."

"She's almost here—I still can't believe Addie undertook this journey for me." Kate staggered to the window and stared down at a double-decker trolley bus now sporting maroon paint instead of the usual red. "Mr. Tenney, you're going to like her a lot."

Her employer pulled out his watch. "I believe that prophecy as reliable as my offer to drive you to the station. The train arrives at six-thirty, and I planned to check some debris on Hammersmith, anyway. What say we make this an official visit?"

Kate suppressed a wild yelp. "Thank you. I hope you expect me to accomplish little in the meantime?"

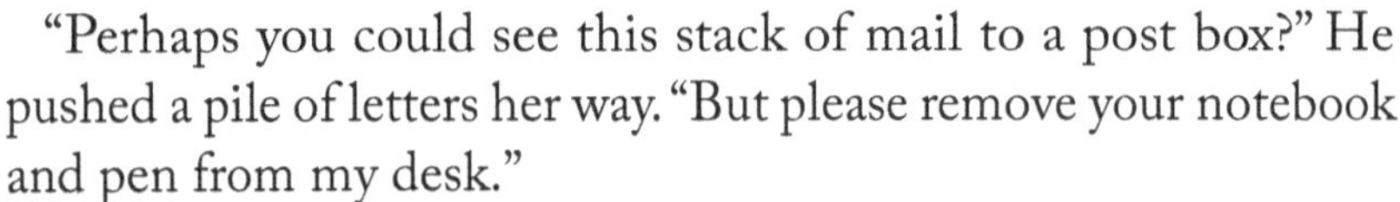

"Perhaps you could see this stack of mail to a post box?" He pushed a pile of letters her way. "But please remove your notebook and pen from my desk."

Cheeks blazing, she obeyed.

"Do be careful—hoards of taxis and busses out there."

After her outing, Kate noticed the W.C. needed a good cleaning. She rummaged for a mop, scrubbed the floor, and tackled the hallway.

When the office cleared, Mr. Tenney searched her out. "Mrs. Isaacs, exactly what do you think you're doing?"

"I had to keep busy."

"Scrubbing like a washerwoman? Mum would have a conniption fit."

"I have as much energy as ever, maybe more."

"But if you slipped, how would I ever face her? I must say, though, you have invigorated this old hall. Come along, now."

Kate swallowed down a retort. What did he think peasant women did? She would bet their robust outdoor work enhanced their deliveries.

She caught his eye as he locked the door. "You won't mention my cleaning to your mother? So far, I've managed to be a suitable tenant, and wouldn't want that to change."

His grin assured her of his collusion, but his mood changed as they drove through bombed out areas.

"Skeletons all around us. More than a million homes destroyed or damaged, more women and children killed than soldiers, half of them here in London. Make a note—some of those danger signs from open gas or electric lines could be taken down."

He steered around a taxi. "On the other hand, one never knows when another leak will emerge. And look over there, Hammersmith Hospital. Important research takes place there."

Kate imagined him in his RAF uniform, downing Nazi bombers. Like Alexandre, he had no chance to complete what he started. She leaned her head on the side window.

"Depressing, isn't it?"

"Sometimes it seems this war will never end."

"Indeed, yet we must take the long view. At least Hitler failed to launch an all-out land war here, thanks to our hold on Gibraltar. And thanks to your country, we didn't starve during the worst of the Blitz."

Some time later, he pointed out the Liverpool Street sign. "It won't be long now."

Kate's stomach buzzed with activity. "I recall the exact moment we met in the school cloakroom, surrounded by smelly wet coats and boys hee-hawing and jabbing each other."

"One of you moved to a new area?"

"I did, after my parents died. The change to my spinster aunt's home challenged me, but Addie made everything all right."

"Here we are, a bit early. Let's take some air." Mr. Tenney came around the car. "Quite the difficult year for you, first losing Alexandre, and then—"

The baby—his baby. Kate hugged her middle. "Things will get better the instant Addie steps off the train."

"Tell me more about her."

"She's everything I'm not—short, dark haired, tipped-nosed, like Myrna Loy. She has a wonderful smile and dark brown eyes, but she's far too humble."

"Too humble?"

"She's always held back, while I plunge in and think afterwards."

"So, this trip says a great deal about your friendship."

"Yes, but her family was what we call backward. Her father outlived her mother, but offered nothing positive." Kate made a fist and tipped her thumb toward her lips.

"Bound to the bottle?" Mr. Tenney guided her around a group of people.

"That and more. I'm so grateful Aunt Alvina included Addie as much as possible, and I think it made a big difference for her. But Addie's husband, well—he demeans her, makes her feel small."

Oops—she shouldn't have mentioned Addie's marriage. She changed the subject.

"We had such wonderful times building snow forts, going to movies when her mother allowed it, reading every Kathleen Norris tale, Jane Eyre, and Dickens—we out-read our little town library's collection."

"You both liked to read?"

"Passionately. We organized a book club, and our high school literature teacher, Mrs. Morfordson, urged us into the classics. Such serious topics we discussed far into the night when Addie slept over."

"Such an idyllic picture."

"Did you have many childhood friends?"

"I'm afraid not. My discussions took place with my father when he had leave from his tours of duty. I was quite the reserved, studious schoolboy."

Kate stopped herself from saying, *No big change there.*" She remembered her first day of work when she asked about Mr. Tenney's wounded arm.

The staff member gave her a long look. "If you ever find out, tell the rest of us."

Kate turned the conversation back to Addie. "Addie's fearless, though she doesn't know it. She's just swell, the kind of person people are drawn to. It's her kindness, I think."

"Give me an example."

"Oh, that's easy. In New York, she met a woman who works for the Secretary of the Treasury, and learned about Jews suffering all over the world—not the sort of person you'd expect someone like Addie to run into. I mean, she's so downright ordinary. But truth runs through her, sure as sunset, and that woman trusted her."

"She's always right?"

"Just the opposite. Her husband Harold is too bright for his britches—he can never be wrong."

"Sounds like a peach of a girl." Kate's head jerked, and Mr. Tenney explained. "The GIs teach me some of your American terms. I must say, you whet my appetite to meet your dearest friend, and just in time, for here comes the train." His brow wrinkled.

Kate could read his expression. "What is it?

"I can't help but wonder how your Addie could leave her husband."

"He joined the Army, and his mother had married someone who could tend the farm. Addie was left sitting alone in that big old house, and even her mother-in-law encouraged her to come and help me."

"Ah-ha."

Closer to the platform, Kate quieted her urge to break into a run. Her hands turned as cold as post boxes in winter. What if Addie didn't come? What if— Once, she wouldn't have permitted such thoughts, but since Alexandre died, doubts encroached at the most inopportune times.

Mr. Tenney touched her shoulder, and Kate realized she'd stopped breathing. She inhaled and answered his puzzled look. "I remember the U-boat torpedoes when our ship reached the Black Gap—"

"You sailed at the worst time, Mrs. Isaacs. Now, we have huge convoys and airborne radar. No ships have been sunk since—"

Over the loudspeaker, a clipped male voice announced, "Liverpool Express, in on track six."

Kate's entire body quaked.

Mr. Tenney whispered, "Do stay calm, for your baby's sake."

Stay calm, exactly what she told herself through all those long weeks of waiting for word about Alexandre.

A dark grey engine hissed to a stop. Two cars emptied. Breathing became difficult. When the third car's doors opened, Kate bowed her head and closed her eyes.

Mr. Tenney steadied her. "All will be well." Finally, when she thought too much time had elapsed, he nudged her shoulder.

"Does your Addie wear one of those modern hats the office girls call *cute* and sport freckles across her charming nose? You're right, she does rather resemble Miss Loy."

A strangled cry left Kate's throat as she opened her eyes and spotted Addie. She tore through the onlookers, waving her hand in the air.

"You *have* come—you have." Everything else faded amidst hugs and tears. Then Kate held Addie at arm's length. "You're all dressed up and looking fine."

"Berthea decked me out in this new coat and hat."

Mr. Tenney strode up and cleared his throat. "Mrs. Bledsoe, I presume? I am most happy to meet you."

"Me, too." Addie swiped her eyes with a hankie. "Forgive me. You must be Mr. Tenney. How do you do?" She freed one arm and shook his hand.

"I—er, yes. Let me see to your baggage." He held out his palm, and Addie dug in her pocket for the ticket.

Her fingertips grazed his as he took the ticket, and something sparked in his expression, something akin to hope.

Charles arrived late, just as Mrs. Tenney declared, "Saint Swithin's Day will be perfect for Addie's welcome party."

Addie looked up from sweeping the bricks and cleared her throat. "Please, I'd so much rather—"

Charles faced the girls with a smile. "Mother believes that old myth, no rain on July fifteenth, so we shan't have any for forty days." A look passed between mother and son that piqued Kate's curiosity—was Charles teasing or filled with resentment?

Addie paused her broom. "Saint Swithin?"

"An Anglo-Saxon bishop, patron saint of Winchester Cathedral. A century after he died, they moved his body to the new basilica and incited some supposed miracles."

"I'll take you there someday, Ad."

Mrs. Tenney scowled. "Too much activity can be dangerous. I've heard the influenza is about, so we have to be extra careful."

Kate clamped her mouth shut, but noticed Charles glare at his Mum. She had used *we*, as if this baby were her responsibility.

"It's just that—" Mrs. Tenney's expression grew wistful. "With such wee ones, one cannot be too careful."

Addie came to the rescue. "Don't worry, Ma'am. Kate can be reckless at times, but never with her child."

Charles coughed and reached to the iron table for the teapot.

Mrs. Tenney continued unfazed. Last night, she vowed before Addie and Kate to make him promise to attend the party. "He inherited his father's stubborn nature, so I doubt he'll even come by tomorrow."

But he had, and she was underway. "We'll gather right here, what? I shall exchange my petrol coupons for sugar and extra tea. Dreadful to find only blue and red tins of dried eggs and milk in one's pantry. What if the cherry crop doesn't ripen by then?"

Addie patted Mrs. Tenney's arm. "I noticed apples on that tree down the way. Maybe the owner would—"

Kate burst out, "What a chipper idea, Addie, you could make pies!"

Mrs. Tenney puzzled over the suggestion. "Why I never— you mean that James Grieve tree that bears early, just past the crossroads?"

"That's the one."

"Charles, do you suppose I might ask—?"

"I doubt anyone could stop you." He studied Addie. "You make apple pie?"

Kate answered for her. "The best in Halberton County."

"I should love a taste." He lifted a brow toward Mrs. Tenney. "Do you propose a round of croquet then, Mum?"

"If you like. We need a bit of relief from constant war, war, war."

"Lucky, aren't we, when the soldiers get none?"

Mrs. Tenney ignored his implication. "We can count on you then, Charles?"

"Barring a bomb attack."

"That's settled then. You'll come to the party." Mrs. Tenney poured some tea and sighed, "Now, the only problem is this courtyard. With all the gardeners employed at the Liverpool munitions plant—"

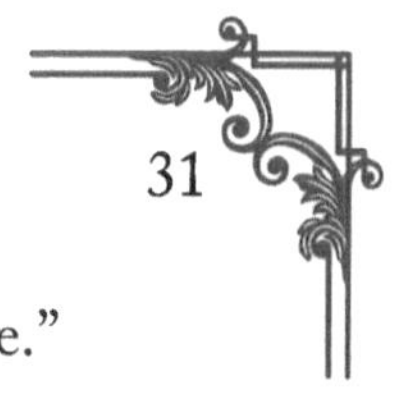

Kate gestured at Addie. "We have an expert right here."

"Addie?"

"I've been itching to start, but thought maybe you'd rather—"

Mrs. Tenney drew up an extra inch in her chair. "As they say, all things fall into place if you have faith."

"Quite." Charles fixed his eyes on Addie. "You like to garden?"

"More than anything. I'll start straightaway, as you Brits say."

Charles' face flushed. "Such an accomplished young woman. I may actually enjoy this party."

Addie's cheeks, bright as window box begonias, matched his. Flustered, she set aside her broom and perched next to Mrs. Tenney.

"Could I ask one favor, Ma'am?"

"Anything."

"I'd feel better if we call the party Saint Swithin's, so I can meet your guests on my own, one-by-one."

Mrs. Tenney opened her mouth, shut it, and pursed her lips. "Surely."

Addie hugged her, and Charles' jaw dropped.

His mother turned his way. "Well, then, it's settled. Thank you for coming, Charles."

"My pleasure, Mum. If I find some extra time, maybe I can help with the courtyard."

Charles' interest fascinated Kate, but a sudden twinge caught her attention. "I think I'll go upstairs and rest a while."

She dozed, but sharp pains wakened her. Then, a spike drove through her abdomen. She struggled from bed to study her flushed reflection. Did influenza hit this fast?

Her abdomen convulsed, and Kate clutched the bureau until the onslaught passed. Her mother's picture trembled against the wall, then settled again. "Only a few weeks to go. I can't be sick now."

The next pain lasted longer. The third staggered her. She stumbled across the room, but another zigzag, like the direct bomb hit at a cinema the other night, sent her to the floor. The walls swam in dizzy circles.

The next thing she knew, Addie knelt beside her. "Are you having pains?" Kate fought to answer, but locked her jaws to hold back a scream.

"I'll be right back." Footsteps clattered on the long stairway, with Addie's shout faint in Kate's ears. "Mr. Tenney, please hurry—Kate needs help!"

Cool fingers stroked Kate's forehead. "He's ringing the doctor." Then the world went black.

A strange man and nurses with crisp white caps hovered over Kate. "She's conscious. Take her vitals now."

Fingers prodded her neck. "Low pulse—she lost so much blood, doctor."

Voices wafted away, but snitches of conversation carried back.

"—wish we could have saved the baby."

"Hopefully she pulls through."

Kate's neck rebelled when she tried to look around. She flattened her chin against the plain white sheet draping her like snow on a landscape. The whiteness closed in, and someone screamed, an unearthly, eerie sound. But Kate Isaacs never screamed, not even when she learned Alexandre was gone. Something stabbed her arm, and she drifted away.

Later, white hat-topped female faces showed above her, and a pinprick claimed her finger. She slept, wakened, slept, and wakened. In between, the ache of one more loss ripped her soul. Finally, Addie's voice soothed her, and she wiped away Kate's tears.

A lifetime later, Kate lay propped up with sun pouring in, and a nurse mentioned the date.

"St. Swithin's. Your party, Addie—it's supposed to be today."

Addie grinned. "Here in this land of lime trees, no limelight for me."

"Oh you!"

"Today, they're letting you try to walk. That's far more important to celebrate—enough of you lying in bed."

Later, Mrs. Tenney tiptoed in, and Addie welcomed her. "I'll be down the hallway. Kate will be so glad to see you."

"Hello, Dear. I've hesitated to come, but we miss you so."

"I've missed you too."

Mrs. Tenney's nose reddened and the vein that intersected her forehead pulsed. Kate felt sorry for her, but couldn't think what to say.

"We so look forward to having you home. I—I'll be going now."

The next day, Charles stood near her bed, fumbling with his hat.

"I thought not to bother you, but Addie—er—I've brought some books to help you pass the time. I am dreadfully sorry for your loss."

She waved him closer. "Thank you for coming. Ah, Emerson."

He set the books down and clasped his hands. How hard this must be for him, with his memories of war hospitals.

"Is everything going well at the office?"

"Perhaps some day my best stenographer will return." Charles forced a smile.

"Addie's working out fine, isn't she?"

"Oh, yes, I didn't mean to imply—that girl has a way of—" He turned his hat brim like a nervous schoolboy.

"Thank you so much for the books." Truth be told, the last tangible evidence of Alexandre's love had vanished, and nothing else seemed to matter.

"Well, then—" He raised his fingers in a feeble wave.

Kate's heart claimed a stark truth. Office work could never satisfy her again.

Chapter Four

Domingo swallowed the first bite of heavy bread in a single gulp. Weary from clawing over rock ledges with Gestapo collaborators in pursuit, he slumped exhausted in a peasant's cottage. As he'd been told, the missions grew more and more dangerous, but he'd led another pilot to Spain. The young fellow was probably en route to England right now.

The peasant eyed him askance, but his simple, hearty fare strengthened Domingo to engage him a bit longer. "How many have passed this way so far?"

The peasant pointed out forty-nine notches on one side of his window frame, fifty-seven on the other. In the recesses of the kitchen, his wife's stirring wafted a yeasty smell. The odor of farm animals came from the barn below the farmhouse. This was how Maman grew up—no wonder she spent so much time in the barn now.

Above the door, an etched sun stood within a circle, and another circle within the sun centered a crude cross. Surely this householder's grandfather carved it when the Basques turned Catholic in the generation of Aitaita's father.

Domingo saluted the matriarch with his empty mug. "Merci, Madame."

The man followed him out, and a few yards down the path, murmured, "Our son Abarne guided Basque children here after the terrible bombing of Guernica in the Spanish Revolution of '37, when thousands fled. He saw our people's ancient oak tree with his own eyes.

"Abarne watched the Heinkel 111s raze the town, killing so many innocents, but when the attack ended, our ancient tree still stood." The peasant wiped his eyes. "If only Abarne had stayed home the last time, he might have fulfilled his name, *Father of a Multitude*."

His reverence for Guernica's tree, the Basque symbol, lived on despite his sorrow at the loss of his son. It was the same with Maman when they lost Ander.

"But he went to fight then. 'If Germans can bomb Guernica, they can bomb us, too,' he said. Partisans brought word months later, when we had only potatoes to eat and Spaniards flooded the countryside."

Domingo stood arm in arm with him, like father and son. Then his thoughts turned to Sancha.

The peasant sensed his urgency and pointed down the path. "About a kilometer that way, you will find berries."

Night doves cooed and owls' winter calls kept Domingo company through slumbering farmland and villages. Then, a few kilometers down the path, a whistled singsong message from the brush alerted him.

Tonight, in a nameless round meadow, a parcel would land. Could Domingo attend?

Domingo lifted his palm, and before turning down a sharp descent, the courier brushed near to whisper the precious password. Knowing the code's magic, Domingo repeated it aloud three times.

Gabirel would have to manage the sheep a while longer, but those who fought for Basque freedom in Spain, like their brother Ander, left young brothers behind, too. Since then, his family had shrunk to him, Maman, and Gabirel. A pang niggled Domingo, for he ought to be teaching Gabirel the old ways, as Aitaita, Ander, and Papa had taught him.

But with the Résistance sending desperate Jewish children to Switzerland from the Massif Central, and ever-expanding OES circles, a tightening Milice noose in the foothills demanded more certain radio contact. Thus, nearly every recent drop included wireless sets. Still, Domingo vowed to stay home for a while after this mission.

At the meadow's edge, Domingo rested under a spreading oak and pondered how these valleys and plateaus formed. His people arrived here before much of written history. What eternal forces brought them centuries ago?

The moon's position had altered when he woke from dozing. He snoozed again; images of Sancha filling his mind.

This very night, she might be guiding refugees past Annemasse in southeastern France across the Swiss border or huddling with Jewish children near a haystack's hidden trapdoor. Oh, that he could protect her.

Domingo turned to stare across the field, alight with moonlight and dew, and practiced the code name he must repeat if this package contained a Résistance worker. The ungainly words would keep the hapless parachutist from fighting him or cringing.

How terrifying it must be to throw oneself to the earth from those winged zephyrs. But to have someone approach with no password would be worse than the fall.

A distant low hum sounded. Domingo crossed himself and repeated the code. The welcoming committee shone their lights, and he stood ready for the parcel assigned him but would rather take a radio if he could choose.

People presented more challenges. They tripped and snagged their knees on thorns or refused to cooperate. Worse, their lives hung heavy on him—one careless decision could lead to death.

The delivery point, several kilometers north, posed few obstacles. He would return home before dawn, and if God willed, Gabirel could rest tomorrow.

Suddenly, he heard a sound like a coat being zipped, and then a parachutist whooshed down, swayed like an aired bed sheet, and landed at the field's west edge. Domingo rushed to cut the chute loose and stuff it into his pack—the fabric would protect Maman's tender vegetable patch next spring.

Several other partisans moved ahead to shoulder their loads.

Then, *ka-ziing!* Something whizzed through the air and searchlights strode the sky. Domingo froze amidst gunfire and shouts. The parachutist zigzagged across the meadow. Heavy booted soldiers thundered after him, and someone yelled, "Schnell!"

A woman screamed—French women could not even vote, yet risked their lives out here every night. Fifty paces away from Domingo, the parachutist dodged for cover, but German shepherd dogs lunged after him. A shot felled the hapless fellow.

Breathless, Domingo snaked backward, away from the lights. By the time he inched into a thicket, the soldiers shooed their haul to the other side the meadow. They took time to investigate the crates and pulled out radios, munitions, and who knew what else.

Domingo watched the Gestapo tie the injured parachutist's hands behind his back and shove him into the forest, paying no attention to his limping. If only he could rescue that poor wounded fellow. But facing six Nazis—what could he do?

Finally, their thrashing through the woods faded, and when insects set up their racket again, Domingo set out in a wide, cautious circle. An hour later, he dared to rest. Around him, nocturnal animals made a last provision dash, frogs croaked pre-dawn songs in a shimmering pond, and a fox scrabbled for breakfast.

A new day, yet different from all the rest—bloodshed had arrived here. That Brit would face interrogation, and likely, death, and the enemy would employ the valuable goods dropped.

As Domingo neared home, a small shed belched acrid smoke. An accident, or had the Milice found a Résistance cache? No sign that Maquisards scuffled here in the night, but for good reason. They took their name from the brush into which they disappeared and left little trace.

Aitaita's final words soothed Domingo. "Before the Revolution, our *fueros* governed us well, but, the revolutionists strove for a new France and felled ancient borders. Spain and France pitted

Basque against Basque, yet our men were slow to kill for Franco's sake, and were blamed for the failure."

"Our hopes stirred when Aguila took the oath of presidency under Guernica's tree, and with him now governing from Amerika, we foresee peace. Your father and Ander died in the freedom fight. The banner now passes to you, Domingo."

Light waned as Domingo entered the barn. Maman was right—having cows on the first floor and living on the second would provide winter heat. Still, he liked sneaking in all alone to remove all trace of his terror before he faced her. But a while later, espadrilles scuffled outside.

That sound might have calmed him once, but the shifty Milice had learned to trade their boots for Basque footwear. Domingo searched the stanchion's underbelly for a knife and melted into the shadows at a knock on the door.

"I bring news of Sancha." The half-light hid the messenger's face. "High in the Massif-Central, the Résistance killed a Gestapo operative, so in reprisal, they took children and workers from a safe house. You have heard of the Cévenol School at Le-Chambon-sur-Lignon?"

Domingo waited in silence.

"Many have found safety there, the holy book's city of refuge. But your Sancha was among those taken."

Lightning burst in Domingo's head. Finally, he croaked, "Taken where?"

"Near Saint-Paul-d'Eyjeaux, a holding place for God's Chosen."

"How many?"

"One other worker, six or seven children."

"Saint-Paul-d'Eyjeaux?"

"In Limoges, across the Garonne." Domingo groaned. Long days away, and first, he must seek information in Le-Chambon-sur-Lignon.

A sturdy post steadied him. "Can you take me there?"

"Surely you have heard the Gestapo, using our own *gendarmes*, takes all French Jews now, with their citizenship revoked. We launch retribution attacks and have killed more than thirty French policemen since July—my duty lies here."

Domingo dug his fist into the crusty stall divider until his eyes smarted. "As surely as Basque blood runs in my veins, I will bring Sancha back."

"Give me a full day to see if someone travels that way."

Swallowing his emotions, Domingo strode to tell Maman he must take a long journey.

Chapter Five

A few days after Kate left the hospital, the temperature reached only 15.3 degrees Centigrade, but by the end of the month, oppressive heat reigned.

Mrs. Tenney prepared lunches that proved her potential for clandestine work. A boiled egg graced the tray she carried to Kate's room.

"How did you manage, when we're each allowed only one every two weeks?"

"With your green ration card." Mrs. Tenney beamed. "And Charles helped."

"But I'm not expecting now. Shouldn't my card be buff-colored?"

"Recovering from—an illness requires nourishment, Kathryn. Later, you will enjoy a real vegetable soup and fresh pears and plums. My friend Blanche promised us some almonds in September, an exciting prospect, what?"

"You've taken such good care of me. I'm feeling stronger every day."

"These things take time." Mrs. Tenney's eyes glossed.

"May I ask how you know?"

For once, Kate's landlady allowed her shoulders to droop. "Before Charles was born, the Colonel and I—er—lost a baby. And then two more."

Kate sucked in her breath. "I'm sorry. I had no idea."

"How could you? Even Charles doesn't know."

"You had your hopes dashed three times."

"I always wanted a daughter." Mrs. Tenney bit her lip. "When

Charles mentioned you needed a room, I feared I would become too close to you, and then you would—"

Kate patted her hand. "But look. Now you have both Addie and me."

"Something about me drives people away, I'm afraid. Charles calls it my propensity to engage in others' affairs, but I only wish to help."

"I lost my mother and so did Addie. It means so much to share your home. I really don't know what I'd have done without your generosity."

Mrs. Tenney colored. "People all over the city open their homes."

"Yes, but you took in Addie, too. Two wild Americans—we'll always be grateful." For the first time, silence between them became a beautiful thing.

Monsieur le Blanc's note, flimsy from Kate holding it so often, lay on her bureau. She stared at her mother's picture.

"What shall I do? I don't think I can stand much more of being nurtured, but I mustn't hurt Mrs. Tenney. Addie says the office has plenty of work for me, but—"

Maybe a cup of tea would help. She dressed and wandered downstairs. They'd run out of the tea Addie's friends sent from the States, but Mrs. Tenney pilfered some from somewhere. Grateful she'd gone to a meeting this morning, Kate set the water to boil, but jumped at a knock on the door.

"You're feeling better?" Charles brought in more hot air.

"Almost back to normal, but I'm under doctor's orders for another week."

"And Mum's, I daresay, for the rest of your life? She went out, I presume?"

"To her regular warden meeting. I've gone with her a few times, but—"

"Falling incendiaries, oil bombs, and warden duties have lost their attraction?"

Kate gulped down a torrent. "Yesterday, I'd planned to visit the woman who helped me when I first came, but your mother—"

"Ah, yes. Evelyn, wasn't it? I'd guess Mum held you back because of the heat."

"You know her quite well. I'm ever so grateful to her, yet envy Addie when she goes to work in the mornings."

"I can understand. You've considered coming back to the office?"

"Yes, but—" How could she explain?

"We could use you, although I just heard one of the civilian staff at joint military headquarters must leave his position. The work requires excellent stenography, communication skills, and an unflappable personality." His sideways grin showed that he read the question on Kate's tongue.

"This insider opening might be more your cup of tea—constant tension, incoming generals, ever-changing orders, and working far more than the regular five-day week—"

Generals, ever-changing orders—Kate could barely sit still.

"You have the ideal temperament and would come highly recommended."

He tapped his fingers on the table. "What do you think?"

She might have crushed him in a fierce hug, but tried to appear calm as she steeped the tea.

Charles pressed his thumbs together.

"I would work here in London?"

"Downtown—a secure location."

Kate walked to the window. She and Addie could still have late-night talks and Sundays together, though she'd have to guard her tongue. Down the way, a chestnut tree created a mass of shade, and one swatch of leaves started to turn.

"I'd like to apply." She turned back to Charles. "Could I still do that today?"

"As I thought. I brought copies of your work record and processing documents. Make yourself as businesslike as possible while I savor some tea."

A good thing Mrs. Tenney was out, for Kate tackled the stairs three at a time.

August temperatures rose and fell, and the first morning in September, Mrs. Tenney sent horehound lozenges along with Kate and Addie. "To ward off colds—my father swore by them when the weather became so changeable."

Every day brought something new. Midafternoon, Kate entered a secret underground passageway leading to the secretarial room, number fifteen. Voices drifted from the hall's end with heady cigar smoke—the honorable Mr. Churchill?

Her supervisor loaded her arms with a delivery, so Kate climbed the stairs into unpredictable weather. But clouds couldn't dampen her high spirits. She addressed the heavens.

"Thanks for Charles seeing my need and for this opportunity."

A cohort of American soldiers marched down a nearby street, and she fell in step. Every uniform color and style imaginable crisscrossed this area—such a conglomeration. In the never-ending stream of dictations, typing, and deliveries, her distant meeting with Monsieur Le Blanc retreated to a dusty mental shelf.

But by night, her mother's picture transformed into a moonlit message, and she wondered if he would still see courage in her eyes. Working so near Parliament, she contributed to the war effort, but *Many people need your help* still piqued her curiosity. Just last night, she and Addie discussed Monsieur's note.

"You ought to do more research about your mother, Kate."

"Sure, but it's bad timing for a trip to France."

Now, moisture threatened the toes of Kate's shoes and a siren screamed, prompting memories of the Blitz. Sometimes she felt more British than American, having endured the last five months of heavy bombing.

Under her umbrella's covert shelter, Monsieur's words rose once again. *You have your mother's courage.*

"Who did he mean, and what could I do for them?"

Between buildings, bushes still wore summer green. Two months ago, she'd lost her baby, and imagined nothing could pull her from her grief.

She looked to a miniature blue patch in the sky, heralding warmer breezes. A minute later, strong rays broke through, and with sun warm on her forehead, Kate closed her umbrella, lifted her arms and turned a full circle.

When she picked up her umbrella, a burly man approached, and a familiar French lilt caught her ear. "*Prendre un peu de soleil?*"

"*Oui, exactement.*" Yes, precisely—taking in some sun.

He lifted his hat—Monsieur Le Blanc. Her heart leaped to her throat.

"*La fille du Madame Dumont— voilà!*" He slapped his hand over his chest. Exactly what he'd said the first time. His teeth showed brown stain, his wet-wool, tobacco, and seasoned leather scent reminded her of their first meeting. Her knees went weak.

"You are well?"

"*Oui.*"

He swiped a kerchief over the sodden seat of a nearby bench. Kate's ears buzzed as her most insistent question popped out.

"*Le Renard Intrepid*—he was truly my father?"

Crinkled cheeks gave way to a smile. "*Oui. Les Américaines* called him that, because he moved swift and sure, impossible to track."

"He was French?"

"*Oui.*"

"What work did he do?"

"Espionage." The sinister word caught in his mustache, inviting Kate closer. An inner puzzle piece slipped into place, as fragile as raindrops perched precariously on grass blades—her own true father.

All this time, she had held him at arm's length, but now the intrigue touched her soul. A faint recollection trickled in, a man speaking French with her mother. Shivers raced down her arms.

"You haf more questions?"

"I must get back to my desk soon."

Monsieur's dark mustache twitched and his eyes summoned her curiosity.

"My parents married in France?"

"In Chaumont. I witnessed their vows."

A bound spot in Kate's abdomen released. She could find this place on the office map.

Monsieur unlatched his briefcase and produced a photograph of a slender, dark-haired young man. Under a jaunty black beret, a wide leather strap crossed his shoulder, as if any second, he might take off running.

The photo carried a signature: Gérard Isaacs, November 19, 1918. Black eyes plumbed Kate's curiosity, and she recalled another of Aunt Alvina's photographs—her mother with a man on a stone bridge.

"Where was he born?"

"In Haute-Loire." Mountains—gurgling streams, snow-covered peaks—"

An officer passed, rousing Kate from her reverie. "Oh, my. I really must get back right away." The picture quaked in her fingers. "Monsieur, you mentioned suffering people. Who needs my help?"

He slumped against the bench. Emotion contorted his features.

"I must know something else. Do you still see courage in my eyes?"

He threw back his head and looked heavenward. "I have prayed for you, *ma Chérie. Oui,* your mother's courage lives in you."

"What shall I do?"

He pulled a packet from his briefcase. "Read these. Meet me tomorrow at nine, at this address." He scratched something on the top article.

"Could we meet earlier? I—I start work at eight."

"As early as you wish. I will watch for you." He put a thick finger to his lips. "Let no one see you enter." A cloud covered the sun, sealing their pact.

One shoulder lower than the other, he ambled away, but his request lingered. It wouldn't be hard to arrive in secret. Addie took an early walk every morning, so she could write her a note and leave a few minutes later.

Kate scurried to work, but when she left the building to go home, her thoughts returned to Monsieur. The rendezvous seemed dreamlike, yet the packet under her coat testified to its reality.

Her heels tapped the sidewalk in staccato with the conversation burbling inside her. Mrs. Tenney's kitchen offered a still-warm meat pie and a note—*Bandage rolling with Mrs. T, come if you like. Addie.*

Kate wolfed down the pie and wrapped in a blanket near her bedroom window to devour the contents of the papers.

1942—Vélodrome d'Hiver received 7,000 of 12,884 Jewish family members seized in July raids. Two doctors attend internees—five days' thirst, hunger, dysentery, diarrhea, daytime heat and cold of night.

President Laval briefed, original goal of 28,000 Parisiene Jews unreached.

Doctor—recorded 5,500 children from unoccupied zone, separated from parents—in broad daylight. Taken to camp Drancy in sealed cattle cars, severe diarrhea.

Wooden dog tags for some so young they could not give their names. Perpetual crying, no soap, soiled clothing, children on filthy mattresses—transports to Germany on four August dates, parents interned in Pithiviers and Beaune-la-Rolande.

The raft of newspaper and magazine articles, smaller encyclicals, and official reports made her head throb. She peeked through the blackout curtains, but this other darkness overwhelmed her far more.

"November—Mortality levels rise, German sanitary team investigates. Officer frees some prisoners, more than a thousand seriously ill, worse than notorious Dachau camp—July '43, Germans take over administration, material conditions improve. Deportations continue.

"American Friends Service Committee beseeches State Department and German Foreign Office for immigration visas, Secretary of State Hull offers one thousand entry visas, five thousand more pending French approval. Sluggish negotiations. Quakers receive no exit visas in Marseilles. Finally three hundred children for safe houses."

Vichy regime closes its eyes, Berlin disappointed with August 1942 roundups. German diplomat finds French police clumsy (ungeschickt) in publicly separating families. Laval, concerned with Vichy reputation, orders children to accompany parents to Auschwitz. Over 6,000 in 1942.

Children separated from their parents—

A hazy childhood memory wiggled into Kate's consciousness. Her mother's flowery scent, a suitcase, and a hasty, "Dear, don't cry. Mommy always comes back, doesn't she?" Cold feet tiptoed the back of Kate's neck, and her sigh echoed the room.

"Where did she go, and why?"

"Auschwitz designated to deal with Jewish Problem. Archbishop of Toulouse, Monsignor Saliège declares Jews 'real men and women—part of the human species, our brothers—Jewish and other war veterans return World War I decorations to protest Vichy complicity.

"Cardinals' and archbishops' protests proclaimed throughout France. No action taken—Monsignor Theas, Bishop of Montauban, reads pastoral letter—outrage of Christian conscience, proclaims all men brothers created by the same God. Protestant protests added—Laval ignores them all."

Suddenly Kate remembered Addie writing about this from New York. Kate rummaged through her desk for her last letter.

—met Esther Goodman—works for the Treasury Secretary, Henry Morganthau, she was meeting a Swedish diplomat—to save European Jews.

—Bermuda conference—Roosevelt met Churchill, but immigration laws and Palestinian quota remain the same.

How could this happen?

"Child deportations resumed, February 1943—no further official protests—huge roundups into the present in unoccupied zone and the north."

Kate didn't hear Addie and Mrs. Tenney until Addie entered the room.

"Kate? What are you reading?"

"Do you remember that lady you met in New York?"

"Esther Goodman—my first Jewish friend."

"And she told you—"

"Mr. Morganthau bemoaned Hitler's agenda with the Jews, but no one could convince the President to change our immigration laws."

Kate patted the floor beside her. "I've been reading something someone gave me today. Things sound far worse in France than I imagined." She stopped. Monsieur warned her to keep tomorrow's meeting secret, but not this literature, and Addie was as trustworthy as Gibraltar. "We may have a long night ahead of us."

Chapter Six

After navigating the stairs at 64 Baker Street, Kate knocked at the third door on the right.

"Come in." Brylcreem-laced, ash-brown hair shone in a bare bulb's light, and an officer eyed her through wire-rimmed lenses from behind a desk stacked with papers.

"Have a seat."

A straight-backed wooden chair quieted Kate's jitters. Unremarkable furnishings bespoke seriousness, as did the officer's approach.

"They sent you up from intake?"

"Yes, sir."

"You look a little underweight, but that's London living. Do you exercise often?"

"I walk fourteen blocks between busses, and most of the time, I'm energetic."

"Most of the time?"

Heat razed Kate's cheeks. "All the time."

"Special Operations Executive agents train in Scotland. Can you shoot?"

"My husband taught me some basics."

"You're married?"

"I—he died in battle. He was a Canadian pilot."

The officer blinked. "So I need not inquire as to your motivation."

Kate hid her relieved sigh, although four days of tests should have revealed her inmost secrets. Alexandre's death played a large part in her decision to join the Secret Operations Executive, but so did her desire to discover more about her father, who was now as tangible as if he stood here beside her.

"Once we receive your credibility report, you could become active in Churchill's secret army late this year."

"Active?"

"Sometime in early winter, Mrs. Isaacs, you may enter southern France. Your language ability makes that location obvious."

Kate forced down a surge of excitement.

"But utterly tight-lipped we must remain. If certain military quarters heard of women training in gunnery and parachuting—"

He drew a thick forefinger across his throat. "We commission you in the politically acceptable First Aid Nursing Yeomanry—FANY, and indeed, you will receive first-aid medical training." He cleared his throat.

"Neither the Geneva nor Hague Conventions considered women in wartime service. Behind enemy lines, you'll enjoy less protection than a POW. Do you quite understand?"

A cloudy image surfaced of *Madame Dumont* at the dangerous front twenty-five years ago.

"I believe so. What does the credibility report require?"

"Your visa, passport, birth certificate, family history, and work records." He handed her a stapled stack of papers. "Fill this out. We need your work documents by the day after tomorrow. We keep everything in a safe box until your service ends, at which time you may retrieve them. Ah—depending on the circumstances."

Whether or not she still breathed. But now was no time for cowardice. Her mother turned her back on ease, and her father took incredible risks to earn his nickname.

"Isaacs sounds Jewish—are you?"

Abraham, Isaac, and Jacob—Why hadn't she considered this before? Her shrug satisfied him, and the long day's interviews ended.

Kate rode the bus to pick up Addie and by the time they reached home, explained what she needed. As usual, Addie asked few

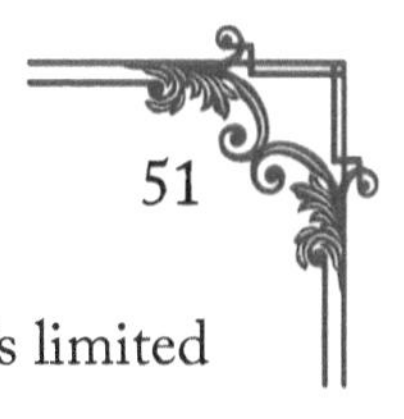

questions and offered unconditional acceptance to Kate's limited information.

"I can't discuss the details, Ad, but I've thought about this a lot, and the need is so great—"

"You've been through so much, Kate—your long search for Alexandre, his final crash and death, and losing your baby." With glistening eyes, Addie finished with, "Whatever this mission is, and I bet it's full of danger, you'll do it,"

To Kate's silence, she added. "You'll risk everything."

Finally, Kate choked out, "I have to. Do you see?"

"You're your parents' child. You can't sit by and do nothing, Katy-did." Alexandre's old nickname brought tears, like Addie's hug. "How can I help?"

"You'll be the one to face Mrs. T." Kate swallowed a sigh. "I'd rather jump from a hundred planes than disappoint her after all she's done for me. She may never want to see me again."

"You exaggerate. This must have something to do with helping Jewish children, so maybe she and I can get involved somehow." Addie stopped by the courtyard to check her plantings. "Remember the money Norman Allen left me when I nursed him before he died?"

A wayward curl hit Addie in the eye. "All this time, I've wondered how I might use it, but Jane said I'd know when the time was right."

"Have you heard from your mother-in-law and George lately?"

"Not for a while, but Berthea and Jane told me to let them know if they could help. So far, I've only asked for a pound of sugar and some spices for Mrs. T. But they have so much more to give."

The next day, a different officer frowned at Kate through a window separating his office from the main room. "We only need your work records now. If anyone follows you here, let us know." He scribbled on a paper and handed it to her. "Our phone number, day or night. Alert us if anything untoward occurs. He squinted at some forms. "Your parents—deceased. No specifics?"

"No, sir. I learned more recently, but my childhood memories serve me poorly."

His forehead wrinkled. "Airplane crash. Where?"

Kate shook her head.

"That's all you know?"

"They both served in the Great War. Mother's code name was Madame Dumont, an Allô Girl, and my father was a spy—*le Renard Intrepid.*"

"I may do a bit of research."

"I'd like to know if you find anything."

"You'll reside here. Pass by the residences to get your bearings."

He released her, and though it was the middle of the day, Kate stopped by to see Addie.

"Can you take a minute?"

Addie gathered a letter packet. "I'll walk you out." In the hushed stairwell, Kate whispered her request. "By tomorrow, I need documentation that I worked here."

"I'll do my best."

Kate parted with her at the post box and waited for a bus. Against the hazy London sky, one column of undisturbed bricks waggled from its foundation like an accusing finger—Old Bailey's spire. An afternoon shower washed the city as Kate's thoughts drifted back to her early days in London. After Alexandre's second crash, she found him again, only to lose him forever. And then their baby.

Raindrops funneled like tears down the steamy bus window. "That might have been my only child. I'll never love anyone like I loved Alexandre."

She departed the bus and hurried home. When Mrs. Tenney stepped from the library to greet her, Kate flinched.

Only the beginning of deception, but at least Addie shared a bit of Kate's secret. That made the undertaking bearable.

Addie closed her desk drawer, tidied her paper tray, and scanned the empty office. Final footsteps faded out into the hallway—except, of course, for Mr. Tenney's.

A sliver of light created a slender L where his door gapped a couple of inches. How could she keep her word to Kate? Knowing how to run the A-Pe-Co "Photo-Exact" copier was only half the battle, since employee files stayed in his office.

Maybe she could tell Mrs. Culver early in the morning, but she wasn't one to veer from the rules—nothing to do but throw herself on her employer's mercy. Addie ran clammy palms down her skirt and crossed to his door.

"Mr. Tenney?"

"Ah, Addie." He glanced up. "You've not gone home yet?"

"No, sir. That is, I—" She bit her lip.

"Something troubles you. Do sit down."

Aware of wasting valuable time, Addie fought for breath. "It's about Kate."

The fold between his eyebrows deepened. "You may speak freely." He perched on the edge of his desk—

"I have a conflict of loyalties, sir."

"War complicates things, what?"

A tight-drawn place in Addie's chest loosened. "Kate stopped by earlier. I hate to involve you, but I—she needs help."

He leaned forward. "By all means."

Words came spilling out. "By tomorrow morning, she must have her work records, but I don't know how—"

He put a fingertip to his chin. "Ah—the SOE. I wondered how long it would take them to engage her."

"You know?"

"Before hiring her, I familiarized myself with her history, and accompanied her when that Frenchman presented her parents' photographs. And actually, I did a bit more sleuthing—"

"I'm so relieved. I've learned secrets can kill you, little by little."

"I regret whatever taught you that." His kind expression urged her to continue, but she kept it simple.

"It's just that I'm very pleased you understand."

"The secret side of war touches many of us." His eyes took on a faraway look, and the little muscle in his cheek fluttered into a spasm.

"Well, then—Kathryn's papers. I expect they're filed here." He unlocked the second drawer of a tall wooden file and grinned.

"Now, if you'll guide me with that new-fangled machine, we shall succeed at this or die trying." His statement transformed the mood to jovial. He turned the light switch to illuminate the outer office.

Addie flipped the duplicator's ON switch while he placed the first sheet in the trap. She snapped the holders shut.

"An incredible invention, what? And an American, Chester Carlson, patented an improvement last year. Soon, the process will update to electrophotography." The machine set up a terrible racket, so he raised his voice.

"The clatter and that chemical smell mixed with the ink leave something to be desired. But to think of reproducing—hiring someone to retype even one week's documents—"

A final click signified the machine's readiness, so Addie pushed the red GO button. In less than a minute, Mr. Tenney waved one copy to dry. Addie removed the original and fastened another paper in the holder.

"Soon, we'll have duplicated Mrs. Isaacs."

Mr. Tenney's engaging smile removed Addie's last shred of discomfort. "Duplicating Kathryn—an impossible job, what? I shall stamp these, and you'll be on your way." He went to his office and returned with a manila envelope.

"Less than five minutes. The machine did cost $55.00, and convincing the board we required one took its toll. If I have my way, within the year we'll move to dry photocopying."

"Does that work like a camera, without all this odor?"

"Quite right." He handed her the envelope. "Please allow me to walk you out."

Addie found her purse and coat, and they left the office.

"How are you adjusting to London?"

"It's very different from Iowa."

"No doubt. Tell me how." He motioned her toward the hand-rail side.

"There's a lot more space, and it's all green, compared to—"

"I do hope during the city's renovation, we retain our parks and create a few more. Does Iowa look like a park?"

"You'd have to see it, I guess. Miles of flat farmland, roads set around sections, green, red, and orange tractors in the fields, endless rows of corn and soybeans, pastures of thick yellow hay—"

"I should indeed like to see your beautiful homeland. Do you miss it?" He held the outside door wide.

"I do miss my garden and a couple of friends, but London has so much to see, and being with Kate—"

"Your friendship impresses me." He donned his fedora and claimed the street side of the sidewalk.

Heat crept into Addie's cheeks as their hands accidentally touched. "Kate's the best thing that ever happened to me."

"How so?"

"When we were growing up, she invited me over nearly every week, and we could talk about anything."

"Ah. Mother kept me inside with lessons and tutors until I went off to school." The stark blue of his eyes matched wistfulness tugging at his lips.

"I'm sorry to hear that."

"Many London boys grow up that way, but I treasure this opportunity to watch how a friendship works. You will feel great sadness if Kathryn leaves?"

"Even though it's for a good cause, I expect I'll be lonely."

"After all, you planned to care for a baby, not work in an office." He stopped at the crosswalk. "You do like your work, though?"

"Oh yes."

A break came in the traffic, but something in Mr. Tenney's eyes held Addie. "I .... Perhaps we could be friends?"

"I'd like that very much."

"With only one stipulation." His brown wool hat reminded her of Spencer Tracy in—*What movie was that? Kate would remember.*

"Outside the office, I should like you to call me Charles."

"Charles."

"You did that very well. This is where I turn off. Will you be all right?" He scanned the distance ahead of her.

"Oh, yes. I walk fast. I love being out in the fresh air, the time whizzes by."

"Mmm—" He tipped his hat. "Do take care, and please greet Mum for me."

Stricken with wordlessness, Addie crossed the street toward Westbourne Grove. When she glanced back, Charles still watched her from the curb.

Chapter Seven

D omingo's heart lurched as he thrust an extra knife into his boot and reached for Maman. "Before you know it, I'll be back." His jaw tightened at the quiver coursing her thin frame, and his reassuring whisper echoed empty.

He struck out eastward. The messenger returned last night and promised a companion would meet him on the trail. The Résistance kept its word. About an hour away, as if he and Domingo met regularly, a slender partisan appeared.

"Domingo?"

"Yes. You are—?"

"Philippe, bound for Haute-Loire." Questions rose, but hearing this older man's name in Euskara calmed Domingo. "You seek a woman called Sancha?"

"*Oui.*"

"Then we go."

Domingo's pulse returned to normal as Philippe lunged down a path like a nocturnal animal. His style appealed to Domingo—he spoke only when necessary. At full daylight, they dozed in a granary and wolfed down porridge a child brought them.

Traveling from midmorning until the next daybreak formed their pattern. Six days later, after hiking with little sleep, Philippe pointed to a village perhaps a kilometre away.

"There lies Le Chambon-sur-Lignon, with the old volcano *Le Lisieux* directly behind—over 100 kilometres south of Lyon and that far from Clermont-Ferrand, too."

He gestured southeast. "This road leads to Valence."

How he catalogued these details mystified Domingo, but he seemed always aware of their exact location. Domingo made friends with the high point, a signpost of the west, the direction of home.

A shiver took Domingo, though the sun already warmed the earth. Perhaps it was the stones testifying to all those who sought refuge here. Philippe's eyes revealed no trepidation beyond his normal wariness, so Domingo breathed a little deeper.

In the strong light, he noticed the grey at Philippe's temples. After all these days on the mostly uphill trail, the goal of finding Sancha united them in an almost spiritual connection on this grassy plateau. Whatever other mission brought Philippe here, he set it aside, and they started their descent.

A road took them directly to the main square. The white lettered train station sign proclaimed *Le Mazet* and *Le Chambon*—twin villages sharing a stop. Philippe's solemn tone alerted Domingo to their shared focus. "Someone here will remember your Sancha."

Domingo imagined Sancha skipping these gray cobblestones, grasping the hands of small, forlorn children while teaching them some childhood chant. Perhaps she drank from this same fountain. He sniffed for her scent, but detected only raw milk, the day's bread baking, and cow dung.

A shrill whistle blew in the distance, and a great iron beast tickled his toes from afar. Closer, fierce rumbling sent vibrations up Domingo's calves. Some minutes later, a shriek pierced the peaceful scene, and the charcoal engine chugged to a stop.

Philippe allowed the smoke to clear before he shunted onto the platform. A few people descended, shoulders hunkered down, scarves tied, bags clenched in taut fingers. Some faces shone firm with resolve; others gave furtive looks before deciding on a direction.

One well-dressed woman's bright orange scarf caught Domingo's eye, for Sancha possessed a similar one. Under her father's sessile oak, she had once teased him with its fringe. That day, he stole the sweetest kiss, but vowed to wait for the divine blessing.

"God will honor our obedience." Sancha's voice suddenly came so real, so strong, she might have stood here beside him. Domingo touched under his chin at the memory, and the unique mix of lavender and fresh milk that accompanied her wafted from somewhere, or he imagined it.

Seconds later, Philippe approached a stranger and gestured for Domingo. Always more comfortable on the outskirts, he halted in Philippe's shadow to listen.

"They arrested Monsieur Trocmé, the cleric, in February, but let him go after a month. Now he hides in the countryside, for everyone here unites in this cause. His wife perseveres with regular trips to Switzerland with the children. For word of your Sancha, you must first visit the Presbytery, down *la Rue de la Fontaine*."

"Here, one feels safer than in Paris, yet we stay on guard. A double agent they call *la Corneille* has been spotted on this train, but no one knows whether he is a man or a woman."

La Corneille—the Crow. A shudder rocked Domingo all the way to his toes. That crow he witnessed when he returned from the border crossing, perched over the last rise before Sancha's home, had given such a garrulous cry. Had it issued him a warning of what was to come?

Someone guided passengers away from the hissing train. Philippe and Domingo followed them on *La Rue de la Fontaine*, the street of the fountain, and refilled their canteens. At a grey stone church, a black-eyed youth with a heavy shock of hair greeted newcomers, so Philippe questioned him.

A door closed, and Domingo looked up into another fellow's hazel eyes enlarged by scholar's glasses. His hair, parted on the left and slicked back, emphasized the outward turn of his ears. Following Philippe's lead, Domingo shook the stranger's hand.

Nothing was remarkable about the other buildings, but someone spent long days perfecting that carefully crafted window. Like Domingo's church vestry icons, the careful artistry radiated a shaft of comfort.

Clearly these Protestants his ancestors labeled heretics cared for God's Chosen. What would Aitaita say to that?

The man Philippe conversed with spoke Sancha's name and waved across the street. "There, the Milice herded them into automobiles, along with boys from the House of the Rocks."

An itch started between Domingo's shoulder blades. Finally he could hold his question no longer.

"And now?"

"Although our teacher, Daniel Trocmé, lives in hiding, we continue, with the help of many good people, to protect *les innocents*. It is good and right to do so. Our Heavenly Father provided cities of refuge, even for those with blood on their hands. His mercy is from everlasting to everlasting, so here in *Le Chambon*, we offer ourselves and our homes."

A cool wind wisped Domingo's face, but at the word *mercy*, something hard formed in his chest. Did mercy watch when the Milice stole Sancha away? And this fellow ignored his question. *Now, what are we to do?*

Philippe thanked the man and clapped his hand on Domingo's shoulder. "Come."

Not knowing their destination mattered little, since Philippe secured a trail with confidence. How he ascertained their direction was a mystery, but to follow Sancha's trail filled him with excitement.

In the first few hours, the kilometres fled like running water. Some bushes already showed yellow, gold, and rusty orange. Domingo's breath caught in his throat at the beauty—another part of *La France*, with its own unique spell. To the inhabitants, these hills and valleys were as dear as his.

Brilliant day became cool twilight, but his mind refused to rest. A few hours later, he drank ground roasted chestnut powder Philippe dissolved in water and boiled over a hasty fire in a secluded cave.

"Tomorrow we overtake them."

"You see signs?"

Philippe merely grunted, and on the trail at dawn, Domingo sharpened his scrutiny. There, a boot print pressed into the moss. Here, a twig had snapped under pressure.

Past a main thoroughfare and through a ravine, they climbed toward a bramble pile. Philippe squatted, fingers to his nose. Domingo sniffed something chemical before recognizing wheel tracks on the ground. *A vehicle out here, so far from—?* A relentless weight bore down on his ribcage.

"They stopped here." The tracks veered into a winnowed field, its harvest stubby pencils rows. It was all Domingo could do not to break into a run. Farther on, a smell tinged with copper alerted him.

He fought sickness as the tracks led into the brush. Domingo ran ahead, thorns tearing at his trousers, hands, and face. Then metal burned against his kneecap, and terror overcame him at its smoothness—an automobile's sleek surface. He razed its covering with his bare hands.

Black, shiny, and cold as death, this vehicle had not stalled by chance. Someone backed it here. He surveyed the tracks. No, in a hurry, they pushed it, then concealed its bulk. Philippe panted behind him.

"Stop, it is too dangerous."

The iron smell now soaked the air. Domingo rounded the brazen hood, raised like a wanton woman's skirt. Odd, exposed motor parts stared up at him. He bent to rancid oil and rusty radiator water.

"They ran out of petrol or *gazogene* and the engine overheated." Then Philippe dared to speak the truth. "Someone died here not long ago."

A knife chiseled Domingo's chest. He tore at defiant branches strafing his face and hands like razor straps. Papa administered harsh discipline, but Domingo would choose a thousand beatings rather than uncover this auto. But laid bare, the seats lay empty. He stood panting as Philippe plowed into a nearby bramble pile.

Domingo stood for a minute before joining him. There would

be no coming back. A permeating odor ate up his oxygen and dipped his soul in dread.

Philippe straightened, took a long breath, and scanned a mound of earth and rocks scattered like barn refuse. He fell on the heap and Domingo followed, clawing at the earth until something bony, small, and delicate touched his fingertips.

Stunned, he fell back. In a cold sweat, he panted against a tree. Gratitude filled him as Philippe continued pawing the site. Finally he probed the thrown-together pile with a stick.

A foot protruded—a child's foot.

"*Mon Dieu.*"

On Philippe's next probe, something orange emerged, far too alive with color and nuance, a floating, silken persimmon the shade of ripened peaches and the middle line of sunset. Domingo stared, transfixed.

A sound he could not own sailed the breeze. Philippe grabbed him and pushed him back. What seemed like hours passed as he exhumed the inconceivable. Finally, he twisted and held out the scarf. His voice scraped the edges of his throat.

"Sancha's?"

Domingo nodded, his mind vacant as an empty potato cart. Yes, that scarf defined the rich scarlet in her cheeks, her lips—

"Five lie here, all dead for a few hours. *Quel horreur.*" Tears tunneled Philippe's four-day beard.

All dead. What if those swine buried them alive? Or tortured them and took from Sancha what she had saved for him, as those Nazi beasts did with the little girl whose attacker he blinded?

He ran, willing the thorns to scrape even deeper, to kill him now. His legs, a separate power, thrust him up a hill, around a curving path and down again, panting, racing, lost, desperate. Then the bushes parted.

Boots thrashed through the break until two peasants emerged, picks and shovels in hand. One removed his beret and clasped Philippe's arm.

"What do you seek?"

His question made no sense. Spoken words belied the mêlée in Domingo's head.

"Let us help you."

His lips formed a response, but Philippe brought forth the answer.

"Over there—" He pointed in the general direction.

"So, you found them? You know them?"

Slow of speech, the peasant's yellowed eyes drew Domingo back into this world. These aged eyes treasured truth. "The Milice skulked by with bloody uniforms. We knew they'd caused suffering and waited until they left. Show us the way."

As usual, Philippe led, and like a worthless shadow, Domingo fell in behind the peasants, who used their shovels as walking sticks.

Through a last thicket of gnarled bracken, Philippe waved Domingo back. No use trying to argue. He could only stare as Philippe helped the farmers make sense of the bodies.

"Bury the young woman on the end ever so shallow." Philippe's instructions forced Domingo's helpless sob. "We will return and take her home."

The men left, and Philippe pushed Domingo into a cold mountain creek and bade him wash. The right thing to do, but Domingo couldn't have said why.

The sun slipped away and, alive with the cold, they dressed. Then Philippe handed Domingo something—fabric aflame with the color of tempestuous oak leaves at their autumn height, sailing on a current like the souls of the dead.

Domingo crushed the scarf in his palm and fell against Philippe's shoulder. When his sobbing finally stopped, Philippe folded the scarf back into his hand.

"She will travel with you always, my friend."

Back at the site, six small, branched crosses marked the graves in the twilight. The workmen's sober faces communicated the camaraderie of silent fury.

Philippe faced Domingo with an unspoken question. Domingo

knew he viewed eyes turned to stone, his own eyes, for they had seen far too much this day. But in the dusk, after they had scented out the killers' trail, Philippe twisted again.

"Shall we act alone?"

Even as Domingo assented, energy inundated him. They passed another peasant leaning on his fence.

"The Milice have been here—ransacked a house and barn down the road, and left only two hours ago, brandishing guns. Our neighbor said they stank of blood. Do you need my help?"

Philippe surveyed the darkening sky. "We have the advantage of night. Stay here and protect your family. Who knows if they will return?"

Power emanated from Philippe's shoulders. Through bracken higher than their heads, trees stooped in fortresses. But muscled and stealthy, they became wolves on the hunt in a night too painful for moonlight.

Once they stopped, but only to refill their canteens. A swift breeze cooled their necks, and rising fog lent the evening a fitting shroud.

With no warning, what we once saw clearly reveals only haze and fumes. Still, we know what we are about. Père Gaspard's words from a sermon swept Domingo.

We know what we are about. Exactly.

Distant firelight drew them. A few stars blinked in a careless wind. Domingo thought he would never see the sky the same again, for this night cut to the division of bone and marrow, soul and spirit.

Strangely, verses from the Holy Book sustained him. *Vengeance is mine, saith the Lord. I will repay.* The ancient teaching dwelt in him, straight from Aitaita's lips. "Leave vengeance to the Almighty."

But now, war upended the teaching, and God's servants transformed into leaping, pouncing, indomitable weapons. Another story lived in Domingo: even as a boy, King David, a man after God's own heart, took human life at the Almighty's bidding. David slew the evil giant Goliath who taunted the children of Israel.

Yet the Savior taught men to love each other, and the

Commandments condemned what he and Philippe planned. Still, Domingo sensed heaven lighting their way.

Ancient warrior words merged with the knife he slipped from his boot. *Vengeance is mine*— They melded with the hungry tip of Philippe's blade and some time later, caught the enemy's firelight.

Sated maggots, the *Miliciens* and Gestapo sprawled in their cooking fire's afterglow, heavy bears full of liquor. Humps of worthless flesh.

As if stationed far above, Domingo viewed the scene. This night, divine vengeance flowed through human hands. Evil stumbled and fell headlong in this beautiful valley.

He tamped his desire to call out to the stars, *"Innocent blood has been shed. Hear it cry from the earth!"*

He and Philippe edged forward until the fire's sparks became their own. Then they sprang on the men. Even before their blades made sure, sharp slits, the swine were essentially dead. Philippe felled two, Domingo one.

Then Philippe touched Domingo's forehead. *Are you all right?* He received his answer in silence and bent to rip at a uniform. Domingo gulped. Why dirty his hands touching such filth?

But Philippe was right. No reason to leave them easy to identify. Hadn't the Gestapo killed a line of men in Paris for the deaths of two SS troopers?

Like a fiend, Domingo riddled smooth manufactured wool trousers and shredded a shirt into the fire. He turned to Philippe with a long, supple leather boot.

"For the Maquisards." Philippe paused. "Pocket the buttons and medals."

Domingo slashed at polished brass as if filleting fish, threw a jacket into the fire, then another. Flames spit in protest. Philippe stashed one full uniform into his backpack.

By the time Philippe pulled him back, Domingo could have continued all night, but he found his posture and strode away. Once, he looked back at faces never again to view the sun, and stark pink flesh reflecting dancing flames.

Sleek and purposeful, he pulsed through the blackness behind Philippe, feeling nothing. Then, as clouds overcame the stars, and night deepened into indigo, an inner storm mingled sorrow and anger. The mass grew until Domingo could barely contain it.

Deserted automobile chrome guided them. Philippe knelt on the cold earth to strike a match against his boot. Strong sulfur stung Domingo's nostrils as he watched mounds of earth gently cupped from one frail, dirtied body.

Tears traced Philippe's cheeks as Domingo held out his arms to lift Sancha from that shallow, cold spot, her knees all bone, her back a hapless curve. Philippe tore off his coat to wrap her, and with one long look into Domingo's eyes, made the sign of the cross over Sancha, beautiful even stained with mud and blood.

Eventually, faint starlight shone once more, enough to transform towering branches into cathedral arches. Philippe led the way past the peasant's farm.

The man stepped into their path, and Philippe croaked. "It is done."

"We will bury them deep in the forest. Godspeed."

All night they traveled, the next day, and that night. When Domingo had to relieve himself, Philippe stayed with Sancha. Keeping her warm was all Domingo knew—and taking her home. Time stretched into hazy hills and valleys until familiar land appeared.

A small family plot sat at the homestead's edge, away from pecking hens and wallowing pigs. Here, Sancha would lie with her people.

Straight to the barn, Domingo carried her. Her sisters clung to her hands. Then her mother ran to rock her like a small child. Domingo could watch no longer, but he took in the aura of her home, pungent with lavender and milk.

Her father, his features crushed, embraced Domingo, but silence fettered Domingo's tongue. What was there to say?

The graveyard, where they would bring fresh flowers, and in winter, brush the snow away, called to him. Someday, children would play nearby—Sancha's nieces and nephews, as she rested until her family joined her.

Philippe drew back, allowing Domingo time. Sancha's father sheltered his own, and her mother's wail rent the night air. Then the circle closed around Sancha, and Domingo backed away, turning toward Aitaita's land. Running was all he knew.

Just as dawn transformed into full day, Philippe held Domingo's shoulder before veering toward his own home to the north. Domingo stood still as he faded into the morning light, and then, one last time, twisted westward to once again give his heart to Sancha.

Chapter Eight

After days of climbing up and down bomb craters in the Scottish wilds, Kate ate supper one night and went straight to bed. Lying there, she recalled an instructor's response when she mentioned her father.

"You must be proud of such a heritage. Not many get to follow in a parent's footsteps, especially when that parent was a spy."

If only she knew for sure the path her father took. Here in her narrow bunk, the single wool blanket hardly dispelled the drafty cold wind rattling this old estate's windows. In one of three other beds in the large room, someone snored. Kate turned from the sound, but her muscles ached.

Today's exercises challenged even the strongest participants. Thankfully, no rationing was observed here, and a hot meal waited when she staggered in from hard morning and afternoon workouts.

You must be proud of such a heritage. Her phantom father flitted like a shifty breeze, but opening her mind to him only strengthened her hunger to discover more. If only she could remember her early years, but she'd been over this a thousand times.

Maybe she *could* learn more. At least, it couldn't hurt to try. The next evening, she asked one of the older instructors about him.

"*Le Renard Intrepid*, you say?"

"He was in espionage, at the front."

A few days later, he pulled Kate aside after a weapons class. "T'was highly unlikely, but I've found a little information." Kate's heart rattled against her ribcage.

"Not much, mind you, but a report mentioned him."

*A French underground worker they call Le Renard Intrepid
keeps us abreast of chemicals shipped to Germany. Before the
war, he studied there, and no one raises an eyebrow when he
crosses the border. Uncanny how he wins the trust of both sides.*

"Your father sounds like quite the professional."

Kate pictured *Le Renard* blithely deceiving German guards time
after time. She would give anything to know what he studied, and
if her mother's interest in the same subject drew them together.

The officer directed her to a vision check. Kate read the eye chart,
and the woman administering the test grinned.

"You must be eating your carrots. Maybe they'll put you in the
radar brigade with Cat's Eyes."

"I'm sorry, I don't understand."

"You've not heard of John Cunningham, the night fighter ace?
In the Blitz, he shot down the first plane at night."

"The propagandists posted carrot signs everywhere—in the tube
stations, in windows—*eat your carrots, improve your night sight with
Vitamin A1*. Didn't you see them in London?"

"Oh yes."

"Don't spread it around, but by now, some people probably real-
ize that was a ruse to throw off the Nazis. A1 actually refers to
Airborne Interception Radar, A1 Mark VIII, but the Ministry of
Information shortened it to A1 for the newspapers.

Word got around that Cat's Eyes' success came from eating
lots of Vitamin A, especially carrots. The Kitchen Front literature
campaign probably helped. This is a food war, you know?"

"The gardens spread to the States, too—victory gardens. My
friend grew one."

"I've heard government warehouses have a massive carrot surplus
now, and of course, we have carrot cake and a host of other recipes.
They've even tried to introduce carrot flan—strange how the war
changes even the smallest things."

Kate walked away shaking her head—war trivia. In fifty years,
no one would even remember.

A pleasant fire glowed and the mealy smell of cooked potatoes warmed the cottage. Domingo hung his coat on an iron hook behind the door and rubbed his hands. "We'll have a hard frost tonight." Gabirel sat by the fire reading, and Domingo ruffed his hair. "A good fire for us on this cold evening."

Maman looked up from her knitting, but Gabirel hardly stirred. The look in Maman's fiery eyes alerted Domingo, so he sank on the hearth. "What are you reading?"

The boy flushed and bit his lips.

"Here, let me see."

Gabirel revealed a tract that Domingo read aloud.

—you believe joining the maquis is an easy route away from forced labor in Germany? Perhaps you need some facts. Joining the maquis entails a grave commitment— when you sign yourself over to the Résistance arm, what you can expect is far from an easy life. Hunger, strong discipline, no soft bed at night, with little reward. And be assured, Vichy will hunt you down.

"But my friend Valencia says Allied bombs will kill you if you submit to work in Germany. Since we will all rise up against the Reich in the end, why not join those loyal to France who already fight against the invaders?"

Maman set down her knitting and withdrew to the cooking stove, the tightness in her shoulders apparent. What would Aitaita say to this fourteen-year-old—too young to fight, yet facing Vichy's ever-tightening noose?

But Gabirel lanced his own question. "Have you joined the *Maquis*?"

"Whatever these tracts say or what you hear in the marketplace, there is still something in-between."

"What do you mean?"

"The press pitches Vichy against the Résistance. Those who resist the quotas have become *refractaires*, unmanageables. But I go at a moment's notice if the *Maquis* calls, and right now, they need guides for pilots bailing out over Germany and Belgium.

"Joining the bands that scavenge in the forests is unnecessary. You already do a man's work here, and because the *gendarmes* have not reached into our valley since the last quota, I still go in and out without fear."

Across the room, Maman set out plates and lighted another candle. "But if they do, what will happen?"

Candlelight reflected Gabirel's youthful intensity.

"Then, as Père Gaspard instructs us, I will join the fighters."

Maman turned to the stove, and Domingo lowered his voice. "But she has lost one son already, and I will stay close as long as I can."

With the steaming pot in the center of the table, Domingo and Gabirel took their seats. Maman nodded to Gabirel to pray.

"*Notre Dieu*—" Instantly, he realized he used French instead of Euskara and pleaded, "I am sorry, Maman."

But she flew into a fit. Domingo understood Gabirel's unwitting shift to French, but to Maman, the slip represented all the trouble of the past few years. She could not separate herself from its curse, and Franco's Fascist oppression enveloped the table in those two simple French words, *Our God*—

Franco hated the Basques, restricted their language, and branded Spanish the *Christian* language. But worse, after the Nazi Condor Legion bombed Guernica, with over 2,000 casualties, Papa and Ander joined the fight.

How could they not? Under the ancient oak in Guernica, the Basque laws were written centuries ago. But Papa and Ander sacrificed their lives, and now the Nazis controlled Spain and also occupied French Basque lands.

Never had Domingo seen Maman in such a state. She half-rose from her chair, and her voice shrilled. Gabirel shrank back, and when at last she stopped, she looked as bewildered as Domingo felt. She rounded the table and shook Gabirel by the shoulders before wrapping his head in her embrace.

They ate in silence. Gabirel's fingers trembled, and Domingo's breath came hard, as though he'd climbed a rough stretch. He ought to say something to right things, but what?

When Maman cleared the plates in silence, Gabirel followed him to the barn. Aitaita would know how to soothe his hurt, but Domingo's brain turned as dry as his mouth.

Just before they crossed back to the house, he attempted. "You are her youngest, her last hope, and Euskara her only language. We must try to—"

"To what? Be something we're not? The old ways mean everything to her, and to you. I may be the least of us, but I am a person, too. She and Papa sent me to school—how can I never speak French? Even Père Gaspard uses both."

What Gabirel said was true—every Sunday morning, Père said the mass in Latin, of course, but gave the homily and greeted the people in Euskara. When he discussed matters with local officials, however, French flowed from his tongue.

Domingo laid his hand on the lad's shoulder, but Gabirel shunted him off and made for the house. Domingo turned up his sheepskin collar against the frigid November wind and took a turn around the sheep pen.

Gloom rode the cold gale. He stroked the sheep dog. Maybe he, too, realized things were amiss.

Surely, he missed Papa and Ander, and most of all Aitaita, who sat on this stone wall often to ruff his fur. As twilight darkened, Domingo considered sleeping in the barn. The dog nosed his palm in commiseration.

No, he was the man of the house now. He thought he'd faced that long ago, when Maman remained outwardly stalwart no matter how many new graves they dug. But tonight, something altered in her, a transformation beyond Domingo's understanding.

He startled at an airplane's indistinct hum, as common north of here as the bleat of a wayward sheep. They veered this far south now?

Inside, all was quiet except for snores from the back bedroom. Domingo stole to the archway and surveyed Maman's sleeping form, so small in the bed she and Papa always shared. Not long ago, her black hair would have contrasted with her faded quilt, but it had turned white. A flood of sorrow washed Domingo, and his whisper turned raw.

"Don't leave us yet, Maman. I need your strength."

He extinguished the single candle on the table and lay beside the fire rather than climbing to the loft beside Gabirel. He would stay near the door, like their sheepdog at the pen's gate.

Not long after he stilled his mind enough to fall asleep, a tapping came, and Domingo opened the door to a slight partisan he'd seen a few times before. He gathered some bread, dry cheese, and a bladder of milk and ushered the fellow under the eaves, lest they wake the others.

"*Ongi etorri.* Where have you been?"

"Your welcome in our blessed tongue refreshes me. I have traveled from Saint-Jean-de-Luc, where the navy and the Luftwaffe have taken over. One of our people lives up the coast, within sight of forced laborers building gun emplacements, bunkers, and a long dock far out into the sea. The Nazis hide the installations with artificial sand dunes.

"But another of us collects intelligence and travels a regular route across the south. This time, they needed help packing the reports into parcels—maps showing the latest armored equipment, bivouacs, even sketches of uniform insignia. These agents are like our people of old—professionals at smuggling. They even put negatives and what they call microfilm into toothpaste tubes."

Domingo chuckled. "Aitaita learned some of his tricks from his own father, who used to say, 'Basques are smugglers and thieves.' He told us, 'Funny how the government calls us the worst but contacts us when they need help.'"

"Not much has changed. As Aguierre proclaimed, 'The territory may have been vanquished, but not the soul of the Basque people. It never will be.' I have heard he works with the FBI to coordinate espionage." Seeing Domingo's puzzled look, he explained. "*Bureau d'intelligence d'Amerique.*"

"Ah—nothing would surprise me."

"Some Ingelesak come all the way across the Atlantic. Who could have imagined Amerikans fighting with us?"

"You mean pilots?"

"No, espionage."

"So you go back and forth along the border?"

"Usually not this far inland. With my slight build, I pretend to be an elderly man's slow-witted charge. We watch the Atlantic fortifications, the Todt Wall—it means death in German. Little do they know that many view their installations in our photos." He gnawed a hunk of bread and drank his fill.

"No one ever bothers us. Who knows how many miles we have covered, but the photographs—ah—troops, six-foot steel reinforcements around Bosche bunkers wired for telephones, guns and ammunition, whatever we see.

"Their wall covers 500 miles between Spain and Normandy, but we concentrate on the south." He handed the empty jar to Domingo.

"So far, we have only success, but headquarters gets nervous. Surely, they say, someone will suspect, so they sent me on a new task, *hanhemenke.*"

Here and there—Domingo recalled Aitaita's tales of his youth and his injunction to disobey the rulings against their language. The roll of his words ran through Domingo's mind like a potent premonition.

They cannot understand our dialects, so they try to thwart them. Our way of speaking is so difficult, it is said the Devil studied seven years to learn Euskara, but finally gave up the effort.

The wayfarer wiped the last crumb from his whiskers. "So it is with the Basque Information Services. I hope to help one of the *Ingelesak* on this mission. Who knows? Maybe someday, I will visit his country. I have heard of one such who fought on our side in '37. He left Amerika illegally to champion our cause, and fled when we were routed. I wonder how he fares now."

He reached for his *makila*, a hand carved walking stick much like Domingo's, and stretched his shoulders and arms.

Here and there—the familiar term described Domingo's life right now. He'd become a butterfly, flitting from one place to another, always accomplishing another mission. But in the safety of his homestead at this moment. Details of the war seemed far away.

"I hear mention of *l'Invasion*—"

"Ah, yes. The German defenses prove how much they fear an attack, and refugees from everywhere seek safety in Spain."

"So you have no lack of work?"

"Indeed. The French may scoff at our penchant for smuggling, but what would they do without us?" He pressed his beret onto his head. "As the old saying goes, *Before God was God and boulders were boulders, Basques were already Basques.*"

"I wish I could offer you more for your journey, but—"

"You are lucky to have cheese, even dry. In the cities, people starve to death. In the camps—"

Domingo stepped back. He'd heard enough of the camps.

"But across the border, I fill up, and often carry something back for my family."

He jammed down his beret and lifted his chin. "*Gero arte.*"

Domingo echoed his good-bye, and the friendly fellow took off as quickly as he appeared.

The wind cooled even more, a sign of winter. Domingo's sigh wafted into the night. If only Gabirel would remember the old ways and refuse to forsake their ancient Basque tongue.

At least the sublime bowl of this valley endured.

Chapter Nine

En route to the Ringway hanger, the bus driver motioned toward a long field with a tall steel tower at one end.

"You'll practice here in the evenings, to protect your identities."

A circular platform ranged at least 200 feet high, and miniature figures descended an endless ladder. Above them, a long steel arm protruded, and a white fabric canopy billowed over another doll-like figure suspended in mid-air.

"Dangling like bait on a fishhook. That's what we're volunteering for, chaps."

Kate ignored Pencher, a talkative fellow, and pondered a recent newspaper report.

General De Gaulle became President of the French Committee of National Liberation, and the Red Army liberated the city of Kiev on the sixth, the anniversary of the Russian Revolution. The Nazis overran British forces on the Dodecanese islands off Turkey. So much was happening with November barely half over.

A loud jerking noise brought her back to the present. A tower cable released, and another man floated to the ground.

Pencher's voice turned reflective. "Best be ready for the real thing, blokes."

A few feet before impact, the jumper lowered his hands to his chest, bent his knees, flexed his forehead to his fists and hit the ground with his boots. Almost imperceptibly, his knees turned so he landed on his thighs and buttocks. In one smooth action, his back connected with the earth, head, arms, and feet pointed up.

Pencher announced, "There, mates—that's how it's done." A murmur passed between would-be agents gawking out the windows.

Kate whispered her excitement. "Looks like jolly good fun to me."

The driver opened the door, and an officer entered the bus to address them. "A little background. You may or may not jump into your locale, but must learn how. Some of you may jump in a second or third time. But even if you never parachute, you may meet jumps or prepare others for them."

Across dewey grass toward the hangar, Kate's thoughts became a commentary. *What happens here will change me forever, like that bomb hitting Evelyn's house.* Since Alexandre died, she hadn't seen much of the new British friend who'd helped her find her way during her first days here.

But now, in light of her training so far, an unexpected insight occurred to Kate. Evelyn's appearance and manner might be a cover for something. As she filed behind the officer, an inexplicable discomfort descended.

On that recent Sunday when she introduced Addie to Evelyn, all the signs that Evelyn was hiding or feared something became evident—dark circles under her eyes, a jerk of her hand when someone walked by the window, a muffled gasp when she noticed a set of automobile keys at the back of her table.

She came off as a dyed-in-the-wool commoner, but might be attached to Research and Analysis, or even to—? Several other possibilities ran through Kate's mind as her group entered the hangar, but she chided herself.

Evelyn's dark circles might result from chauffeuring dignitaries across London under cover of darkness, with her vehicle's blue-capped headlights almost unnoticeable from above. Those drivers, mostly women, put themselves at risk, and Evelyn seemed the sort to handle that sort of stress.

"Line up over here, and we'll begin."

For a fleeting moment, Kate wished she hadn't introduced Addie to Evelyn, but her motives had been right. A born Londoner,

Evelyn had plenty of practical wisdom to offer Addie. And these days, anyone—Mrs. Culver, for example—might dabble in danger on the side. Kate swept her ponderings aside and glanced up at the lofty rafters supporting the hangar.

If only Alexandre could see her now.

"Memorize France's twenty-one regions. Focus on the Auvergne, the Limousin, and the Midi-Pyrénées, Basque Country in the Departments of the Lot, Aveyron, Haute-Loire, Cantal, and Puy de Dôme. You will most likely enter the Auvergne somewhere in the Cantal.

"The Limousin and the Auvergne form a peasant's straw hat, and the Midi-Pyrénées, taken with the Auvergne, resembles the state of Kentucky. But conjure your own metaphor to solidify them in your memory. The Causses—great limestone plateaus, three in the Lot, three in the Aveyron, appear in yellow, as they do covered with summer wheat."

Kate's instructor moved his long wooden pointer along the Department of Lot. "The Gestapo has difficulty navigating here, and the Ségala highlands over the Cantal border host a vital camp, impenetrable to the Nazis thus far.

"The ninety-six departments most commonly originate from rivers within their borders. Southward in Haute-Garonne near Toulouse, the Waffen SS refurbishes its tanks as we speak, and *Résistance* agents relay increasing troop movements to Allied headquarters."

Kate's word picture came in a flash. The Auvergne and the Limousin formed Addie's scarecrow hat a couple of summers ago, when birds threatened to strip her cherry trees. And the Midi-Pyrénées resembled her crooked kitchen stovepipe.

"In the Midi-Pyrénées, Basque shepherds-turned-*Résistance* guide our downed pilots over the Pyrénées. Note the heavy black line stretching all the way from Belgium to Gibraltar."

The instructor glided his pointer along a railroad line and into the mountains.

"You will encounter the *Langue de Occident*, Euskara, and circumstances may force you to deviate from your initial assignment, for the Gestapo ever seeks to infiltrate our circuits. Once a circuit is blown, the organizer signals the alarm code, and fleeing is the only alternative. You cannot learn too much about the locals, upon whom you must ultimately rely.

"We find the Basque tenacious, reliable, and utterly knowledgeable. Their fiery independence and hatred of the Nazis drives them. Tireless and patient on the trail, they have become irreplaceable.

"You will need the same qualities. As the Invasion nears, nothing is guaranteed. If your circuit's cover is blown, trust no one easily. But the Basques prove themselves over and over.

"Every mountain range, river valley, city, and hamlet Kate tucked into her memory called to her. Many nights, she fell asleep with a map over her chest, like a capsized tent, and dreamed she fell through a night sky toward a sparkling meadow.

From the first day, jump training became her favorite. Each step of the process made instant sense, and the connections between theory and practice intrigued her.

"We employ all the contraptions this hangar can hold. With no airplanes available, we make do. I cannot over-stress the necessity of following instructions precisely. They may call this place Kilkenny's Circus, but we abide no tricks. Roman candles sputter out when they hit the ground—we do our utmost to learn from failure, and aim for you to eject in the upright position."

His word picture—an upside down paratrooper landing on his head, couldn't have been more motivating. He stopped the group near a sort of harness.

"Arrive here alert and rested. Not too much to eat beforehand. We've had that sort of spill from on high, too." The instructor ignored a stifled guffaw.

"All paratrooper training concentrates here at Ringway. You enjoy some leniencies from Scotland's rigors, but risk falling from the sky like punctured balloons." He made eye contact with each participant.

"Enjoy the rides and learn as much as you can. During the day, lines of would-be paratroopers form at each post, but though you practice in secret, you accumulate more practice hours. Commander Kilkenny himself devised your training, which we constantly update."

He swept his arm toward a black chute hanging in midair, and Kate flashed back to the cattle chute on Addie's farm. Forced to run down the narrow alleyway into a holding pen, the cattle fought every step of the way, but succumbed in the end.

"You see before you an actual Whitley fuselage, also a Dakota. Tonight, you will swing in a trapeze while learning correct flight drill, play on the wooden chutes, and do a great deal of falling and rolling. Tomorrow, you attempt the real chute. By week's end, with your head for heights developed, we shall acquaint you with the Fan. Follow me."

The Fan drew Kate's eyes to a cable with an attached harness wrapping a big drum suspended by steel cables. The instructor climbed a ladder and harnessed himself into the drum.

"Watch the vanes. They control my speed like air brakes, allowing me to land with the same impact as if I employed a chute out in the open."

He pulled on his goggles and jumped from the twenty-foot platform. The drum revolved, and slowed by the vanes, the cable unrolled. Someone gasped and others changed their positions, but Kate memorized his movements and pulled her hand from her pocket, in case he asked for a volunteer to go first.

Darkened London streets shone with mist, a fitting night for Sherlock Holmes intrigue. Spires and tall buildings interspersed with searchlights scanning the moonlit expanse. No drone of airplanes in the distance, no flares this night.

Kate and three other agents hovered in a cold vestibule, awaiting their ride with her mentor, Miss G, plus all their baggage. Several vehicles passed before their lorry arrived, and they all scrabbled in.

The driver's profile seemed oddly familiar, but the hat obscured the individual's face. While the others shoved their backpacks inside, the mist turned to rain, and Kate brushed it from her hair as she scrabbled between Miss G and the lorry's cool wall. Miss G leaned over and whispered.

"You can trust the artists at the house. The dye smudges in your hair to aid your disguise should last about a month. Water won't fade them, but when they diminish, you can always rub in a little mud."

After three aborted attempts to cross the Channel, Kate's expectations cooled, but just in case coastal storms cooperated tonight, she allowed a smidgeon of anticipation. Southern France prepared a place for her, she knew it.

Its roads, railways, and physical contours were imprinted on a silk map in her pack, and in a few hours, she might finally take up her French milkmaid role. Or not. The past three weeks had tried her patience, but everyone shared the same conundrum.

The lorry headed out of London. The closed-in space gave Kate a suffocating feeling, but one of the agents hummed *Wish Me Luck*, and someone else joined in with a whistle on the high parts.

Through tears, Addie did just that the last time Kate saw her. Saying good-bye to Mr. Tenney was difficult, too. She'd never forget stopping by his office the day before cutting off all outside contact. His greeting sounded as normal as ever.

"What brings you here this afternoon?"

"I'm walking home with Addie."

"Good enough." He pulled her to the corner. "Do come back to us alive." His eyes glinted. "My father would be proud of you. He carried war secrets to his grave."

"Like my father." *My father*—at least she could speak of him now.

Out on the street, a double-decker bus screeched to a halt, and Mr. Tenney gestured toward it with his chin. "Did you know a woman received her license to drive one of those a couple of years ago?"

"Truly?"

"Yes, a Phyllis Thompson. Women do most everything now, but not many go as far as you." He pulled her farther into the shadows. "I've spent plenty of time at the Scottish training center and at Ringway, Kathryn. The latter is much improved, despite its rather grisly humor. Hopefully those with uneasy stomachs turn back right off."

"You think that might include me?"

"Not at all, but I do hope you consider one request." He lowered his voice even more. "Avoid becoming a wireless operator if you can. The Gestapo continually upgrades their detection devices, and once they locate an operator, there's little hope of escape."

He leaned closer. "I no longer risk my life in the air, but might still be of service."

"How would I contact you?" Kate's eyes blurred as the bell signaled office workers to go home.

"Memorize the phone number here. If you fail to reach the Baker Street offices, contact me."

The idea fit with the S.O.E.'s flotsam approach. *Random information, insignificant at first glance, might prove invaluable in the long run.*

An instantaneous flicker lighted Mr. Tenney's eyes. "I am not quite old enough to be your father, nor I daresay, brave enough. Yet I believe you came to us for a purpose. Now, you carry out another."

When Addie knocked at the door, Mr. Tenney waved her in and placed his hand over his heart. "We shall take care of your Addie."

"She's doing well, isn't she?"

"She does well at everything. Mum positively adores her."

Kate grinned. "I could say 'I told you so.'"

Charles' expression softened at Addie's approach. "You've completed your duties, what, like a good Iowa girl?"

In contrast to blue and black ink smudges on her chin, Addie's smile revealed sparkling teeth. "Today whizzed by, but it'll take a while to recover from all the ink and chemicals." She quickly added, "I'm not complaining, though."

The lorry jolted Kate back to the present. They bounced over a dip in the road, and Kate considered these drivers who worked day shifts, but drove night OES missions. Bad weather had botched four trips to the airfield, which meant four drivers gave up a night's sleep so she could meet her plane. Hopefully this one would return to London with an empty lorry and some Benzedrine to keep her awake.

She'd seen a worker in Mr. Tenney's office take a Benzedrine tablet more than once. Who knew what she sacrificed at night for the Allied cause?

When they finally lurched to a halt, Kate was the first into the cool night air. One agent whispered, "We're somewhere near Sussex. I can smell the cattle."

An obscure moonlit runway highlighted two high-wing monoplanes.

Miss G said, "I believe this Lysander is yours, Agent Merce."

The dull-green plane won Kate's heart. *Please, please let tonight be the night.*

The pilot strode over. "Looks like we won't have to abort this time. Get your gear."

Miss G gave her a final hug, helped hoist Kate's pack into the Lancaster, and handed her one last tiny package. "Use only if absolutely necessary. *Au revoir.*"

A lipstick with cyanide for dire circumstances—Kate's heart lurched into her throat. She'd waited so long for this moment, why such a wave of trepidation? She secured her seatbelt and stared out the window at the agents and Miss G. Gathered like a kit of pigeons in the cold, they would soon disappear—one more family she left behind. The difference was, pigeons had an uncanny knack of finding their way home.

The pilot twisted toward her.

"Ready?"

"Ready."

The next time he asked her, she'd bail out into a sea of stars.

Chapter Ten

The plateau took Domingo across the border into Cantal, where glimmers in the northern sky led to silvery wings. Then two white canopies sailed the night sky.

In case the Milice also waited, he staggered his advance. The way this 'chutist floated tightened his sense of responsibility—his first female. He couldn't have said how he knew. As with an agent in an earlier landing this week, she grappled with the knots, so Domingo bent to assist.

Her shushed intake of breath reminded him that for all she knew, he might be Milice, or worse, Gestapo—the Secret State Police.

His whispered, *Code Name Merce,* brought a sigh that broke his heart. The girl's eyes glowed dark, like soil on a northern slope, but the gold in her hair reflected the moon. Domingo soon freed her leg.

Like Sancha, did this foreign girl's blood stir for *les Juifs?* Or perhaps she was one, though few had hair this light. The code name brought to mind Aitaita's medieval tale of Pedro Nolasco rescuing his brothers, held captive by Catalonian infidels and pirates. *La Merce*—Our Lady of Mercy—appeared to him with oppressed children under her cloak.

Had this modern stranger come for the children, too? She took a step and crumbled against his ribs, then startled away like a frightened lamb. He eased her to the earth, and because she sought no sympathy, her pain catapulted through him as he pushed up the pantleg of her ungainly parachutist suit and untied her boot.

A sprain. Common, but so painful. The agent flinched, yet certain he could trust her to remain quiet, Domingo lined his kerchief with Aitaita's remedy: a handful of mud.

Another sigh rewarded him—this war made ascertaining right from wrong difficult. The girl's eyes glistened, perhaps from pain, perhaps with gratitude. He had no need to know, since all eyes melded into Sancha's, those eyes he would never again see in this life.

While she loosened a collapsible shovel attached to her pant leg, Domingo took stock of her weight and the radio's bulk. He pretended to bury the silk canopy in the bushes, but whisked it up his sleeve for Maman.

The girl removed her drop jacket and gestured for him to bury it. When he swung low for her to clamber on his back, her drawn expression communicated dignity, even as paleness bespoke her discomfort. Good—she detested relying on him.

Strong to have come here, she must become even stronger. He cringed at that reality, so like Sancha's, and adjusted to the agent's weight. He shifted the radio into his arms, thankful he inherited Aitaita's powerful girth. Moonlight made the going easier, and at their destination, the girl emitted no cry as her feet touched the earth.

In the brittle haystack, Domingo fished for a waiting peasant's fingers, and like a hungry field mouse, a sinewy hand latched onto his. He dropped the radio and then reached for the girl's soft palm and guided it inside.

"*Merci.*" Her breath tingled against his ear.

He troubled his tongue for words. "Allez avec Dieu." The English rendition filtered through his mind from his studies—*Go with God*.

The haystack swallowed her in a rush. A passerby would never guess what pulsed within that innocent pile. Domingo rested his hands on the cool grass to stretch out his back and his spirit lightened at this small triumph against the Reich.

Merci. The girl's whisper edged his flight as he embraced the night. Domingo's throat filled, and he sent up a silent plea for the agent's safety.

A time years ago came to him, when he knelt beside Aitaita and Maman in the cushion of wet churchyard grass.

"My firstborn, my boy-child. Oh, Ander."

Domingo entered into Maman's cry—one could claim another's spoken thoughts.

The same thing happened after he and Philippe departed from Sancha's family. All the way home, and until Père Gaspard came to weep with him, grief swarmed Domingo, but Père's presence brought deep solace.

In sorrow's dank communion, he confessed he and Philippe had killed the Gestapo men. Père waited to respond, though what he said, Domingo could not recall. But the rhythm of Père's voice lifted Domingo back into this world. Later, Maman's hand on his shoulder lulled him to sleep.

Before recrossing the meadow where the agent fell to earth, he slowed to make sure no signs remained. There, amidst frost-coated grass, something metallic sparkled, so he reached to its unnatural coolness—a silver ring that flew off in the jolt?

Maybe she kept this in the sole of her shoe. Perhaps her beloved gave it to her, or maybe it was like the *Lauburu*, the Basque cross Aitaita always carried in his breast pocket for reassurance.

Domingo circled the ring's tiny ridges with his thumb before pocketing it. Then he lowered his head and carved a sharp line home through the remains of darkness.

No questions and no complaints, became Kate's motto that first night. The next day, she rested her ankle before a peasant fashioned her a makeshift brace. Then for days, she followed a guide through reckless, wild country. Mornings, afternoons, and evenings ran together, filled with views that stole her breath.

Her sense of time slipped away. Faces replaced rigid deadlines, practices, schedules, and memorization.

Addie, the Tenneys, and her mother and father, now almost

clearer than Alexandre, appeared. And finally came the high brow of the guide who met her drop and tended her ankle. Intense private pain chiseled his eyes. Could he also sense the weight of her grief?

As with others who joined this hike, she knew she would never see him again. One by one, they dropped off at this village or that until only the guide continued ahead of her. Could they be passing the village where her father was born? At last, after rough climbs through stunning gorges, the guide scanned the horizon and turned.

"Only a few kilometers left."

Rugged terrain finally shifted into cobblestone as a village unfolded like a travel flyer. Steep roofs and slanted stone fences scooted down hilly streets boasting a *charcuterie*, a *boulangerie*, an *épicerie*, a *bibliothèque*, and a *bureau de poste*.

Butchery, bakery, grocery, library, and post office—everything she might need. From her apron to the second-hand stockings the Baker Street disguise artists had matched with her simple cotton dress, Kate metamorphosed into an unschooled milkmaid who had never left the area. She smoothed the folds of her skirt, brought into England from Southern France.

She had rubbed sour milk into the fabric at the last farm, after traipsing uphill through temperatures too cold to think of bathing. The perspiration of days on end mixed with the milk taint—surely no Nazi in his right mind would come near her.

Farther on, her guide glided around a stone church. Etched in stone at eye level on the right, a simple inscription: *Le Presbytère*. The guide motioned her to wait.

Miss G had described this destination in great detail. "Three thousand feet in altitude, on the Viverais Plain with the volcano Le Liseaux in the background, the whole community welcomes Jewish refugees. A preacher and his wife formed a school, and the Garel Network, the former Jewish OSE, operates there, although they renamed it when it went underground. Madeleine Dreyfus chaperoned children to safety in Le Chambon.

"In August, 1942, after the Paris round-ups of Jews, Mr. Lamirand, the General Secretary for Youth for Vichy and the Haute-Loire prefect, received scant welcome in Le Chambon. The older students protested his speech and admitted they sheltered Jews. They declared their refusal to defy gospel teachings to obey deportation or registration requirements. Yet, the Gestapo round-up yielded no Jews.

"Last year, stipulations worsened, rendering searches more brutal. The merciless Pierre Laval, Général Pétain's second-in-command, launched a fatal round-up on June 19th. But Chambon's Huguenot Protestants still pursue this endeavor, with Catholics from all over France."

The juxtaposition of two intersecting eave spouts now symbolized Miss G's observation. *Protestants and Catholics.* Together, the two spouts protected the roof. Kate breathed deeper as twilight encroached the courtyard and a heavy doorway on the far side of the house with a smaller door carved into it.

Beckoned by her guide to an open space through thick green vines partially shading another wooden door, Kate rubbed her finger on a hewn stone archway. The smell of damp earth and moldy leaves gave way to a mélange of aromas—yeasty bread, heavy cream, nutmeg, and cinnamon. In a sudden rage, her stomach bellowed.

Tap, t-tap tap, t-tap. A slight woman in a gray dress ushered them into a kitchen with lavender and garlic bundles hung from rafters and cookware on great iron hooks over a massive iron stove. The guide murmured something to the woman and fled through another door without a word to Kate.

The bright-eyed matron gripped Kate's hand with surprising strength. She sat Kate down in a sturdy wooden chair. "You are hungry?"

Steam from a lidded pot and a tantalizing lavender honey scent from a large pottery bowl made Kate weak. The woman slathered thick, creamy porridge with golden butter and pushed some crusty bread her way.

It was all Kate could do not to grab the bowl like a mug and gulp, but she controlled her urge and dug in with her spoon. Her hostess poured from a small pitcher of hot milk.

"You are American?"

Her question sent panic through Kate. Could it be that obvious? Her full mouth prevented a response, so Kate nodded. American, yes, but she felt British and might also have claimed French citizenship.

A steaming mug of a thick, chocolate brown drink wakened Kate's insides and smoothed the way for every last lick of porridge in her earthenware bowl. Over another full mug, she posed her own question.

"How did you know? Should I change some part of my dress?"

"*Non—non.* Perhaps it was your bearing." Eyes the color of a moonless night reminded Kate of the powerful, patient guide who nursed her ankle.

When she finished her porridge, a slab of cheese appeared on a small board with a cutting knife, next to a wintered-over yellow-green apple.

"*Bon appetit, Mademoiselle.*"

A woman shorter and wider than the first entered the room and spoke in low tones. Kate made out only *Des Grillons* and something about a seven-year-old.

Her hostess peered Kate's way. "Wait here. I will return."

The phrase ignited Kate's imagination. Returning to England seemed a distant dream, and returning to the States, inconceivable. She enjoyed some mellow cheese and leaned back against her solid chair, achingly full.

Adjusted to the shadows now, she smoothed the table's uneven edge. *Hand-hewn* described the entire room. The earthy hominess declared that whole lives played out in this room. Many people passed through here, and traces remained of these benevolent ghosts, like the scuffed canvas pack draped in one corner.

A worn path in the plank floor revealed a thoroughfare from

one part of the house to another. Outside, a rooster crowed, pails clanked, and a door scraped on garrulous hinges. Faint light peeked through a gingham-curtained opening.

Warmth lingered here, creating an aura of safety. But Kate stiffened at a sound from the door. Better check her papers, just to be sure. She unlatched her pack and lifted her *carte d'identité.*

Nom: Dumont
Prénoms: Merce
Profession: Sans.
Nationalité: Francaise
Née le: 21 Avril, 1918

Everything in order—name, no profession, French, born in '18. *Guard your identity card above all else.*

She knew she should check the window for the woman coming back, but her head became a ponderous weight. She angled forward and bent her neck. In an instant, she was riding the night sky over the Auvergne once again.

The pilot chute jerked free of her backpack. The inflation *whoosh* and frigid air took her breath as the wind claimed her.

Release the main canopy. Extended lines parted the binding at the shock of her weight and cast her to the heavens until the main chute billowed.

Eyes open, chin tucked, knees locked to the rear—so far, so good. Time suspended, melding her body with night's indigo blanket and an odd sense of comfort. Between two very different worlds, the ache in her chest let go momentarily, and she declared her new identity to the universe.

"I am now *Merce Dumont,* descending to the land of my father." Perhaps *Le Renard Intrepid* observed her descent, with her mother, Aunt Alvina, and Alexandre. Perhaps her family, all deceased, cheered her on.

Months earlier, the SOE officers exchanged looks when she requested Code Name *Merci.*

"How about *Merce? Résistance* Spaniards and Basques know her well, and celebrate her festival every year. Besides, your mission will aid the oppressed."

Merce—rhymed with scarce, a pleasant sound where Nazis were concerned.

Bend slightly forward from waist, elbows tight into sides, hands over reserve parachute ends, fingers spread.

With all four risers secured, the canopy came under control, and a vast starlit dome embraced her. Below, misty valleys surrounded a plateau—her destination.

Turn into the wind, let go the toggle—balls of feet, calves, thighs, buttocks, and side of back must touch down in a continuous roll.

The story of her life. If only she could hover here longer between worlds. But the earth loomed closer and closer, until trees reached eye level, and then silvery grass glistened with dew.

The shudder of impact burned her calf to the knee. The chute puffed and fluttered, canopy release assemblies clicked, and, jaws clenched against the pain striking her ankle, Kate recalled her instructions.

Lift latches to free parachute from pack and roll over.

Back on earth again, but she already needed help. Her nerves grated—a pathetic landing, despite her perfect training performances.

A shadow approached, Kate's heart knocked against her ribs, and one seven-letter word focused her attention. *Gestapo.* But warm breath grazed her ear with *Code Name Merce,* and Southern France's subtle scents niggled her nostrils.

A different concern overwhelmed her at the tangle around her ankle. A sharp sting radiated her calf, but the stranger loosed the cord and in one efficient movement, balled it with the chute and buried them in the brush.

She tried to stand when he returned, but fell against him. He explored the pulsing spot with warm fingers and dressed the ankle with cool moss. Veiled obsidian eyes under heavy brows calmed her as he retied the string and leaned low, waving her onto his back.

Heat flushed her at causing him trouble, but the guide's calm demeanor tamped her anxiety. *Must be Basque—wears beret flat on head, not to the side. Dark coloring, powerful build, patient, and controlled under pressure.*

He shouldered her 110 pounds, ten more in boots and clothing, plus her pack and the radio, without hesitation. She made herself as small as she could against his wide, rock-hard shoulders.

Once, Alexandre had carried her like this after a foolish fall had sprained the same ankle. In those long-ago days, adventure equaled a late evening walk along the creek in the security of Halberton, Iowa.

What a difference here, with capture a breath away. But that kind of thinking would do no good. Kate trained her eyes east to snowy Massif Central peaks. Westward lay the Pyrénées foothills.

You drop south of Vichy, Pétain's occupied capital, where villages harbor Jews, downed allied pilots, and others of Gestapo interest. We may eventually set up forest camps to contain the growing number of downed pilots seeking safety.

Perspiration washed the back of Kate's neck when she realized she'd forgotten to shed her trousers. But electricity sizzled up her leg, and the pants kept the blessed coolness in place.

If you are found out, your errors may cause the deaths of others.

The guide's worn wool jacket absorbed her prayer. "May he not suffer on my account."

What seemed like hours passed through stark thickets. Prickly broom bushes clawed like night phantoms, but the guide paid no attention. Finally, another meadow shimmered before them like spun glass. He dropped her radio and pack with a solid thunk and eased Kate against something scratchy but yielding.

She caught at the stuff and sniffed a handful—hay, the same as in Addie's haymow. The guide's muffled password roused a response from inside. He hoisted her pack and radio over, guided her fingers to a rough hand, and then his thick Basque-accented French brushed her ear.

"*Allez avec Dieu.*" The blessing soothed her like a benediction. Then, like a moon-shadow, Kate's deliverer disappeared.

The Presbytery door scraped and she shook herself awake at Madame's touch. "Come. I will show you to your bed."

Chapter Eleven

"I need to check north of Wilmslow. Would you mind taking notes, Addie?"

Six weeks had passed since Kate left, and Mr. T was asking her to take her own notes, not simply dictation. Maybe someday, she'd be able to write even more.

"What time should I be ready?"

"Three-fifteen. I'll drop you at Mum's on the return trip."

At five minutes of three, Addie scrubbed ink stains from her hands and pushed back a stray curl. Her breath misted the mirror.

"Your first trip through London, maybe even into the countryside. And maybe Mr. T will cheer up his Mum—she'll never recover from missing Kate."

She grinned, recollecting how a slip she made had led to a change in the office. At home, she and Kate always called Mr. Tenney *Mr. T*, but never at the office. But one day, while talking with Mrs. Culver and some of the other staff, she forgot. Before she knew it, everyone used the more familiar term, and Mr. T seemed not to mind.

Addie rubbed a finger across her freckles as an old memory surfaced. Once, years ago, Kate showed her Aunt Alvina's store of new *pancake* make-up and told them how a Hollywood artist named Max Factor created it with his son Frank. The girls smoothed the thick substance on their faces, but soon rubbed it off.

Afterward, Kate declared, "There, that's better. For a minute, I thought I'd lost you, Addie. Wearing this stuff is like having a scab all over your face—I don't know how Aunt Alvina stands it."

Now, Kate probably had to wear make-up, and life in Westbourne Grove wasn't the same without her. But with Allied troops landing at Anzio and Mr. Churchill recovering from his pneumonia, all was well, or soon would be. Addie applied a bit of lipstick and returned to her desk.

Mr. T came along a few minutes later. "Don't forget your pad and pencil."

He led her out the back entrance and opened her door. The auto's cushioned leather seat invited her to settle back through mild traffic onto Altrincham Road.

"Our path lies near Oversleyford. In the olden days, Mum and I came here to see father off to the wars, so it holds mixed memories. I suspect since you've seen photos of Father and gotten to know Mum, you have questions about our family?"

"I wonder about things sometimes, but it's not my place to ask your mother."

"Mum can seem a bit distant, yet she's taken to you like fog to England's coast. But you may ask me anything you wish."

"Your upbringing is so different from mine, with your father in the army."

"I daresay."

He shifted around a double-decker, and Addie immersed herself in the sights and sounds. Every few blocks, another bombsite turned up, with buildings showing their insides like a little girl's dollhouse.

Finally Mr. T turned down a road flanked by vast fields with a tall steel tower at one end. "Welcome to Ringway Field, Addie."

"Where Kate trained?"

His eyes twinkled like a small boy guilty of mischief. "Quite. Your sharp intellect has found me out."

"Sir, you brought me here on purpose?"

A pained look crossed his face. "Must you call me that?"

"Oh, forgive me. It's just that—"

"Quite all right, but we're out of range of the office now." He parked the car outside lines of Army vehicles. "I thought a peek might do you good, since I had to check on some things up here."

"Thank you so much. So Kate learned to parachute here?"

"Yes, and I once trained here, myself."

"And your father, too?"

"He fought before we learned to parachute. Come along, then. I'll show you the lay of the land."

He opened her door, and an unexpected attack of shyness struck Addie. Thankfully, the large RAF RINGWAY sign provided a focal point.

"Maybe Alexandre was stationed here, too?"

"Quite possibly." Charles pointed west. "See there, along the North side? The white-walled hangar used to be the terminal. Now its flat roof sports a MANCHESTER RINGWAY sign. And the Air Transport Authority employs the black one, built early in the war. Those six small buildings mark the old Firtree Farm."

"And that huge black one?"

"That one houses parachute ground training. The Bellman over there serves as a hangar, and the one next to it, the Number One Parachute Training School for the RAF. They parachute over Tatton Park, with permission from Lord Egerton, the owner, but keep the women's involvement very hush-hush."

"How do you know all this?"

"I maintain some connections and have done some checking. After all Kathryn has been through, I—"

He fiddled with his hat brim. "I hope you don't think me a meddler, but Mum and I have little family. I feel a fatherly protectiveness for Kathryn." His cheeks colored. "Not to say I am old enough to be her father."

Addie touched his arm. "You have no idea how hard I prayed for protection when she first came here, Si— Charles."

"There you go. I feel certain you can learn to call me Charles." His eyebrows danced with approval. "After all, the entire staff addresses me as Mr. T."

Addie imagined the brilliant ruby of her face. "Anyway, I prayed for people who would watch out for her, and God gave her you."

"Mum became so involved, and then with Alexandre's crashes, his death, and the latest complication—"

The softness in his face sent a shiver through Addie, but a watchful inner voice held up a hand. She must remember Harold's final injunction the last time she saw him, the day he attacked her friend Jane and threatened his mother. The scene went through her mind as if it were yesterday.

"Son, Addie's taken care of everything since you left. George and I have been married since February."

The vein in Harold's forehead nearly ruptured. "Ma!"

"Yes. Sooner or later, you'll have to accept it. And about Addie—if she doesn't want to see you, that's her right."

His upraised arm stark against blue sky, Harold sputtered. "You would stand against your own son?"

"And you would hit your own mother?" Not a tremble in Berthea's voice, but her unmistakable sad undertone drifted to Addie.

"You don't want to miss your train, do you? You can still make the afternoon one out of Waterloo. I'll drive you."

Simon gave another push with the gun. Berthea pulled Harold to the Chevy and shut the door, but as she opened the driver's side, he burst out again.

Addie's mind said, "Run," but her feet froze.

Like a villain in a movie scene, Harold pushed Simon aside and the gun fired. Harold's fingers bit into Addie's wrist, and his gravelly tone imploded in her ear.

"You will do as I say." He nearly wrenched her arm from its socket, and ire wakened in her. She kicked him in the shins and clawed his face with her free hand. Berthea sped toward them, and another loud crack sounded.

Harold sagged against Addie as Simon raised the gun butt. But Jane held out her hand over Harold's crumpled figure, gentle and steady.

"Simon. Simon. Now, that's enough."

The recollection still made Addie squirm, but at least Simon had only fired into the air, and Berthea was able to corral Harold and get him to the troop train in time. She put the awful experience out of her mind, but Harold's "You will do what I say," remained.

Then it occurred to her that Charles might be privy to information about Harold. "Would you consider me brash if I asked for something along military lines?"

"Not at all."

"Would an American private stationed along the coast ever visit London?"

"Right now, you mean? In light of coming events, I very much doubt that."

Her sigh came out stronger than she intended, but Charles bent her way. "If you wish, I can attempt to find out more. I—Kathryn told me a bit about your husband."

Words failed Addie. Hopefully he read the gratitude in her eyes.

He shuffled his feet and peered out at the field for a while. "All right, then, we must proceed. But if your—ah—husband should ever find his way here, I—"

His skin flamed as ruddy as a directional flag on a distant pole, and the muscle in his cheek hollow worked like a small machine. It wasn't like him to leave a sentence unfinished, but Addie claimed his meaning.

"Thank you."

They turned back, and when Charles opened her door, Addie ducked to get in. She slipped on some wet leaves, so he steadied her with a hand to her elbow.

"Do be careful, dear girl."

Their eyes met, and she recalled how Harold's changed color when he became enraged, a daily occurrence during their last year together. Like thunder clouds, that darkening served as her warning. But this crystal blue-black, like a raven's shimmering feathers, revealed only caring and concern.

The next afternoon at closing time, Mrs. Culver held the street door for several workers, and as Addie passed under the massive brick and mortar archway to open her umbrella, something struck her from the side. She toppled against Mrs. Culver's arm.

"Oh, my goodness—whatever for—" Mrs. Culver helped her regain her balance, and Addie bent to pet a shaggy mongrel dog that was slobbering all over her leg.

"Why, hello, you big old lovable powder puff." The oversized mutt gave her a dripping lick across her cheek and roused a giggle. A familiar matted-hair odor took her back to the farm and Old Brown, an equally scruffy hound dog.

"Mackie, come back here—you know better than—" A stocky redheaded young woman in men's overalls shook her head apologetically.

"I see you've found a pal. Sorry, he usually stays right with me."

"Oh, it's all right, I won't break. Did you call him Mackie?"

"Yes, Mackie the wonder dog. He's rescued more than seventy people from the rubble during the past two years."

As though he understood every word, Mackie surveyed his growing audience and gave a thorough shake, covering Addie's leg with mist. Mrs. Culver applauded while Mackie's owner caressed his muzzle.

"You're a good old friend, aren't you, boy?"

That voice—Addie had heard it somewhere before, and when the woman looked up, Addie recognized her as Evelyn. "Aren't you Kate's friend? We had tea one day—"

"For sure and certain. And you're Addie from Iowa—nice running into you—or having Mackie run into you."

"Proud to meet you, Mackie." Addie hadn't realized Charles had joined the gaggle that gathered in the doorway. The slant of his twill Fedora Trilby revealed a glint in his eyes.

"This is Mr. Tenney, my employer, and Mrs. Culver."

"And I'm Evelyn Brown. When Mackie's family was bombed out, my Home Guard adopted him. Now, he helps search bomb debris."

They shook hands all around, and Charles turned to Addie. "Do you suppose this fellow has an American bloodline, seeing how he ran straight to you?"

"Possibly, although Evelyn's the expert."

Evelyn cracked her gum. "Oh no, nothing like that. Mackie's only a British mutt."

"But a hero, no matter what. Where would we be in these perilous times without such loyalty and determination? Speaking of that, I hear Mr. Churchill made a sudden appearance at the House of Commons today, with his usual, *Never give up*."

He leaned down to ruff Mackie's fur, tipped his hat, and disappeared into the crowd with Mrs. Culver and the other workers, while Evelyn turned to Addie.

"I haven't seen Kate for a long time."

"No." Addie fidgeted with her purse handle. "You're the one who helped her find this job in the first place."

"Righto." Evelyn lowered her eyes. "Never dreamed I'd meet so many folks from across. I remember when Kate first came, and last time, she'd heard about her husband and discovered she was expecting a wee one."

"Um—she lost the baby, Evelyn."

"Sorry to hear that. I was making a little sweater for him."

"It took some time for her to recover, and she started working for the Allies. Mr. Tenney told her about the job."

"Jolly good. I'd best set about my business. Why don't you come over sometime? I'm usually working at our local guard station."

"Really? I do need to get out more."

"Well, then, I'll draw you a map. Come prepared—it's not the cleanest." Evelyn took a pencil from behind her ear and sketched on a scrap she pulled from her pocket.

"These are directions from here. I'll look forward to seeing you." Evelyn ushered Mackie down the street, and Addie watched them out of sight. Something about petting him made her lonely, although he'd probably wrecked her second-to-last pair of silk stockings.

In the distance, Old Bailey's spire towered above burned out buildings, a sight Addie observed every day on her way home. When she first arrived, Kate told her how the landmark gave Londoners hope during the air raids.

Hope. Such a powerful word. Addie automatically glanced behind her before she started down the street, but chastised herself.

"Kate would say I mustn't worry about Harold suddenly coming out of nowhere. He's 150 miles away, and Americans don't get passes to come way up to London. Even Charles said so, but—"

Still, she gave another look behind her.

The night before Kate left, she'd received a letter from Berthea. Mrs. T left it on the table, and Addie tore open the seal. "Oh no—she enclosed a note from Harold."

"Would you like me to do the honors?"

Addie handed over the letter.

"Tell me if you want me to slow down or stop."

"Stop." A nervous giggle escaped Addie's lips. "It's been so wonderful, two whole months with no word from him, and then comes this reminder."

"Why don't you see what Berthea has to say first?"

"She and George are making my garden into a showplace. Oh, my—this year, for the first time, the garden club's visitation extends into the country, and guess who's on the agenda?"

"You and Jane? That'll give those haughty town ladies a little honest competition. They don't stand a chance. As you say, there's no better fertilizer than horse manure."

"And George is retiring from his mail route. Thirty-seven years, rain, snow, sleet, or shine. He's excited to farm and garden. Pure fun for him, Berthea says."

"Not a bad prospect." They sat in the quiet. "So, tell me your decision. Hear Harold's illustrious letter in full, or a professional stenographer's summary?"

"Go ahead. I have to stop being a baby."

"You take that back. You survived more than three years of his shenanigans. I'll always be proud of you for that—some women would have died in the effort."

Two blocks from the office, Addie had passed a newspaper stand blaring details of the three German planes brought down the night before and Mussolini's wife fleeing to Switzerland with three children. Things could always be worse, and listening to Kate read Harold's letter that night proved it.

"August 27, Brixham, England. Now we know precisely where he is—we'll find a map later, but don't worry. The trains are swamped with troops on missions. Mrs. Tenney's friend told her she tried to visit someone in Hastings, but couldn't find standing room."

Addie exhaled a shaky breath and Kate patted her arm. "Here we go. Drum roll, please." Kate swept her arm in a dramatic gesture and her wheat field bangs made a fencerow over her dark eyebrows. Addie leaned back and squinched her eyes shut.

"Well, what do you know? A surprise, right off the bat. He doesn't begin with *Dear So and So.*

I would write, 'My dear wife, like other soldiers, but their spouses, obedient and humble, submit to their husbands and their God.

Mother will only tell me that you help Kate. Does a mere friend deserve this, at the risk of your life? We prepare to fell a cruel oppressor, and my wife cavorts far from home for the sake of a childish friendship. Your "Myrna Loy" beauty, as Kate says, goes only surface deep. Before I deployed, you hid from me. How bitter a pill that was, having my own mother side with you, and in front of Mrs. Pike, too.

One day, you will answer for all this before our Maker, no shilly-shal-lying and no excuses. Mark my words. "Kate needed me," will fall on deaf ears.

I command you, as your lawful husband, to return home by any possible means.

PFC Harold Bledsoe

Kate made a gagging sound. "Going to seminary really humbled him, eh?"

"I must be dotty, but I'm still thrilled he can write *PFC* before his name. He wanted to join up for so long. Sometimes, I truly thought he'd lose his mind, but he prevailed. I have to hand him that." She opened her eyes to Kate's frown.

"You always put the best light on him, even now, after the horrid things he wrote. He seems to have forgotten a few minor details—he called you horrible names, threatened you, and physically attacked Jane, a lame woman with a cane." Kate's eyes flashed. "She hid you because he would have forced you that night, and I doubt his main concern was an heir—it was all about power. Now, supposedly concerned for your safety, he orders you back across the mine-infested Atlantic. Argh!"

"I finally realize Harold honestly believes he knows what's best for me, for everyone." Addie leaned into the mattress, and Kate scrunched down beside her.

"You've suffered enough under his tyranny, kiddo. No matter how often you call a skunk a kitten, it'll still smell like skunk."

"You're right. I'm not taking his side, Kate. I see how he wore me down, but I was so weak. I bet he'd win an argument on this, even with you."

"Don't be too sure."

Addie giggled at Kate's menacing face.

"Weak, my foot! You endured his endless whining about being a cripple, but now look at him, deployed with a fighting unit. He did have an injury, yes. But he made it into a *condition* and used it for his own purposes."

"Nobody forced me to believe him, Kate."

"True, but that was then. Now you're free of him. Maybe you could picture him like a balloon heading toward the clouds, monarch of his own world of rules—"

A blustery wind gave a bully push against the house, and Addie closed her eyes again. "That balloon's floating away—now it's close to the window—" She jumped up, opened the window a crack, but slammed it as a draft raged in.

"Gone!" Kate clapped her hands and Addie started laughing. Kate joined in until they both held their sides. Then Addie sobered.

"Oh, Kate, Mrs. T's going to be so upset when you don't come home tomorrow night."

"I know. That's my one regret, leaving you to face her alone. So here we are again, each with our challenges. Only I don't know exactly what mine will be."

Addie gave a rueful grin. "And you're about to leave again."

"It's your fault, you know—you helped me figure out what I should do."

A horn blared and someone pulled Addie back from the curb. In the chaotic crowd, she couldn't even tell who to thank. London filled up more every day, with such a hodge-podge of uniformed men and women coming from all quarters. She let the crowd sweep her along, catching snitches of conversation.

"Who can tell what will become of the Polish and Russians?"

"Do you think the Allies will attack Monte Cassino?"

"They have to, don't they—at least the town? Ten to one, the abbey's loaded with Nazi ammo."

"That gunfire Saturday night was deafening—did you ever hear what those confounded Messerschmidts hit?"

"—don't know, but what I wouldn't give for a decent night's sleep."

She shook off thoughts of Harold's proximity and considered Mackie, such a plain old dog making an enormous difference. Probably many in this crowd were, too. In the end, it all would surely lead to victory, and she was happy to be in the thick of it.

Chapter Twelve

A petite, tow-headed child shared a wide upstairs room in Des Grillons with several young women and children. The tiny sprite's enormous eyes spoke of wisdom beyond her years, and she boasted a nose like Addie's—drawn up at the end. Fragile blue veins traversed her pale forehead, and her chin, the size of Kate's thumbprint, balanced cheeks as rosy as the shrinking apples stored in the fruit cellar, or dried cherries filling large glass jars on the Presbytery's pantry shelf.

The child weaseled her way into Kate's heart on her very first morning in Le Chambon-sur-Lignon. One of the older children carried her to breakfast. Little Linden locked eyes with Kate, and that was it.

Unpasteurized milk—that's what made her cheeks so rosy. Nondescript facts like this entered and left Kate's mind like a revolving library, trivia she'd learned during training or back in Iowa.

But this cherub with perfect china features carried a different air, and something told Kate they belonged together. Knowing her situation's impermanence, she shook off the sensation. Still, she was meant to meet the child, and she made up a singsong rhyme to express just that. She crooned it to little Linden every time she held her.

You and me, lost and found.
Put your little hands around
Around my neck, and off we'll go
off to dinner through the snow.

Daily life involved walks to gather firewood, trips to the *bou-langerie* for yeast, and to the market for supplies at Madame Claude, the cook's, behest. Taking their meals in the Presbytery entailed another long walk from their room, but Linden had no strength for the journey. Kate gathered her up like the orphan lambs Addie sometimes fed from a bottle. Linden trembled like those lambs, too.

"Do you have some long stockings and an extra blanket for Linden?"

The dark-eyed mistress of the household gestured for Kate to follow her to a great chest in an adjoining room. There she found what Linden needed and carefully clothed the little one for the cold weather. The girl clung to her, often falling asleep in her arms. Kate had to pry her fingers loose at bedtime.

As days turned into weeks, the Presbytery table where Kate devoured her porridge that first night expanded with each meal, making room for whoever appeared. Helpers fetched extra chairs for unexpected guests, and the bench under the window seated four comfortably, or eight children if necessary.

Aware of the chatter around her, Kate relaxed, feeling almost guilty with this life of leisure. The rest of her training class might not be having such an easy time. Yet she was following instructions, and as Miss G warned her, sometimes that would involve waiting. Linden, she decided, helped her to feel purposeful, as did the mountains of dishes she washed for Madame Claude.

Linden reached a potato-laden finger upward, and Kate guided it to her tiny mouth. Around them, *au Père* girls helped the others eat. *Au Père*—of the Father—such a fitting name for these young women devoted to caring for the children. Two of them hailed from Switzerland, another from Norway.

One Swiss girl named Laura, a Girl Scout, sat beside Kate often, so they had struck up a friendship. "I've been all over with the Scouts, and volunteered when I heard about the need here. At home, there's courier work to do, with Germans in and out across the border, and statements to be made against their beliefs, but this is where I belong."

"Statements?"

"The Nazis know Switzerland's a neutral zone, but still brandish their propaganda. In my city, they set up a bookshop with little to offer except *Mein Kampf* and a huge poster of Hitler. But we're free to ignore it or show our displeasure to the man who runs the store. On our soil, the Germans can't do much about that."

"How do people show their displeasure?"

"As Scouts, my girlfriend and I felt duty-bound to do something, even though we were just twelve. So we pried the door partway open one day. The proprietor ran at us and shooed us away, so we told the Swiss guard, and voila! No bookstore."

"Amazing. And you were free to travel here?"

The girl nodded and guided a chunk of bread to a hungry little one's mouth. Several conversations mingled, and Kate felt content being involved in none. She sipped her *potage*—a thin potato soup—and let her mind wander back over her time in France.

From the haystack, a short, wiry fellow had guided her to a stone house. There, she slept on a featherbed in a nondescript room until a hazy figure carrying food hovered over her in semi-darkness.

That house gained and lost people like flies—she never figured out who lived there. Later, the peasant who first welcomed her brought his offering to protect her ankle.

Easing leather and wood around her leg, he pulled heavy string through holes and crisscrossed the contraption into a sturdy brace. She stood without pain then clapped her hands, and he lapsed into a broken-toothed smile smelling of onions and wine. He pointed her to bread, cheese, and fruit and bid her take what she liked.

A long trek, always upward, began an hour later with a fresh guide. With whispered instructions, scrambling footsteps and hasty retreats, they progressed steadily upward to thinner air. In a safe cottage, the mistress fed them lavender shortbread with a steaming herbal *tisane* that smelled like Aunt Alvina's closet and cleared Kate's sinuses.

Several hours later, another cottage welcomed them, and she

collapsed beside the fire near a battle-weary dog with a clipped ear that reminded her of Addie's farm dog, Old Brown. In the evening, a tableful of peasants and *Résistance* partisans feasted on a chicken and onion dish with the mellow aroma of onion broth and chicken, tarragon and rosemary filling the house.

Linden dropped her bread, so Kate leaned down to fetch it, then resumed her recollections of her trip here. Already December seemed long ago.

One by one, people dropped off at various sites until late afternoon when she began to wonder if her guide knew the way. But finally, they viewed a house set back from a larger one. There, a slim-nosed man with a deep chin cleft introduced himself.

"Call me Maurice, and this is Eugene, our radio operator. I apologize, but plans have changed overnight. The danger here has mounted. The Gestapo has devised a mechanism for listening to radio transmissions, and someone in our circuit has been found out."

He held his forehead. "Hopefully, we'll be back in operation soon, but until then, the best place for you is Le Chambon-sur-Lignon. I planned to welcome you with a cup of *noisette* and some other local delicacies, but this alert came up awfully fast. We're glad to have you though, and believe me, we need you."

He paced to the window and back as Kate's mouth watered for that mentioned cup of chestnut tea. Eugene, a tall young man with a great shock of thick black hair, scurried around the room packing his gear.

"Your identity will remain the same." Maurice tapped his fingers on the table. "Yes, that should suit us, but first we must move the transmitter farther up the mountain and change the mailboxes. For now, Jacques will take you to a temporary home."

And so she had arrived here, sore of foot but in high spirits. Across from her, two little boys dipped their biscuits into rich yellow custard. A gangly urchin that came to the Presbytery only yesterday passed the basket, and Kate helped herself as the au Père girls toted a carafe of hot tea to the table. With no

need to concentrate, these idle moments again took Kate back to meeting Maurice.

He gestured through the window toward her guide. "He will show you the new transmitting location, too. Check the butcher shop for messages every morning. Use this code: *Est-ce-que vous avez le canard frais aujourd'hui?*"

Kate had never asked for fresh duck in a *boucherie* before, but one day, her inquiry would yield information or instructions. Some rough-looking men appeared to usher away Eugene and his transmitter. Maurice spoke with them in hushed tones before he pulled a chunk of yellow from his bag for Kate.

"At the very least, have some cheese. I'd planned to fill you in on the circuit, but you must forgive me. I have several things to accomplish before nightfall.

"Wait in Le Chambon with people we trust totally. The Gestapo knows full well the village protects Jewish children, but so far, all is well. We won't forget you, and by the way, you've done jolly well with the dairymaid disguise. You look a far sight older than you are, and—" He raised his eyebrows and sniffed. "I daresay, right down to—"

Kate chuckled. "I only hope the smell deters the Gestapo."

He paused at the threshold. "If you receive a message to move, it will probably be back up here, and a bicycle will be provided. If that should be the case, modify the dairymaid image just a bit, for polite company."

Kate blinked. "I should purchase some common women's clothing?"

"Yes, you'll most likely be out during the daytime and won't be the only bicycler. If you're stopped, say you're going to a relative's funeral. However, the roads between here and there are too dangerous to tackle at night, especially if it snows. That's likely, so be sure you have enough wraps, and take your time.

"You'll have to seek refuge along the way, at Tence and Montfaucon, where you'll view the Rhone. On the outskirts of each village, safe houses watch for the likes of us. Often someone wearing a

Basque beret will sit outside in the evenings. The last town is Firminy. Most peasants in these parts are sympathetic to our cause."

He dug in his pocket. "Here. These franc notes should suffice for the clothing and buy whatever else you need."

He took a step and then halted again. "You'll be all right?" Genuine concern etched his brow.

"You recall my training to use my ingenuity?"

He tipped his beret. "Soon we'll be working closely. Take this as rest time."

As she helped Linden clean her plate, Kate chuckled. *Rest time.* Miss G certainly knew what she was talking about when she warned that periods of inactivity might challenge her most.

Chapter Thirteen

Several weeks had passed since Kate's guide deposited her in the Presbytery, and she became accustomed to life in this hilly village on the Lignon River. But every time she caught sight of Le Lisieux with its brilliant snow-cap sparkling in the sun, the urge to be more involved with her circuit gripped her.

After supper one night, she washed dishes, went to bed at the same time as the children, and slept without disturbance, as she had since she came. Maybe she was making up for all those sleepless months of searching for Alexandre and enduring the noisy Luftwaffe.

The next morning, her twenty-seventh day there, she walked to the boucherie to ask for fresh duck. A jovial man she hadn't seen for a few days responded to her question with a tweak of his wide nose.

"For whom?" The rest of the code came as easily as Addie's name.

"*Monsieur Chambert, Rue des Oranges.*"

Something extra bulged under the string of the bulky package the butcher handed her. Kate left the store and turned off the main street, making sure no one followed. In a cranny leading to a courtyard, she wiggled out the note and read it in the shadows.

"*Demain, le matin. A quatre heures et demie. Des Grillots, sud. Vacances au Clermont-Ferrand.*"

Tomorrow morning at four-thirty, on the south side of the stone house where she slept. Vacation. That must mean travel to Clermont-Ferrand—no small undertaking.

Another small folded sheet carried coordinates for a landing strip. This she must deliver to Eugene as soon as possible. She memorized the numbers, lest she lose the note or be captured. *Must be a Lysander, to require such a small landing field.* Shivers tracked the backs of Kate's arms—her first delivery.

She pushed the notes under her sleeve and glanced around. All was quiet except for normal shopping chatter from the main street. Suddenly, Miss G's words came to her. "Use your creativity, and always remember, the message matters most. Memorize it. Eat the paper it's written on if the Gestapo finds you."

Next, she'd better purchase some traveling clothes. Across the street, a dress shop's sign welcomed all comers. Kate hadn't expected to be shopping so soon, and the perfectly coifed clothier eyed her askance.

"*Madame, excusez moi.* I need to buy a dress."

The clerk's expression starched even more as Kate's sour milk odor reached her, but when she saw her franc notes, she halted her retreat.

"I need something appropriate for travel, *si'l vous plait.*"

Keeping her distance, the well-tailored woman brought forth several suitable garments. Kate chose a burgundy heavy cotton with a shine to it and a navy blue with white trim. The clerk cringed when she touched the fabric, and Kate almost chuckled. Money was power—isn't that how the saying went?

She couldn't blame the poor clerk, but if she hadn't needed to deliver the message to Eugene, she might have played the game a bit longer. Instead, she asked the store's closing hours, promised to return, and left the package of meat with Madame Claude.

In the courtyard, she memorized the radio operator's message, tore the paper into bits, and looped her arm over the fence. One by one, the shredded paper slips disappeared into the pig pen.

Grunting sows attacked them as they would potato scrapings. Kate made sure they faded into the gooey muck before she adopted a normal pace out of the village and across a meadow. She turned right at a smattering of trees and paused to orient herself. A cowbell clattered, and in spite of the cold, the low rush of icy water from a small stream and winter birdsongs accompanied her.

The left fork led down a steep embankment, then up again. Kate took the right fork through a meadow and across a rock-studded stream. There, she followed a cow trail along the bank. When a pine gnarled into an artful masterpiece appeared, she paused.

Rugged snow-patched countryside splayed a colorful prelude to spring, and these hills muted the strong wind. Her next move would take her directly to an old barn with a transmitter hidden in its loft. How many times had her instructors warned her to move slowly, especially approaching a transmitting station?

Ten minutes passed. Fifteen. She meandered, a milkmaid in search of a lost cow, for that would be her story. The truth was, she'd only viewed this site from afar when her guide pointed it out. Finally, the unremarkable building came into sight.

Through a thickening spruce grove, speckled light added to her mission's mystery. The guide told her only that here, she was closer to Saint-Agrève in L'Ardèche, than to Le Chambon, and pointed a finger at *Pont d'Arc*, a distant natural arch sixty meters wide and nearly that tall.

"This canyon boasts thousands of caves, if you ever need a spot to hide."

Kate looked every direction, then rested for a few minutes on a fallen tree before ambling to the door.

Unlocked.

She slipped inside.

An unnatural crackling met her ears, but her basic radio training rendered the sound inviting, a bit of Great Britain in the middle of this vast wilderness. She picked up a board and hit a stall divider. *Bang.* The hollow resonance made her shudder, but in seconds, a profusion of black hair swept over the haymow's edge, and a rope ladder dropped to within three feet of the dirt floor.

His thatch of black hair disheveled, a pencil tucked behind his ear, and the whites of his eyes veined from lack of sleep, Eugene prepared to write in a small notebook.

"*Bonjour.* You have something for me?"

He recorded Kate's whispered message, and disappeared into the mow. Then Kate stood outdoors again, her heart thumping as though a Gestapo agent hid behind every tree. Mr. T's warning thrummed—"If you can, avoid being a radio operator."

Her return trip cut her time in half. With the misshapen tree behind and Le Lisieux in sight, she gave herself to memories of Miss G, the women's mentor after their paramilitary training in Scotland. This officer helped determine their long-range assignments, suggested identities and disguises, and had a say in whether agents landed in a plane or by parachute.

One day, Miss G invited Kate to the Oxford Street Corner House for lunch. "Your intelligence, ability to think on the spot, and determination bode well."

She drew on her cigarette and waved her hand around the restaurant. "But success sometimes translates into a disadvantage. You see how I have dressed?"

Re-entering Le Chambon, Kate's thoughts wandered back and forth to London. She kept an eye out for brown-suited characters lurking in obscure doorways under soft dark hats. France crawled with Vichy collaborators, so most likely, this was no exception.

At the same time, she recalled Miss G's outfit that early December day. Her perky, forest green felt hat brim nested a silk flower, and her make-up showed effort. From hat to silk suit to stylish pumps, she exuded a lady-about-town aura.

"Let this outing stand as an example to take care of yourself out in the field. If you don't, what good are you to the effort? You must avail yourself of whatever cover you need, even if it requires expense."

Miss G must be thirty-five or forty, but unmarried as far as anyone knew.

Peering at Kate over her teacup, she interrupted herself. "You have a question for me?"

Cigarette smoke curled like heavy white fog through an open window behind her mentor as Kate eyed her fish and chips. Miss G gave her another opportunity.

"Go ahead. Ask whatever you want."

As Kate crossed through the center of Le Chambon, the town clock announced the hour—enough time for a bath before the shops closed. She hurried toward Des Grillots, still mulling over that conversation with Miss G. some months ago.

Even though Kate had curtailed her curiosity, Miss G's frankness had taught her something. "My uncle brought me here as a displaced child during the Great War. Perhaps that is why your background interested me so much."

So she was an orphan, too.

"Your work ethic and personality fit you into any slot, so we doubled you up. You are content with your roles of courier and organizer?"

Kate nodded as Miss G signaled the nippie. "A pot of tea, please, with lemon and sugar."

"When you start out, your deliveries can make or break certain operations, as you are aware. The organizing will come in due time. For the sake of clarity, you also ranked high in radio operation." She snuffed her cigarette and leaned closer.

"After you jump in, someone will speed you through the mountains to your organizer. With the Gestapo influx, they take extra precautions, so prepare for an uphill journey. The circuit operator will relay your landing information back to us. What stands out from your studies of Clermont-Ferrand?"

"The black lava rock cathedral."

"Yes. The *Résistance* has an outpost within sight. With the build-up to—"

Miss G dropped her voice even more. "—the invasion, recruiting new members from the south is vital. Some agents never change identity, but you're likely to. If that happens, cast off the old and slip into the new like a fresh dress.

"As an organizer, remember the *Résistance* needs women as badly as men, especially for courier work. Some organizers set up as many as thirty airplane reception committees a month, so jobs exist for everyone. How many greeters are needed to receive a Hudson?"

Kate recalled her week's training at Medmenhan. "Ten."

"Why?"

"To point their torches so the pilot knows where to go."

"How many torches for a Lysander?"

"Three, placed in an L shape to form a flare path."

"Which way will the pilot turn once he lands, and how long will a Lysander remain aground?"

"Right. Two or three minutes, since cargo is not larger than the size of a suitcase, and the plane only holds three people."

"In both cases, time is of the essence. Clothes, boots, coffee, grenades, sten-guns, bren-guns, ammunition, medical supplies, and food must be exchanged with cargo headed for London—downed pilots or agents needing rest or training. All must occur with split-second timing, and organizers bear full responsibility for the outcome. We're counting on you, and you have our utmost support."

"Thank you." Kate drained her teacup as Miss G pursed her lips.

"Your most difficult trial may be to accept necessary waiting before your next challenge."

"You know me quite well."

"Above all, never forget your other identity, your unchangeable code. This may seem repetitive, but we cannot stress it enough. Contact us that way only in dire emergencies, day or night. Although you've memorized the code, repeat it ten times each night before you fall asleep."

Les jonquils sont en fleurs ce matin. Kate had chosen that code since daffodils were her favorite flower, morning her best time, and because it reminded her of Addie, who loved yellow. *The daffodils are in blossom this morning.*

That special luncheon might have occurred years ago, although only two months had passed. Now, the same intensity Kate felt that day filled her as she climbed the steps of *Des Grillons.* Its three chimneys belched smoke, and she shivered at the thought of a long bicycle ride. *About a hundred miles*, she figured, *and it might snow.*

She drew a bath, relished the warmth inside *Des Grillons*, and borrowed a dress from one of the other girls to wear to the shop. That snooty clerk would definitely welcome her francs.

The mistress worked alone over a whopping batch of bread dough when Kate stopped by the Presbytery. Fresh rolls for Linden in the morning—oh, how she would miss that sweet child.

"All is well?"

"I leave sometime during the night."

"Take plenty of food, and go with God. Gestapo activity heightens. Be wise as a serpent, innocent as a dove."

Madame Claude waddled in under two burlap bags of potatoes and turnips. Kate helped her with one and walked downtown.

How many people have passed through here since France fell to the Nazis? June of '40—such a long time to live under occupation and harbor children—especially as some Gendarmes from the French army joined the Milice as collaborators.

Children warbled a merry song from the side yard, where Linden skipped in a circle with several others.

"Le Chambon-sur-Lignon, l'on y danse, l'on y danse
Le Chambon-sur Lignon, l'on y danse toutes en ronde."

The delicate child clung to one of the older girls' hands, sang her heart out, and even smiled. A couple of weeks ago, she had hesitated to smile and play, but now belted out the singsong tune like the others.

The melody jogged something deep inside Kate. *Le Chambon, where they dance, where they dance, all in a circle.* A vague memory arose of a throaty male voice murmuring mellow French phrases in her ear to a rocking beat. For a moment, she could almost detect his countenance.

Could that have been her father? She opened herself to this figment of the past, but it receded as quickly as it surfaced. She smoothed her collar. If she stayed here long enough, soaked in the rhythms and nuances of the language, would her soul dredge up more recollections?

She arrived at the dress shop ten minutes before closing The clerk glanced up with beneficence, and Kate tried on the two dresses. She settled on the burgundy because it offered enough flare for bike riding, and purchased a practical olive drab raincoat.

Along the south side of *Des Grillons* she hummed the children's song. Tomorrow morning at four-thirty, when darkness still ruled the land, a sign would come to her here. She paid careful attention to the road's ins and outs—every minute piece of information might help.

Six or seven small torches lay in her purse, but she wanted to avoid using them unless absolutely necessary. What else could she do to prepare for the trip? No matter how she schemed, whatever happened would unfold without her effort, like the butcher slipping that note under her package this morning.

No use speculating how tomorrow's meeting would occur. This might be what Miss G meant about resting when she could. But how could she relax when her whole being leaned into the traces?

She couldn't help conjuring what might take place, though she understood its uncontrollable nature. Scenes kept coming to her—someone would approach on a bicycle. For some reason, she envisioned a man, but the messenger could as well be an old washerwoman.

That reminded her of Toad disguising himself like a washer-woman in *The Wind and the Willows*. With his penchant for taking impossible risks and making a fool of himself, he'd always been her favorite character, whereas shy Moley had won Addie's heart.

Perhaps a cart would fake an accident, or a peasant would wave a bevy of pigs across the road and slip her directions to a hidden bicycle. Her mind created several other scenarios, but it was no use imagining. Now came the waiting, as it had when Alexandre left on his final mission and when she discovered she was with child and again after that. Always waiting—someone ought to write a book about waiting, to place next to all the other psychology books Kate had discovered on Mrs. Tenney's shelves last winter.

After dinner, she squatted on the floor for Linden to climb on her shoulders, and everyone sang on the walk to *Des Grillions*, as usual.

Au Clair de la Lune
Mon ami Pierrot
Prête-moi ta plume
Pour écrire un mot.

In the light of the moon, my friend Pierrot brought me a feather pen to write a word. If she could only write a note to Addie—pouring out her thoughts and concerns in letters when she first came to London had helped so much. But that forbidden luxury was no more.

Later, Linden splashed through her bath and snuggled in Kate's arms for a bedtime story. Those sweet eyes closed, the other children slept, and finally the *Au Père* girls went to bed. Kate listened to the old building's creaks. Then she crept to a roomy closet she'd spied on one of her solitary tours.

Only old mop heads, brooms, and cleaning rags lined the nook, so she had carted her belongings there. Truth be told, she would rather not leave this safe village. Eating in the warm kitchen, sleeping in the large dormer room, and listening to the rise and fall of conversations gave her a sense of belonging. In her new post, she might live alone, with few human connections.

She fingered her milkmaid's dress and frayed petticoat. Did she dare leave this smelly garb behind? No, technically she still was Angelina, and hopefully her new clothes wouldn't attract attention if a *gendarme* viewed her identity card expecting a milkmaid.

Through dusky streets to the Presbytery, Kate let herself into the kitchen. A tub of cold milk sat beside the breezy doorway, so she drank a glassful and filled her knapsack with bread crusts and cheese, two apples, and a water flask.

Her pack over her shoulder, she trekked down the back path for the last time, wondering how the tall old fortress earned its name. Crickets probably infested its crumbling walls during summer and fall, but why call a building after an insect? Probably the name had a hidden meaning, like so many other places.

A three-quarters moon rose through the trees, a good omen. Better to bicycle in moonlight. Another good sign, the snows had held off so far. The nocturnal quiet seeped into Kate's being.

Maybe through this experience, she would attain to patience, that wayward virtue she seemed to have missed. Suddenly, boots struck cobblestones, and she rushed into the bushes as two men conversed in French.

"Three to four thousand. We should double that number—more than double it. Mid-March, the White Mouse will drop in to conduct explosives training. She made it safely to Scotland, did you hear? From here on out, we can only grow."

Two men moved down the side road in Kate's direction. "Even now, the SS masses more troops around the plateau above Chaudes-Aiguwes. No artillery, mortars, or mobile guns, but when the spring rains cease, intel says they'll even employ airplanes there.

"So many recruits have joined us, we must guard our supplies even closer—no trusting anyone until they prove themselves worthy. We receive up to three drops a week now, and that can only increase."

Odd these two met so openly, though darkness had fallen. Kate's heartbeat seemed loud enough for them to hear.

One figure skulked away, and Kate froze until he disappeared into a garden along the main road. A minute later, another set of boots sounded. The rhythm seemed familiar. Could it be the man who had carried her all that way when she sprained her ankle?

No, that man had worn soundless espadrilles. Besides, he met drops far, far from here, and these boots shuffled, as if worn by someone old and weary.

Probably every night saw this much activity out in the streets, for Le Chambon's array of underground organizations went on and on. The Swiss children's home, the *La Cimade* refugee center called *Coteau Fleuri*, or flowering hillside, and others—the *Guespy, Faidoli, L'abric,* and *La Maison des Roches.*

A breeze stirred crisp leaves still clinging to trees. Kate hugged herself and let her freshest recollections flow. So many caring people here, down-to-earth, yet intrepid, like her father.

Another full minute passed before she shook fresh dew from her shoulders and set out for *Des Grillot's* side door. In bed, she considered the White Mouse, alias Nancy Wake, an Australian-born agent who had escaped the Milice numerous times by crossing the Pyrénées.

Once, captured and interrogated for four days, she managed to trick her captors into releasing her. No wonder the Nazis had bestowed her nickname. The last Kate heard, Nancy fled into Spain—good to know she'd made it to Scotland.

Some day, she might meet her, or even work with her, if those men's whispers proved true. From the large room's shadows, where snores and turnings marked the others in their beds, another possibility emanated.

Or you might become another Madeleine Dreyfus or Nancy Wake.

Even with all the qualities her mentors saw in her, becoming a threat to the Germans or winning their respect would take more than her slim courage. Leaving this safety sent shivers through Kate, though others viewed her as independent and unafraid—she'd even had to explain to Addie the difference between her outward bravado and what went on inside.

Had it been like this for her mother when she crossed the Atlantic in the Great War, and shuddered at the reverberations of battle nearby? Threadlike moonlight trickled across her bunk from a high, barred window. As surely as crickets would chirp here next summer, this night would bring no sleep for her. But she would rest, even if Miss G said she didn't know how.

Chapter Fourteen

The sheepdog rubbed Domingo's pant leg more than once on his first morning back home. Domingo ruffled his fur and took his head in his hands.

"You've taken care of things while I've been gone. You're a good dog."

The air smelled of spring, even though more snows would come—about the time he got another call to cross the border, Domingo guessed.

No use thinking the worst. Enough bad happened without him conjuring it ahead of time. From the farmyard, Gabirel lazed over a rise, toolbox in hand. *Ah, yes. He'd promised to help Jean-Luc Edorta build some stalls today.*

A wave of satisfaction welled in Domingo. This morning, his brother's eyes looked clearer than they had in weeks. Still, he avoided conversation.

It wasn't right, him missing school and having to do the work of two men. Sunlight shafted through stark poplars bereft of their leaves, highlighting an ungainly spot near a ewe's leg joint. Domingo hurried to examine the area. All manner of ailments might beset a sheep at any time and for no apparent reason. Disease could travel through the flock so fast, they might lose several animals before he even analyzed the cause.

When the sun reached its height, Domingo left the flock to eat with Maman. He was glad for Gabirel's opportunity to get away but also for time with her, for she shrank with every mission he took. Her shoulders curled inward a bit more each passing day until he wanted to stretch them from her collarbones, forcing her back straight again.

"Gabirel will eat with Edorta today."

He realized her habit of stating what he already knew, but the sound of her voice soothed Domingo no matter how often she repeated simple facts. When Aitaita still lived, meals became lively with his pronouncements about the weather, the sheep, the government, and all manner of other topics.

Now, Domingo gave thanks that Maman eased the long silence of familiarity. She ladled creamy potatoes from a tureen and sat down.

"Tell me where you went last."

"A short delivery, only to the edge of the Ségala."

"To the *Résistance* camp?"

"Below there, to a training area for new recruits, in the chestnut forests between the Lot and the Cantal."

"The Milice know about this training?"

"Who knows what they know?" He could lie outright to the Milice, but to his mother—that was different. To tell the full truth would keep her awake at night, so he mixed truth with caution.

"What did you carry?"

"Some batteries. The rest, I am not sure." As usual, partially true—one packet marked explosives, one grenades. But his questioner knew he hedged.

Her eyes blazed. "The danger grows?"

He sucked in his breath. Isolated as she was, Maman knew the situation like she knew her kitchen cupboard.

He nodded. *Yes, like a pestilence attacking a perfectly healthy flock of sheep. No hiding from this war that ballooned like a pestilence out of control.*

Maman's upper lip rippled as she chewed, black hairs frolicked on its surface, and Domingo swallowed down a wad of trepidation with his potatoes. She had aged far too fast, probably from so much grief.

When Aitaita died, she had remained so strong, even though she'd already lost Papa and Ander. But something about this ongoing loss they traipsed through each day, like the pigs in their mud wallow, bore down on her and stole her spirit little by little.

This constant, anticipated grief became a vast thing, an overall losing beyond earth's normal trouble and sorrow. A perpetual sense that what was being lost could never again be regained stalked Maman. Domingo knew, for the same dread haunted him.

Neighbors vanished overnight, without a word of farewell. Young men headed off to fight, and once-conservative parish priests plunged headlong into the struggle, in spite of the dreadful cost. He could take such things in stride, but how much more could Maman bear?

"Edorta says the *Ingelesak* will come. He speaks of *le débarquement*." She pushed back against her chair and forced Domingo to meet her eyes. "Do you believe this?"

The faces of Amerikans he'd guided through snow-filled passes ran through Domingo's mind, along with recent confirmations of exactly what Maman described. And then one other face appeared, that female agent, *Code Name Merce*. Out of all the codes Domingo memorized, hers alone stayed in his memory. And he remembered her thoughtfulness to say, "*Merci.*"

He cut a hunk of cheese and tore the end from a bread loaf, suppressing the rising tide in his chest, a tangled emotional mix. He hardly knew what to call this blend of ferocity, anticipation, and confusion ranging just below his breastbone.

He finished his milk and set down his cup. "Others call it *l'Invasion*, and argue whether the Allies will come from north or south. But most believe that, one way or the other, they will come. I think Aitaita would call this our hope, Maman."

Her eyes held steady, reflecting the same longing that coursed through Domingo, yet her posture demanded a clearer answer. "But do *you* believe they will come?"

He took his time answering, knowing how many times she had

hoped—for her sister to heal from the fearsome influenza in the Great War, for the end of that terrible fighting, for victory over Franco, and for the return of her loved ones.

In this tempestuous late February, 1944, everything rested on the Allies invading. If they forsook France or held back, the struggle of the past four years would be a waste, as happened with Guernica's victims—so many people perished, yet no victory occurred.

"I do believe, Maman. I do." As the words left Domingo's mouth, something slipped in place inside him, like a bone mending. How two shattered pieces melded again into one, he had no idea, but he'd witnessed this miracle in downed sheep.

Here with Maman, in sunlight from the kitchen window, he could almost hear Aitaita say, "The time has come—" Maman's glance shifted then, but though he tried, Domingo failed to read her thoughts.

Light had yet to tweak the horizon when Kate rose from the floor beside Linden's narrow bed. She'd spent her last minutes here, relishing the steadiness of the child's breathing.

She brushed the smooth china cheek, and Linden's dark eyes fluttered for a second, giving Kate a final glimpse of her gentle spirit, like Addie's, made tender by suffering. Maybe that was one reason this child stirred Kate so irrevocably. Once again, in that last moment beside her bed, she felt as though Linden might not be quite real.

But now, she must say good-bye to such innocence—the thought created an avalanche of emotions. Kate curled down to kiss Linden's forehead and took in one last whiff of the cherub's scent, clean and sweet. The ensuing sensation went deep, beyond words, and burned the backs of her eyes. Linden's sleek tawny hair, startling against her translucent skin, flowed under Kate's fingertips.

"You are one of the chosen—you ought to have dark hair." Her whisper rode the air like quicksilver.

And so should you. Her parents' photographs passed through Kate's memory, both with hair the color of coal.

But Miss G proclaimed her coloring a boon. "It's such an obvious difference, the Gestapo might not even think to check you. In Basque country, you will find anomalies, light-haired individuals with blue eyes and fair skin. Just be sure to wear a headscarf in public to show a milkmaid's place."

An anamoly. The four syllables gamboled on Kate's tongue. An oddity. An aberration. In a way, that word described her whole life, but at least she had her mother's eyes. Now, she paused to consider what the supervisor told her about Linden.

The fragile waif came in on the train with her brother, a few years older, wearing tidy clothes and carrying a small fabric bag. But last year, her brother came of age and left the school with mountain guides taking people over the Swiss border. He vowed to find their parents and come back for Linden.

"That hollow look in her eyes deepened after he left. She's different from the rest, an old heart. You can tell she thinks beyond her age."

How many times had a teacher said something similar to Aunt Alvina about Kate? Back then, Kate basked in her Aunt's pleased response.

"You're very grown-up, Kathryn. Your parents would be proud of your behavior, a fine example for the other girls in your class."

But was that somberness a blessing or a curse? Didn't people think like adults enough, once they aged? Was this, in essence, what drew her to Addie and now tied her to Linden?

She had debated again about what to wear, but a cold draft told her the milkmaid garb, with its long, thick stockings, would be warmest for this first cold day.

She tied a wool kerchief over her head and crept back to Linden. One last fingertip to the little girl's tipped-up nose, and Kate hoisted her knapsack onto her back.

The baby she lost last summer would have grown into a precious child like this. If only she'd been able to see her—or him. If only she'd touched the baby's skin, or smoothed its hair, even for a second.

That tiny individual's skin color, her hair, and the shape of her nose would have blended Alexandre's attributes with hers in a new human being, unique in all the world. The imaginary, fleeting outline of those features waltzed in the room's shadows.

Slipping on her coat and descending the narrow, frigid stairwell, fresh grief assaulted Kate. She would never see so many people again. Everyone left her—or she left them.

Addie said it so well, *and you're leaving again.* In Mrs. Tenney's upstairs, Addie slept right now, like Linden. And Alexandre's baby—Kate's sigh echoed up the three-story, enclosed space. At least her infant knew no trials in this world—slim comfort. Her arms ached with the loss.

The frosty doorknob stuck to Kate's hand, but she opened the side door without a squeak and stepped out to meet whatever lay ahead. Across the back yard and through the gate, she stole up a little ditch toward the movement she'd spied from upstairs.

Damp night air took her breath away. Stealing away like this, she felt like a criminal as murky darkness enclosed her.

Miss G's voice sounded in her head: *Keep your wits about you.* Such an unusual saying, as if one's wits were small separate beings requiring herding.

No one appeared when Kate reached the roadside, her thumb laced through a loop on the side of her pack. Night creatures skittered through the brush, and though the slim moon dropped, it still revealed the roadway. About an eighth of a mile ahead, a curve like a lizard's tail beckoned her, so she decided to walk. Better than standing still in this cold wind.

Only her own footsteps kept her company, but spectral questions rose, as if from the ditches. *What if no one came? What if dawn brought light, but no one? What if—* Yes, her wits did need herding.

"Calm down. Someone will come. Didn't the butcher hand you that note? Didn't the guide find you when you hurt your ankle, and didn't the man in the haystack take care of you? Have a little faith—remember you are the daughter of *le Renard Intrepid*."

In the early morning stillness, she felt like anyone but a renowned spy's daughter. Her memories drifted back over life's panorama like movie scenes. Her childhood formed a mere pinprick in the film, but after she moved to Aunt Alvina's and met Addie, things perked up. Then, during high school, Alexandre visited from Canada with his parents, and something in her changed after he left.

Impatient with the school authorities, she lost her determination to be class valedictorian, and her desire to attend college dwindled. All her dreams paled in comparison with the dashing Alexandre's exciting plans. When he returned, he declared his love for her, so she succumbed to elopement and gave up all her chances, even her graduation.

What had she been thinking to leave Addie alone like that? She ought to have known Addie's good-for-nothing dad wouldn't even show for the ceremony.

A night bird let forth a song she'd never heard before—or was it a morning bird? Step by step, Kate's introspection plumbed deeper. Why did she always make choices that led to missing out on things? Her graduation, her opportunity for college and a career, and she had even missed saying a last good-bye to Aunt Alvina before her death.

Something glinted up ahead, so she stopped to listen. *Was that a horse's nicker?* Questions continued to careen through her head.

What ailed her that she kept setting up good-byes? Addie came all the way from Iowa for her, and what did she do? She left. Mr. Tenney did so much for her, and she liked working for him, but tired of it. Would nothing ever satisfy her?

A steady clop-clop began, and then something sparkled again. A few steps later, a cart appeared, a squeaky wooden contraption pulled by a scraggly work horse with great clumps of hair around its hooves. Kate's pulse raced. She took the road's slanted edge, where weeds and wild grasses brushed her stockings.

The cart moved abreast of her and halted. A muffled whisper, "The time is ripe," washed a tingle over her neck and shoulders—the code for this mission. The figure, under a wide farmer's hat, looped the reins and circled behind the cart.

Something rattled, and soon Kate's fingers wrapped around chilly handlebars—a bicycle, just as Maurice promised. Without a word, the person, whether male or female, pointed toward Clermont-Ferrand.

A second later, an envelope brushed Kate's hand. She'd already made a slit in her hemline for this purpose, and bent to insert the envelope. The sour milk smell almost nauseated her.

Surely no *Miliciens* or Gestapo in their right mind would pursue such a stinky old milkmaid. She secured the envelope inside the hem with a safety pin. The messenger waited until she finished, pretending to check the horse's hoof—*must be a man*. Then he climbed aboard the cart and shuffled toward the village center.

For a long moment, as the moon sliver disappeared, the darkness threatened to suck Kate in. How far she ought to bike today, what would happen when she got there—more questions. But surely, the envelope contained guidance. It would be late tomorrow before Clermont-Ferrand's volcanic mountains came into sight—and its dramatic black lava rock cathedral. Plenty of time to read the envelope's contents.

At least she knew the landmarks, thanks to her training. "Nothing to do but head in the right direction." Kate straddled the bicycle, aware that this might be how her whole time in France would go, moving from one spot to another with such little sense of destination and meeting people like little Linden, only to leave them.

"What did you expect? You have your promised bicycle and a delivery to make, and before you winds the road." She shook away her apprehension. Her pack held a lunch and her heart fresh memories, good memories that would suffice.

With one foot positioned on a pedal, Kate shooed away her doubts and set her mind on the journey.

Chapter Fifteen

Restless sleep captured Kate. Her dream, so realistic it transported her back to the day she'd been accepted into the Secret Operations Executive, remained with her long after she wakened.

"You have passed your initial interviews. Report to F Section on Monday at seven for the first phase of your training in Wanborough Manor near Guildford. Your language skills and determination will aid you in learning deception for a worthy cause." Miss G paused and raised her brows above her glasses. "Do you understand?"

"You're training me to be a good liar?"

A nod confirmed Kate's impression. "That's not often a plus, but we count it a necessary virtue. If you're surprised at your power to deceive, it's not the last thing you'll learn about yourself here."

Kate held her tongue as past deceptions haunted her. Running out on Aunt Alvina and Addie to elope with Alexandre brought a grimace. *A good liar*—she'd certainly proven that. But now, even that questionable skill would be put to good use.

"Your physical prowess is satisfactory, though we hope training will improve your musculature. Thank you for your husband's sacrifice, and welcome to the S.O.E."

Kate fixed her eyes on the speaker's sleeve. The orange, yellow, and white floral pattern radiated cheer in the midst of such serious business. Miss G lit a cigarette and scanned the papers before her. Her silk stockings swished under her desk. Everyone remarked that even her hosiery seams always stayed ruler-straight.

"Any questions?"

Kate shook her head, although she had plenty. Not the least was the reason the staff sent a trainee named Margo home yesterday with no time for a word with her before an officer whisked her from the building.

"All right then. Take the number sixteen bus on Monday morning, and you'll arrive in plenty of time. Here is my phone number. Rather than lose sleep, call me with any sudden concerns. You're going to need your rest."

Miss G smiled, but then her mouth transformed. A diagonal fissure broke across her face. Kate stared in wonder, then horror, as her mentor stripped off a mask to reveal a wizened elderly crone like those Kate and Addie had conjured when they first read stories about witches.

The dream—or nightmare—ended, and Kate woke gasping.

Her heart pounded nearly out of her chest. Where was she? Her forehead dripped, and not more than a few inches from her face, five fingers extended. She stopped breathing, but then realized with a start that the fingers belonged to her. She moved one, another, and dropped her hand onto the blanket as her pulse gradually returned to normal.

Faint moonlight shone through a gabled window. *Ah, yes.* She'd ridden all day and arrived after dark. She'd had to dig a path for her bicycle through heavy snow drifted onto the road. A flickering light glowed in this farmhouse window just when she considered abandoning the bicycle and walking the rest of the way.

Someone strong walked toward her, helped her down—she hadn't realized her numbness until then—and took charge of her bicycle. In the shelter of a cottage, her appendages tingled as they thawed, and she entered yet another temporary home.

Hours later, her sopping gloves draped over a radiator not far from the narrowest bed she'd ever seen. When she dropped them there, along with her drenched coat, the scent of warming wet wool filled the room, but her fingers still trembled. She made a mental note: *buy a pair of fur-lined leather gloves as soon as possible.*

After meeting her hostess, Celeste, and her three almost adult children, Kate satisfied her hunger with hard bread and a creamy soup. But from her present perspective, the food seemed as much a dream as her recent nightmare.

Pattering sounded above her, and two short thuds—probably squirrels landing on the roof. She recalled little else after Celeste led her to this miniscule room in the upstairs front corner, for it had taken four long days in biting cold winds and the help of strangers to make her trip. Kindness laced those peasants' faces. Clearly, they had hidden others before her, and would hide more in days to come. Her last refuge, a snow-covered shack back from the road to Clermont-Ferrand, had even featured an inside pump.

Early the morning before, a pale, earnest young woman brought Kate a hot chestnut brew and provided bread and cheese for the final leg of her journey.

"Word has come about Allied soldiers killed at Malmedy and Baugnez. Americans, word has it—shot in cold blood as they surrendered. I hope when *l'Invasion* comes, the Allies show the Nazis no mercy."

Of course, this girl could not know she was American, but for safety's sake, Kate submerged her reaction. *Shot in cold blood.* The phrase made her shiver again in the warmth of her bed.

The snow had stopped during the night, but another storm hit midmorning. Seeing the road six feet in front of her was all she could do, and her expectation that the black lava cathedral would guide her to Clermont-Ferrand fizzled.

Aware of a clock ticking somewhere, and snoring from another room, she sat up and peered into the hallway. At the table a few hours ago, a boy about fifteen sat silently beside another perhaps a year older, taller and more dignified, and a girl closer to twenty. Surely they slept up here, and she must not disturb them.

The vivid image of Miss G's mask replayed. Except for the mask, all the other details matched real life. If only Addie could help her analyze this visitation.

The second day of her journey wouldn't have been so bad without the snow. At first, glorious huge flakes made designs on her coat and splashing her face. After an hour, though, the downfall turned menacing.

After several slips and falls on a road turning ever more icy, something felt not quite right down in Kate's chest, and when she found safe shelter that first night, Kate gladly accepted a peasant woman's remedy. Brandy and lemon juice ensured both sleep and healing.

But then came another day of working her way over slick passages. That odd pull in her chest came again, and she whispered an ultimatum.

"Oh no you don't, Angelina Dumont. You will not catch a cold. Do you hear me?" Her chiding bounced back to her in the silent upstairs. But as she tried to sleep, her breath came harder and heavier. A cup of something hot—that's what she needed.

She slipped out of bed and down the narrow, steep stairs. Luckily her room sat first in the hallway, but the old house was rampant with cricks and creaks. Someone turned over in one of the rooms above, so she halted for long minutes before continuing to the first floor.

The teakettle's gleam guided her into the kitchen, where the open cupboard produced a saltshaker. She dared not hope for a lemon, but honey, she might find. She smelled the honey before she saw it, mixed a spoonful in steaming water and sat down to sniff the concoction.

Objects she hadn't noticed earlier caught her attention—a wide pottery mixing bowl with ridges as deep as Maurice's chin cleft, a bound basket trailing apples and cloth, a folded tablecloth, slices of thick torte on a small plate at the back of the table, pottery mugs lining a lone wall shelf, and a wide butcher knife hanging underneath.

"*Ma Chérie*, is everything all right?"

Kate startled and recovered her breath. "I think—it's a cold in my chest."

"*Tch. Tch.* I have some syrup."

Prepared for an awful taste with a powerful healing element, Kate waited. When Celeste handed her ginger tea laced with in table wine, the drink gave her an instant shove in the right direction.

"*Merci beaucoup.*"

"You need the bathroom, *oui?*"

Celeste led her out the back door into a small shed attached to the house. Shivers hurried Kate back into the kitchen, where Celeste grasped her shoulders. "Do not forget. I am your aunt." Her hazel eyes held a trace of fear.

"*Oui*, Auntie. I won't forget."

"Sleep well." Celeste moved past her down the hall, and Kate revisited her dream about Miss G. Her memories took her back to Wansborough Manor, not far from London, where her training began. The other students lined up in her mind. Out of fourteen beginning in the French section, seven had completed the training.

At Wansborough's Special Training School 5, or STS5, as the students called it, instructors taught shooting, Morse code, sabotage techniques, observation skills, and even how to handle certain explosives. All seven studied every subject, for no one knew what needs might arise in their circuits.

Some of her fellow students might be blowing a bridge tonight, or breaking into a Nazi headquarters.

When a girl named Cherise left for her flight, looking quite the lady about town, Miss G supplied a real fur coat, an expensive watch, and the most stylish heels.

"I may have to slip under the covers with government officials, if necessary," she'd confided. "Pray my nerves will hold their steel."

Feigning romantic interest in a German officer or a collaborator made Kate wince. Right now, Cherise might be risking her life in a far more intimate way than she and with greater likelihood of being found out.

As Kate sank deeper into her pillow and a thick goose down comforter, an odd contentment washed over her. She was an undesirable, stinky milkmaid, but gratitude filled her for this bed, the hot drink, and an Auntie.

"Keep Cherise safe, and Addie, and Mr. Tenney." Just before she drifted off, the tender, dark eyes of the guide who waited for her the night of her drop floated near.

"Keep him safe, too, wherever he is." Instead of focusing on the dreadful mask from her dream, she recalled the blessing he bestowed on her. "*Allez avec Dieu.*"

Scuffling in the granary drew Domingo closer. He'd told Gabirel to sleep late this morning and rose before dawn to tend the animals. But once he entered the barn, he knew all was not well.

In the quiet before daylight, an unusual stir alerted him from sleep, and now, lantern light showed flakes of mossy soil on the ladder rungs. He took a long breath and touched the still-wet stuff to his nostrils. Not from around here—drier and rockier.

Above him, the door stood ajar—strange. Nothing to do but go up and check. Probably someone who needed a little sleep—he'd taken naps in so many barns, he felt no particular fear. But just in case, he flicked open his knife and started the short climb. Near the top, thin breathing drifted to him, like someone was ill.

Under a slanted bin of corn, the worn toe of an espadrille peeked out, and Domingo breathed deeper. Basque, though the wearer's exact origin remained a mystery. But seconds later, he knew unmistakably when he'd seen this precise pattern, and a pang crossed his chest at the fearsome memory it evoked.

He took another step, causing a loose floorboard to creak, and cautious eyes glinted up at him from a pile of straw in the granary's depths. The man uttered a single syllable and fell back. "Dom—"

Domingo fell on his knees. "Philippe?" He checked for blood and breaks. Philippe was so limp he hardly noticed.

Could this indeed be the warrior who tore into those murderers with him the night of Sancha's death? The peculiar bump on the bridge of the man's nose told him it was. But Philippe must have run even harder than then, for he fell here in exhaustion. In this condition, how had he even climbed the ladder?

Of course, he sought refuge and had no idea Domingo lived here, since they'd parted a distance west. But perhaps Providence had led him this way.

Domingo stole back into the house for a blanket and food. *Good, Maman and Gabirel still sleep.* Once again, he gave thanks that Aitaita never rebuilt their house into a proper Basque abode. If he had, Maman would surely have heard Philippe open the barn door, and Gabirel might have heard him climb the ladder.

Whomever Philippe fled might still be tracking him.

Domingo fed the weary traveler some cheese and bread with a little wine and issued severe instructions. "Stay here. Sleep as long as you like. I will bolt the door and return soon."

Barely able to utter his thanks, Philippe sank back against the straw.

A plan formed while Domingo fed the animals. He would hurry to Jean-Luc Edorta and engage his help, for Gabirel must not see Philippe. He didn't know exactly why—he only knew it was true.

With Edorta's pledge to busy Gabirel far into the evening, Domingo schemed how to keep Maman from the barn. A look at her garden patch gave him the necessary idea, and when he went in for breakfast, he made an offer.

"Today we will clean up the garden for spring."

"This early? Planting is weeks away."

"You never know how the weather might turn. With Vichy's new quotas and rationing, your garden means even more than ever. We can organize the fruit cellar, too, and see what will last for seeding. We'll hide whatever we can from the authorities."

She accepted his logic and once Gabirel left for Edorta's, walked toward the shed with purpose in her step. Domingo called, "First I need to visit that sick ewe."

He rounded the barn toward the sheep pen, but scrabbled

through the back barn window instead, up to the granary, and beside Philippe, who sputtered through half-sleep.

"Pilot's and guides in danger—Gestapo—called to execute a double agent—two days ago—completed, but—" He groaned and held his left wrist. "Fell from a—Gestapo trailed me as far as Grezes—lost them there—no danger now, but *shhh.*"

A chill swept Domingo. So, the *Maquis* required Philippe's killing skills again, and now the Gestapo sought him. Domingo gently worked with the injured wrist—the wrist that had most likely wrenched an unfortunate double agent's neck.

"I'll be back at midday with food. Keep your arm up on the straw."

Before he reached the doorway, Philippe already snored again. But the lost look in his eyes haunted Domingo as he worked with his mother over burlap sacks full of potatoes, carrots, and turnips, some rotted, some sprouting green as if ready to be planted.

Hearing Philippe's voice and touching his wrist brought everything back from their revenge that night in wild Haute-Loire country. It was as though for a time, they both became other men—killers.

When the sun shone almost overhead, Maman mentioned the noon meal, so Domingo said he must check that ewe again. But he passed through the kitchen first and carried Philippe a bowl of stew. Sound asleep, the older man looked so docile against the straw.

When they amassed enough vegetables and Maman took some to the house for supper, Domingo relished the trip alone across the frozen meadow to the sod cave Aitaita fashioned long ago. Here, they stored extra food, and when necessary, Basques sought by the authorities. Perhaps he ought to move Philippe out there tonight, but since Vichy had started requisitioning more of their produce, Edorta used it too, when his own hiding place overflowed.

The cold air quieted Domingo's doubts. He never wanted to revisit his experience with Philippe. Having gone too far into the darkness stretched tentacles around his heart, but Père Gaspard's words brought him back to this beautiful countryside, preparing for spring's renewal.

The sublime sky reminded him of Père's clear eyes, washed with sympathy after Sancha's death.

Forgiveness visits us in spite of our guilt, our shame, and our fears. Yet we must allow it entrance into our hearts.

He returned to the yard through the barn, but Philippe had gone. His bowl lay empty. Relieved and disappointed at once, Domingo forked fresh straw over his sleeping place and crossed himself for Philippe, the sort of man these times required. But he also beseeched the Almighty for this warrior's soul, lest all the bloodshed destroy him.

Chapter Sixteen

"Charles, good to see you, but I must be on my way." Mrs. Tenney huffed and whisked out the kitchen door to one of her meetings, and Charles grimaced as he closed the door behind her.

"I ought to be more patient with her, but how could she imply I had something to do with Kathryn leaving?"

"Oh, she just misses her, Charles. I'm sure it's hard for her to think Kate chose to leave without some outside motivation."

"Maybe. Well, Mum thinks you top them all, Addie, and has entrusted her pitiful courtyard to you. Could you use some help?"

Dingy London sky backed the barren trees of March. The arbor looked miserable, the vines were brown and damp, and the gate's iron hinges rusted into crumbling wood slats.

"I hadn't put any thought into it yet, but I'd better do something before she returns from her bandage rolling. I wouldn't want to disappoint her."

"Ah, no. We must avoid that at all costs." His exaggerated *all* was not lost on Addie, but he changed the subject. "Did you work outside every day back home in Iowa?"

"Yes. The temperatures here are so mild, my hands think it's spring, and I should be puttering at something."

Mr. Tenney set his cup down. "Too bad we can't put the whole of London under a tent, like the gardens, and burn pitch to keep plants from freezing."

"Would you like more tea?" Addie made a move to push her chair back, but he leaped up for the thermos.

"Let me get it." He filled their cups and sat again. "You like to work, don't you?"

"I wouldn't call it work, just not lazing about, as your Mum would say."

"Indeed she would." He set his elbows on the table. "Lazing about troubles her greatly. If you can't come up with anything to do here, we might volunteer for any number of projects. Would you be game?"

Excitement shot through Addie. Since Kate left, she'd had to fight to keep Saturdays from becoming glum. She enjoyed getting to know the bandage-rolling ladies, but longed for something new and different.

"Oh yes. I'd love to."

"By the way, you called me *sir* a while ago. I hope it was only because of Mum?"

She nodded, and his voice became brisk. "Well, then. I shall ring someone up and check on possibilities. And I'd better rummage in father's things for suitable work togs. When I brought Mum those papers to sign, I hadn't expected to stay long." His glance wavered between Addie and the door.

"I'm glad you did, Charles. I'll finish the dishes and get some clothes from the garden shed. Your mother said I could use any-thing I find in there."

"By all means. Granger was a slight man, but still—" He eyed her head to toe. "I doubt his garb will fit you very well."

By the time she found what she needed, Charles tapped on the shed door and peeked in at her. "Ah, now you look the part, and my contact tells me the gardens rarely turn down an offer of help."

"Good. What a dapper dresser, you are." She couldn't hide her grin at the change, down to denim overalls rolled up at the hem and a moth-eaten khaki shirt.

He tucked a faded handkerchief into his pocket. "You think they'll accept me like this?"

"You might pass for an Iowa farmer, especially if you wear that beat-up hat."

"I shall do so at your suggestion. I can't see what we might do in the courtyard yet. Did you think of something?"

"We could pick up twigs from the latest rain. I hate to tell your mother I did nothing."

"Let's have at it. And after that, I've discovered a place we might help out. Have you heard of the WLA?"

"Let me guess. Workers' Landmine Authority?" Addie brought out the wheelbarrow and threw in a few twigs.

"Close. The Women's Land Army, a dedicated crew of produce growers who take the place of men gone into the forces. It's official service, actually. Every female must register when they turn twenty."

"The National Service Act of 1941?"

"How did you know?"

Addie smiled. "Guess."

"Kathryn Isaacs, or I'll be snookered." Charles unlatched the back gate and started filling a burlap bag with fallen twigs.

"When she heard about the act, she was up in arms that the States hadn't conscripted women yet."

"I find her ire easy to imagine. Last summer, our legislators revised the parameters here, did you know? Now, ninety percent of single women engage in some sort of civilian army or other. I believe eighty percent of married women are involved, too."

"American women can work in factories, and now we have WACs and WAVES to fly supplies in the States, at least. But we're a little behind you Brits."

"Ah, you'll catch up. After all, we've had four full years to attain our present state. At any rate, it's time we gave our valiant girls a hand, wouldn't you say?"

The promise of gardening sent a thrill through Addie, and she hurried around the yard, grabbing every twig she could see.

"This spot north of the city hauls in earth from the country and operates greenhouses year-round. I wish I'd thought of going there sooner, with your penchant for this kind of work."

"You've thought of it now, and that's good enough for me. If they welcome us, I'll want to go every Saturday."

A few minutes later, the bus hissed to a stop, and Addie clambered on in Mr. Granger's old plaid shirt and trousers, secured at the waist with several safety pins. A few looks passed between well-dressed riders, and Charles leaned close to her ear.

"I expect the others think us rather dowdy."

Addie adopted her best British accent. "Raaaaather." More people entered at the next stop, and Charles edged a bit closer. "Do you wear such clothes on your farm?"

"Yes, my husband's old overalls. I'd been thinking it was high time I bought my own when Kate wrote about her pregnancy. Besides, Harold wouldn't have approved."

"No?"

"He—ah, he doesn't believe women should wear men's clothing, even in the WACs and WAVEs."

"Hum." They rode for a while in silence, and Addie imagined Harold blowing a gasket if he had to take orders from a female. She giggled thinking of his chagrin.

"What is it?" Charles looked into her eyes. "Something tickled your funny bone?"

"Yes, it's—well, something Kate would appreciate. I just imagined Harold having to take an order from a female over here."

Charles opened his mouth, but the bus stopped at a corner, and several women entered. He grasped a pole and motioned for one of them to take his seat. The woman, about Berthea's age, huffed and puffed her ample hips between Addie and another passenger.

The black underneath her nails reminded Addie of Jane, her neighbor back home. She stuck out her hand.

"Hello, I'm Addie Bledsoe."

"Nice to meet you. I'm Mrs. Noelting. Goin' out to work on my cousin's farm."

"How fortunate for you."

"That it is, Miss. Sends me back fixed for the week. An extra egg on Sunday mornings." She eyed Addie. "Looks like you've tried your hand at farming too."

"I surely have, in the United States. I like nothing better."

By the time Charles chose an exit, Mrs. Noelting shared her address and an invitation to tea. Addie and Charles headed west, turned north at the corner, and entered a country lane.

"You found a new friend?"

"Yes. She lives in a flat, she says, a couple of blocks from us."

"On Afton?"

"Yes. I suppose you know every street in all of Westbourne Grove."

"When Mum let me go out, which wasn't often, I gawked around a lot. And in my later years at home, I made it a point to learn the lay of every possible area."

"That comes in handy now, with all your responsibilities?"

"Indeed. Especially since I've never liked maps, but think it rather pleasant to organize the pieces in my head."

"You'd make a good secret agent, then, or a spy."

Charles stopped short. "Why do you say that?"

"A spy would have to get around without asking a lot of questions or relying on others. That's what Kate has to do right now, don't you suppose?"

"You think about her often, don't you?"

She nodded, and he led the way down the road again. "With Mum's impertinence this morning, I neglected to give you some important information I learned recently."

"Oh, do tell me."

"In preparation for the Invasion, which I'm guessing will occur soon, The Special Operations Executive has jogged down into the Auvergne for recruiting purposes. Kathryn may be located that far south."

"What does that mean?"

"I take it as good news. She's out of the main loop, off from the Parisian activity a bit."

Unspoken questions turned thunderous as they approached some tent-like structures in an open field. But Addie didn't want to try Charles, since he had already given her so much news.

"I believe it best not to mention this to Mum. But I think Kathryn might be in less danger than I expected, at least for now."

"Can you explain?"

"The *Résistance* there has stymied the SS more than any other section, but the enemy is bound to press in on them sooner or later."

Addie let out a long breath. "Thank you so much. And of course, I'll keep this quiet."

"Far better for Mum to picture her here in England, awaiting transport, than let loose in the French countryside."

Without thinking, Addie threw her arms around Charles in a heartfelt hug. Then she stumbled back.

"Forgive me. It's just that—" Heat rushed her cheeks, but Charles rescued her.

"Come now, you expressed your joy at good news about your best friend. Completely appropriate—don't worry yourself about it."

But she did. As he unlatched the big iron farm gate, Charles carried the dialogue, as if he knew she might be troubled for a while. "My father used to bring me up here to ride horses once a month, when he stayed home for a period, that is."

"Did he ride with you?"

"He always had other business, but never failed to collect me three hours later. And he planned out my progress with the owner."

"You tried hard to please him?"

"Ever so hard."

Addie remembered her one fateful so-called horse ride, when her older sister Rose and she ended up on the ground beneath a horse with a loose cinch.

"I've always wanted to learn to ride, but Har—"

"You owned a horse?"

"Yes, but—" Why spoil the day discussing Harold's attitude toward horses as work animals, or his intolerance of her fear? "I got to witness a foal's birth last year with a neighbor. I named

her Missy, and before I left, she came to me when I walked into the barn."

"You miss her?"

"I hadn't thought about it, but I suppose I do. She won my heart with her first breath. I miss our old farm dog, too."

"That sort of longing can be remedied—while many dogs have been absconded and trained for military missions, we surely could locate one."

"That reminds me of Mackie—Evelyn invited me over, and I haven't yet."

"Evelyn?"

"Remember that big dog outside the office—it was a while ago, right after work."

"Ah—" Charles touched Addie's arm as they turned down a drive, but said no more about Evelyn. "We're entering a wartime vegetable project that supplies food for part of the city, so you mustn't think it typical."

Canvas covers, situated like buildings over the property, protected vegetable beds. The scene didn't fit Addie's picture of a British farm, but the smells did—earth, manure, and growing things.

"Some day I shall arrange for a visit to a real farm, complete with a crowing rooster, a horse, and barn cats lapping milk."

He opened a door and ushered Addie inside, where a girl not more than fifteen lifted her head.

"Do you have work for two stray farmer-sorts?"

She waved them toward rows of maturing lettuce plants. "Weeding that section is on today's list. Choose your tools over there."

With a grand gesture, Charles signaled Addie to go first. "Lead the way, oh fearless gardener."

A wayfarer approached Domingo as he warmed his feet at his campfire after delivering a parcel far up into the Aveyron, much farther east than he liked to travel. Beyond the border, uneasiness rode his back, but on the return trip, the twin steeples of Clermont-Ferrand's black cathedral orientated him.

Snowfall increased and bitter March winds buffeted, but now, he dipped along the Cantal border, near the *Résistance* camp. The stranger stood near his fire and took off his hat. "Where is your home?"

Domingo might have laughed. He seemingly had none, since day by day, his orders changed. Often, simple deliveries enlarged to embrace any number of additional missions. His visits home had become overnight stays rather than sojourns to provide relief from Gabirel's constant responsibility.

Before he left this time, Maman had labeled him with the Basque word for stranger. He kissed her wrinkled forehead in reply. What else could he do? Word had it the Allies would invade early this summer, so preparations escalated. That meant the *Resistance* required his services almost daily.

But this man asked only where he originated. "In Lot. And you?"

The man's appearance hinted at the answer. What had once passed for suitable clothing in some large city had dwindled to tatters offering little protection from the cold. Domingo could have guessed the wanderer's story—plenty more like him appeared over the fall and winter.

Two other men straggled to the fire, and a while later, two more. Domingo pushed aside his desire for quietude. At first, partisans trickled into Midi, but recently, with tighter city restrictions, the floodgates opened. Now, a gaggle of hungry-eyed, hollow-cheeked men crowded around.

"How long has it been since you've eaten?"

The leader shrugged. "This morning a farmer gave us cheese and bread."

"Tell me what goes on in the cities."

"Surely you must have heard?"

"Maybe not. We come from a remote area, and I only act as a courier when necessary."

The dark-bearded man sitting next to the leader grinned. "That is what we used to do before *Le Releve.*"

Domingo feigned ignorance.

Murmurs passed among them. "He does not know what came to pass in Paris?"

The bearded man continued. "They demand that we work in Germany, even women, from twenty years of age to sixty-five. They transported a million and a half prisoners there in '40. Now, Laval proposes trading prisoners of war for skilled workers."

"What skills do you have?"

"Supervising rail production. Steelworks. Machinists."

"But no matter what Darnand threatens, we won't go."

"Darnand?"

"The head of the Milice." The man spat in derision.

"Ah." Domingo put on a placid face. He could describe his own exploits with the Milice, but to what end?

Spittle sailed into the flames like miniature swords, sizzling and swirling upward in small cyclones. "Our opinion of Joseph Darnand. Surely you have met *Miliciens?*"

"*Oui.*"

"But you do not know their leader?"

One of the men guffawed. "And we thought you would be able to help us! The government sent 250,000 of our compatriots to Germany, so we fled to the mountains. But what do we find? Men who know nothing."

The leader shushed him. "Voices carry up here. Keep your tone low."

Another man took his turn. "Then I suppose you do not know Phillipe Harriot, either? That propagandist pipes his lies to every home. You have no radio?"

"Harriot's lies are well known, but I've never listened to him. I concentrate on stopping the Milice when I can."

"Stopping them? What do you mean?"

Domingo leaned back against a tree stump and changed the subject. "I am only a simple peasant, but I will help you if I can."

The leader took over. "We have left our homes, families, and work to volunteer. Fritz Saukel, the detested Reich Minister of Labor, will receive none of our sweat or blood. Instead, we offer ourselves to the *Organisation de Résistance de l'Armée.*"

Domingo sought to respond without offering them false hope. He scanned the sky. *Donnez-moi les mots.* He translated his prayer into English—*Give me the words.* The image of that female agent he left in the haystack came to him. Along with an odd serenity.

Strange that war would bring heaven nearer, but the disaster lurking everywhere reinforced Domingo's dependence on the Almighty. Who else could he trust? He had not set foot in his church for weeks, yet felt the Holy Presence near and called for help with the most common decisions.

"M*es amis*, things change day to day. One moment I think I know something, the next it has become two opposites."

Several men nodded. In their world, so different from his, this war produced the same effect.

"Until now, only the *Résistance-fer,* from within the Railroad workers, and the Communist FTP performed sabotage. But now, the *Résistance* needs your particular skills. In the hills northwest of here, you will find the *Maquis.*

"*Les Chantiers de la jeunesse française,* organized for young people by the STO, meet in St. Jean du Gard. Vichy wants the young to collaborate with the Germans, but they drift to the Maquisards." Domingo gestured behind him.

"This steep trail winds toward their camp."

"Why there?"

"Vichy supplies *Les Chantiers* with weapons, ammunition, and food, trusting they will work for the Nazis. But the Maquisards pick off the volunteers and steal their supplies. So what Vichy sends *Les Chantiers* supports our cause in the end.

"Farther north, our leaders have had more freedom to learn the Gestapo's ways, while in Midi, small bands and individuals only anger the local *gendarmes.*"

Someone fed the fire, and Domingo glanced around the circle. "They'll teach you to survive out here."

"How do we find them?"

"Beyond the Cantal's chestnut forests, the camp guards will find you."

The leader leaned close to Domingo. "You travel at night?"

"Mostly."

"Can you lead us out of here?"

"As far as the next village where you'll find food and warm barns for sleeping. These peasants hate the Milice and share what little they have. Vichy has stolen their sons, their seed, their fertilizer, and their animals."

"So we depart in darkness?"

Domingo yawned. "At midnight, when the moon is bright."

Fleeting thoughts of slipping away tempted him, but hunger and cold hounded these men. If he gave them instructions to the next village, they would become lost on the winding trails, and the sure scent of snow tinged the air.

No, he would not leave these patriots helpless. He would keep his promise. They would seek him later tomorrow, but he dared not wait. Traveling by day meant no hardship, only more watchfulness, and Maman and Gabirel needed him.

One by one, the would-be partisans lapsed into exhausted sleep. The rising silver moon seemed clear and certain. Day and night still followed their usual pattern—sunrise to sunset. War's complexity had changed Domingo, but this decision beside the crackling fire assured him that compassion still lived in him. Aitaita would be pleased with his choice.

Chapter Seventeen

Addie pinched off spindly lower leaves before positioning a tomato plant on its side and covering it with soil. Sunshine drenched her back and shoulders, and she could hardly believe the springlike feeling in the air.

"May I ask why you do that?"

"The fewer lower spikes, the stronger the root system, to support the branches."

"And let me guess—you position the plant on its side because more roots will grow that way?" She nodded and Charles leaned on his hoe. "You certainly know a lot about tomatoes."

Addie didn't even try to hide her grin as he locked his brows in mock consternation.

"Laughing at my pronunciation of tomaaa-to, are you?"

She ignored him.

"Be honest. I am your employer, you recall."

"Yes, sir."

"And now you have defied one of my most heartfelt requests, calling me by that blaaaaasted title again." He scratched his ear, tipping his father's stained hat. "Whatever shall I do with such an impertinent American?"

At Addie's chuckle, he flapped his hat against his knee. "But I am presently under *your* tutelage. You know the answer to my every question."

"Anything else I can do for you?"

Addie reached for another tomato from a wooden pallet, but

Charles touched her wrist. She looked up into blue eyes streaked black. Perspiration dotted his temples.

"You could—" He pressed his top lip against his teeth, and his voice deepened. "You could allow me to take you to dinner tonight."

A mix of emotions flooded her, too. Dinner—oh my, how she would love to say yes. But down on the coast, she had a husband.

"There's nothing I'd like better. But the expense, and would it be—do you think—?" She flopped her arms in a futile gesture. "Oh, you know what I mean."

What she meant was Harold. He hadn't written again since he'd ordered her home, but his ultimatum left her no choice. She couldn't allow him to rule her every move again—that would dishonor everything the past four years had taught her.

"Would it be appropriate in your married state?"

Addie closed her eyes.

"Dinner would merely express my gratitude for your lessons today, and your companionship. Before we discovered these gardens, you cannot imagine my stuffy weekends. I did paperwork, like every other day. I can't even begin to express how much better this is."

He dug a hole for the next tomato, and Addie picked off the fragile lower branches. Late winter sun sent the garden into a frenzy of growth. Spinach, lettuce, and kale plants bushed out, great bunches of baby string beans hung from their vines, and by next week, the peas would be ready to pick.

Though they set out for the gardens earlier each week, Saturdays went by far too fast. Addie lost count of how many weeks she and Charles had come here, but she wouldn't exchange them for anything. And now, he proposed adding one more delight to the day.

The silence remained comfortable, not tense and fearful as it would have been with Harold. Charles moved ahead, giving space for her to ponder.

Three more plants nested in their new earth homes before he caught her eye again, but without the slightest impatience.

She leaned another tomato plant into a perfect-shaped hole

and pushed earth around the roots and stem. Nothing else gave her this sense of satisfaction, and it was Charles who brought her here. His head bobbed up and down above his shovel as he created more holes. Time expanded—she could take all day to decide.

Thinking of Harold created a pain in the back of Addie's neck. If he cared at all about her, he would surely have responded to her letter by now. Of course, she wrote what he didn't want to hear, that God had led her to London for a purpose, and with his mother's blessing. Where did this leave them?

The conversation of several girls hoeing a few rows over provided a diversion. One wore jeans with shoulder straps, the other a sweater tied around her waist.

"My cousin went to New York for safety, and she's working in a garden there, too, although it's as big as a farm, she says, fifty or sixty acres."

"Girls from all over—England, France, Holland, and elsewhere, board with an older lady. My cousin says in the cities, some apartment-dwellers plant a garden atop the building, and everyone living there chips in to work."

"How old is your cousin?"

"She was sixteen when her parents sent her. Now she's qualified as a grey lady in a hospital, too, so she works double-time. The good thing about being over there is they have eggs several days a week—can you imagine?"

"When this is all over, I'm going to raise chickens and never go without eggs again. We'll feast on sweet custard once a week, and flan whenever I feel the urge."

"I wrote back and told my cousin to stop with the food news. But what's interesting is her social life, even with the two jobs. The girls go to the U.S.O. on Friday and Saturday nights and dance till midnight with whatever fellows happen to be around. She says, 'We're still young. Even though the war's going on, everyone needs a little fun.'"

Addie yelled over, "I envy you your overalls."

At the girl's puzzled look, she clarified, with gestures to her shoulders. "Your trousers—where did you get them?"

"Never thought anyone would think this clobber desirable! My aunt pulled them out of an old clothing box. Want me to see if she has more?"

"Oh, no thanks—that's all right."

Charles returned without Addie even noticing until he squatted beside her. "If I spoke out of line, please say so, Addie. We need never revisit the subject."

"You never speak out of line." She sat back on her heels and rolled up Granger's well-worn shirtsleeves as the next-door girls continued chatting about that cousin in the United States. But one statement still rang in her ears.

We're still young—everyone needs a little fun.

She had turned twenty-two last year—still young, although she'd felt much older at that time. Berthea remembered her birthday a few days late, and Harold ignored it altogether. Thankfully, Kate sent her a card from England that arrived the day before.

The chatter seemed timed just right for her quandary. "I agree with your cousin. Let's go out tonight and meet some American chaps."

Sunlight accentuated the deep glint in Charles' eyes, and Addie gave him her answer. "I accept your invitation. I know you mean nothing more than friendship."

His left eyebrow quirked, but his forehead creases decreased by a few lines.

"But how shall I manage my landlady's curiosity?"

"Ah, Mum—I understand. We'll come up with something."

"You think so?"

A mischievous glimmer entered his eyes. "There's a hospital fundraiser less than half an hour from her house tonight. I might press into service an old friend who works there. He could call Mum with a tale requiring her services at the money-taking table."

"Positively brilliant."

"This fellow and I attended school together, rather a rowdy bloke.

More than once, faithful, obedient Charles Tenney covered for his escapades. Surely he hasn't forgotten those days when I rescued him from certain danger."

Before long, the tomatoes all stretched their roots, and Addie surveyed them with satisfaction. That's what Charles gave her, too—room to stretch. As they walked back to the bus stop and boarded, she determined to relegate all thoughts about Harold until later.

Kate often said she thought about things too long and hard. Addie imagined her hand on her hip. "Stop analyzing, Addie. Enjoy this day and look forward to dinner."

Her mind flitted to a happy quarter—plenty of time to wash her hair before evening. After all, she was going out! That sounded almost impossible, like some exotic bird suddenly appearing. Then, another twinge crossed Addie's heart. *Harold would call eating dinner with a man sin.* An iron vice tightened around her chest, and she sent a plea heavenward. *Show me what to do—if You want me to stay home, I will.*

As the brakes squealed and passengers filed out, tranquility overwhelmed her. Overhearing those girls today was no coincidence, Kate would say, but a sign of divine care and guidance. She did need some fun, and by the way, Harold didn't know the meaning of the word.

As usual, Kate was right. For one thing, Addie'd never really gone out to eat. It was a big treat for Harold to stop at the Halberton drugstore for nickel cherry cokes. During a clandestine trip to Cedar Rapids their senior year, she and Kate had stopped at a Dairy Queen, a new restaurant that started in Joliet, Illinois. Hearing how it had caught on in Cedar Rapids was exciting, but they kept that a secret from Harold.

Fresh air filled the bus, and Addie breathed deeper. The other night during an air raid, Mrs. Tenney's crew chief announced directions through his megaphone. Now, a personal megaphone targeted Addie. "You were born for new experiences. It's all right."

Charles turned her way. "You don't mind stopping by the hospital?"

"Not at all—I'll get to meet someone new."

To that tired, peevish inner voice that reflected Harold's suffocating perception of life, she sent her own message. *Friendship with Charles is a gift from God—if knowing Kate taught me anything, it taught me that.*

"You came to Clermont-Ferrand with Pétain?" The Nazi's razor-edged voice assaulted Kate's ears as his tall leather boot blocked her path. Celeste, a few steps ahead, glanced back wide-eyed.

"With Pétain?"

"*Oui,* the government was once here, you know?"

Fit and perfect in his pressed grey-green uniform, with collar flashes for General Service and Poland, he turned over her hand, and Kate gave thanks she pulled some weeds this morning to be sure she looked the milkmaid part.

He reached for her elbow, and his heavy cologne stopped her breath in her throat. "You are French?"

She nodded.

"You have been here how long? Since Général Pétain?"

Think fast. Général Pétain had moved his military government here from Paris briefly before establishing offices in Vichy.

"No, after that."

"You are political? You detest Pétain?"

"*Oh, non, Monsieur.*"

"You are La Résistance *française?*" Flat grey eyes pierced hers, but Kate looked away. *Never let them look into your eyes.*

"My aunt's husband left to work in Germany, and she has many cows, Monsieur. Maman promised her sister one of us would come—"

His left eyebrow shot up. "You milk the cows?"

"*Oui Monsieur,* morning and night."

He wiggled his nose and snorted. "I believe you, *mademoiselle. Ach du lieber Himmel!* Rather smelly for a proper officer's taste."

Oh, my heavens. Kate burned with a desire to slap his face, but maintained her composure until he sauntered back to his post. From the corner of her eye, she observed Celeste open a shop's door with her foot and fake an interest in a display of scarves and gloves just inside.

This was no time to hurry, though Kate wanted to run like a deer. Still eyeing the officer from under her matted hair, she crossed the threshold and forced her breathing down. Celeste made room for her while the Nazi repeated their conversation to another officer who guffawed.

"*Ein Milchmadchen?*"

Kate understood enough German to catch his meaning—"Yes, she could be beautiful if she would take a bath—just your style, fine-boned, blonde hair, and dark eyes. But she smells like a cow."

"You are certain she is not a filthy *Judenschwein?*"

A Jewish pig. Kate edged closer to the center of the building. She'd like to find him asleep and slit his throat. But at least he hadn't asked for her papers.

The second officer straightened his peaked cap, revealing a Luger automatic in his leather belt holster. *Never forget the destructive power in an oiled cartridge clip.* In Scotland, Kate loaded Lugers and earned an Expert in marksmanship.

"Come along." Celeste hissed her command and wove out a back door, down a side street, and through a gateway. A distance farther, she entered into a tiny church that lurched toward its surrounding wall as if it might crumble any second.

In a high-raftered foyer, she whispered with a tall, slender vicar who turned to Kate. "Tonight at ten, someone will come for you."

Celeste answered Kate's unspoken question. "You have a new delivery, a very important one, so rest here today."

The vicar handed Kate a folded note, and Celeste touched her arm. "Goodbye for now."

The gangly vicar led the way to a small cottage. "Find whatever you like to eat in here. I must run some errands, but should be back before dark."

An avalanche of doubt inundated Kate. Had she compromised her mission on the delivery she made this morning, a straightforward mission that only took an hour and occurred before most households awakened? She'd learned to navigate the stairs without anyone stirring—that was an accomplishment. Her task came to her when she weeded in Celeste's garden.

A youthful messenger boy slunk into the yard from a nearby pasture and handed her an envelope she hid in her hemline. An hour later, she'd returned from making the delivery, and Celeste barely raised her eyebrows.

Would she have brought her here today even if that uppity officer hadn't examined her? As usual, no answers.

Sunlight from a high window created a light shaft all the way to the sanctuary's stone floor. Otherwise, the dim space lapped as cold and dank as a murky river. The dark grey stone might have formed a prison as well as a holy place, just like Kate's frame of mind.

Carefully, she went over everything—after the morning's delivery to an obscure chateau, she made sure no one followed her to Celeste's house. Meeting that obnoxious Nazi had probably been just a coincidence.

She wandered down a low hallway. Through the kitchen's calico-curtained window, the great cathedral of our Lady of the Assumption, seat of the Archbishops of Clermont, rose against nondescript sky. The city sprawled below its twin Gothic spires, more than 350 feet tall. Built and destroyed several times, the spires forced Kate to look up, even from this distance.

"I counted on you to lead me here, but you failed me in that miserable snowstorm. At least today you show your spires."

Melancholy shrouded Kate as a cloud covered the sun. She'd made Celeste's house her home. There, she helped with household chores when she had no courier duties, and one of Celeste's sons seemed like the younger brother she'd never had. She'd even learned to make a few French dishes, and everyone praised her crêpes.

Nothing to do, though, but accept her circumstances. Miss G

would say this presented an opportunity to rest, but Kate had plenty of energy. Out back sprawled a woodpile, so she found a wood box faded an odd shade of blue—something to keep her busy.

Back and forth, she filled the cavernous wooden trunk and low slung iron arms beside the fireplace. Every load lightened her spirit. On her next-to-last trip, words came to her, silent but strong.

Your real life is hidden with Christ in God—last Sunday's text in Celeste's small home church, read with great enthusiasm by an elderly pastor. The French version helped Kate rethink the meaning, and now she lifted her eyes to the spires just as sunshine broke through the cloud cover.

"I'm like you, a long time in the making. But there you stand, whole and beautiful. I must not let this lost feeling overwhelm me."

Chapter Eighteen

To Kate's left, a cavernous desk monopolized an alcove in the parish house. When she sat down and picked up a newspaper, the writing mesmerized her.

"*L'Echo de la Montagne*" and another smaller paper titled "*Le-Chambon Pages*" brought to mind the Presbytery and Linden.

"*The confessing church and its persecuted ministers. We must care for foreign peoples, as Holy Writ instructs.*

"*Sunday June 23, Pastors Trocmé and Theis preach: The duty of Christians—to resist the violence that will be brought to bear on their consciences through the weapons of the Spirit—We will resist whenever our adversaries demand of us obedience contrary to the orders of the Gospel. We will do so without fear but also without pride and without hate.*

"*The Pastorales, our regular meetings, inform Pastors of the Plateau. They educate their parishioners of our activities through sermons and Bible study groups.*"

This morning proved that Kate attained to no such standard. One haughty German officer mocked her, and she was ready to kill him.

"*July 1941 - Detention camps.*

Gurs. 12,000 internees, many transported east. Still 7,000. 90% Juifs.

Rivesaltes, created January, '41. 8,000 families. 3,000 children. 3,000 Juifs.

Noé, 17,000 sick, old, infirm.

Récébédou, same as Noé.

Internment Camps.

Vernet - 3,200 men, 25% Jews, political prisoners, refugees.

Argeles – 200 Juifs. 700 Spanish cripples

Rieucros – 400 undesirables (feminine)

"Cripples … undesirables …" Kate's whisper sounded hoarse to her own ears. Many at the Presbytery would qualify.

Doctors and charities reported living quarters badly constructed, no windows. Huts 50-60 meters long for nearly 100 internees. People sleep on straw, rarely changed. Filth. Rats. No disinfectant. Loathsome latrines.

No changes of clothes, worn for six months. No access to adequate water for washing. Dreadful stink and continual infection risk from rats, flies, mosquitoes.

Poor food. Hardly 800 calories daily. Cold conditions.

Children – only milk coffee in morning. Rice twice a week. Swede and turnip soup. Children weak and nervy. Dysentery, tuberculosis, high death rate. No medication, unstocked hospitals.

At least the final section showed something being done.

Actions:

Opening of Abric for internment camp children

November '42 - opening of Faidoli, same mission

November '42 -L'atelier Cévenol– workshop to teach woodcutting to young men

December '42 - Swiss Aid rents two farms,

1. teach modern agriculture techniques.

2. Alleviate foodstuff shortage. Run by Swiss national and wife, former nurse at Rivesaltes."

So many people, and by now, many of them likely inhabited German prisons or camps.

Undesirables.

Kate's head swam with visions of frightened parents and lost children—children like Linden. Deep in thought, she grasped for some way to aid them when the vicar suddenly stood beside her. She startled up.

"Forgive me. I couldn't stop reading about the camps."

He leaned on the doorjamb and wiped his brow with a kerchief.

"No doubt conditions have worsened since those reports. Gurs, where many perished in the Spanish conflict, has been reopened. Thousands have been hauled to Drancy, near Paris, but most on to Germany. His voice dropped. "To death camps."

"You know this for certain?"

"Informers have no reason to lie. One camp they call Auschwitz." The hall clock marked time. "And as if the *Chantiers de Jeunesse* were not enough, Vichy established the *Service du Travail Obligitaire* on February sixteenth."

"All French men are to take the places of conscripted Germans. Young men refuse, and many come to us. A large group from Bolbec, whose Pastor once lived near here, has joined the *Résistance*."

"This is not good?"

"Yes, but also dangerous. Who can tell what is good any more?" He raised his palms. "The whole world has turned around. What we once thought evil masquerades as right."

"I stayed in Le Chambon for a while."

"You know about the YMCA? A man named Charles Guillon settled volunteers in Camp du Joubert. Some young Jewish men work with them in cooperation with the Maquisards."

He pulled long fingers through his thinning hair. "These times require so much discernment, with enormous consequences and few, if any, parameters. I long for simple Sunday sermons and visiting the sick." His limbs sagged. "Forgive me, but you know how to listen."

"I've learned a great deal today."

"You may be hungry?"

Suddenly, Kate realized that toting wood had worked up her appetite.

"I'll brew some tea." He entered the kitchen. Through the hallway window, the spires shone like a *guidon* bathed in sunset.

Hot tisane, thick baguette slices, jam, and a plate of cheese made her stomach growl, and a smile softened the vicar's angular face. "You neglected your needs for knowledge?"

"I guess so, but how can we help the internees?"

"Outside aid and more food drops. But making a difference inside the camps is impossible unless one knows a worker."

Overhead scuffling sent his forefinger to his lips. "We give temporary shelter to as many as possible. You may never know the impact of your deliveries."

"My English and American friends would give if they knew—"

"I'll provide an address to give them."

"I mustn't send any mail."

"Ah yes. If you leave their addresses, I will contact them to send their donations via the Quakers. Don't worry—I travel far and wide and mail letters from different areas. Every small gift helps." Deep forehead wrinkles belied his hopeful words.

"It's no coincidence the *Resistance* beckoned you on this full moon. I would guess you carry news of a new commander coming to set up military training, a Spanish woman, expert in guerilla warfare." He took a sip of tea and rubbed his temples. "Also, there is word—"

He stared above her head. "One of our agents has turned on us—for how long, we don't know. They call him—or her—*la Corbeille*. Every time I hear a crow call now, I think of this. And I must admit, I hesitated when Celeste spoke with me. For all I know, you could be this double agent."

"True."

He gave a hollow laugh. "Well, if you are, you can kill me, and then my troubles will be over. If you aren't, then beware—it seems this crow crosses France like a dance floor."

La Corbeille. Wasn't it Iowa crows that pierced Addie's cherries in early July one year?

"In the end, we will fight. I find comfort in the Psalms, where King David confronts vile enemies who kill *les innocents*. And the other day I realized again our Lord's all-encompassing love, when He healed the daughter of a Roman soldier, a man who surely had taken innocent life."

He eyed Kate's empty plate. "Pack some food for your journey."

Out the window, the cathedral disappeared in the darkness, yet its outline remained in Kate's mind. She refilled her cup. The well-steeped concoction eased the pressure in her head, so she started her list of names and addresses.

"You think our agent believes?" Philippe scraped snow onto their campfire.

"You mean, the way we do?"

The woman they just took over the mountains through bitter cold had faith in the Allied cause. Chattering teeth, raw skin, too thin a coat—but she refused help until she had to let Philippe rub her legs before the fire. Even then, she turned her head away.

Beautiful Sancha rested with the saints, having sacrificed her life for the Chosen. This British agent, blue eyes afire with intensity and wild tawny hair massed under a beret that offered no protection from frostbite, was willing to give up everything, too.

But did she believe in the gift of forgiveness? After he and Philippe killed Sancha's murderers, that forgiveness embraced Domingo like the plant tincture Maman boiled to soothe cuts and deep bruises, or her slippery elm and aloe cream for sheep sores.

In this budding season of *Paque,* did the agent believe in the restoration of life, redemption, and the resurrection? The fire sputtered out, and Domingo would have shrugged away things too deep to utter in this wet cold, but Philippe waited for his reply.

"Others would have turned back, but she lunged into the cold—is that not faith? You led us well, Philippe."

"It seemed heaven itself fought us. But after five attempts, we simply had to succeed."

Heaven itself—Lately, Heaven seemed adrift and whimsical to Domingo. Yet, the Creator protected them through this long winter, the coldest he recalled.

The wind increased, but an hour down the trail, a south breeze carried a putrefying odor. Some animal must have died. A while later, Domingo decided several animals surely perished together in a terrible storm, and their carcasses thawed a bit today. With each step, the stench grew.

"Only a couple of kilometers left to that pass I used last winter." Philippe lowered his head like a bull and plunged ahead, but the smell almost gagged Domingo. He recited the past weeks' events for a diversion.

He'd longed to return to his valley before this latest series of trips. Due to treacherous snows, the final one wound through unknown territory. Never had a border delivery been thwarted so many times. But finally, he and Philippe prevailed.

The agent balked when they turned back the last time, for she carried vital information for London. But fierce winds blocked trails and froze noses and toes.

Philippe overruled her and sought shelter—a cave away from the wind, where they lighted a fire and waited. The snow stopped, but an hour after they started walking again, a wall of white swirled around them like thick soup. When the woman's legs became raw, Philippe hovered over her in yet another fire's glow.

Why did she come so ill prepared? Geography lessons taught Domingo that Great Britain lacked mountains like these, but cold, its citizens ought to know. Maybe the Nazis outed the agent's circuit, and she fled with nothing but her clothing.

Even on their last attempt, Philippe considered retreating. But when the wind died down, the agent swayed on her wobbly legs and proclaimed, "Only a few more hours—I almost know the way myself."

When they finally left her at a safe village, Philippe suggested they try a southern pass. But Domingo didn't know which was worse, the formidable snow or this overwhelming *odeur dégueulasse*. He would never even use that word in public.

He choked back a cough. "That atrocious smell—what is it?"

"Gurs."

The name knocked against Domingo's breastbone—this was where Ander died. Philippe waited a few steps ahead.

"You mean—?"

Philippe's pointing finger replied. Below them, organized rows of wooden buildings resembled felled trees against the snow. Philippe pulled his kerchief over his nose.

Gurs. After Ander's death, that same syllable rolled from Aitaita's tongue. Now it roiled in Domingo's stomach.

"Someone you know perished here?"

"My brother, after Catalonia fell. He survived the fighting and started home, but the French built this camp for the International Brigade and sent him here."

No use detailing the experience—straggling survivors brought back word, and Aitaita translated—dysentery or pneumonia wasted Ander's precious life. On the day the news came, something altered in Aitaita, as though saying the words meant he bore a portion of the blame.

That spring, he shrank back from carrying the *Olentzero*, a straw figure left over from the ancient *jentillak*, in the Saint Joseph the Workman's Day parade. And in the local summer festival, he refused to take his place as one of the *bertsolariak*, the revered storytellers. Always before, he improvised rhymes with the best of them.

Combined with line after line of low windowless structures, these memories ignited a dark sickness in Domingo. Far from home and family, Ander, whose name meant *warrior,* breathed his last. Dear Ander taught him the valley, the hills, the paths, and how to hunt and care for the sheep. Domingo still sensed his presence, like Aitaita's.

That Ander now lived in glory seemed paltry comfort as Domingo gaped at this place that wounded his mother forever and diminished the luster in Aitaita's eyes. For weeks afterward, Maman inhabited a shell, cooking, tending her garden, picking herbs, and kneading bread, a mere remnant of her former self.

Papa, Ander, Aitaita, and Sancha. Aitaita had been ready to leave this earth, but not Papa or Ander, and surely not Sancha. But Père Gaspard maintained that their deaths also afflicted the Almighty, and heaven grieved along with Domingo's family.

A wind gust strengthened the foulness. Domingo crushed his fist against Philippe's shoulder, and Philippe turned downhill so fast Domingo raced to keep up.

Down, down, down, faster and faster they scrabbled through rocky outgrowths, slippery inclines, and fearsome brambles. Up a bit, then down again, two dots in the wilderness, strong and evasive as gazelles.

Anything to get away.

Philippe never paused, but ran even faster. Finally, he paused and gasped. "They brought German prisoners and common criminals here at the war's outset. Now the Chosen fill it.

"Nearly a year ago, I passed closer and saw some children and trembling old women, their ribs accordion pleats, their bellies protruded. Some witless soldiers constructed a two-storied latrine, so prisoners carry their own excrement out in carts."

He swiped at his nose. "When the wind turns, the smell is not so bad."

Cold sweat traced the back of Domingo's neck, and he wanted to scream, "Enough—no more talk of the camp." He thrashed into the bushes and braced against a tree. A cavernous breath quelled the distaste in his throat, and the urge passed. He leaned back to study the heavens, blue and glorious in spite of this mangy earth.

A new determination rose in him. He'd always thought to travel south some day, to view the famous tree at Guernica. But now, he reconsidered what it would mean to stand before his people's emblem, the lone tree that withstood such fierce shelling from the *Luftwaffe*.

The South reeked of violence, and he'd seen enough for a lifetime. Aitaita's recollection of the tree sufficed for him. Above all, Domingo longed to embrace the sweet scent of his own valley. That alone could satisfy. He found Philippe, and they took off, men strong to run a race, oblivious to everything but the call of home.

Chapter Nineteen

Kate knew she ought to stop for a few minutes, yet the road spread before her, inviting her on. At least she knew her way, having biked the route between Maurice's headquarters and Clermont-Ferrand so many times. Her raincoat and gloves, well used during the past weeks since she met up with him again, kept the sharp March wind at bay.

Moonlight presented a trail off the road, so she stretched her legs, munched a hard biscuit, and remounted her bicycle. A dark blur crossed the road—probably a raccoon or fox. Ten minutes later, she circled the back way into an abandoned chateau garden.

To her relief, a guard stepped out of some bushes. He recognized her, no need to prove her identity with passwords. Often, one of his replacements called for the password even though he'd seen her several times.

Down a dank, creaky stairway and through a maze of tunneled hallways, Kate gave her own personal tap at the door. Maurice opened it—his eyes had shrunk back into his head even more since her last visit, and his latest instructions came in ghost murmurs as furtive as this cellar room.

"We've issued you a new identity card for this mission, and you must go by train, almost to Toulouse." He held out the card, and Kate perused her new persona as a French teacher.

Nom: Dumont
Prénoms: Marguerite
Profession: Institutrice

Nationalité: française
Née le: 16 Juin, 1919

"Leave your bicycle behind the Issiore station. In addition to the Auvergne *Maquis*, I work with another unit near Tarbes. You will deliver a vital message almost all the way to Spain."

Tiny somber lines around his lips and his chicory-laced breath seemed as familiar as his tone. Maurice laid out her mission in a terse sequence Kate had become used to. The thought of leaving gave her a fearful twinge.

Almost all the way to Spain.

"Recent Gestapo patrols captured the circuit leader at your destination, but regardless, messages must be delivered. Chances are, another leader will rise by the time you make contact. Yet we must face the truth—once the enemy finds a worker, two more may fall. Be wary as a vole hunting food."

Maurice's eyes glinted from the shadows cast by a lantern hung from the ceiling. "Tell me again the care you will take."

Kate recited her instructions, lined the broken hemline of her burgundy dress with the message, and threaded her needle into her canvas backpack for future use. She showed Maurice her identity card. "I am Mademoiselle Ansel, lately of Haute Loire, where I aided my bereaved aunt, but now I am headed home."

"Where do your people live?"

"West, close to Bordeaux, but my father died in the Spanish war, and my mother stays with her cousin now."

"Why do you travel these mountainous roads in winter?"

"My sister's husband has been called to labor in Germany. She has many children, and I go to help her."

"Your card proclaims you a teacher, but you resemble a milkmaid I once saw—smelled—on the street." Maurice gave a wicked grin.

"Ah, no *Monsieur*. I am a teacher, and have never milked a cow."

"All right. Keep in mind that though the northern *Résistance* expects the onslaught via Normandy's coast, many in the south believe the Allies will invade from the Mediterranean. Village people near the sea climb the *Aigourd Massif* to view the landing. The liberation of Corsica is near—this fuels their belief the Allies will soon invade France.

"Let them believe. But no matter where the invasion takes place, every railroad bridge blown and every supply factory disabled will slow the Nazi machine."

He rubbed his eyes. "Detonators line your pack. And perhaps, for your other contraband, you ought to find—" His eyes lowered.

"A more secret place?" Kate touched her top sweater buttons. "Don't worry. Whatever treasure you entrusted to me will stay as close as my heart's secrets."

He referred to a small, cellophane-wrapped package he had fished from his desk drawer and carefully handed to her. "Take care with this." Perhaps a supply of cyanide pills, or something worse.

"They've become so strict with papers here since the arrest, you'll need to catch the train from Issoire. Before your final stop, someone will pass you more information. Do whatever they say. Then walk through the town and eastward about a kilometer. Stop at a wide meadow between two haystacks, and someone will take you to meet a drop."

Maurice consulted a train schedule on his desk. "The train should leave there at, let me see—ten-thirty in the morning. So—only fifty kilometers—leave at first light, to be safe. Breathtaking views of the Livradois Forest await you, but don't let them become a distraction."

He gripped her shoulder. "Be ever so careful." He hesitated before letting go, and in that space Kate realized this might be their last meeting. Overnight this whole circuit might become history.

Now, early morning light sliced through heavy pine forest, and Kate rehearsed her lines once more. Gradually the air warmed, so she shed the gloves Celeste gave her and rounding a curve experienced the strange sensation of having traveled this road before.

For some reason, she felt at home. *At home*—what did that phrase mean? Her rooms at Mrs. Tenney's and in Aunt Alvina's house took on a fairytale quality.

Her mother's image rose before her, prim and bright-eyed in her Hello Girls' white shirt and black skirt, hair trapped at the nape of her neck, and high-buttoned boot tops showing below her skirt. Kate smiled to herself. Her own mother, sworn to serve on the front, in the thick of the action—and so many years later, Monsieur Le Blanc revealed this to her.

It seemed improbable—no—impossible that she would meet him. Yet she did, and those photographs could not lie.

If only she knew more—what hardships her mother faced, what travels, what dangers. And her father's exploits—a great hunger to explore their paths thrummed like a constant yet tenacious drum in Kate, but how could she discover even the bare details of their lives a quarter of a century ago?

Right now, she traveled the wrong direction to learn about her parents. Most of the fighting took place in the north, near the German border. Once again, she found herself headed the wrong way.

"Take heart—at least, you found your way to France. Alexandre would be proud."

The humble scent of snow on wet bark embraced her as daylight stroked the sky. The people in Le Chambon, Celeste, the long-faced Vicar in Clermont-Ferrand, and so many more risked everything. A massive unseen army all across this vast nation abandoned their futures to the same cause. They chose to go beyond fear, beyond reason, and listened to their hearts.

When she'd run off to marry Alexandre, she'd listened to her heart, too. Wasn't that the way to live? Yet because of that choice, she missed so much. And then, the war took Alexandre away. Listening to one's heart guaranteed anything but ease.

Morning birds twittered as Kate swerved to avoid a low-lying branch. It would take a miracle for her to discover more about her mother. But then, had it not been so for Monsieur Le Blanc to find her in London? At that time, she prepared for her baby's birth, with no knowledge of the *Résistance*.

One might say she headed in the wrong direction then too, but how was she to know? Still, directions could be altered—her presence on this lonely winding road offered proof.

Long after her legs begged for relief, she pedaled into a village bathed in full sun. Along cobblestone streets, curtains drew back and windows opened to receive the new day. This should be the last village before Issiore. In the city park on a bench scraped clean of snow, Kate unwrapped her bread and cheese and drank a thermos of hot chicory.

Twenty minutes later, she found the Issoire train station and checked for dark-suited watchers lolling about. Then she parked her bicycle against the back side of the building and entered some brush leading to a waterway below.

Better to relieve herself here. Filthy floor drains the French called toilets offered nothing to keep her bag out of harm's way. She climbed the ravine, filled her pocket with francs from her pack, raked her fingers through her hair and straightened her dress. Automatically, she sniffed her fingers—no milkmaid smell. From here on, she must wear her public face.

She purchased her ticket and waited on a wooden bench until the platform vibrated, and the train engine belched fumes that stung her eyes. While descending passengers retrieved their valises, a shiver travelled up Kate's back.

Cover me with Your mercy. Make my journey successful.

A minimum of food lay in her backpack atop items that could change the outcome of the invasion. But she must act nonchalant, like any old teacher on her way to her sister's house.

The conductor announced destinations and waved passengers in. As Maurice predicted, no Nazi guards checked identity cards, but one fellow in a dark Fedora leaned against the stone building smoking a cigar. *Gestapo, maybe.* Relieved to be up the steps, Kate settled into the back seat of the first car.

The khaki trousers and flannel shirt Maurice had jammed into her pack's side pocket at the last moment said more than words—she might end up traipsing those gorgeous vistas he mentioned. That brought to mind the Basque guide from her parachute drop.

Maurice's final warning rang in Kate's ears as the conductor advanced down the aisle. He stopped beside each passenger, and when he barked, "Ticket please," she was ready. He studied her identity card for what seemed far too long, but Kate tamped down the anxiety that rose in her.

Finally he passed on, and she rehearsed Maurice's directions.

"Get off at Brens. Before you disembark, someone will give you another message and instructions for delivery."

"You won't let them destroy the track ahead of me?"

"Humph."

Half a day past Gurs, a figure emerged from the brush along the steep path. Philippe stopped to speak with the ruffian, so Domingo sank on a rock.

All around them, Spring made her entrance, increasing his hunger for home—only one day more. He wished they had stuck with their original route, formidable snow or not. They might have arrived by now.

An afternoon breeze brushed low-hanging branches, and a meadowlark called. Philippe and the newcomer conferred longer, but Domingo waited a distance away, content with ignorance. The stranger gestured when he talked, but kept his voice low.

Knowledge had become a bane, not a blessing. The more Domingo learned, the more he had to traipse where he'd never wanted to go. The more he knew, the more he had to hide.

The man left, and Philippe's expression said *more instructions.* Another drop. Another delivery. More time away from home.

"Welcoming reception. Train into Brens, Department Tarn, a woman alone—high priority delivery after moonrise tonight."

Philippe and Domingo had developed a shared intuition, like the chamois they'd seen climbing above them yesterday. Hunted for their supple golden-tan skin, the swift-footed animals alerted each other of every human footfall for miles.

Philippe went off the trail for a couple of minutes, so Domingo chose the opposite direction. Gone nearly a month this time, he longed for the comfort of his own barn, Maman's bread and Gabirel's companionship.

Philippe, as close as a brother now, showed little sign of similar desires, but in that instant when he paused to deliver the latest message, his posture revealed utter weariness. With a wife and children, he ought to go home if anyone did. Domingo made his decision. What difference would one more reception, one more delivery make?

When Philippe returned, Domingo leaned forward. "I will go with you. Perhaps there is much to carry."

They turned southeast, and Philippe rested his hand on Domingo's shoulder an extra few seconds.

"Will we ever watch our sheep and weed our fields and vegetable patches like we used to? Do you think these hills and plateaus can ever be rid of the Milice?"

If Domingo listened to his deepest fears, he would have to say no.

With no idea how long she'd slept, Kate surveyed the railcar for suspicious faces, not that she knew how to tell. That woman with the crimped velvet hat might be a spy as easily as the man with the fedora shadowing his face.

An elderly lady left the car, and a younger woman in tasteful, well-designed clothes took her seat. Kate smoothed her rumpled dress and studied passengers' heads spread like mushrooms in the narrow space. Men's hats told her little, but women's apparel related tales to feed on—she and Addie could write a novel for each outfit.

A lady wearing a dressy coat crossed her ankles and pulled at her hemline, revealing her demure profile. Her smooth brow and slender nose offered no noticeable secret agent attributes. Kate chuckled—what attributes? The people in her training were plucked from all over the world.

The train lurched, and so did Kate's stomach, so she reached into her pack for a biscuit. Her fingers confirmed everything in place.

A conductor passed through the doorway. "Next stop, Albi, Gaillac, Brens."

The landscape's ever-changing spectacle stunned Kate, even after Haute Loire's beauty. A new season. Where would she go from here? Back to her circuit, of course, but more than once, Maurice hinted at its vulnerability. Who would meet her here, and where would they lead her? To a drop site, Maurice said. But what then?

Haute-Loire, even though she'd stayed only a few months, had a hold on her. The region had become Kate's home, even as little Linden and Celeste had become her family. Had Linden's brother returned yet, and what would become of the child if he never did?

This country, more Mediterranean even from this distance, drew her, too. Maybe, after all, she was perfect for this job. Home met her wherever she went.

She got out for the short stop in Albi, to avoid any time lapse at the Berns station. The lady with the green hat used the facilities before her, and for a moment, Kate thought of searching for a place behind the building. Managing the volatile backpack while squatting over a detestable drain unnerved her, but drawing attention by going behind the building might be worse.

The green-hatted woman emerged, but seemed aloof. In the restroom's fetid odor, Kate decided if she moved to France after the war, she'd lobby for better public facilities. She chuckled at her private joke—people lost their lives all around her, and she criticized the bathrooms.

A bulky older gentleman claimed her seat, so she took one on the opposite side. At Gaillac no one else boarded, and the green-hatted lady got off. Only six people remained besides the man who took her seat. Who would deliver her message?

The older man's ample weight overflowed his seat—being heavy might help an agent hide messages and contraband. Kate told herself not to hurry things, to keep her thoughts in rhythm with reality.

But the more she studied that older fellow, the more he seemed familiar. Coldness crept her shoulders, but she shook off the sensation. What if he were that double agent?

With his hat shadowing his face, she couldn't see much but tried to pinpoint what seemed so common about him. *Trust no one.*

Mid-car, a middle-aged woman with a young boy stared out the window. Kate stared too, and every meadow she saw became her meadow, the fixed rendezvous point. *Walk east out of town, a wide meadow between two haystacks.* So far, every time she needed to meet someone, they came. Why should they not this time? Still, she would feel better once her contact made this delivery.

She checked her bag again. Of course, all was there—why wouldn't it be? She was reverting to the way she behaved when she first moved to Aunt Alvina's, hiding leftover food in her room with plenty in the pantry.

The memory broadsided her. Why had she done that? Had she known scarcity in her parents' home? The question brought up others, but the engineer applied the brakes and the name *BRENS* appeared, painted in white on a grey background over a small wooden platform.

But the delivery hadn't reached her—what should she do? Her most frequent prayer pirouetted from her lips. *Help me. Show me.*

She gathered her coat, hat, and knapsack. If she exited without receiving any contact, what then?

Chapter Twenty

Halfway down the aisle, the heavy man with the hat pushed in front of Kate, collided with her, and twisted in the narrow aisle, knocking her purse into the seat. His voice issued low, quiet, and oddly musical.

"*Pardonez-moi, Madame.*"

Just then, another traveler with dark beady eyes entered and surveyed the car. Kate's heart pulsed in her ears. The portly man who bumped her glanced ahead. His neck stiffened. He turned back and increased his volume.

"How rude of you!"

First he said he was sorry. Now he declared her rude to the whole world. What was going on here? A curt reply poised on her tongue, but Kate's sarcasm transformed to gratitude when he slipped an envelope into her left hand.

"Stop in the second *boulangerie*. *Bonne chance.*" His whisper barely met her ear.

Good Luck. Stunned, Kate covered the envelope with her coat.

He waddled ahead and plopped into a seat near the front. The newcomer stood aside to let her by, but her shoulder brushed his stiff coat sleeve. She controlled a shudder until she passed down the steps.

Away from the afternoon sun, she followed the main street past a bakery boasting long loaves in its window. She continued, pausing here and there to window shop. Finally certain no one trailed her, she slipped into the next *boulangerie* and purchased a quiche and tea.

Only one other customer—a solitary older woman. Kate took a table near the back and sipped her tea. If anyone did follow her, they would think she was in no hurry. Besides, she needed to know that envelope's contents. She might be headed in the wrong direction again.

She pretended to read a newspaper while opening the envelope to a handwritten letter addressed to Maurice. Another folded paper listed needed supplies, with a note at the top: *For Lysander pilot.* Kate memorized the list, just in case. Meanwhile, the other customer paid her bill and departed.

The tea had a calming effect, and the quiche satisfied her need for comfort like Aunt Alvina's homemade vanilla pudding. Now, for a way to raise her skirt and sew in Maurice's message. When the clerk, a middle-aged woman, went into the kitchen, Kate finished her food and approached the counter. She stretched her leg to reveal her raveled hemline.

"Do you have a—?"

The woman gestured her around the counter, and Kate perched on a chair in a small back room. She could have used her own needle, but gratefully accepted the woman's. When the clerk turned her back, Kate memorized the coordinates, tucked the letter underneath her dress lining, and stitched away.

But as she looked up, a man sauntered in. Not the Gestapo type, Kate thought. He spoke to the worker in a low voice and with such furtive glances, Kate knew she mustn't go out again. Instead, she slipped through the kitchen to a door on the far side and out into a courtyard. Which way to go?

Charming streets led out of town, but maybe she should disguise her path.

She walked three blocks north into a residential section and turned right. Six more blocks—this huge rectangle ought to get her near the village's east edge.

The whole time, she mulled over the train encounter.

That agent's quick thinking may have diverted a dangerous

situation. Her mentors back in Scotland often mentioned diversion, the first tactic of espionage, and that agent accomplished it with ease. But something else about him stayed with her.

With dark hair, a mustache, and thirty fewer pounds, he would resemble Monsieur le Blanc. But of course not—Monsieur acted as a recruiter, he was too old for this sort of work.

Twice she took a path off the road to be sure no one followed her. By the time the first haystack came into view, afternoon waned, and she hesitated at the edge of a thick wooded area opposite the meadow. With no sign of a contact, she feasted her eyes on small purple, white, and yellow flowers peppering the field. A few minutes later, a figure appeared from behind the second haystack.

The wiry man hurried behind the first stack, not far away. Kate waited a while longer before walking that direction, and a flurry of *What ifs* nearly paralyzed her. *What if that man in the boulangerie sniffed out her trail? What if—?*

Hurry only in imminent danger. She rounded the stack and forced herself to stay calm. Steel-colored eyes held hers. "Move quickly. We must climb that cliff." He gestured to a sharp rise.

"Give me a minute to change clothes." Kate switched into her trousers and flat shoes. This promised to be a long night, but the climb looked like a challenge she could enjoy.

Domingo and Philippe approached the landing field from the north, drank spring water from a bubbling oasis, and waited. Normal evening sounds broke the stillness until Philippe spoke.

"A perfect place for a landing, but climbing down in the dark with an agent might prove a challenge."

"Nothing could be harder than our last trek."

"My Aitaita often said things could always be worse."

Dusk faded into darkness. One by one, the welcoming committee arrived, a scrappy crew, old and young and in-between. The organizer counted only nine, but one man spoke up.

"Another man is guiding an agent from the train in Brens."

"All right. This shipment will take a bit longer to unload. Take extra care with these parcels—grenade canisters, ammunition, and explosives. Make piles and hurry back for more."

Philippe jabbed Domingo in the ribs. "Explosives—*quelle chance!*"

"You call that luck?"

The organizer stationed them while Domingo ruminated on his choice to accompany Philippe. If he had gone on, this committee would be short a person to hold the guiding lights for the plane to land, forcing the organizer to postpone the landing. Lysanders seemed so simple—they took off almost instantly, sometimes with only the dropped agent seeing them off. Domingo hardly knew they'd come, except for the remaining cargo.

Hudsons, much bigger than a Lysander, took longer, and required a clear space at least 600 yards long to land. For their own safety, onlookers received orders to leave, because the Hudson pilot and co-pilot followed orders to clear the strip of anyone standing between light A and light B. That could mean being shot, and a partisan once witnessed a bystander being run down by a Hudson.

Still, people sometimes appeared to satisfy their curiosity. Tonight, though, the plateau stood so high, Domingo doubted anyone extra made the climb.

Philippe voiced his thoughts. "Wonder how many other flights this Hudson has already undertaken tonight? I've heard some of them fly over the Channel and back all night long on missions."

Domingo wondered, too. And he often considered these pilots' loved ones. Did they know their son might crash on some isolated French plateau tonight, or that the Gestapo might bear down on his plane once it landed?

The sky's vast bowl rained stars, and images of Maman and Gabirel troubled him too. But at the same time, a sense of divine presence remained. Had Ander felt this way during the Revolution or even at the edge of death in that miserable camp at Gurs?

Down the field, a small glimmer revealed newcomers hurrying

to the landing site. Just in time, for Philippe and Domingo soon hunched down at an unmistakable drone from the heavens.

"A Hudson. And surely no Bosche climbed up here tonight."

Domingo agreed—he could not imagine a *Milicien* or Gestapo agent tackling the sharp ascent. And yet, the enemy often did the exact opposite from what he expected.

Lights blinked in the northern sky, and the command to shine their torches came down the line. When the Hudson landed and the door opened, the welcoming committee surrounded a voluminous metal belly. By the time Philippe and Domingo neared, workers had piled heavy boxes to one side and cylindrical containers end on end.

From the corner of his eye, Domingo observed the pilot reach back inside and hand a package to the thin latecomer—*Must've set up this meeting before he took off from England.* The agent gave him something and retreated into darkness. After the plane roared away, canisters lined the meadow like stanchions in a barn. The organizer lifted a bazooka and several carbines, nodding to an assistant to lead the way with a certain canister.

Peasants carted off the Hudson's contents, and within minutes, the field cleared. Philippe leaned close to a partisan for instructions and turned to Domingo.

"We have two tasks. Guide the agent east, with an urgent message for the Clermont-Ferrand circuit. The original plan was to take him to Albi, but the railroad bridge is scheduled for destruction later tonight. If that occurs, we must find the nearest train station beyond there for the agent. Second, deliver explosives, much needed, to a cell far north of Albi. Choose your task."

Domingo gulped as the agent fell in behind Philippe. Good— Domingo had had enough of fiery agents set on their willful ways. He would take a desperate downed pilot any day. What difference did it make whether he guided an agent or delivered enough explosives to destroy several small villages—villages like his own?

Charles said good-bye to Addie at the Westbourne Grove stop. "I'll pick you up at six-thirty. Can you keep a straight face with Mum?" Intrigue twinkled in his eyes.

When Addie opened the door, Mrs. Tenney was putting on her coat. "Hello, dear. I do hope you won't be terribly lonely tonight, but an emergency at the hospital fundraiser requires my presence. I'm afraid I won't be home until late. Do lock the door, won't you?"

Addie nodded. "I'll be fine. If somebody asks you to dance, say yes."

Mrs. Tenney gave her a raised eyebrow, but Addie noticed a lilt in her progress down the sidewalk. In her hurry, Mrs. Tenney hadn't even asked about her day. Charles' friend must have cooperated fully. Clearly, his mother only needed to be needed.

With the house all to herself, Addie did a pirouette in the kitchen and whirled through the parlor in her socks. "Just time enough for a bath and a hair wash."

Forty minutes later, she stood before the mirror in Kate's room. Although her own room had a similar long mirror, something drew her here. She toweled her hair dry and let it fall into natural curls.

"I would give a month's salary to talk with you right now, Kate Isaacs. What would you say to this? Mr. T has asked me out to dinner."

Arms akimbo, she angled her head as Kate would and imitated the rise and fall of her voice. "Bully for you! God gives us all good things to enjoy."

"We agreed it's only a friendly outing, but Kate—" Addie stepped forward and looked into her own eyes. Her voice trembled. "I wish you were here to talk this over, not because I feel guilty, but because I don't. I love being with Charles. I feel so free with him. You would understand, I'm sure. He's like a strong older brother."

She opened Kate's closet. "And just for fun, I'm wearing something of yours."

Fifteen minutes later, Addie slipped on her good shoes and surveyed her image. "Your best skirt—the red and brown tweed—and your red cardigan. If you were here, you'd offer me some jewelry, I imagine, but simple suits me just fine."

The doorbell rang, and she twisted to check her seams. "Please, please come back to us safe and sound, Kate, so I can tell you all about today, and about tonight."

She ran down the stairs. Charles stepped into the room and stared at her in silence. Finally, he found his voice.

"You—you did something different to your hair."

Addie turned a circle. "I didn't have time to put it into a roll."

"Your—those curls are delightful." He cleared his throat. "Let me get your coat."

Outside, he turned her way. "I'd say my old chap repaid me well, wouldn't you?" He promised to keep Mum busy until at least half past nine."

A cool evening breeze fluttered Addie's pleated skirt, and Charles offered her his arm as they neared the bus stop. "How about something homey tonight? A luscious beef pastry pie would suit me well."

The night air entered Addie's lungs like a blessing. "Homey sounds perfect."

At the bottom of the raised plateau where the Hudson landed, the agent went into the bushes, and Philippe turned to Domingo. "What have you decided?"

Domingo hesitated. Delivering the explosives offered fewer complications, but would lead Philippe farther from his home. Philippe was in no hurry for his reply.

"I learned something tonight. The local police and the Milice have spent countless hours traipsing over hills in search of young *refractoires*. Some went to work in Germany, but when they returned to visit their families, they joined the *Résistance* and became backsliders—*recalcitrants*.

"Recently, someone intercepted a letter from the *Intendant de Police* to a regional authority. Over six weeks, the Milice have interrogated families and scoured the countryside in vain—all for one *refractoire*." Philippe snorted. "So their frustration grows.

Parents who once obeyed Vichy's command and sent their sons to work in Germany now attack the government over its new policy."

One truth throbbed at the base of Domingo's neck. Soon the Milice would be seeking Gabirel.

"They offer amnesty to those who refused to join the work force and promise them jobs here in France rather than in Germany. I can see how angry this would make parents who complied with their demands from the beginning."

Domingo had been completing his teacher instruction when the first call came, so Vichy left him alone. Then he taught for a year, but with so many students leaving since '41, the school closed.

This new information meant that furious Milice would be tougher than normal. This reality took him back to his decision—which would be worse, being caught with explosives or with an agent? And which of the two meant more to the organizers north of here?

Domingo thought perhaps the explosives. With his ability to slip through enemy hands, Philippe should deliver them. Besides, if the bridge blew before they made it to Albi, taking this agent to the next city could take days.

"I will guide the agent."

Philippe's arched eyebrow showed in the moonlight.

"You're certain?"

"This way, I can circle back home. I've had enough of mountain passes for one winter."

"All right. No doubt we will see each other again." Philippe cuffed Domingo's shoulder and chuckled. "Unless the war ends in a week or so, we may never meet again, except in the afterlife. I'm afraid you chose the worst of the load, my friend." He gave Domingo a sly smile.

"Who knows? Loads can change during transport."

The agent approached, and Domingo detected only the outline of a straight nose, high forehead, and straggles of light hair. Then a longer strand escaped, and the agent removed a hat. More flaxen hair fell out, catching the moon.

Philippe exchanged a glance with Domingo. Did he still stand by his decision?

Domingo shrugged. Luckily, she was slim. *Chicken bones*, Aitaita would say. That meant she could travel faster, and she'd already made it down that steep descent in the darkness. Besides, she had the sense to wear pants.

"Millau is about eighty kilometres, through the Cevennes foothills. If the Albi station blows tonight, perhaps you can pick up the train there."

Domingo's throat tightened. He hated to see Philippe leave. Always before, the instructions accompanying packages had been simple to follow. *Memorize this code name. Take this parcel so many kilometers in a given direction. Look for a certain landmark. Wait and watch for someone.*

But this time, he and the agent would have to find their way like ants in a garbage heap. If partisans succeeded in destroying the Albi bridge, by morning the border between Tarn and Aveyron would swarm with gendarmes, Milice, and Gestapo.

Philippe gave him a salute. "Like the tree at Guernica, conquer whatever comes."

East. That was all Domingo knew. He shouldered his pack and waved for the agent to follow. But his thoughts dwelt on the old tree at Guernica that survived all odds.

They'd replanted it through the centuries, of course, the last time in 1860, before Aitaita was born. So *survive* actually meant to endure for an extended duration. Until the Allies invaded—until they freed France from the Nazi stranglehold.

Domingo found a trail and after half an hour, squatted beside a gurgling stream to fill his water bottle. He addressed the agent, whose face was shaded. "*Vous êtes fatigue?*"

The words roamed his mouth before coming forth, for he surmised they would sound odd to her, since she most likely learned precise, proper intonation. She had arrived on the train—perhaps she hailed from Paris or some other large city.

The agent pulled her scarf closer around her forehead. "*Non*. I am not tired, but the air is cold." Flawless French, but the frankness in her tone marked her as Amerikan. She filled her canteen, and Domingo struggled to translate the exchange into English.

Translating had become a habit from his contact with Britons and Americans, and his language training weaseled into his consciousness. If necessary, he could bring his English out, but even if not, the practice encouraged him—he had not forgotten everything, at least.

The agent adjusted her pack, and something niggled at Domingo. Had he seen her before? He brushed the possibility aside and set off, thankful for moonlight almost as bright as day. If he had his way, they would range into the Cevennes hills before the explosion, beyond the reach of the disturbing Milice.

Chapter Twenty-one

"Not too exciting an evening for you, eh?"

"I like this restaurant, and the food tastes wonderful. I'm surprised so many eating places and theatres flourish."

"People have lived under the bomb threat for more than four years. This latest Mini-blitz has almost done some of them in, but in spite of it all, businesses rebuild and adjust." Charles' left eyebrow danced. "What do you think of this restaurant?"

"Quiet, just my style. I've not gone out for dinner since—why, since I met the ship in New York."

"What did you think of New York?"

"Have you ever been there?"

"Never."

"I wouldn't want to spoil it for you, and you have to remember, I'd never even left the Midwest before that trip." Addie gathered the last flaky crumbs of her piecrust with her fork.

"I'd still like to hear how you perceived that great city."

"The vastness didn't thrill me, although it's always exciting to meet strangers. A Jewish woman showed me some of the city, but what I remember is her sorrow."

"Ah. Somehow that doesn't surprise me."

"No?"

"You've a tender heart, that's clear enough." Charles motioned for the waiter to refill their teacups and bring the bill.

Addie glanced around the corner restaurant and thought a family resemblance ran through several of the staff's faces.

"Thank you for bringing me here tonight. You have a tender heart, too."

"I suppose so, if you count shedding tears during war." Charles blinked as though he'd suffered a sudden shock. "I can't believe I said that. You make me feel quite at home, Addie, an effect you also have on Mum."

"But I'm the one who moved in on her."

"Ah, yet your arrival has rendered her more—shall we say, approachable? Kathryn started that off, but Mum didn't soften much until Alexandre died. And then Kate's other loss—I don't pretend to understand Mum's reaction, but something about that brought out the best in her. A side appeared that I'd either never known or wholly forgotten—gentler. Perhaps Father motivated Mum to buck up and hide her emotions, as he did me. But thanks to you Americans, I do believe she's begun to thaw."

"So you think Kate and I have been good for her?"

Charles emptied his teacup and settled it in its saucer. "Very good. And good for me, as well." Addie's neck heated under his amiable scrutiny.

"I don't know what Kate would have done without her job, and then you led her to your mother. She wrote me right away about your kindness."

Charles played with his knife. "We all step up and do what we can during this horrendous time when people are cast about like ships in a storm. Still, I am more than pleased to know we could make a difference." He pulled some bills from his money clip and set them on the table, then helped Addie with her coat and hurried her to a bus across the street.

When he unlocked the back door, he took off his hat and turned it in his fingers. "Would you mind if I stayed a while? For ages, I have neglected to check on something in Father's study."

"Of course I don't mind. I don't want this evening to end. You've shown me a wonderful time."

"We got frightfully dirty at the gardens, and it was only a simple wayside restaurant."

"But this day has been perfect." Addie avoided the dark creases forming in his eyes. He helped her off with her coat and hung it in the closet.

"I won't be long. Just some papers I've been thinking about. I keep forgetting to ask Mother—or perhaps I rarely find myself here without her present. I presume she's got the blackout curtains closed in the library?"

"She never forgets—does it right after dinner every night."

"Well then—"

"Will you mind if I switch on some music?"

"Not at all." He walked into the library.

Addie climbed the stairs to put on her slippers and bring some paper down to the parlor. It was high time she answered Jane and Berthea's letters. She hadn't yet thanked Berthea for the package that arrived last week. It would be quite the challenge to properly describe the light in Mrs. T's eyes when she tasted Berthea's rhubarb-cherry jam.

Soon the scratching of her pen engrossed her, and she didn't hear Charles slip into the room. "Addie?"

"Oh, sorry. Did you call before?"

"Yes, twice. You must be writing a manuscript."

"Only letters to friends back home—first, to my mother-in-law, who sent the homemade jam."

"Tell them a true blue Englishman appreciated its taste. Would you please come in here when you've a moment?"

Addie joined him and looked closely at the library furnishings for the first time. The room had always seemed a private place where Mrs. T retreated.

"Have you spent any time in this room?"

"None at all."

"I'm sure Mum does. That's one reason I decided to look for these papers tonight—information about Father's military connections. I don't want to cause her any disturbance."

"You've found them?"

"I have. So much of his life remains a mystery to me, but every time I learn one more iota, it does my constitution good."

"I understand that. Last year, some things about my father came into focus. Knowing facts, even difficult ones, is so much better than imagining them."

Charles patted the arm of a chair near his father's desk. "Sit, won't you? Can you share any of what you learned?"

"You won't think the worse of me?"

"Where we come from is not our doing, Addie. Truths about your father have no reflection on you." Charles leaned toward her. "I doubt I have the capacity to think badly of you, actually." His voice thickened.

Addie lowered her gaze and began. "Jane, my neighbor down the road has the most beautiful flower garden—that's how I got to know her. I was bicycling one evening and stopped in. We became friends, and she helped me see that my father probably gambled. Strangely, though, the knowledge didn't weigh me down, but freed me to be a little more patient with some of my reactions."

"Not to intrude on private matters, but did your father ever—hurt you?" Charles's angled head invited her to admit the truth.

"He hurt all of us. My older brother Reuben ran away in the middle of the night after a beating. I've never seen him since."

"I cannot imagine." Charles cleared his throat. "I wouldn't wonder, you might be afraid of men?"

Addie shrugged. "Always. And living with Harold did nothing to improve that tendency. Or maybe it did. I've seen plenty of men's bad sides, so I appreciate someone of integrity."

"Hmm." Charles tapped his forefinger on the desk. The radio played a tune Addie recognized from somewhere. A sonata, she thought, something she'd practiced in her piano lessons, slow, methodical, and quieting.

"I found some notes from a lecture Father once attended at the Royal Institute. Would you like to hear what he wrote?"

Addie smiled. He was going to read to her, like Kate.

"'It is possible to believe that all that is past is but the beginning of a beginning, and that all that is and has been is but the twilight of the dawn. It is possible to believe that all the human mind has ever accomplished is but the dream before the awakening.' January 24, H.G. Wells, The Royal Institute, London."

The clock ticked in comfortable silence. Finally, Charles spoke. "Is it possible, do you think, to see the past—yours and mine—in this way?"

A delectable sweetness stole over Addie. An austere upbringing, Charles's lonely childhood, and even the misery she'd known with her dad and Harold, could be viewed as dreams before an awakening. The gentle light in Charles's eyes relaxed her completely.

Once again, she thought how different things were when she was with him. An explosion could occur any moment with Harold. All she had to do was say the wrong thing, and her honest opinion always qualified. Sometimes, conflict ensued if she only *thought* the wrong thing, since Harold constantly sought to read her mind.

But tonight she felt no need to produce an answer. Charles accepted her as she was, with no preconceived expectations. She could be herself without wondering what he thought of her, or comparing her thinking with his.

When she didn't answer, Charles busied himself at the desk. Harold would have demanded a response. Words from somewhere in the past ran through Addie's consciousness—*for in Him we live and move and have our being*—The way God made her was all right. It was fine to be exactly who she was.

The next thing she knew, a key turned in the kitchen door lock. She must have fallen asleep, and Charles—he'd turned out the light and let her rest.

"Addie, are you awake? How was your evening?"

Addie started up and ran into the kitchen. "Good. I fell asleep writing a letter to Berthea."

"I am absolutely famished. The fundraiser took every ounce of my energy, with not a stitch of food left for the workers. You

do look weary, better go up to bed while I prepare myself a little snack."

Addie said good night and stopped by the library for her things. How could she have dropped off, with Charles right here in the room? But it was true—she pictured him stealing out while she slept. His scent—leather, wool, and ink, still hovered near the desk, and he left a note on the stationery that slipped from her lap to the floor.

Dear Addie,

Thank you for a splendid day and a lovely evening.

Charles

With a sense of wonder, she folded the note into her pocket and climbed the stairs.

"We can rest only a few hours. We still have far to go."

The agent lifted her chin in agreement. Domingo wondered at her quietness—she spoke only when he initiated conversation. He pulled a bread loaf from his pack—and some cheese.

"You are hungry?"

With a nod, she sank onto a rock and untied her pack. Traveling with her might not be so bad, after all.

She accepted the food and drank from her canteen. Behind her, the area around Albi reflected pink in sunset's afterglow, and the agent turned to survey the odd light.

"What a spectacle."

Domingo ripped some bread off and drank a draft of water. Though he averted his eyes, he felt the agent's on him. Several minutes passed before she spoke.

"I believe I know you. I think you rescued me."

Rescued her?

"Code Name Merce." The three syllables floated between them like dry leaves on an autumn wind. As soon as she said the code, her recalled her.

Lights speckled her dark eyes, her smooth skin radiant against the sky's rosy hues. "You wrapped my ankle after my drop and carried me to a haystack. I remember your eyes, *Monsieur*, and your kindness."

Domingo felt like a youth found out in some plot. But he recalled the night of her drop. She'd made a light load, and hadn't complained.

"Your ankle?" He bumbled like a shy adolescent.

"The sprain healed quickly, because you knew just what to do. *Merci beaucoup*."

Hot squiggles attacked Domingo's neck. "Good—it was the sheep."

He hadn't spoken with a woman since then, except Maman. "I mean, working with our sheep has given me practice with injuries."

The agent gave a slight nod and turned quiet, but sleeping arrangements weighed on Domingo. She would expect him to initiate their camp.

He pulled out his wool poncho and knelt to gather pine needles. "You have a blanket?"

"*Oui.*"

Philippe always slept close on cool nights, for body warmth. But with this agent's graceful facial bones already etched into Domingo's consciousness, he gave thanks that the worst of winter had passed. Night slanted down, so he must allow no distractions. He alone must gage this mission's danger and make appropriate decisions.

"Let me help." She scrabbled for needles like a cat until they amassed a pile a foot deep.

"I'll be right back." Domingo found a private spot not far away, but far enough. He dared not leave the agent alone, yet now that she'd communicated their shared history, this new responsibility lacked the feel of a burden. He breathed a prayer into the night. "Help me with this woman, Almighty One."

When he returned, she left for a time, so he leaned her pack against his. He ought to speak to her about their circumstances, but how to start? After she took her place, he was about to explain his precautionary decision not to make a fire when great rockets blasted the southern sky.

Next, flames embraced the heavens in a vast inferno. He turned toward the agent as another mighty blast filled the horizon.

"They did it."

Her breath grazed his cheek as she peered past him, taut and ready to flee. "Will we stay here?"

Domingo stared dumbly at the firestorm. He attempted to judge its distance by how far they had already travelled, but the figures jumbled in his head.

"They must have blown more than a railroad. It's a factory or something with gasoline reserves. See—Albi's great brick cathedral reflects the glow." Then he remembered the agent's question. "For now, we rest here."

"Um—" She leaned back against her pack. A few minutes passed, and in the interval, Domingo marveled that she knew how to keep quiet. Anders always complained about females being so talkative, but like Sancha, this agent must be an exception.

The hefty breeze sent a chill up Domingo's legs. Surely, she must be cold, too.

As if to answer his unspoken question, the agent nudged her pack closer and arranged her blanket over her legs. Domingo did the same with his poncho, and they watched the fire for long minutes. When she spoke, it was only a brief comment.

"Now I remember—they built Albi entirely with orange-red bricks." Her observation brought to mind a vague recollection of Aitaita describing this city on his return from a southern pilgrimage.

For the next hour, tired as they were, Domingo and the agent stared in awe. She shifted her shoulders once or twice, but made no other movement or sound, and her composure took Domingo back to that night last winter when he had met her drop.

Her heavy radio had forced him to carry her in a crude way.

Still, she hadn't whimpered. Even with her pain and her harsh introduction to the haystack, she had uttered only *Merci.*

He relaxed into his pack. She held her silence, and after some time, her altered breathing told him she slept. Questions flooded Domingo. How far had she traveled before the long climb to the landing field? And before that, what dangers had she faced? After the haystack, where had she gone? She came to Bren by train, but from where?

The red sky highlighted her profile, firm but soft. Probably she had her life after the war all planned. But he couldn't help but wonder if she were promised to someone. If so, what would cause her to risk her life in this faraway place?

He reached for the blanket slipped from the agent's shoulder. Back home, Gabirel would be making one last check on the sheep, and Domingo felt that same concern as he tucked the wool around the agent's neck, careful not to touch her face.

Every draft of night wind fluffed the distant flames. He breathed deep and considered how long the blaze might last. For their purposes, the longer the conflagration busied the Milice, the better.

Philippe shared another bit of intelligence during their wait on the plateau. An Allied general named Patton had earned fame during the battle for Sicily and now waited with his forces in the Greek islands. With them so close, most locals believed the invasion would come on the Mediterranean coast.

And if that were true, Domingo and Philippe's worst fears might become reality. With the Nazis dug in far to the north, fighting might occur on their ancestral lands.

To have armies on their own humble soil, heavy tanks rumbling through their streets—the fearsome vision made Domingo shudder. Philippe felt the same consternation.

"We must take note of these things and protect our families, our homes. The Germans make regular raids on farmers when they cross an area. We cannot imagine our valleys will be exempt."

Like an omen, the orange and black sky above an inferno

completely out of control signified other far-reaching disasters. Fires in the sky, traipsing like wild men across unknown lands, enemies around every corner—what would happen next? And Domingo sat on a windswept hillside beside a secret agent who had dropped in from the sky last December and re-entered his life tonight.

Struck by his lack of power over anyone or anything, he might have been one spark in those Albi flames. This sense of smallness reminded him of those would-be fighters from Paris. Had they found a *Résistance* cell to join?

One thing he knew, if waves of Allies stormed this countryside, he would aid them however he could. The flames rose and sank until his eyes drooped. Tomorrow, the Milice would be even more than vicious with stragglers. What if they widened their search to Millau? Finally, he drifted off, aware of the agent's warmth against his back.

Some time later, something startled him from sleep. He half-turned, but only a swatch of the agent's head peeked from under her blanket. The moon had started its descent, yet still highlighted pale streaks in her hair.

Starlight strained through still-rising smoke, but an acrid breeze permeated even this far afield. Domingo rubbed his eyes as the agent poked an arm from her burrow and blinked up at him, but said nothing.

She rolled her blanket and prepared to leave, so he split the last of his bread with her. From now on, they would resort to strangers' kindness. He hoped to come upon a Basque settlement at daybreak, when farmers tended their animals.

Within minutes, the agent shouldered her pack and thanked him for the bread. Under the circumstances, hot chicory was out of the question, but she drank from her canteen without complaint in the crisp early morning.

Domingo struck out as though the night's excitement had not stirred his fears, but at the slightest sound from the brush, he stiffened. Surely the Milice remained engaged nearer to Albi, and yet— He wished Philippe were here, with his innate wisdom. If they suddenly encountered Nazi collaborators, what would he do?

Conquer whatever comes. Philippe's parting words made Domingo grin, but then he remembered something he'd said earlier.

If we get separated, remember la Corneille is still about. He is spotted here, then there, and his reputation—or hers—has grown. The crow for which he is named is known for encroaching on other birds' nests. Just so, la Corneille has a knack for claiming territory for La Résistance française, *but channeling it to the Nazis.*

Just beyond the six-kilometer signpost for Millau, the thick of night gave way to a gray compromise. A little farther, Domingo nearly stumbled on something heavy and soft blocking the path. He flailed for a branch to avoid falling headlong.

The agent ran into his pack full speed and bounced back, but kept her balance. At first he hoped an injured deer slumped here, but an arm, an elbow, and fingers met his touch. His breath caught in his throat.

Kneeling beside him now, the agent touched his elbow to steady herself. Domingo fished for his torch in his coat pocket and felt the man's fleshy neck for a pulse. Faint, like a placid clock.

"He is alive."

He focused the light at the victim's pupils. "So much blood—"

The agent stifled a gasp. "Monsieur Le Blanc."

"You know him?"

"A little. *La Résistance française.*"

A copper tinge in the air took Domingo back to the Gestapo campfire where he and Philippe pillaged Sancha's murderers. No— not death again.

Kate unbuttoned Monsieur's coat to find a thick blanket wrapped around his middle, making him appear heavier and older. A sudden realization took her breath away. He had been the man in the train, whose expertise she admired. She should have realized when his voice sounded familiar.

Domingo grasped under his arms, and she gained a hold on his legs, dragging his middle as they carried him to a poncho. Kate sat back on her heels in the protection of a tangle of brambles so thick they hid the trail.

Checking around Monsieur's head increased the concern in Domingo's eyes. "He has lost too much blood—I must find help." He guided her hand. "Press here to stop the bleeding while I—"

A gash traced from Monsieur's temple to behind his ear, warm rivulets still flowing. Domingo bound a kerchief around the wound, handed Kate his canteen and groaned.

"Not much water left—give him a little at a time."

"*Oui.*"

"Do not leave this place. Promise me."

The mix of care and authority in his voice tightened her grip on their patient. "I promise."

Domingo lowered his shoulders and raced off. The sticky wetness of blood clung to Kate's fingers, and in growing daylight, Monsieur's face appeared pasty from shock. She palpated part way down his back, but found no more gashes.

The final shift between dawn and daylight rolled in heavy fog as Kate hurried for her bag and pulled out her blanket. Fiery determination raged in her.

"Monsieur Le Blanc, you cannot die. Do you hear? I have far too many questions for you."

She covered him chin to toe and held her canteen to his lips. No response. She tore a strip from her shirttail to wash his face and neck. His cheek felt cool—no, cold. There was only one thing to do. She squirmed onto the poncho, opened her coat over his arms, and laid her face against his chest.

Without him, she would not be here on this trail, or even in France. She would know far less about her mother and nothing about her father. Her throat constricted with the weight of her request.

"Please, dear God, keep him alive." She focused on Monsieur's heartbeat, faint but steady, as sunshine made pathetic attempts to conquer the haze.

Fine mist hung like lace over the rocky descent, and Kate realized her guide had found the one flat place visible from here. Monsieur's skin appeared like small raised rocks scattered over a patch of earth. Pebbles embedded his forehead where he must have slid headlong.

Did someone attack him, or had he suffered a bad fall? Was he traveling a higher route and rolled onto this path? Brush and rocks were everywhere, and through the mist, dark smoke still curled from the southwest.

Monsieur lay much too still, his breath almost imperceptible. Dry blood matted his hair, shirt, and coat. His pockets revealed nothing, not even identification.

His helplessness melded with hers. Kate got to her feet as a single ray of sunshine won its battle with the haze.

Back toward the trail, only her own footprints showed, and then she spied larger ones that matched Monsieur's boots. Her guide wore espadrilles, leaving no trace. Dense underbrush packed the path's other side. She took time to study every inch of terrain, for Monsieur must have carried papers.

Another few feet up the path, a denser patch showed in the brush, black and unnaturally solid. Spines and nettles fought her, but she strained and eventually touched leather—a case. With one last arm thrust, the bunglesome object came loose. She held on and pulled, though thorns poked through her shirt and trousers.

Bloodied but victorious, she raced back to her patient, whose one hand unfolded to the sun like a fleshy blossom. When she removed his second boot, a small gold key fell out and the latches gave way easily. Inside she found an identification card.

Charles Garonne, lately of Nîmes. Fifty-three years old, from Toulouse, a teacher by trade. Everything else was marked "*Moyen*"—unremarkable.

But her heart told her there was nothing average about this

man. His papers, envelopes, sealed and unsealed, maps and charts, some bearing names of Vichy officials, produced one name she recognized—Doriot. Another letter mentioned Pétain himself. Scrawled logistical notes covered scattered papers—*railroad south of Clermont-Ferrand, insane asylum in Milleu, rendezvous the twenty-seventh near Decazeville collerie.*

Numerical columns indicated amounts of supplies, a file of railroad routes, name lists—*Résistance* workers or collaborators?

Kate's speculations bounced in circles. What if he collaborated with Vichy, carried these names for surveillance and reported partisans to the authorities? Yet why did he deliver that message to her on the train? An icy thought stymied her for a few seconds: perhaps he was that double agent the vicar mentioned.

She traced her way back to where she found the case. If someone attacked him, why had it flown so far? There ought to be signs of a scuffle, but moving him erased all evidence. If someone tackled him from the left, he might have had time to throw the case as far as he could. She finally found a boot mark, wider and longer than her own prints by far, and to the south, where an assailant might have climbed, two more prints.

Those sharp points belonged to no peasant, nor to a German soldier—no round-toed Fallshirmjagers, these. Her training had familiarized her with various Nazi uniforms, including boots, and she had even tried some on. Made for show, these boots belonged to someone very rank-conscious.

Back beside Monsieur Le Blanc, she sank to the earth. Milice, always conscious of rank and out to impress the Gestapo, had an eye for the flashy. A *Milicien had* followed Monsieur, no doubt, with no time to change into climbing boots. Perhaps the blast took him off-guard. She searched again and found more boot prints up the slope.

If her guide sought assistance transporting Monsieur, he should be back soon. Her blood ran cold at another possibility—that whoever attacked Monsieur would attack him, too. A rabbit or fox scrabbled on the path, and the wind changed direction. Saplings shook their new leaves. An involuntary tremor passed over Monsieur Le Blanc as Kate checked his pulse.

"Please, don't let him run straight into them." There was nothing to do but nurse Monsieur the best she could, but she resolved to find out her guide's name when he returned.

Chapter Twenty-two

One Monday morning in mid-March, Addie woke at dawn to prune and transplant in the courtyard before going to work. She stood hands on hips when Mrs. Tenney emerged with her hair rolled to perfection, ready for a morning with her lady friends.

"This courtyard looks better every day, Addie. By summer, we'll have flowers everywhere."

"I hope so, but there's no guarantee, of course."

"The guarantee shines in your eyes. I've never known such an energetic young woman. But you don't want to be late for work. I've packed you a lunch—"

"Oh, thank you. I do get carried away out here." Addie brushed her dirty hands on her pants and hurried toward the gate. "One more bush that grows, say, six feet tall, would make all the difference. I'd plant it over in the far corner to cover that old pipe."

"I'll mention that to my bandage ladies today. One never knows." Mrs. Tenney stepped back inside. "The other day someone needed a new hose for their fire pump, and Mrs. Wright found exactly the one."

"Your contacts seem able to come up with anything."

"Oh, I don't know about that, dear. I've a run in my stockings, my very last pair, but I doubt they could supply a new one." She waved and stepped over the threshold.

"You will lock the door—? Oh, I know you will. What comes over me at times like this?" She grimaced and flushed, but returned Addie's smile.

"It's all right, we all get into habits. Have a good time with your friends."

Half an hour later, Addie hurried out again. She felt so much better when she got her hands in the soil before going downtown. She could work in the courtyard all day, but one good thing about the office—Charles would be there.

With especially heavy foot traffic this morning, she took a couple of shortcuts on the bus route, loped up the back stairway, slipped into her desk before eight-thirty, and set to work on a stack of files. An hour later, Mrs. Culver called her over to the copy machine and flicked the ON button. The machine belched its usual clatter, but Mrs. Culver insisted on whispering.

"Mr. Tenney sent a message that he will be gone today and tomorrow, so we shall catch up on our backlog."

Her tight-rolled hair stretched her wide cheeks into a severe look, but Addie had grown to respect Mrs. Culver's administrative ability.

She gestured for Addie to bend with her when she reached under the machine for more paper. Now, her forehead resembled a street map of London.

"I wouldn't be surprised if the Army called Mr. T for special service."

"Special service?"

"With all the secret operations going on before—" Mrs. Culver gave a furtive glance to each side. "Before the invasion, and with his war experience, I put two and two together. I thought perhaps you might know—"

"Not about that sort of thing—remember, I'm an American."

Addie rose with Mrs. Culver, who locked a sheaf of paper into the feeder control. A rosy hue suffused her face. "I thought, since you live with his mum, you might have heard something."

Addie chuckled. "She's the last person he would tell about a secret mission."

But all day and the next, she wondered. Charles owed her no explanations, yet it seemed strange he'd said nothing on Saturday in the gardens.

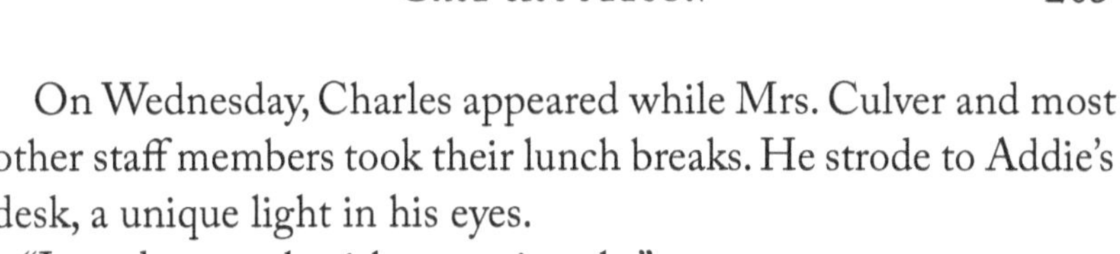

On Wednesday, Charles appeared while Mrs. Culver and most other staff members took their lunch breaks. He strode to Addie's desk, a unique light in his eyes.

"I need to speak with you privately."

"Why, of course."

"What say I walk you part way home tonight?"

"All right. Shall I stay late?"

"Yes, I shall—er—arrange to occupy Mrs. Culver toward the end of the day."

Addie gave him her brightest smile. "It's good to see you." She held back what she wanted to say—*I missed you.*

But Charles said it for her, after scanning the nearby empty desks. "I must say it has been highly irregular not seeing you these past few days."

Before she could reply, the main office door swung open. "Oh, Mr. T—welcome back." Charles swung around and met Mrs. Culver.

"It looks as though you've held things together, as usual. Something came up on Sunday with little warning, but we shall make up for lost time this afternoon."

Mrs. Culver flew into an organizational frenzy, and by afternoon posting time, she handed Addie an enormous packet. Her eyes blazed with purpose.

"We've jolly well got to keep the postal service running, dear. Please stamp these and get them out before the collector comes by."

Then she added to Addie's prospects for time outdoors. "I would like you to stop at the bookseller's, too. Mr. Firth, you know?"

Addie nodded. Kate would be jealous if she knew.

"Here is a list. Mr. T keeps a running tab there, so don't trouble yourself concerning payment."

Addie left her light coat behind. Blatant blue skies promised a lovely outing, and she wondered again at how many birds made dingy London their home. Their darts from windowsills, hops through potholed streets, and cheerful songs took her back to Iowa.

Yesterday, Berthea's latest letter had arrived, three hand-written pages. Jane fared well, and her husband Simon kept at his games between his cabin and the house. Berthea and George took to inviting them over to play five hundred in the evenings.

"For so long, people have called Simon weak-headed, but he plays cards like a whiz. He remembers the trump for each round, which took me ages to learn. George has become his special friend, and I see the relief in Jane's eyes.

As for Harold, the Army Air Force has discovered his managerial talents and attention to details, so they've turned him him into a spotter. He studies photographs of the terrain before a mission, to devise precise bombing targets.

I shudder to think of those dangerous missions, but he sounds very proud. I imagine this would be easier, with his handicap, than the Infantry. Lately, though, I keep remembering that day he leaped to my rescue during haying season ... do you recall?

A bale fell wrong in the new elevator, and hurtled my way. I've asked myself time and time again how Harold could have moved so fast to grab that bale. It's a mystery.

He did mention you: "I see little hope where Addie is concerned. Though our Methodist roots frown on divorce, we cannot live together if she refuses to submit to me. She won't even accept what I know to be the will of God."

Harold won't like my reaction, but I was honest with him. Now, I see how I contributed to his rigidness. I always let his father rule the roost.

Maybe you never witnessed Orville in one of his religious rants. But through my silence, Harold picked up on his prejudices. The past is past—no use trying to change it, George says, and he's right. I can only try to persuade Harold now.

Please promise me you'll stay in my life, even if you and Harold part. You've become a friend I cherish, and we share similar growth experiences, although it took me much longer to learn to listen to my own heart.

Berthea's reference to Harold clouded the fine afternoon, but Addie gave herself from the office to the post box to ruminate, and no longer. If only she could discuss all this with Kate, who would spout her opinion with style.

"Of course, Harold has a higher, holier stance than us normal peons. If he didn't hate Catholics so much, he might claim to be next in line for Pope.

"As for his handicap, the Army physical proved it existed mostly in his mind. How could the Air Force accept him if he couldn't bail out of a bomber? As for his attention to details, oh my, don't get me started …"

Kate's animated narration punctuated by air punches and severe voice inflections produced a giggle, causing a passerby to flash Addie a curious look as she slipped the letters into the post box. She whispered her response to her best friend, as real to her as that London citizen.

"Even in your absence, you keep me out of the wallows, Kate. I do pray this afternoon finds you safe and fulfilled."

Mr. Firth ushered her into the bookstore like a long-lost friend. "You're that chum of Kathryn's aren't you, working for Mr. Tenney? Addie, isn't it?"

"Yes sir. Here is his list."

"Delightful. Do have a seat. I shall pass this to my assistant and join you for some tea. Do pour for us both, won't you?"

A worn leather chair invited Addie to make herself at home, and fragrant steam soon rose from delicate china teacups. The ceiling-to-floor leather-bound volumes reminded her of Aunt Alvina's library. As Mr. Firth took his seat and his cup, she savored the fine, mellow flavor.

"Tell me of Kathryn. I've not seen her for ages."

"She—she was called away—an urgent matter."

The shopkeeper swished a finger over his temple. His inquiry came slow and quiet. "To do with the war?"

Addie let silence answer for her.

"A dangerous mission?"

She offered only raised eyebrows.

Mr. Firth hung his head for a moment. "Quite. Whatever that girl takes on, she will do well, I daresay. With thousands of secret undertakings being carried out, we are bound to win, as our prime minister often reminds us."

"I surely hope so. I cannot imagine the opposite—what would become of us?"

"Precisely, not to mention the rest of the known world. If the Luftwaffe's all-out attack in '40 and '41 didn't deter us, nothing will. You should have seen the thousands of fires they started down at the wharves, but just as many firefighters won the day."

"Kate wrote me a little about how many died in the effort. It must have been so frightening."

"Indeed, it was. And Mr. Tenney? How does he get along these days?"

"He whisks in and out like a bee in springtime blossoms."

"Ah, you Americans do create the metaphors."

The assistant set some books on the counter then dove back into the stacks, and Mr. Firth finished his tea. "And his mother? Am I correct in recalling you and Kathryn board with her?"

"Yes, sir. She has been more than gracious to two vagabonds from across the ocean."

"I daresay she enjoys your company. With the colonel gone and Charles so occupied—" A distant look entered his eyes, but his assistant waved him over, so he stood up. "I think your order is ready, but take your time."

For another few minutes of luxury, Addie curled into the genteel chair and closed her eyes. When she collected the package, Mr. Firth sent his assistant on another task, beckoned her close with his finger, and handed her a folded note.

"See that Mr. Tenney gets this directly, will you? Do come again soon, and please greet him for me?" He handed her a note addressed to Lieutenant Colonel Charles Tenney—maybe they were old war buddies.

The bustle of late-afternoon London, full of hurrying strangers, swept Addie back to the office. Mrs. Culver met her on the stairs, umbrella in hand. Such a proper English lady.

"Oh, Mrs. Culver—you're going home? It must be later than I thought."

"No, I've an errand across town, near where I live. Mr. Tenney is still in-house so you can deliver his books—his office door is ajar. I'll see you in the morning."

Charles looked up when Addie handed him the note. "From Mr. Firth."

"Thank you. I shall be ready soon."

She finished some filing and tidied her workspace when the rest of the office workers cleared. Within a few minutes, Charles settled her jacket over her shoulders, and they walked for a while in silence. Past the bus stop, pedestrians scattered, so he motioned her toward a bench in a small, grassy wayside rest and folded his hands over his briefcase.

"I have some things to tell you, Addie." He took a deep breath. "I have never totally left off military involvement. Recently, they've required me for intelligence purposes."

"That's where you went?"

"Yes, on the southeast coast, across from the Channel's narrow point." He looked all around, revealing the puffiness around his eyes, and he turned a shade paler. "Directly opposite the Pas-de-Calais region. I trust you will not mention this to Mum, but I may be gone regularly until sometime in the summer.

"My transparency may surprise you, but life has become somewhat complicated, you see. I—we spoke before about war altering our loyalties—" He made another visual sweep of the area.

"I have become involved in another cause of dire necessity, but these new responsibilities with the forces hinder me from fulfilling some of my obligations."

Her mind swam with possibilities and questions.

"Mr. Firth's note could not have arrived at a more opportune time. Clearly, I must assign certain duties to someone I trust. That is, if you are willing—"

A wave of curious satisfaction enveloped Addie.

He pulled his hat brim lower. "I suffer some trepidation, since a degree of danger is inherent." His eyes creased with black.

"I trust your judgment."

"And I strive to be worthy. But not to warn you—I could never live with myself if anything—" He bit his upper lip.

"You realize that on Saturday at midnight, your Mum and I were out patrolling, and noticed some incendiaries just down the street. We tamped them all out in time. We watched our rocket guns fight back, and the sky lighted like daylight with flame showers. Then they made their big bang. In a yard down the way, someone spotted a time bomb, so your Mum called the authorities—"

"Stop—I forget you face danger here with every warning, and who knows when a bomb will land right on Mum's house? I wish she would go to the Tube station more faithfully, but she has a certain hunger for risk, it seems."

"She says this mini-blitz is the same old thing as back in '40 and '41, and she's worn out with running to the station. Some of our neighbors still hurry down there, and a couple of them sleep there as a matter of course. Another one installed an Anderson shelter right in her house, but—"

"Yes. Well, then. I shall try not to worry. I speak of a different sort of danger, though, since Mr. Firth and I join other Londoners in sending aid for displaced children. Word often passes by devious means, and spies traverse the city. Der Führer seems unsatisfied to leave any place on earth safe for innocent youth, and is willing to reach far and wide to punish those who offer aid."

A dark-haired woman wandered onto the grassy expanse, and Charles lifted his elbow from the back of the bench to shade their faces. "Would you be willing to deliver messages from time to time when I am away, most often between Mr. Firth and myself?"

"More than willing. Ever since I met Esther in New York, I've wanted to get involved somehow."

Charles nodded. "Your story set me to thinking, and when Bertie approached me, it seemed too coincidental not to have been part of some plan."

"That's how I felt when I met Esther. Do you believe God was in it?"

A deep blush rose under his tan. "Quite."

Addie took note—he kept his generosity close, and his beliefs, too. How like him to show his faith through risky action.

"Mr. Firth may ask you to contact Esther and others who might be of assistance. Although things have gotten so out of hand that—"

A handful of children skipped onto the green, and the woman casually took a seat a few yards away. *Out of hand—?* Addie's spine tingled at this inference. Maybe she could make a difference, on a much smaller scale than Kate, and in the safety of London.

"No use dwelling on the dreadful facts filtering in from Poland and parts of France, not to mention Germany. One can scarcely believe the dire situation. Still, we can have an impact."

Charles sought her eyes. "Unfortunately, we are limited to supplying finances and never have the satisfaction of knowing who is helped, but individual conscience can make a difference, even in the face of such advanced evil."

"Knowing there's actually something we can do gives me hope."

"Deliveries usually takes place on Sundays. Someone will bring you an envelope, and your drop-off point, unless you receive other directions, will be Mr. Firth's office. He waits there between twelve and one for our code, four knocks on the alley door."

The sun caught the blue of his eyes. "You understand, I would never involve you except for this other—"

"I feel privileged to have some small part."

His tone turned husky. "There's no one on earth I would trust more."

Emotion swarmed Addie, but she couldn't resist teasing Charles. "By the way, do you go to the Tube station every time an alarm sounds?"

Red overtook his face and he gave her a shamefaced grin. "Um—may I say that amounts to an unfair question, with my duties?" Then he chuckled. "Mum is right, as usual. You are a smart girl."

Chapter Twenty-three

Reciting Scripture passages and the catechism from her confirmation classes sustained Kate throughout the morning. Monsieur's condition seemed to stabilize—at least not to decline.

"I believe that I cannot by my own understanding or effort believe ... but the Holy Spirit has called me through the Gospel, enlightened me with his gifts—"

During their confirmation studies, she and Addie bounced that tenet back and forth a hundred times. Finally, Aunt Alvina clarified the concept of grace. "Every human being depends on the Creator for life, breath, and inner strength. If we accept the Almighty's omniscient wisdom and allow for His leading, a whole world of opportunities opens. Do you see?"

Later, in her room, Kate had contemplated, and now she revisited the explanation in light of watching over someone who might well be dying. As a young adult, she had felt full of her own inventive strength, but now she'd lost Alexandre and their baby. She could do nothing to prevent either death, and this situation underscored that grueling lesson.

Her stomach churned as she hoped for the faint shuffle of espadrilles on coarse stone, for even in this bramble patch, any passerby might spot them, and all would be lost. Her training had introduced her to the typical Basque shoe, but seeing Domingo in action gave her new appreciation for espadrilles. In contrast, the Milice sought the showiest uniform to flaunt their fake authority.

If one of them appeared, how could she veil her distaste? These former French army gendarmes enabled the Nazis to live off the hard work of French citizens. While French children went hungry, these collaborators made sure Nazi officers feasted on the best pork, Roquefort cheese aged in nearby caves, and fine wine. Of course, the gendarmes received their reward.

Just in case, Kate hid Monsieur's case behind a boulder. Burying it in this hardscrabble soil would provide a challenge to pass the time, but her guide should see it first.

Their patient's temperature rose with the sun, so Kate swabbed his forehead and neck with a wet scrap of fabric. He refused water, or more precisely, showed no reaction.

Midmorning, the scratchy sound of boots alerted her. Then, like Monsieur le Blanc's soothing heartbeat, came the shwoosh, shwoosh, shwoosh of espadrilles.

When her guide's dark beret topped the rise, rimmed by his black curly hair, Kate breathed again. Two men bearing a stretcher accompanied him.

His glance communicated confidence—he must have found a safe place for their patient. The men prepared Monsieur for travel and the guide turned to Kate for information.

"He has a fever and gives no response."

The men lifted Monsieur, whose skin shone rosy-blue in the morning sun, and Kate whispered in his ear. "I will be there soon." He gave no sign he heard, and a sense of helplessness invaded her as she turned to Domingo.

"I found tracks over there—a *Milicien's* boots."

"Show me."

She stumbled on a root, and Domingo stopped her fall. "Your hunger is great." He pulled some crusty bread from his pack and held out his canteen. "The men must move slowly with him. Take your time. Point me to the prints."

"That way, about twenty paces. And behind that rock, I hid his briefcase."

Domingo brought back the case and immersed himself in the

contents. He seemed not to notice Monsieur vanish, but Kate knew he held the keys to her past. She wanted to go with him and urge him to stay alive

Domingo caught her eye. "He will have no use for this, and it will only hinder us. Shall I bury it?"

That seemed the wisest choice. She nodded and prepared to set out.

Half a kilomètre down the trail, Domingo veered north. The taut place between Kate's shoulder blades loosened—he'd found a back way to their destination.

She stopped imagining a *Milicien* patrol demanding them to open their packs. Thankfully, the message and detonators she carried yesterday had reached *Résistance* hands, and she carried only the message for Maurice.

An hour passed before her guide dropped his pack to rest.

"How much farther?"

"A few more kilomètres, near a village. A man there said the Clermont-Ferrand organizer has gone into hiding."

"How did he know—?"

"When I said we needed a doctor, he asked if I saw a young woman on the trail from Bren. I told him nothing, but they must be looking for you."

"Did he mention the organizer's name?"

"Maurice. He said even if you travel to Clermont-Ferrand, finding him will be impossible." Domingo rubbed his temples. "I can take you to this man if you wish."

"But what about Monsieur?" Kate's throat filled at the thought of losing him.

"Don't worry, I'll take you there, but this other fellow—what do you want to do?"

Kate bit her lip. She should have known simplicity could not last forever.

Domingo angled down a steep ravine beside the River Tarn and

Kate caught her breath. Not a murmur from her, even though she sincerely cared for that wounded agent they discovered.

He made an alteration to Aitaita's warning about foreign women. "Take care, my son. Those women think differently than ours—they can be cold and cruel."

But this agent was no kin to cruelty. Her eyes met his when she looked up, and her smile warmed him. "You must be part mountain goat." She reached for her canteen. "Would you mind telling me your name and when you joined *La Résistance française*?"

Beginning with the Jewish child ravished by the Gestapo and culminating in Sancha's needless death, a panorama of events flooded Domingo. How could he say when?

"For someone born in this country, it is not so simple."

How could he explain the impossibility of knowing for sure who sided with whom? Some gendarmes provided partisans with foodstuffs, weapons, and information at the same time they carried out raids for the Milice. In an ever-increasing web of deceit, friend and foe inextricably mixed.

Weariness invaded Domingo like a sudden cyclone. He sank on a fallen log, and the agent joined him. Sunlight dappled her fair skin, and a slight breeze lessened the afternoon's heat. He longed to crawl into the brush and close his eyes.

She read his hesitation. "You don't have to answer my question."

"How was it for you? Did you join one day and never look back?"

Some small rodent fished its way through their camp. Domingo rubbed a bruise on his wrist. Perhaps his question sounded ignorant to her, so he tried again.

"You were brave to come here, so far from home."

Her voice softened. "Farther than you know." Her shoulders rounded, and she dropped her chin into one hand, pealing alarm through Domingo.

"My curiosity has troubled you. Accept my apology."

"Oh, no. It's just that—I joined in England, but I come from the United States."

As he had surmised from her bearing. Amerika, he knew better than England, since their Basque leader Aguila sent regular reports from there, and Domingo's distant cousin worked as a sheepherder in the land called Idaho. Before he could think of a reply, the agent went on.

"My parents met in the Great War and died when I was young. My father was French, but I have only faint memories of him."

Ah—to speak of this must bring her pain. Domingo latched onto the most comfortable part of her answer.

"Where was he born?"

She stared into the brush. "I don't know."

God's chosen, dispersed from their homes and hunted like vermin, at least knew their origins. Domingo wanted to ask how the agent's mother met her father, why she crossed the ocean, what she would do when—

Just then, she jumped at a raven's loud cry. *La corneille*—Domingo's chest hairs curled tighter. What if this Monsieur le Blanc was that despicable double agent?

Her next questions startled Domingo. "This man you met, the one who mentioned me, was he Basque? Do you think all Basque are trustworthy?"

"No, he wasn't. And mostly, I think so." A simple lie, for how could he be sure? Only one thing to do, keep moving. He shouldered his pack, and then remembered her first request.

"My name is Domingo."

Down to a break in the trail, over a meadow peppered with spring flowers, past a pond, and through a hedgerow of low pine saplings, he halted and pointed.

"See that church spire? The organizer lives there." She said nothing, so he moved on, but a sharp edge of worry badgered him. Something about this Frenchman provoked uneasiness he couldn't temper. What was his connection with the men who carried Monsieur's litter, and why had he been so eager to connect with this agent?

As the path turned to cobblestone, the agent jabbed Domingo's shoulder.

"I have a bad feeling. This man could have known Maurice's code name without being *Résistance*. He might be a collaborator."

Domingo pulled her off the trail into pungent pine shadows. "I have a bad feeling too, but the stretcher bearers recognized him."

Her forehead still bore worry lines. "That doesn't mean we can trust him. What if I send him a false message—tell him I took ill?"

She plopped on the forest floor and took pen and paper from her pack. "His reaction to this note will show us the truth."

Her pen moved easily against plain white paper. Domingo marveled that agents could trick one another with words at a moment's notice. It was one thing to run the heights like a chamois, but to deal in those secret codes, quite another.

She held out a folded paper. "One word in this message is wrong. If he doesn't recognize the error and asks you to bring me back, I'll know we must flee. Tell him I need an immediate answer."

Perspiration broke out on Domingo's head, but he took the note. The agent touched his sleeve. "Be careful—he'll have someone follow you."

"Maybe we should meet somewhere else." He glanced around. "Wait for me on the other side of town, beyond the spire. When you see the cross directly above you, hide in the trees."

For a brief moment, he hesitated. If someone arrested him, she would be left all alone out here. But he could think of no other plan. He plunged toward the village, a whispered plea in his throat and the agent's eyes burning his back.

A few furtive steps at a time, Kate worked her way to the other side. Finally the cross towered above her, so she crouched under heavy branches raised like powerful arms against the sky.

The forest seemed too quiet, and she started at the slightest echo. Then, her mind started playing tricks. She could have sworn muffled human tones emanated from nearby.

Be still. Stay quiet. Wait. So few choices, but controlling her emotions was one of them. *Let Domingo come soon. Please, let us reach Monsieur Le Blanc before darkness falls.*

For some reason, Alexandre seemed so real right now, and she longed for his embrace.

The voices came again, closer.

Sound carries much farther in a forest, especially low pitches. Make yourself as small and silent as possible.

"Attack precisely at five a.m. as the workers arrive. Rough up the supervisor with a small black check mark on the right side of his yellow helmet. He promised to put up a struggle. Make it look as though he obeys you at gunpoint, so when the Germans inspect, he will be able to tell the truth."

"At least part of it." A guffaw echoed through the grove.

"Shhhh. These woods could be full of Milice, especially after three raids this week. They've increased the guards at the plant from five to thirty-seven. Take every precaution, and communicate that to your people."

"I've heard that four of those guards side with us. What fools the Vichy police are! At the City hall two villages over, we netted thousands of dollars worth of ration coupons. The Mayor kept them in his house, and even gave us the cupboard key. At Lyon, a savings bank made itself available to one of our units. And—"

"All successes, true. Still, this is no time to boast—no, it's the time to act. The long, demoralizing winter has nearly ended. Now we strike, with many railway and factory workers on our side."

"Last night that Harriot fellow called *l'invasion* a delusion."

"A collaborator extraordinaire." The other speaker hurled a curse. "Why listen to his garble? He hates *la France*. Of course, they want us to believe the *débarquement* will never come. But it will, have no doubt."

"How can we trust the English? They destroyed our ships, remember?"

"You'll see. Corsica fell to the Allies six months ago—keep that in mind. Now, they fight bad weather to secure our liberty."

Branches crackled as though one of the speakers sideswiped a tree.

"Remind your men of Sicily's liberation. Like the Corsican Maquisards, our work behind the scenes makes all the difference. Hum the *Marseillaise*. Wait in earnest."

A long pause followed, with a vehicle moving, stopping, and backing. Something heavy dragged the ground amidst clipped orders. Next a *slap-thud*.

"Enough to blow two-thirds of the plant. How many men do you have?"

"Twenty on the outside, and only you know how many inside."

"Three. Do they all live in the camp?"

"Thirteen. The rest operate from their homes as *sédentaires*."

"Last night many *sédentaires* raided a manufacturing company up north—a large take of tents, khakis, and jackets. Furious gendarmes and Gestapo lurk everywhere. After tonight, lie low until you receive further instructions."

"By then, the men will be more inclined to obey that order."

"True. Now the Nazis know our recruits not only flee the German factories—they stand and fight. Call your men in."

In another minute, the forest echoed grunts, soft mumblings, and curses. Kate visualized men lifting heavy loads. Then silence. Her left leg cramped, but she waited to stretch it.

The forest cleared. Ten minutes later, the unmistakable *swoosh* of espadrilles—Domingo. Finally, a pine bough spread. Kate drew back, but then his forehead showed, and the sparks in his eyes.

"He said for you to come." He brandished a sheaf of ration tickets. "He sent francs for your hotel room and said to meet him late tonight in the dining room."

"He mentioned nothing about a certain type of food?"

"No."

"You are sure?"

A flush rose along Domingo's neckline, and Kate tucked away this lesson. Above all, he hated being doubted.

"He should have said something about chicory coffee and croissants."

Domingo's mouth worked. "So we go now?"

He was asking *her*—for a second, she could have crumpled into his arms. She swiped at unbidden tears.

"*Oui. Merci.*"

His name sat ready on her tongue, but seemed too personal. It didn't matter, anyway. He bolted at this glimpse of her sudden emotion.

Pine forest rose into windswept rocks, down a slope, across a splashing creek on a wooden footbridge, and into a spacious valley. Domingo twisted at the end of the descent. The agent's breath came hard, but she quietly groped for her canteen.

"I'll be back."

Lengthening shadows darkened into looming strips traversing the rocky path like piano keys. Domingo returned and bent to work with his pack's strap, so Kate asked a question she'd held back.

"Where did you learn to run? You ought to try out for the Olympic team."

"My older brother Ander always started late for school." He swung his pack onto his back. "And we played pelota."

"Pelota?"

"A boys' game. Our church had a court next to its outer wall."

"They trained your bodies as well as your souls?" She imagined a quaint stone church like le Chambon's Presbytery, with children at play.

He dropped his pack and tinkered with the latch again.

"Did your family watch you play?"

"On procession days, perhaps."

"Procession days?"

His expression tightened. "The sun lowers by the moment. We must hurry."

Like Moley following Ratty, Kate fell in step. In her favorite *The Wind in the Willows* scene, adventuresome Ratty led timid Moley through a fierce snowstorm. When they passed the turn-off to Moley's old home, nostalgia overwhelmed Moley, but instead of verbalizing his desire, he suffered in silence.

The mesmerizing scent faded, yet his anguish increased at the lost opportunity. The grandiose General Ratty urged him on until he collapsed in a heap of misery and spewed the truth. To Moley's surprise, Ratty retraced their tracks, and they spent the winter night in the mole's humble home.

Now, following Domingo's steady zigzag, Kate wondered how far he had wandered from his home. How long since Domingo had been there? When he stopped to sniff the air, did it call to him?

Roots rose from the path and branches whipped her face, but the sky offered a golden-orange spectacle. Headlong into growing shadows, Domingo shot ahead, unswerving and full of certainty.

Somehow, he knew where they were. His beret became Kate's anchor. Bright rays lighted clouds over the sinking sun, calling up water. That's what Aunt Alvina always said—"The sun's drawing water, so it's going to rain."

Domingo slowed over a steep ridge as the world took on dusk's hazy, lingering light. Then he fell back beside Kate, his breathing regular and sure.

"Just over there. See that roof?"

Golden thatch peeked through the forest—if only Monsieur le Blanc held on.

Chapter Twenty-four

"After those miserable raiders last night, I feel awfully cheap today—I must admit, I had trouble focusing on the sermon. Surely a day must come when Hitler has no more bombers to send." Mrs. Tenney took off her Sunday hat and slipped off her pumps.

"I know what you mean. After we finally got in from last night's patrol, I couldn't fall asleep. I can't imagine how tired you must have grown during the blitz. Kate wrote me a little about it—a cinema near her hotel was hit, but she spared me the details."

"One night, over 3,000 fires broke out, but the very beginning was the worst. September 7, 1940, just before five in the evening, a month after the Colonel passed. It wasn't the first strike, but that day, they targeted the waterfront. The Ford Motor Plant and the gas works went first—the first hits only lasted an hour, but two hours later, the planes returned.

"My neighbor at the time worked as a courier for the firemen. We didn't see him for days and assumed he lost his life in the blazes."

She started upstairs to change clothes, and Addie followed. "What did couriers do?"

"Because all normal communications were knocked out, they carried messages on motorcycles from station to station, with just a twinge of light coming from their blackened headlamps. When we finally saw Donald again, he said they'd worked all night in the stations by candlelight and set up a thousand pumps at the Thames for the next influx of bombers."

Mrs. Tenney stopped at the top of the stairs. "And of course, it came the next morning, a Sunday. From then on, for fifty-seven days straight. I thought I might go off my trolley, but by then Kathryn arrived. She helped save my sanity."

"It must have been terrible, being so exhausted, yet I think I'd have been afraid to go to sleep."

"Exactly. But when I realized Kathryn's burden, with her husband on air raids, it calmed me down. She bore up so well. And then, she—"

Addie waited, but Mrs. Tenney started for her room. Then she turned back and asked, "What do you have in mind for this afternoon?"

"Such a beautiful today. I think I'll take a long walk."

"And I shall take a nap." Before she shut her door, she added. "Addie, you wouldn't disappear like Kathryn, would you?" So many lines crisscrossed her forehead that Addie ran to hug her.

"No. Kate's always needed an extra spark of adventure, but I feel so at home here, I might stay forever."

Mrs. Tenney's shoulders relaxed a bit. "You are most welcome, my dear."

Twenty minutes later, Addie entered the April freshness. Not many people ventured out yet, and the sunshine warmed her back. After a few minutes, she tied her sweater around her waist.

For some reason, Esther filled her mind today. The morning they met in the New York hotel restaurant seemed like a figment from a novel. But the tingle down Addie's spine reminded her their paths had crossed for a purpose. Esther had wired money for the underground. So had Berthea and Jane, and she still waited to hear from Teddy, the Indiana lawyer she met in Chicago.

Donations bulged in her purse, along with another letter she found on her desk Friday after a post box run. Speculating about who left it was useless, so she tucked the envelope away for today's delivery.

The sun's rays permeated even bombed-out buildings today. Strange how three houses stood untouched, but a neighboring one gapped open on one side or lost its roof.

The glories of this mid-spring day caught Addie up, taking her back to this time last year, when she readied for her voyage. She could never have imagined all that was to come. Even though her original purpose to help Kate with her newborn had changed, knowing Charles and his mother made the whole of London seem friendly.

At the office, little by little, Charles had allowed her to compose messages—one here, one there. When he was pressed to produce a report, sometimes he asked for her help putting the information together. At those times, a unique satisfaction filled her—her high school English teacher, Mrs. Morford, would be so proud to know she used what she'd learned in class.

Her route took her southwest, bringing Harold to mind. His AAF unit might already be making survey flights for the Second Front. Try as she might, Addie couldn't envision him jumping from a stricken airplane. Kate, yes, but Harold—never.

"I can't imagine him giving up his insistence about being crippled, even for the war. Still, he must have been trained to parachute. He can't fly with the Air Force without learning that. Ah well—one more unanswerable question about Harold to add to my ever-increasing pile."

At the bombed-out house where a white-haired man always wandered, caught in the past, Addie allowed herself to theorize about the future. In Harold's note, things looked hopeless. They'd come to a dead-end, barring some sort of war miracle.

A complicated concept—a war miracle. Battles wreaked devastation and destruction, but produced their own kind of miracles, not the least of which was her presence on this London sidewalk today. How many times had someone told her about the incredible deliverance at Dunkirk—civilians working together to rescue the entire beleaguered British army?

As Mrs. Tenney quipped, "Even Mr. Churchill, not known for his faith, called that a miracle."

A woman toting a baby approached. She also had a toddler in

hand, a little boy with a blue felt cap, ruddy cheeks, and a smile like sunlight.

"Nice day."

The woman had hardly noticed her, but Addie's greeting caused her to look up. Even with such sallow skin and dark circles under her eyes, she managed a, "G'day, ma'am."

The little boy reminded Addie of Michael, the child she held on the train to New York. His poor, weary mother—she voiced such gratitude, yet Michael brought the perfect diversion against Addie's second thoughts. That day, she'd left behind everything familiar.

Even after nearly a year, it seemed impossible that she had actually left Halberton, where she'd assumed she would live for the rest of her life. Now she'd taken London in, heart and soul—staying here seemed possible. Nearly everything seemed possible—except Harold transforming into the kind of man she could respect.

Past the office bus stop, Addie continued on toward Mr. Firth's. Everyone she met looked cheap, in Mrs. T's words—worn out from lack of sleep.

Down one final street, the alley entrance came into view. At her fourth knock, the proprietor opened the door.

"And how is our Addie today?"

"Well. And you?"

He slipped her envelopes into his inner coat pocket. "The same, but another engagement beckons me." He patted his pocket. "Thank you for rousing people to our cause. I hope you come again next week, when I shall have time for a cup of tea."

With no reason to hurry home, Addie lingered in front of a corner yarn shop.

Maybe she should start knitting for the troops again—she might be able to convince Mrs. T to start, too. She seemed so much happier when something occupied her hands.

Hurried footsteps sounded, and someone touched Addie's shoulder from behind. She turned and gasped.

"Why, Charles!"

"Hopefully, I didn't startle you too much. I thought I might find you here, if I waited long enough. I didn't want to risk running into Mum." He gave a sideways grin. "Could we talk for a while?"

"Why yes. I'm surprised to see you."

"I intended to leave earlier but need to attend to something. A possibility has been nagging at me." He glanced around. "Let's cross over to that bus stop."

He took her elbow, and Addie forced down her feelings. No matter how seeing Charles excited her, Harold remained her legal husband. She couldn't lie—God knew her thoughts. But how long could she balance such opposing thoughts?

Charles dusted off the bench, something she couldn't imagine Harold doing. No, she would be dusting the slats for him. Charles fidgeted once he took a seat, and troubled lines smattered his brow.

What could be wrong? Something about the Invasion plans? Small brown wrens twittered from a nearby tree, and a few vehicles passed, but this Sunday afternoon rendered the usually busy scene restful. The deep scratch on Charles' hand reminded Addie of their gardening yesterday. He'd turned into a natural at weeding and transplanting.

He seemed so perturbed, that might be a good start to their conversation.

"I so enjoyed yesterday, especially meeting those local people at the pub. I felt like a real Englishwoman."

"You're the stranger here, yet you brought cheer to those down-in-the-mouth folks with their tales of rocket bombs. How did you learn to make others feel at home?"

"Probably a backhanded gift from my dad. I wanted to become his opposite."

"A most positive attitude. I marvel you carry no bitterness. Is your father still alive?"

"Yes, my sister takes care of him in California. About bitterness, I don't know—maybe I have some down inside me, like germs waiting to attack. Mainly, I'm glad that part of my life is over. Maybe some day I can help some children in a similar situation."

Charles tipped his head, and his voice softened. "You already are. Pardon my asking, but do you wish to have children?"

"I would love to, but not with Harold." The backs of Addie's eyes burned, but she couldn't call her words back. How could she say such a thing, especially to Charles?

His face flushed. "I know what you said bothered you, but it's all right. I understand—in this cruel world, every child deserves a kind father. I hope to become one some day." His darkening eyes declared that he truly did understand and wanted to help her fight those inner accusations.

He looked away, then back again. "Whatever you suffered in the past, you deserve only the finest." He clenched his fists. "A possibility has occurred to me—"

He turned so quiet—too quiet.

"I have an idea, but—"

For an awkward few moments, she waited, but finally spoke. "Whatever it is, I can manage it, Charles. Really."

His left eyebrow shot skyward. "I hope so. I'm off to Brighton. Army Air Force installations scatter about down there, and I wondered—"

Addie's breathing went shallow.

"If you wish, I could explore information about your—about Harold."

Such a kind offer, but what good would it knowing more details do? She turned away, bereft of words.

"I've done it, haven't I? Disturbed your peace?"

"Not any more than it already is. It's wonderful of you to be willing to—I don't know how to answer you, Charles. I'm sorry."

"Would it help to know something about his plans? I mean, his unit's plans?"

"Maybe. He left without discussing anything with me. We—we couldn't talk. I always said something to make him angry. I couldn't even carry on a conversation with my own husband."

Charles crossed his arms. "With your gift for communicating, I cannot imagine you at fault for the miserable state of your relationship."

Addie squeezed her eyes shut. "Oh, Charles." A mix of gratitude and confusion filled her throat like wet clay.

He put his arm around her, drew her close, and before she knew what happened, his shirt stifled her sobs.

"There, there now. There, there."

Finally she straightened. "Forgive me. I try not to think about this, and most of the time, it works. "

Emotion twisted Charles's lips. "I shouldn't have broached the subject." He grasped her hands.. "Believe me, I had no intention—"

"Of course you didn't."

"Perhaps that old saying, ignorance is bliss, proves true for a time like this. Sometimes knowing more can hinder rather than help."

A cloud hid the sun, and the breeze picked up.

Addie drew herself up. "Maybe not. My tendency to bury my head in the sand may not be the best tactic. If there's one thing four years of marriage taught me, it's that. Kate advised me a long time ago to face things head-on, but I always believed things would get better if I only grew stronger, more attuned to Harold's needs.

"Kate saw everything right off—she said our troubles weren't about me. I guess I couldn't face the facts because they hurt too much. I did the same with Dad all those years, trying to put the best light on him."

"After all, our parents are supposed to love us."

"But I'm grown-up now, and your military connections may be more than a coincidence, Charles. Thank you for your willingness to investigate."

A father and his son walked past with a kite in tow. Addie breathed deep, and once again blessed Charles for his ability to sit with her in stillness.

"Harold wrote to his mother that he sees no hope for us. I don't believe in divorce, but can't go back to living the way he demands."

Sunshine found her face again. "I've left it up to God—to the war—to decide. But maybe that's the coward's way."

"You have already made some choices—to come here, for instance. You can't help this bloody war, or a man who refuses to hear what's in your heart."

Charles slowed his words, and his forehead shone with earnestness. "I would like to say so much, but it must wait. Know this—I will think of you while I'm away."

He bent his head and brushed her fingers with his lips. Addie blinked at the force that swept through her, then drew back and met his eyes.

"Nothing you discover about Harold can make things any worse for me, Charles. My life is better now than it ever has been, better than I ever dreamed it could be."

He reached a fingertip to her wet cheek. Her teeth ached as though she'd eaten too much ice cream, and she took a jagged breath.

"Please do find out what you can about Harold's unit. Tell me or don't tell me. It doesn't matter. All that matters is that you come back."

A single candle showed in one window, and barn smells assailed Kate as Domingo tapped on the door. Then Domingo's powerful bicep grazed her shoulder.

"You run well, too. You might want to learn to play pelota." In the darkness, she could detect no expression except the twinkle in his eyes.

A slight, bleary-eyed woman waved them in. Hair bound back under a workman's cap, she whispered, "Your friend woke about an hour ago."

The woman opened a waist-high gate and stepped back. Below a candle's insufficient flame, a feather tick lodged a bulky figure.

Kate's heartbeat filled her ears as she knelt. "*Monsieur.*"

Even in the dimness, their patient's skin flushed deep red. His eyes darted sideways as he tried to raise his head. His lips moved but produced no sound. A water glass sat on a small bench nearby, and Kate tipped it to his lips. His voice, cracked and broken, finally emerged.

"You ... came ... back."

His eyes sent such warmth, Kate's heart fluttered. "Of course I did, *Monsieur*."

His head sank down into the feather pillow wadded under his thick neck. He closed his eyes, and she took his hand. Its soft flesh sent a tremor through her—once, he'd been so strong, but now—

She whispered in his ear. "I won't leave you again."

In the background, Domingo and the woman spoke in quiet tones. After a while, the barn door opened and closed, and espadrilles made their way toward her stall.

"Do you mind if I show her the papers in your pack?"

Kate shook her head, and Domingo unlatched her bag. A singular shadow, he slipped down the alleyway again. A few minutes later, he returned and dropped on the hay at the stall's far end.

Kate embraced Monsieur's tentative breathing. Intermittent scrapings emanated from above, as though someone paced the haymow floor. Addie mentioned the night sounds in her farmhouse, after everyone went to bed, and Harold blamed squirrels in the attic. But here, those sounds could mean anything.

Alexandre, Addie, Mr. T and his mother—all of them seemed so far away. Life in Iowa with Aunt Alvina receded even farther as Kate concentrated on breaths that created only a minute resonance in the barn.

Her parents' funeral, the flag folded into her hand, the endless train trip west with her nanny passed before her like a faraway parade. Even the recent past—that last Christmas with dear Alexandre, greeting Addie at the Liverpool station, and her early months here faded into a distant dream.

But this man whose hand she held somehow united her with the mysterious past that always escaped her reach. Her heart told her that at this moment only those roots mattered.

Her questions muted in odors of raw milk, grain, and animal refuse. Across the aisle, a milk cow raised her head, her bell making a soft *swish-clang*. From the corner, Domingo's heavy breathing announced he finally felt safe enough to sleep, and Monsieur Le Blanc dozed off.

From a low pile near his pallet, Kate picked up a blanket to cover Domingo, espadrilles to chin, and paused to study his face. His strong jaw shone in undulating light, his nose as pronounced as he was quiet, his wide shoulders limp in the straw.

Like Monsieur, he had changed her life, yet in such a short time. His broad, high forehead, firm cheekbones, and thick neck reminded her of a powerful bull.

"Domingo." What did his name mean? She guessed something about power, evidenced by his fortitude on the grueling trails.

Once, Addie wrote her that a neighboring farmer met his eternal destiny from a bull's gore when he made the mistake of corralling the angry animal and entering the pen. At the time, Kate had compared Harold with that bull, penned up and infuriated at being unable to serve in the fighting forces.

But asleep in this obscure place, Domingo appeared utterly vulnerable. He could be handling guns and explosives, like those men in the forest, but acted as a guide. Had that been his choice, or did he simply accept an assignment?

Watching his chest rise and fall, hearing his firm intake and release of breath, Kate breathed deeper too. She blew out the candle and wrapped in a blanket near Monsieur. Feeble moonlight caressed flaxen hay mounds in the cattle stanchions. A second shard entered through the high cupola directly above. She rested her head on the edge of the thin mattress, and silence reigned.

No one in the S.O.E. knew her whereabouts. At one time, that would have disturbed her—surely, the London staff spoke of her tonight as lost en route to Bren or captured with others from her circuit. Perhaps they also discussed *la Corneille.*

Probably they knew more about Maurice's fate than she. He and

Eugene had embodied *family* for her these past weeks, and now the two of them might already have landed in a Gestapo prison.

But inexplicably, she felt anything but lost and alone. Something about Monsieur Le Blanc's presence, and Domingo sleeping nearby—something far beyond her comprehension spoke security.

Chapter Twenty-five

A raucous rooster startled Kate from her straw bed. In a corner of the stall, Domingo still slept. She feared to look Monsieur Le Blanc's way, and when she did, his weak sprawl proclaimed an unwelcome truth.

But everything in her cried, *No. He must not die!*

Something creaked in the dark alleyway, and she made her way toward the phantom-like figure of their hostess. Yesterday, a band of rough-bearded Maquisards took instructions from this woman in the barnyard when Kate stepped outside for air.

Perhaps, like some women, Madame Chalomet covered for her husband, alive or dead, and carried out his plans. Likely, she also produced ration and identity cards, fed ravenous partisans, and took care of her family and this farm.

The breakfast tray she toted contained precious egg crepes, fruit, and the tantalizing hot chicory that had addicted Kate. As always, she inquired about *Monsieur*.

"How is he?"

"Still alive, and not in pain. Do you know anything about him?"

"His love for *La France* goes back to the Great War, when he served in a spy ring. His papers gave us some other essential information. Fortunately, you found him instead of some *Milicien*—you did the right thing bringing him here."

"It was Domingo. I didn't even know our location by the time we found *Monsieur*."

Madame angled her head toward their patient for a long moment.

"He has given his all for liberty." Then she pulled back into the alleyway.

Domingo rolled over as Kate poured an inch of steamy chicory into a cup. The powerful scent roused even Monsieur. His cold fingers searched for hers, and wistfulness enveloped her, as if Aunt Alvina had entered the barn and embraced her one last time.

"I am dying. Today."

"No, *Monsieur*, surely not. You fought through these nights, and—"

He gave her a half-smile. "I know what I know."

Protest juddered in Kate's throat. "Here." She held the coffee for him to sip, and his sigh ripped her insides. If only they could have found a doctor, but his halting speech declared what she most feared.

"I have a parting—gift for you, *ma Chérie*." He inched closer. "You must know before I pass—from this world. You must know that *Le Renard* loved you."

Breathless, Kate leaned into his scent.

"He was—my younger brother." Monsieur's eyes lighted at her gasp. "I swear before *mon Dieu*."

"You—you are my uncle?"

"*Oui*." He shifted his weight and moaned. She wanted to echo his labored cry—how could his life end just when she had discovered something so important?

"After the war, he still—worked as a clandestine, back and forth from *les Etats-Unis* to Germany." He coughed and sank onto his pillow. "Of course, we—could not—trust them."

Kate wiped his wet forehead. "Oh please, take your rest. You can tell me later."

He raised quivering fingers. "Hear me. Your mother, too—she kept working. She—delivered regular reports to England from *la maison blanche*."

The White House. Incredulous, Kate hardly noticed stirring in the next stall. But what Monsieur intimated about her mother mattered little—what mattered was him.

"A week before his death, we met in London. *Le Renard* spoke of you."

Kate's pulse razed her ears.

"His little Kathryn, with her mother's tenacious spirit. If anything happened to him, and to Madame ... in their travels ... would I watch out ... for you?"

Pasty eyelids closed, but opened again a moment later. Rough, frosty fingers tightened around hers.

"He gave ... an address." His groan made Kate wince. "When I heard about their ... crash, I took a ship ..." A single tear ran the length of his temple. He cleared his throat to no avail.

"The small house was empty ... Langley Park. Someone gave me ... a name, but the woman had gone, and taken ... you with her. No one could tell ... me where."

"To Iowa. Our housekeeper took me to Aunt Alvina's house in Iowa." Kate clenched his hand. With each hungry breath, he weakened. "Monsieur, do not try to talk."

"In '38, we formed *la Résistance*—in '40, with the occupation, I traveled to England. Calculations, plans, meetings—for three years. And then one day, I saw you—the very picture of your mother, as I live—and breathe."

Kate felt a presence behind her, but bent even nearer. "Oh, my very own uncle. But why did you come here now?"

A cough wracked him, Kate's sob tumbled into the stale air. "Oh God, no. Don't let him die, not now."

Without a sound, Domingo knelt beside her while Monsieur's scratchy reply threaded out.

"To organize—to destroy the Reich. To see the end of this ..." Monsieur waved into the darkness " ... impossible evil at last."

He lapsed into labored breathing, yet the faint glimmer in his eyes held Kate when he reopened them. "One last mission ... to deliver your instructions. Your courage, so like ... your father's, your voice, like your mother's ... heartens me to know ..."

His skin matched the blue-white cliff hollows on her fearsome bicycle ride from Le Chambon to Clermont-Ferrand. Domingo steadied her with a warm hand on her back.

Monsieur rasped one final time. "I could not fail *le Renard*, so brave, so ..." He sucked a painful breath, and his throat rattled. "Now you know he ... loved you, Kathryn Isaacs." His voice wavered, his jaw slacked, and his head wagged to the side.

Kate stared in disbelief as Domingo felt for a pulse. He shook his head and closed Monsieur's eyes. Then he stretched his arms out, and she crumbled into his strength.

When her deluge subsided, song gradually emerged, low in Domingo's chest, through his heartbeat, and up into his throat. The heady conglomeration of melody and syllable mysteriously communicated to Kate's stricken senses. He sang of hope, of faith, of family.

The agent's eyes told the tale. Her emptiness had abated. From the instant she told him about her past, Domingo wondered how she could live in a world spliced from the generations, all those looking down on this earthly struggle. What strength would one have, distanced from them cheering like onlookers at a pelota match?

Now, the fine, textured depths of her eyes proclaimed grief's harshness. But even as she experienced that reality, she finally knew the treasure of her own history. The dip of her brow against sunlit eastern morning sky took Domingo's breath away. Words eluded him, so he gave himself to the ever-present farm work.

A hour earlier in the family's plot, after Domingo's last shovelful of gritty earth, Kate knelt beside Monsieur Le Blanc's grave. Madame Chalomet stood with them.

"We are honored to have him with us. He spanned both wars—men like him gave everything. They founded our *Résistance*."

Kate sniffled in a strong breeze. Domingo let out a shaky breath and retreated to the barn. These days altered him, despite his belief that nothing beyond Sancha's death could ever move him. He felt old, yet at the same time, remade. An even more watchful care entered him for this girl so far from her home—with no home.

Oh, he had watched out for her before, but this was different. Now he knew her name—Kathyrn Isaacs. The syllables turned round and round in his head, and like a new batch of Maman's apple cider wine, he tried them out silently with his tongue. Less foreign than so many other names he contemplated over the Pyrénées, this agent's familial roots lay close at hand.

Perhaps her father had been born not so far away. He considered how to trace her family—not impossible, surely. But a host of other questions troubled him. How could Monsieur Le Blanc have found Kathryn on a London street after all those years? A vision of Sancha standing with her mother passed before him.

But of course—like Sancha, this Kathryn bore her mother's likeness. Père Gaspard would term this the Divine Will. Walking London's streets, seeking his kindred, of course the aging spy spotted his Amerikan niece. With every pitchfork of clean straw Domingo nestled into bedding for the animals, this truth sank deeper into his being. He could almost picture the event.

Out in the graveyard, she fashioned a small wooden cross to mark her uncle's grave. Bound together at the center with rope, the wooden piece seemed right for such a patriot. On it, she painstakingly carved the six letters that tied her to him—ISAACS.

And below that, a wayfaring partisan chiseled a sign: Died for the *Résistance*.

Kate sat there as though entranced, clutching the brooch Monsieur gave her. Domingo waited for her and spent the time laboring for Madame Chalomet. A unique solace came to him in busying himself with the animals and needed repairs.

After Kathryn Isaacs slept, she ate the nourishing broth Madame Chalomet brought, strolled into the woods near the farmstead, and slept again. Domingo could not think what to call her, but like a discreet, objective father, he observed her, and when she slept, he did, too. Above all, he asked nothing, for grieving offered work enough.

In the morning, they drank hot chicory, and she told him every-thing, her outpouring like a gushing spring. Phrases, like poetic watchwords, stayed with him long afterward, for she too had known great loss. This expression of what she held inside for so long, Domingo enveloped as holy.

"I recall my parents' deaths in images—a coffin, someone blowing a trumpet, a soldier folding an American flag and handing it to me. Their airplane must have crashed on land, not in the ocean, for they were buried together.

"My caretaker and I rode a noisy train halfway across the country, where Aunt Alvina waited at a small train depot. I still remember her smile and welcoming arms—she took me in, heart and soul."

Her tale entered into Domingo. He could not prevent that, though he knew he would never be the same. Along with her story, he took Kathryn in, for as Aitaita always said, history and life are one.

An alteration impossible to define, but Domingo knew it to be as real as the tree at Guernica surviving those German bombs. It was like Aitaita accompanying him, yet in eternal rest at the same time.

Kathryn—Katarin. But she told him people called her Kate. The names flowed over him for another day. He still longed for home, yes, but a unique serenity stole over him. He cleaned stalls, rear-ranged hay in the mow, shaved ragged hooves, mended harnesses, shimmied up barn poles to tackle cobweb armies—and waited.

When they'd first found Monsieur, and Domingo went for help, he had a terrible thought on his return trip. What if the victim were *La Corneille*, the double agent, and this Amerikan girl was now in his clutches? But Madame Chalomet reassured them they cared for and buried a hero.

What if *La Corneille* was that man in the village, the one Kata-rin—Kate—tricked into the truth? The idea sent a shudder through Domingo, for he'd stood within two feet of him to deliver her message. Perhaps that fellow hunted her now. The sooner they left for parts west, the better. He would breathe easier once they crossed the border into Lot.

On the third day, Madame Chalomet asked for them to come. Domingo relaxed when the flicker of light in the agent's eyes and the set of her chin declared her ready.

In a cellar room, a map spread before them on a huge hand-hewn table. Roads and railroads, hills and valleys, streams and mountains became ink marks on paper, clarifying the distance from their present position in Aveyron to his home across the border in Lot.

Madame cast her stick here and there, pointing out recent raids, and spoke what they most wanted to hear. "L'Invasion comes soon, from the north. The weather has foiled one attempt already."

The rugged woman's lips curved into a faint smile, the first Domingo had seen from her. Then her facial lines ran sharp again.

"The Gestapo has overrun Clermont-Ferrand. Your circuit leader may have escaped, but his radio operator—"

A look of horror crossed Kate's face.

"Hopefully Maurice is close to London by now."

"And Eugene?"

"We have yet to hear, but only danger awaits you in that location." Madame Chalomet tapped her pointer on the table. "Many networks require your skills." She passed north to a corner of Dordogne in the Limosin, bordering Lot on the northwest.

"A woman here, *patronne* of the local *Résistance,* will have great need of your services during l'Invasion. You need only follow the railroad line to Luc-la-Primaube and up to Capdenac."

She looked to Domingo.

"You know the way through Rocamadour?"

"*Oui.*"

Heat sparked Domingo's chest. His first impulse was to clap his hand over Madame Chalomet's mouth. She would send a young woman into such peril? Then, he saw these villages in relation to his home. Perhaps, after all, he could check on Maman and Gabirel.

"You have communicated with London?"

Kate shook her head. "No, Madame. I only carry the message for Maurice."

"You have your password?"

"*Oui.*"

"You are trained to employ a transmitter?"

Kate nodded, and Madame gestured for them to follow.

Domingo motioned Kate ahead and fell in line. He had shadowed Aitaita, Papa, Ander, and Philippe kilometre after kilometre, but he had never followed a woman. Today, though, this agent's straight back, her knot of light hair, everything about her intrigued him. Falling in line seemed natural.

Madame Chalomet's quick, purposeful steps led them through the house and across a vine-dressed courtyard. Where was her husband, if he still lived? Did *Sainte Jean d'Arc* appear like this to her ancient peoples, wise and authoritative? West through a pasture and a staggered vineyard, into a pine grove, Domingo considered.

Here, another stone building, wide and low, butted into a hillside. Madame entered, returned a minute later, and in a secretive hush, addressed him.

"Where is your home?"

"The Department of Lot, south of St. Cère."

"You will accompany this agent to Dordogne?"

"If you wish."

"It is best."

She led the way down some steep stairs and back, back, beyond the building's length, into a cave-like space. At the very end, a nondescript man, not old, not young, occupied a chair pulled up to a radio. "In half an hour they should be listening."

"For this transmission, they always listen."

"You are S.O.E.?"

Kate nodded. The operator stood, so she took his seat. He put his shoulder to the rock wall and lit a cigarette. Domingo took a corner chair, though this close place gave him an itchy feeling in his chest. The smoke made him sneeze, but something told him not to leave. Kate donned the radio contraption and bowed her head and hands to the controls as if in prayer. Then her shoulders tensed and her fingers worked their magic.

The man tamped his cigarette on the dirt floor with his heel. Tapping, like a nervous bird pecking on a window, inundated the structure and tickled Domingo's ears.

These unseen transmissions became real to him only when he attended teacher training. His family's way of life clashed with the outer world, yet Aitaita took the long view and sent him away to school for his good, for his future. That knowledge held him the whole time, as the world of telegraphs and radios opened to him.

Today, a new truth lighted his understanding. This girl communicated with a world he would never see, one she left only for a time, a world as real to her as his to him. His world lay hidden in Lot, between Aveyron and Dordogne, south of Corrèze, north of Tarn-et-Garonne, not so far from a gorge pulsing with water that tumbled with its own vibrant life.

On the route of St. James de Santiago de Compostela's pilgrimage, Aitaita's small parcel of pastureland held meaning for him and his people. The pilgrimage continued to northwest Spain, to Galicia, on the route of St. James the Great, the first of our Lord's followers to be martyred.

Aitaita himself made the trek, and always welcomed other travelers who passed by their homestead. Some inscribed shells in the trees' bark or engraved them on rocks. More than once, Domingo had watched them from a high branch. Far away in Amerika, Basque shepherds who worked with the sheep left their marks in trees, too—it was the way of his people.

But now, Madame Chalomet, like Philippe, warned that the enemy would claim even his homeland, nestled in the very heart of France. A fear deeper than this hidden transmission station engraved Domingo's soul like those shells on bark.

Home. He must get home. The walls swayed in, but he stayed himself by touching their intricate lichen designs. All the while, Kate's tapping tied her to her home, as her sorrow tied her to him.

Madame returned with food for their journey, and Domingo slid the parcel into his pack. A few minutes later, this agent, Kathryn Isaacs, removed the listening posts from her ears, shoved her chair back, and approached him. Shadows from lambent lantern light caressed her features.

Domingo croaked the appropriate question, although he couldn't yet decide what to call her. "It worked?"

Wordless assent leaped from her dark eyes, so he rose. With barely a rustle, she fell in behind him. He would lead, but this time, her image preceded his every step.

The stranger's face glistened in the sun, his dog-like panting matched by the men behind him. Kate could smell them six feet away, where she rested after their journey's violent beginning, with Domingo tearing northwest as fast as his espadrilles would take him. Snatches of conversation wafted as she recovered from the wild run.

"The Gestapo blew a lorry last night, just down the trail. Wounded one of our men. We've used lorries to transport everything from farm machinery to explosives. Now, we must stop. But nearly every night, we receive more heavy containers. They require four men each, and sledges, carts, and mules."

He wiped his forehead. "You have heard about Tunis? The Allies cornered the Bosche there, and now the British First Army has taken the city. The Americans have taken Bizerte, too."

"What about the route to the Dordogne?"

"Intense night movement there. Be watchful. Soon the trees will leaf in full for daytime travel. Jour-J, *le débarquement d'Alie* is only weeks away."

The Allied Invasion. Kate tingled at the thought. Surely the forces would come soon—the very air of France vibrated in anticipation.

"Forming welcoming committees takes all our time. We've had to cut back on direct attacks."

"The Germans trouble even the southeast, in the mountains?"

"Indeed." The man motioned to his followers. "Darnande, Minister for the Maintenance of Order—" He spit in disgust. "He has become very forward, with that dastardly Henriot's broadcasts of Maquisards shot or deported near the Swiss border—tries to make us all look like bandits."

He roughed Domingo's shoulder. "Take all possible care. The Gestapo shows great interest in your route, but keep *l'Invasion* foremost in your mind."

Domingo straightened at the word *invasion*. He turned to Kate, and she lifted her chin, leaving decisions to him. With a slight nod, he accepted the responsibility. *Trust no one, but err on the side of the Basque.*

Her training warned about relying too much on others, yet Domingo knew where they had been and had an idea of their destination—exactly what she needed. A wave of relief swept her with him handling the logistics. Clearly, he longed for *l'Invasion*, too.

Besides, he witnessed everything with Monsieur Le Blanc. After her lack of discretion in baring her past, he knew far more about her than she should have allowed.

Chapter Twenty-six

"Greenham Common must be the busiest place on earth. The RAF requisitioned the entire area next to the airfield for assembling gliders. At present, they complete fifteen per day, and they say the number will triple—all this in preparation for the Second Front. If I could, I'd take you down there. Addie."

Charles' exuberance knew no bounds this morning. But then he raised his eyebrows as he realized he'd just proposed to take her nearer to Harold.

"Oh, sorry. That's the last place you'd like to go."

After a week's absence from London, he overflowed with news, and Saturday gave him time to share it all. Even though Mrs. T predicted an invasion would lead to terrible losses on both sides, it was impossible not to enter into his enthusiasm.

"Thousands of GIs put together Waco CG-4A Assault Gliders, or install some 240 meters of pierced steel planking at the main runway ends to marshal the units. Workers tote wooden packing crates away by the lorry-load, and Generals appear at whim. I might have glimpsed your General Eisenhower yesterday, but couldn't be sure."

He paused long enough to attack weeds intent on decreasing the productivity of some green beans. But at his next words, a suffocating sensation drowned Addie.

"My coworker—we trained together years ago—has agreed to sleuth for us. He commands the 87th Troop Carrier Squadron under the 438th, and I gave him what information we know. He wagers Harold works with the 368th under the Ninth Air Force's 71st Fighter Wing, Troop Carrier Command. On March fourteenth, they already flew their first sweep over the French coast."

All those numbers and Squadron titles made her head spin, and her heart *thump-thumped* like it did last night when a whistling bomb smashed deep into the earth in the next block. She and Mrs. T clung to each other, as the earth shook under their feet, and kept watch. About the time the all-clear sounded, their faithful milkman's pony trotted along the street like normal. For a few moments, life seemed normal again.

But here, tending the vegetables, Addie's pulse quickened at the thought of discovering more about Harold's unit. Her weed slashing became murderous.

To avoid meeting Charles' eyes, she busied herself down the row a distance. What Harold told Berthea might be true—he might really be only fifty miles west of London. A shiver took her, in spite of the warmth. April sixth—tomorrow would have been Mama's fiftieth birthday. Her memory wandered back to the home she had made for their family in spite of her dad.

She did her best, but Ruthie's diligence was the reason Addie even knew Mama's birthdate. Ruthie kept their family alive, though pieces fell off every which way. First Reuben ran away, then Mama died. Ruthie married and took little Bonnie to California, so Herman and Dad looked to Addie.

But I failed them. And then I failed Harold.

Her whirlwind of thoughts spiraled downward. She could no more stop them than wave a magic wand over the gardens to deplete the weeds. Her energy dissipated, and she lost track of time.

"Addie?" Charles squatted beside her. "I've chatted like a dizzy parrot this morning, but you—something is wrong. Can you speak of it?"

She shook her head. "Maybe later."

His pensive look softened into the tenderness she'd come to cherish. "We don't have to keep working. We might take a stroll, go back into town—"

Then he grinned. "Ah—garden work is your best medicine. How could I forget?" He patted her shoulder and rounded the long row to give her space.

What a relief not to have to explain herself. If even the mere hint of Harold's location shook her so, she must still be very weak.

Charles seemed as eager as she to finish the weeding and worked on a separate section until late afternoon clouds flirted with the sun. Addie's merciless uprooting gradually eased her torrent of negative imaginations. Rehashing her feelings did no good, as usual. When would she learn to curtail this useless cycle?

She repeated the same routine, but finally had to let it go. The process seemed to possess a life of its own, as if she must let the wind batter her for a time before breaking free. But the old, familiar progression drained her. Today, though, at least the sun stroked her back, and a friend waited nearby.

She didn't even notice the drop in temperature until Charles peered at her through thick tomato leaves, like a mischievous child at play. In the bright light, his freckles popped out even stronger, fitting her mental image of Tom Sawyer.

"Oh, you." She giggled, and he broke into a smile.

"I've worked myself out. What say we terminate for the day?"

Addie wiped her hands on the new overalls from the girl she'd overheard talking. They fit so much better than the gardener's trousers, whose knees Addie had worn to shreds.

"I apologize for my attitude earlier. The thought of Harold only fifty miles away—I know better than to let it, but it unnerves me."

"Of course. And me engrossed in the grandiosity of it all. What a boor I've been."

"Oh no. The glider-making intrigues me, too."

He offered her his hand, and his storm cloud-blue eyes radiated such calmness that she blurted, "I may need to tell you a bit more about—my former life."

"All right. Where shall we eat, my garden princess?"

"Wherever they'll take us in our grubby condition."

"I might know just the place."

Another thing she liked about him—no lingering over a misunderstanding like a succulent apple pie. His apology was almost too much—Harold never said he was sorry.

Charles shouldered their rakes and hoes. Obviously too old to sign up for active duty, one of the home guard stood watch at the exit, his dingy green Great War uniform stained and hat askew. But he took his job seriously, and he and Charles exchanged salutes.

"What say—have the raids hit close to you?"

"Closer to my office and Mum's than to my flat. I've got a skylight, so sometimes the sky looks incredible from in there."

"You don't fear broken glass?"

"With this mini-blitz, the need for sleep sometimes overtakes the need for safety."

The guard grimaced in understanding, and Charles said good-bye.

A ways down the road, Addie glanced at him. "With that muddy streak on your forehead and more on your nose, you have the marks of a farmer."

Charles turned quiet. Why had she brought up a subject that led to Harold? Addie stemmed her internal tide of accusation—no need to dot her i's and cross her t's with Charles, who had no penchant for categorizing everything as good or bad.

This stillness between them could be pleasant, if she let it. Maybe his change of mood had nothing to do with her, so she could choose to believe the best and enjoy their quiet walk.

Crops spread toward the horizon as they turned onto their usual route. A sheep bleated somewhere, several others answered, and a mild breeze drifted evening scents, a peculiar blend of suppers cooking and dust settling before darkness.

Mama's saying about dusk sifted in. "Evening tide means the earth is going to sleep for the night."

How soothing to be so close to that earth all day long and watch afternoon turn into evening. How good to have worked in the soil.

"England is so beautiful. I'm grateful for all you've shown me."

"You must see more. The area where I went to boarding school boasts hillier terrain, with dense groves and splendid colors as the seasons change."

"I would love to."

"I shall abstain from rash promises, but I do hope to take you one day."

Addie pulled on his arm. "Look! That cloud could be—"

"A spitfire taking off."

"Or a Canadian goose on a lake—"

"They share the same aeronautical engineering, and we share—" Charles turned toward her. "Gardening, earth, sky, work—"

"Your mother, an office, friendship with Kate—"

She almost added, "And the future," but stopped herself in time. Forgetting the facts tempted her, but a few weeks after high school graduation, she had vowed faithfulness to Harold Bledsoe in Halberton's Methodist church and signed their marriage license before witnesses. Before God.

The blue of Charles' eyes transformed to indigo. She wished she hadn't said she needed to talk to him, but he drew her close, and his curlicue chest hairs made bedsprings of his shirt under her cheek.

She knew she could step back any time, yet didn't want to. But he ought to know the truth about her—might as well tell him tonight.

The peasant's nose curved like a comet under his stained beret. "You travel these days? You have great courage."

Domingo shrugged. "Or stupidity."

"Here—eat. Drink." The man waved toward the feast his wife had set—soup, a loaf of dark heavy bread, cheese, and most amazing of all, an apple. They downed their fill, and Domingo cut the fruit to share with Kate. Its mellow scent would have been enough, even after being stored in a cellar all winter. She savored each slice.

The peasant shuffled his feet. "You continue on tonight?"

Domingo raised his chin a half-inch, and the man's wife came forward from the shadows. "Take this."

He and Kate divided more foodstuffs between their packs, and the farmer hovered as they neared his door. "You have word of *Jour-J?*"

"Rumors fly like bombers over London and Berlin."

Silhouetted in the doorframe, two sets of eyes glimmered with hope as the simple folk waved them off.

Nighttime sounds embraced Kate and Domingo, animals on the hunt, insects stirring. After a short distance, Domingo turned his head. "That man was near enough to the trail to spot us because he waits for Allied soldiers, to thank them and offer food. He cannot sleep anticipating *l'Invasion.*"

Down yet another ravine, Domingo tensed and stopped short. Kate scanned the shadowy path and incessant brush. She'd learned to sense shapes and darker blobs against the landscape, but noticed nothing. Still, Domingo poised, his body a single taut spring. Experience had taught her to wait.

She would be dead ten times over if it weren't for him, as this exact scenario had occurred often since they left Madame Chalomet's two days ago. Once, a wild boar emerged onto the trail, and Domingo shooed the animal away.

Another time, something wilder appeared, a grizzled railroad man, an explosives expert. Seemingly unworried about secrecy, he disclosed his destination: blowing a railroad bridge.

Domingo asked about the gun he carried in plain sight.

"When Vichy forbade local peasants their hunting guns, we stole them from the gendarmes. One of our partisans, a local teacher, helps us with information. Domingo's eyes flickered when he mentioned teachers, so Kate determined to explore this later.

Now Domingo formed an impassable obstacle, and Kate stopped so close she bumped her nose on his pack. Within minutes, an entire troop assembled before them.

A friendly fellow shook hands with Domingo. "You work from the Cantal?"

Domingo flinched.

"You have no teaching post this season?"

Domingo kept silent, but his tension emanated to Kate.

"My students turned *Résistance*, so I sleep in the schoolhouse and run night missions." The stranger hailed his men. "Ten minutes rest—quiet."

He gestured toward Kate. "You are *Resistance?*"

The look Domingo gave her solidified her decision to remain silent. Grateful for the chance to relax, she ignored the questions, unstrapped her pack, sat and closed her eyes.

The traveler's opinions filtered her way in snitches. *Locals now paid their tax to his circuit rather than submit to Vichy's impossible demands. Vichy sent the money to Germany, so why cooperate? Milk was selling for eight francs a liter.* At that, Domingo gave a low whistle.

One kilo of potatoes cost two francs twenty in October. Now, that much sold for fifteen francs in Limoges. Finally, the traveler tried again with Domingo.

"How often does your troop meet?"

Kate imagined the lines crisscrossing Domingo's forehead. Obviously proud of his organization, the stranger continued. "We gather every two weeks, all men summoned or dispatched within two hours." He barely hesitated for a reaction.

"Even the priests help us. One keeps a wireless in an unused confessional and suggested I store grenades in the school basement. Men from everywhere join us, even some Great War Spanish holdovers with the revolutionary light still in their eyes. Jewish doctors and refugees find us, and for a time, a couple of Sisters herding the Chosen stayed in our camp."

When his men gathered, Kate strapped on her pack and waited a few feet away.

"Until the trees leaf out, take special care. Only last month, the Gestapo killed 150 Maquisards, including their organizer, near Switzerland."

He clapped his hand on Domingo's shoulder. "You're headed

toward Figeac, *oui?* Last month, their Maquisards netted a huge haul from the Milice barracks—over 50,000 cartridges, explosives, rifles, and machine guns. Made Darnard look bad."

Domingo's reply barely reached Kate. "Sometimes the safest place is under their noses."

The men departed, and Kate feasted on his simple statement. She'd bet he participated in that heist, maybe even led the assault.

When twilight faded into darkness, they rested a while, but not long. She'd become used to night hiking, but hours later, her feet felt far away from the rest of her body. Faint light smattered the horizon, so Domingo signaled a stop and turned to her.

"You heard much about Dordogne yesterday. Do you still wish to go?"

"I know of nowhere else."

He handed her a chunk of bread and bit into one himself. "We could veer east again, but I know far less of that area."

"You are a teacher?"

He told her more than she expected. "I took the training and taught for a couple of years. But many things happened, and Maman needed me at home."

Kate wanted to ask why and how the Maquisards found him. But he changed the subject.

"Now we enter rough country." His eyes glinted in the moonlight as they had the first time she met him.

Rushing water backed his sigh. "With Figeac unsafe now—"

"You know Figeac well?"

He massaged his temples. She took that for a yes and went into the bushes. A cool wind blew waterfall spray. A branch cracked, and she stiffened. At any moment, someone might spring from the bushes.

But back on the path, Domingo's quiet demeanor tamped her wild imaginings. For now, they were safe.

"Somewhere, we sleep. After that, I will take you to the safest place I know."

They trekked another half hour to a homestead perched along a hillside. An alert peasant, already into his milking, urged them to the barn and brought food. Kate climbed the ladder and collapsed in the mow. When Domingo shook her, mid-morning sunshine shone through the windows, and fire lighted his eyes. Whether he'd slept or not, his expression declared that compared to reaching home, sleep meant nothing.

Chapter Twenty-seven

Around noon, a lad's sheep crowded the path near a steep bridge embankment, and Domingo paused to greet him.

"How far to Figeac?"

"Two hours. Someone from there passed by this morning with word of raids."

Domingo's temple throbbed. "What else did he say?"

"Miliciens and Gestapo everywhere, but they moved on."

"Where is your Papa?"

The boy gestured toward the high places. Domingo offered him a hunk of cheese, the last of their supply. Then he lanced west, grateful Kate followed without questioning. His mind raced. *Surely Jean-Luc Edorta has not left Maman and Gabirel alone—*

He could not finish the thought. If Jean-Luc, their *lehen auzo* or first neighbor, had joined the Maquisards, then Gabirel carried too much on his shoulders all this time. But surely, Jean-Luc would never do this, for their families were one. When Aitaita died, Maman sent Domingo to inform Jean-Luc even before the village bell tolled the news.

But these days, common things converted into monsters, and people tossed traditions aside. Could one even trust a *lehen auzo* anymore?

A storm of possibilities pushed Domingo harder, faster. He tackled the steepest pass, where the Milice might not travel. An arduous climb later, he waited for Kate.

"I need to check our route. You will stay here?"

She dropped onto a fallen log and waved him away. Side-winding, he found a slope swathed in spring green, leading to flat grassland. When he returned, Kate had pulled off her wool stockings and swished her feet in icy water.

"I found a shortcut."

He winced at the blisters on her heels. Yet she uttered no complaint, just as on her first rough night here. If only he'd thought to carry an extra pair of espadrilles around his neck, as Philippe often did.

Seeing her ankle brought Sancha to mind. She visited him only rarely now, most often in a dream, when she used to come often during the day as he hastened over a path, ate supper, or studied the terrain for the best route. He hated the idea of her fading, she who had meant everything to him.

But now, impossibly, this girl from Amerika filled his mind. He must get her to Dordogne—he'd promised Madame Chalomet. But with every traveler they met toting despicable Gestapo stories, that quest seemed more and more doubtful. Anxiety swelled Domingo's chest, and the sight of Kate hurting only increased his worry.

Weariness spread through his back and legs as he ripped his shirttail and handed a swatch to her. "To wrap your heels. But first, let me find fresh herbs."

He crawled through the underbrush, crushed the right leaves with his thumb to form the thinnest of compresses, and gestured to her to lift her feet from the water.

Not a word passed between them, but waves of electricity plied Domingo's hands when he touched her skin. She put on her shoes— he could not watch.

"I—Maman will have some ointment and an extra pair of espadrilles."

Her smile calmed him. "Please don't slow down for me."

He forsook the shortcut for the main road, but the closer they came, the more he wanted to run. The forests loomed far too still. By now, sounds from the Ratier bicycle manufacturers in the old sawmill should be reaching them.

A middle-aged nippie washed down the counter at the tiny fish and chips restaurant and waved Charles and Addie to a seat. "Take your time. If you order the regular plate, we'll serve you up in a minute."

"Perfect. And straightaway, two cups of strong tea, please." Charles shed his coat. "I'm ravenous all the time since you introduced me to outside work."

"I gladly take the credit."

The nippie delivered their tea, and Addie took a mountainous breath. She might as well plunge in.

"What do you have to tell me is that bad?"

"I don't want you to—"

"Feel sorry for you."

"How did you know?"

Charles chuckled. "It's rather like those ducks and airplanes we saw in the clouds earlier, coming home from the gardens."

Addie crossed her legs and bumped his knee with her foot. "Sorry."

"Quite all right."

"I tell you this only for understanding's sake. That means everything to me."

He brushed her fingers, clutched around her cup handle. His voice swung low. "And to me."

"I've told you about Harold, but not everything. He seems to have a—a propensity for misery." She bit her lip. "I borrowed that phrase from Kate, but it describes him to a T. Some people do seem to enjoy being unhappy. He called himself a cripple for years, after a childhood accident left him with a slight limp."

"But a bombardier must train to jump—"

"Exactly what Kate would say if I could tell her about this. His mother says he's doing well, but I can't imagine that being true. Sometimes I wonder if I knew him at all."

The aroma of hot fish and potatoes filled the small room. Addie

pulled at her sleeve and Charles leaped to her aid, set her sweater beside her, and returned to his seat.

"That's something Harold would never do."

"Help you with your wrap?"

"Yes. On one hand, he wanted me submissive and always sweet, but he couldn't abide the social graces."

Charles folded his hands under his chin.

"That really didn't bother me much. What did was when he refused to give me time to think things through. You've showed me the opposite, and I'm so grateful. Kate spelled it out for me when she labeled Harold immature." The memory of Kate's vehement verdict, delivered with arms akimbo, brought out Addie's chuckle. "I wish you could hear her rave about him. She saved my life during the worst of it."

"And you'll tell me the worst of it tonight?"

Addie's eyes stung. She must stop it. In the light of last night's rocket attack that set the house shaking and the windows rattling in their sockets, why shed tears over the troubled past? The attack came after their warden patrol, and she and Mrs. T dived under the big library desk until it was over.

Once again, she searched Charles' face and found only welcome. "I'll try. Harold wanted an heir and said it was my fault we had no children, that God was punishing me for my disobedience." She dropped one hand in her lap. All of a sudden, describing their relationship seemed impossible, overwhelming. Why had she even started?

But Charles touched her hand again, and the nippie refilled their cups. Half a minute later, the restaurant owner served their steaming plates himself.

"A good night to y' both. The wife n' me appreciate your visits."

Charles shook his hand. "Mum will be jealous. She stood in a queue for an hour and a half to buy fish the other day. Then a warning blew, so she lost her place making for a shelter."

The owner saluted and backed away. "Tell 'er to stop in. We have our fish connections, and I'll treat her to the best."

After he returned to the kitchen, Charles picked up his fork. "What say we eat? Tales of yesteryear require far more energy than gardening."

Addie devoured her largest piece of fish and emptied her cup. "I musn't get off track. It's now or never."

"By all means, then. You said Harold sees you as disobedient."

"Our childlessness embittered him. He believed I failed to honor and obey him."

"In what sense?" Charles balled his fist around a napkin.

"Oh, I don't mean I refused him—not ever." Heat galloped up Addie's neck. "This is hard. I'm sorry I started, Charles."

"Honesty takes courage. I wish, back when I went through my trials, I had gotten some of it out. Instead, everything balled up inside me."

"Kate says Harold focused on control. To him, obedience meant him directing my every move. He argued with everything I said and resented my friends, especially her. He didn't like me being close to his mother, either. He saw half the town as enemies because of their German blood, and my mother's side was German."

"Yet he chose you."

"His mother had German ancestry too, but he overlooked that when he wanted to."

They ate for a while, and a plethora of scenes filled Addie's mind.

"If women came to church without hats or disagreed with their husbands, he suspected them. I—like to read scripture, but he took my interpretations as an affront. Harold won the state debate championship, and I knew I couldn't hold my own with him, but sometimes I slipped up and shared my opinion.

"Kate says we didn't argue because I let him have his way. She was right, until the last time. Then I stood up to him."

Charles paid the tab and thanked the owner. "Shall we take the bus, or a long walk?"

"A long walk."

The warm evening coaxed bad memories from Addie's mouth

like bats from a dungeon. Harold's insults after she painted the kitchen without asking him, him jerking her arm almost out of its socket, pushing her friend Jane into a wall, and threatening Jane's disabled husband Simon—everything tumbled out.

Charles held her elbow, guided her onto curbs and down again. Something drove her on—the broken china Harold threw at the wall, his belligerence toward Berthea, and his final demand before he deployed—that she conceive an heir.

Mrs. T.'s rooftop appeared behind the row houses, and weariness washed over Addie. Still, she felt lighter.

"You have told me all?"

"I think so. Now you know who I am." The dusky western sky outlined his profile and he bent his head toward her.

"If you ever need to revisit this, Addie, I will be most happy to listen. If you never wish to, I will welcome that, too." His touch on her cheek sent a tremble through her.

"But you err, dear girl." Gentleness softened the lines around his eyes. "You've told me not who you are, but who *Harold* is, and who *he* thinks you ought to be. Yet a year ago, Kathryn chirruped wonderful things about you all the way to Liverpool station. Since then I've seen far more.

"I know who you are when Mrs. Culver describes your efficient work, when you show kindness to that extremely shy girl who works next door, and through our pleasant Saturdays together. And Mum's always been a cold fish, though you may not see her that way. The way you bring out her other side borders on phenomenal."

He pulled her toward him. "I'd as soon never meet this bloke Harold. I don't suffer fools well, men who see no further than their own minds and condemn others because of their own insecurity." His voice cracked and the evening breeze brought a whiff of the Channel. "You described not who you are, Addie Bledsoe, but what you have endured."

At the outskirts of Figeac, an old peasant gripped Domingo's wrist with tobacco-stained fingers. He spoke with a tremble.

"Vichy sent an encyclical two weeks ago. All boys of sixteen must register by the end of May. The Das Reich Division plundered our village yesterday, rounded up the artisans, administrators, and teachers—600 deported to Montauban, others to German work camps, or what they call concentration camps."

"But Gabirel is only fourteen."

"Ah—yes, I remember your brother. Yes, Gabirel, the boy who passes by my house on his way to school. I heard that Jean-Luc took him out of the building and headed to the Ségala."

With a relieved sigh, Domingo eyed the northern heights. Then Kate noted the wildness in his eyes as he flung himself up a fiercely angled cobblestone street, leaving the messenger stranded.

Past a ransacked *boulangerie*, where women and children harvested glass shards, Kate followed him. Past a tall building with five expansive arched windows on the third level, seven smaller ones on the second, and a cloistered walkway meeting a stone wall.

Blood-spattered awnings, foodstuffs, clothing, and china strewed the street. Broken tables and chair legs stuck out, dogs licked leftovers from cobblestones, and smoky dust roiled from burned-out foundations.

Obviously, the attack came in the marketplace as peasants gathered to sell their wares. From all evidence, the soldiers had shown no mercy. A ruined balcony surveyed the smattered street, geraniums and poppies sprawled from their pots, and a hapless featherbed sagged from a railing.

A woebegone tract fluttered along like a dry leaf. Kate snatched it on the run and glanced through, keeping one eye on Domingo's back.

Strong phrases urged women "towards a mobilization *générale, actif.*" At the bottom, The *Union des Femmes Françaises* claimed authorship and called for women to support *L'Armée de la Libération,* as in the Great War. "We can do no less. Mount demonstrations, declare general strikes, provide food and shelter to *la Résistance*."

Bold letters quoted Général De Gaulle. "National insurrection is inseparable from national liberation."

A woman with tangled hair wept on her doorstep, and another comforted her. A small child's hollow eyes ripped at Kate's heart, and from somewhere inside, a baby wailed. Two half-grown boys, obviously now considered local workmen, grappled with a badly damaged front door.

Then Domingo dropped off a street that curved into the countryside and plunged into brush that did violence to her pack. She commandeered her body into a sleek vessel with one mission: to keep him in sight.

Didn't he tell her his father and older brother died in the last fighting on the Spanish border? She shuddered to think that his one remaining brother had been taken, leaving his mother all alone.

Through countryside bedecked in green, Kate's heels cried for attention. But a story about an agent caught by the Gestapo flashed through her mind. Though the woman eventually escaped, the enemy pulled out her toenails. These painful heels would have to wait.

The land burst in late spring growth, but Figeac's scenes haunted her, along with the information about Gabirel. And last night, another wayfarer said Das Reich took 1,200 citizens from Montpelier as they exited the cinemas. The next day, eighty were sent to Germany—perhaps to work, perhaps to be shot to death.

Domingo swooped into a valley, then up again, straight into brambles Kate would have sworn contained no passage. But now they scurried through another valley as idyllic as the *Wind in the Willows* when Ratty meets a seafarer by the riverbank.

In the distance on the far side of a stream, a wide meadow beckoned, and Domingo's posture altered. Surely, they must be close to his home, all he had left in this world.

Monsieur Le Blanc's weak voice wafted to Kate. "I sought you because of my promise to *le Renard* ... you are my family."

The small leather pouch of francs he urged her to open the night before he died lay in her pack. But he had bequeathed her something with far more meaning. The faint glow from Madame Chalomet's barn window highlighted a gold chain threaded through a brooch whose convex glass cover opened and closed.

Monsieur dropped the treasure into Kate's hand, and she opened the latch. Inside, a hazy photo showed a baby and a toddler on a man's knee.

"You and my father, with your father?"

She clung to the tenderness in Monsieur's, "*Oui.*" That moment would live with her forever, signifying all that mattered most—family. Of course Domingo raced toward his people. If she had a mother or a brother alive in this world, she would do the same.

He leaped a six-foot creek, and as if waking from sleep, turned. His expression displayed fury, terror, willpower, and resolve, but he paused to offer her his hand.

She found a rock midstream and grabbed for him as she made the jump to the steep side. Domingo's panting exceeded hers, and fear radiated the moist, shady air. His temples wet and his voice shaking, he hesitated.

"Maman—"

Kate longed to somehow ease his anxiety. When her fingertips grazed his forearm, he blinked and lurched ahead.

On the meadow's far side, they veered left again. Rocks. Brush. Finally, rich green pasture brimming with placid sheep and a small figure armed with a wooden crook. Domingo raced to the diminutive shepherdess and swallowed her in his arms.

The petite, wizened woman dressed in black peered around his thick arm. Domingo swung around, still panting, and swept his hand behind him.

"Our home—Maman."

That one, simple word razed Kate's heart. From his mother's salt and pepper hair to a meadow spiked with rocks, smoke wisps from a stone chimney, and rock walls encircling all, Kate took in the scene. So this was the mother who drew Domingo home. They'd arrived at his place in this world.

She took a slow step forward. "*Bonsoir, Madame.*" Bright dark eyes greeted Kate, and dry, work-worn fingers squeezed her hand.

Domingo hulked over his mother on the way to the farmhouse. Basque chatter tickled Kate's ears. Sprinkled with sparse French, some phrases made sense. Spicy fragrance, vetted and laced into a strong stew, welcomed them into the house, and between grandiose bites, she could tell Domingo recovered recent history.

All of a sudden, Kate wanted to know his family name, and scanned the room. There, above the oven—an inscription on stone hung from a leather strap looped over a nail. She refilled their cups from the cook stove's burbling kettle to get a closer look.

Ibarra.

Domingo Ibarra.

The name made music on her tongue.

Chapter Twenty-eight

Songbirds signaled the end of day as Madame Ibarra glanced out the window. "Gabirel should be home by now—he is never late."

Domingo took a long breath. "Maman, a man in Figeac told us Jean-Luc took him to safety in the Ségala, before the Bosche raided the village."

She swayed in her chair, and Domingo was on his feet, supporting her. "Edorta did the right thing, I am sure."

"The *gaiztoa zara* have come to Figeac?"

"Yes, those evil men left a trail of destruction. But Gabirel escaped. Come, let's milk the animals."

He led her across the yard, murmuring in comforting tones like a father with his young daughter. He mixed in enough French so Kate could follow his meaning. *Took Gabirel from the schoolhouse—"* He was repeating the story to calm Madame Ibarra.

In the stone barn Madame Ibarra pulled a small wooden stool beside a goat. A black and white cat mewed her way to the perfect spot for some milk. Domingo said something to his mother and gestured for Kate to accompany him outside.

"Is she all right?"

Domingo rubbed his forehead, as if it held the world's troubles, and studied the far north.

"I can stay here with her until you return."

His eyes traveled to the earth, to a stone animal enclosure, and back to Kate as if unable to comprehend her meaning. Nothing they'd encountered on the trail had this effect on him.

But Kate persevered. "We can find a way."

"The SS are here among us."

"They are in the Dordogne too. They're everywhere—it's all the same." She held up her palms. "No place is any safer."

Domingo huffed and took off for the sheep pen, but she couldn't let the conversation end like this. "Domingo Ibarra?"

He drew up short and half-turned with a near growl. "You would need to learn a great many things."

"Then teach me."

He ran his fingers under his cap. "Let me think."

She took a step toward the barn, but he reached for her wrist. "No. You are right, Agent Merce—Katarin. *Merci*—"

He stretched his rippling shoulders, and a deep frown etched his forehead. "However, the sheep do not know you, you understand?" As if to punctuate his statement, a bevy of *baahs* broke out in the sheepfold. "And I cannot know how long it will take."

"I will do my best. You needn't worry about your mother. I will stay with her."

His eyes held hers, sending a shiver down her spine as he leaned in with the mellow aroma of stew and warm milk. "You are Amerikan, perhaps, but like a Basque woman, stronger than all others."

He drew back, and a hunger wider than the English Channel catapulted through Kate. She grasped his thick arms, not so much to touch him as to remain upright. A single word left her lips as he let go and disappeared behind the barn.

"Domingo."

Madame Ibarra shut the barn door and crossed the yard to the house, so Kate followed her. Some time later when Domingo came in, he addressed them both. "For now, we must get some sleep."

But long after he left the house, Kate lay awake. In the thick of night, she woke to voices drifting from outside.

"—fighters parachuting in. English, Canadians, Americans, even Poles. *L'invasion* is upon us."

"We have no idea what day?"

"All depends on the Channel weather, but the attack will come from the north."

"And our Maquisards will join them."

"Without question. The ammunition piles rise. In some quarters, we even have bazookas."

"Do you think Gabirel will stay behind if all the partisans leave the camp? Hardly! I must search him out, but to leave Maman—"

"Jean-Luc arrived back here today, torn between protecting his family and keeping Gabirel safe."

"He would not make that decision lightly."

"What about the agent?"

Kate bit her lip. She'd become one more confusing piece in Domingo's quandary.

"I gave my word to accompany her to the Dordogne—"

"Yet the danger traveling there has worsened, and we need workers too."

Kate risked rising from her makeshift bed near the hearth. She tiptoed to an open window and resonated to Domingo's heavy sigh.

"Still, I gave my word, Père."

So this was the parish priest Domingo quoted when Monsieur died. *"Père Gaspard would say the angels carry him away, to rest from his labors."*

"Of course you did. But even the Almighty sometimes changes His mind. Remember, he chose Saul to be king, but later replaced him with David?"

"So keeping one's word becomes a matter of circumstance?"

Père Gaspard's deep chuckle caught Kate off guard. He sounded so earthy, so human, so—*real.*

"The war has taken us over, body and soul, so everything slants toward our deliverance, *l'Invasion.* You'd think the Allies were the Messiah, though we know they're mere men.

"But our foundations still stand, Domingo. Some things never topple, though they may shake. Our calling and the channels we must take have altered, and keeping one's word is more a matter of intent.

"In a way, that hasn't changed at all, for scripture says God looks on the heart, not the outward appearance. Perhaps this war will help us see as He does. I have no doubt He knows your intentions.

"There I go, pontificating in the middle of the night, when you need sleep. Your way will become clear to you. Let me know what you decide."

The priest put his arm over Domingo's shoulder before retreating to the road, and Domingo turned past the sheep pen toward the barn. He stood for long minutes, petting the dog and staring over a hip-high stone wall at a wooly grey mass huddled together against late-May chill.

When he walked on to the barn, Kate crept back to her quilt. Somewhere above, a mouse or bat skittered, and Madame Ibarra's snore penetrated the south wall—such a mighty noise from her petite form.

Men parachuting in—If only she could listen to the BBC tonight. Mr. T had warned against becoming a radio operator, but at least then she would know what was happening. As it was, she was holed up in relative safety but caused even more turmoil for Domingo.

Her thoughts drifted to the sheep, safe and peaceful in their fold. That image juxtaposed with Domingo's conversation with Père Gaspard—two men driven by hope, attempting to make their way through events beyond their control.

She sank into her quilt, most likely fashioned by Domingo's mother or grandmother. Worn cotton fabric as soft as lamb's wool, held together by single stitches. *Parachuting in.* Gradually, the rhythm of Madame Ibarra's snore ushered Kate into sleep.

"Harold is not at Greenham Commons. My comrade discovered him in one of the first infantry units scheduled to cross the Channel."

Glad to see Charles again after three weeks away, Addie wanted to hug him. But the outer office was full of staff, and besides, an old voice taunted her. *You're an unfaithful wife. Your disobedience puts you under God's curse.*

Harold's severe chastisement, still very much alive in her memory, obliterated the safety of Charles' office and sent her pulse racing. A stanza from an old hymn quieted her. *Still, my soul, be still. The Lord is on thy side.*

"I've no idea why he wrote his mother about the Air Force, but this puts him farther from London. Rest assured, infantry privates enjoy no leave before the Invasion, and certainly not to London."

Comforting news, but befuddling. Why would Harold stoop to make up the Air Force story? And why spin it only to Berthea?

By the time she returned from a post box run, Charles' door was closed, and the rest of the day he remained in his office. At least Addie thought so. But when she stuck her hand into her coat pocket on the way home she found his note.

> *Sudden call back to coast. Say hello to the vegetables and pull some weeds for me on Saturday.*
> *I will miss you,*
> *Charles*

When Charles returned on Wednesday, important-looking people visited his office, but five minutes after Addie dove into her stack of filing, he waved her in.

"I have a delivery for Mr. Firth. Do you mind awfully?"

"Not at all."

He lowered his voice to a whisper, and she couldn't miss the strain in his expression, despite his outward cheer.

"The cloud cover slows Channel operations and darkens our spirits, but you will brighten passersby, as you do me."

Heat flooded Addie's cheeks as she took the large envelope Charles held out. "Do bring me word of our favorite bookseller."

"I will. And thank you for locating Harold. I didn't mean to seem ungrateful."

"I daresay I cannot imagine you so."

"And I can't think why he would write such a thing to his mother."

"I puzzle over that, as well."

Addie grabbed her sweater. "Mrs. Culver, I've an errand for Mr. T."

"Will you pass a post box? With everyone on the streets in such a dither these days, I'd rather not make the trip." Mrs. Culver raised an eyebrow toward a pile of mail, so Addie tied it up and descended the stairs.

People headed in every direction. Busses exchanged passengers, office girls streaked by on bicycles loaded down with mail packets and brown cardboard boxes. Charles said young men once held their delivery jobs but now waited at the coast for the day everyone anticipated.

And Harold was among them. It was easier to picture him roaring out of an LST, one of the flat rectangular water vehicles the Allied Command created for the landing, than in a bomber. Surely he knew Berthea would be proud of him being in the Invasion, no matter what his job.

But are you proud? Yes, Addie decided. She could honor his battle exploits without submitting to his ruthless authority. *But if he survives the war, what then?*

She raised her chin into the cool late May mist enveloping London. She simply couldn't think about that—it did no good.

Sometimes, though, in the dark of night, a snakelike hiss assaulted her hard-earned tranquility. And on this dismal, drippy day, that marauder worked overtime. *Estranged or not, how can you think to chum with another man? Harold was right about you—disobedient and worthy of divine punishment. Truth be told, you deserve the likes of Harold Bledsoe, and you're stuck with him forever.*

This accusation stole Addie's sleep, yet morning always brought her back to their confrontation in the chicken house after she had painted the kitchen wainscoting. Harold cursed her that day, and claimed God had, too. But Berthea, his own mother, sided with her and so did Jane.

What happened next couldn't have surprised Addie more. Their church sent Harold to the seminary in St. Louis for the winter months, and there, he kept up his assault on the draft board. Unbelievably, the army finally accepted him, while she ventured to help Kate. Now, she enjoyed her job, and hope ruled her heart whatever the future held.

Reviewing these surprising events lightened her outlook. Besides, now she knew Harold trained at the coast, not at Greenham Commons.

She skipped a few steps, as she and Kate often did en route to Aunt Alvina's house after school. A breeze blew some papers across the street, and an office worker pursued them in a wild chase. So overwrought by lack of sleep from the bombing, no one else seemed to notice.

When Addie arrived in front of the bookshop, Mr. Firth ushered her in where she piled the letters on his counter. When she handed him Charles' envelope, Mr. Firth smiled and whispered, "Just in time. The need has grown overnight. Please thank your stateside friends for their aid."

His assistant, with a butler's bearing, appeared between two tall shelves like a prairie dog coming up for air. At the same time, the doorbell jangled, and a customer entered in a hurry with an urgent request. Mr. Firth led him down an aisle of shelves.

When he returned, he nodded to Addie and retrieved a slim volume from under the counter. "Please inform your employer that one of his favorites came yesterday."

"Thank you." Addie stepped toward the door and Mr. Firth held up her envelopes.

"I shall post these for you at three."

"Oh, my—thank you." She pulled her sweater closer against a quickening breeze that forced curls out of her already straggling Veronica Lake roll. Kate had become the queen of that hairdo, but Addie's early morning efforts led to wayward curls by afternoon.

If only the weather would clear. Tension sobered a jostling crowd of pedestrians, and she searched in vain for a smile. Mrs. T said the tube station queues started midafternoon now, with so many seeking a safe place to sleep.

"After all this time, some older people think of the stations as home. Terrible, yet if they've lost their homes, where else can they go?"

Faces all around Addie testified to the dire times, and she had just delivered money to help displaced Jewish people from all over the world. The Allied Command kept calling Charles to the coast, battle would soon begin across the Channel, and Kate— In London's sea of worried countenances, everything seemed overwhelming.

Nothing changed as she entered the office building. Workers spent their lunchtimes hunched over a radio in the foyer. Addie paused to listen as she rounded the third floor stairwell. "On May 25, Mr. Churchill addressed foreign affairs:

Taking everything into consideration, including men and money, war effort, expanse of territory, we can claim to be an equal to those great Powers, but not, in my view, a superior. It would be a great mistake for me, as head of the British Government, or, I may add—speaking to this Committee as a most respected institution— the Grand Alliance, or for the House, to take it upon ourselves, to lay down the law to all those different countries, including the two great Powers with which we have to work, if the world is to be brought back into a good condition.

This small Island and this marvellous structure of States and dependencies which have gathered round it, if we all hold together, occupy a worthy place in the vanguard of the nations. It is idle to suppose that we are the only people who are to prescribe what all other countries, for their own good, are to do. Many other ideas and forces come into play and nothing could be more unwise than for the meeting of Prime Ministers, for instance, to attempt to prescribe for all countries the way they should go.

Even Mrs. Culver joined the crowd. When she spotted Addie, she leaned out to whisper her response to the address.

"Quite the humbling we Brits have suffered, dear. Once the world was at our beck and call, but my husband always believed we'd gotten too high and mighty for our britches, empiring this and empiring that."

"Well, we all need each other now. There's no other way to make it through."

"Indeed. And now, back to work." Mrs. Culver hailed another staff member and went on ahead. The radio announcer's voice droned on, but on the second stair from the top, a gift arrived for Addie—an epiphany about the meaning of her experiences, including the difficult ones.

In light of Mr. Churchill's humble attitude and Mrs. Culver's commentary, she visualized the man she'd collided with by the post box. He'd blamed the accident on her, but Mr. Firth stepped in and took her part. A panorama of past deliverances swept before her—Ruthie protecting her from Dad, Berthea confronting Harold on her behalf, Jane encouraging her to find her voice, and always, Kate supporting her.

The weather might be nasty, war news might be swirling like cigarette smoke up the stairwell, and tonight would bring more air attacks. But with persistence, things would change. All this individual effort, multiplied, would surely force Germany's come-uppance. Though the Allies suffered trials, they were not forsaken, and neither was she. Not ever.

In the empty outer office, she hung her sweater on her chair and glanced toward Charles, who bent over his desk. On second look, Addie realized he held his head in his hands, and she closed the door so no one would see.

He jerked up when she stepped in with the volume from Mr. Firth. His glazed look startled her, so she slid the volume on his desk and backed away.

"Please stay."

His shaky invitation, more like a croak, jarred her. Something had happened. For a week now, Mrs. T had nursed a cold, but she seemed fine this morning.

"Is it your mother?"

"No, no. Something top secret, down on the coast a few weeks ago. I shoved it into a corner of my mind, but—" She'd never seen him look so glum. "I feel I must tell you, but not a word to anyone."

An icy blast slithered down Addie's neck and shoulders.

"I assume with Mr. Churchill's speech today, everyone is perched in the stairwell as they usually are?"

"Except for Mrs. Culver and a couple others, but they're down at the other end of the office." Charles locked his doors, and Addie's chest tightened even more.

"At Slapton Sands back in April, the forces staged a practice LST landing, to harden the troops with live ammunition. They took soldiers out into landing craft. Officers drew a white line on the beach, behind which the Marines must stay until firing stopped."

He slid his chair back. "As things proceeded, the organizers set the firing time back two hours, but the landing craft failed to receive the message." He stared out the window, at the floor, and finally at his hands.

"Our own fire killed many, and that's not the worst of it. Out in Lyme Bay, carriers constantly defend against German E-boats, but the HMS Scimitar became disabled early on. Word failed to reach the landing craft commanders, so nine German E-boats slipped through and waged a battle. Before it ended—"

He dropped his arms like weights, and Addie held her breath.

"We lost a thousand men." The clock ticked away a long minute. "Ten officers with full knowledge of Invasion plans went missing.

Until we found them, all activity halted. If the Germans captured even one and tortured the Invasion's exact location from him—"

Limited knowledge of Gestapo tactics served Addie's imagination well enough. Charles squeezed his eyes shut.

"Back in December, the command evacuated the village, so they required more men to search—"

Haunting images filled Addie's mind. Charles wading out into freezing, oil-infested waters, dragging bodies ashore, turning over bloated blue faces, grappling for ID tags and burying not tens, but hundreds. *Hundreds.*

The last time at the gardens, he seemed reluctant to get their tools from the shed. She thought little of his comment, "I'll stick to hand weeding today."

Now, more black than blue showed in his eyes. "A gruesome scene, but we finally found the ten victims with the BIGOT clearance." He drummed his fingers on his desk. "Now you know why I've been such debatable company of late."

A chair scraped in the outer office, reminding Addie this was no time to fulfill her longing to embrace Charles. But she did touch his hand.

"You're still the best company I know, Charles Tenney."

His left shoulder sloped more than usual as he stared out the window. She slipped out and closed the door.

The fate of those soldiers consumed Addie, as had the Battle of Dieppe in August of '42 when she heard that nearly a thousand Canadians died. Now, along with sorrow for the lost soldiers' families, sympathy for those involved in the clean-up filled her.

Such a puzzle—why had God allowed the communication failure in the exercise at Slapton Sands? But something else troubled her even more. Why had Charles trusted her with this military secret?

I feel I must tell you, but not a word to anyone. This was so unlike him—what would cause him to violate military confidentiality?

On the bus ride home, Addie tried to block out conversations centered on the much-needed break in the cloud cover. Helpless about the weather, she felt the same way about the Slapton Sands debacle and the war in general.

At bedtime, Mrs. T held her palm out the kitchen door. "Maybe the mist is lifting. Do you think so?"

"I wish I could say yes. But surely, with all of England and France praying, the clouds will lift soon."

"You're honest, yet hopeful. Charles loved *The Little Engine that Could* as a child. *I think I can, I think I can.* So I repeat, *the clouds must lift, the clouds must lift*—

In bed, Addie considered Mrs. T's evaluation. She certainly tried to be honest, although Harold had accused her of deceit.

Hopeful, she could agree to. But during the worst winter on the farm, she almost lost hope. Kate's letters held her up, along with Berthea's growing capacity for joy after Harold's father died. More than once, borrowed faith saw her through.

The hall clock chimed eleven, twelve, two, and three. Grisly scenes floated through her consciousness—no wonder Charles looked so pale when he returned.

At long last, she fell into a fitful sleep, and in the morning, discovered Mrs. T had a similar bad night. They drank tea and ate their toast in silence, then Mrs. T went upstairs when Addie volunteered to set the kitchen to rights.

Still in her bathrobe, she had just cleared the table when someone knocked. Perhaps their newsy early-bird neighbor—maybe the Invasion had begun.

When she opened the door, there stood Charles, looking even more beaten down than yesterday. His bloodshot eyes and unruly hair testified to a sleepless night.

"Sorry to disturb you so early. Has Mum gone out already?" His face paled even more, and Addie's heartbeat tripped.

"She's upstairs, getting dressed."

"Ah. Good. That is—" He turned his hat brim with his fingers. "Perhaps you ought to sit."

His ominous tone froze Addie's insides. "Should we go to the courtyard?"

"A perfect idea." They sat on the bench, and he pulled out a folded white paper.

Her stomach did a jitterbug.

"Please forgive me. Obedience to military rules bogged me down yesterday, but with the dawn, my duty shone clear."

He held out the folded paper. "I don't know how else to break this news."

Chapter Twenty-nine

A pleasant morning breeze accompanied Kate and Domingo on a tour of the Ibarra land. "The dog knows the way through the pastures, but this distance challenges Maman. Normally by this time, we'd have taken the sheep to higher ground, but everything has changed."

By the time they returned to the homestead, a man appeared with word that sparked alarm in Domingo's eyes. "In Toulouse, the tanks are refitted and fueled."

He went on, but Kate could see Domingo hung on *refitted and fueled*. Only 185 kilometers through Montauban to Figeac, straight through this homestead. Time was running out.

The partisan left. Domingo entered the barn, and Kate weeded in the garden until Madame Ibarra gestured for them to come and eat. After checking everywhere else for Domingo, Kate climbed to the granary, where Domingo sat cross-legged, fiddling with a stalk of straw.

"Your mother is calling."

He shrugged.

"I have an idea. Use your contacts to give me a new identity— make me your mother's cousin or whatever will work."

His lips twitched. Was it so difficult to accept this small bit of help from an outsider?

She backed down the ladder, but at the threshold, Domingo suddenly stood close. She smelled the straw embedded in his shirt as he breathed one single word.

"*Merci.*"

The tremble in Charles' hand sent Addie's heartbeat into a wild dance. How could any news be worse than what he had already said? She unfolded the paper once, twice. His left foot beat a singular *rat-tat-tat* against the stonework.

Typed lists filled the paper—names, locations, and descriptions. A third of the way down, three words noosed her neck.

Deceased Identified On Beach.

Alphabetized names blurred. She stopped at *Bledsoe, Harold, PFC.*

No—surely God would allow Harold to storm the French coast. Surely his vengeance could be put to use.

But she read his name again, then let it slip over her lips. A suffocating sensation throttled her.

Charles covered her hand with his. "This must come as such a shock, no matter what you've faced with him."

"I—" An avalanche coiled behind her tongue.

Charles reached for her other hand. "Would you like to go for a walk?"

Addie shook her head, but it seemed detached from the rest of her body. As she re-read Harold's name, heavy mist bled the ink into the paper.

Charles' expressive eyes kept her in reality. "You have all my sympathy, dear girl, but you must keep this quiet. Harold's mother will receive the official news but only months from now, with the Invasion casualty lists."

"I—should feel something, but—"

"At such a time, there are no *shoulds*. Your emotions will sort themselves out."

The plumbing remonstrated as Mrs. Tenney bathed. It was time to get ready for work, yet Harold had vanished from time.

A wanton tide of emotion threatened Addie. "Charles, thank you."

"If you would like the day off, or several, I'll arrange it."

Jumbled thoughts assailed her. Harold, buried in a little English coastal town, while Berthea still saw him as an Air Force bombardier—all his dreams of meting out retribution to the Nazis dissipated in an instant.

The fine haze blanketing London glistened on Charles' forehead.

"Thank you, but I'd rather come to work."

He rose and pulled her up. "Do you want to walk a while? I can stay longer."

"Thank you, but I'm all right."

"You'll be able to come alone?"

"It will do me good." When he turned down the walk after squeezing her hand, she watched him disappear in what had become an incessant drizzle. Prayers notwithstanding, the dripping shroud still hung over the city.

Not ready to face Mrs. T, Addie circled back into the courtyard, where spring invigorated the gnarled wisteria despite the lack of sunshine. She collapsed on the bench under a gnarled honeysuckle like the one in Iowa, and the sweet-smelling pink blossoms brought the Bledsoe farm near.

There, this same sweet, heavy scent wafted during late May and early June when bees sated themselves with nectar. Addie fingered one of the delicate pink flowers.

"Harold will never smell honeysuckle again." The rough wooden bench, flaked by wind and weather, grounded her. Life was like that, offering tender blossoms and old wood full of slivers at the same time.

Tack-tack. She leaned her head to her knees as the milkman's pony trotted by. A few weeks ago when an incendiary set one of the dairy's stables on fire, Mrs. T had bemoaned the poor animals inside. Addie hoped the little pony she'd secretly christened Honey survived, and the next morning, there she was, as if nothing happened.

Something about that same innocent *clip-clop* loosed a cataract of tears. The gurgle of bath water through the pipes told Addie Mrs. T had finished. Soon she'd swing the door open, and a familiar creak would mark her path down the hallway to her room. That was the thing about old houses—they kept tabs on their inhabitants. Living on the farm, where Harold scrutinized her every move, had taught her that.

Her sobbing faded, and clear thoughts re-entered her mind. She'd discovered so much about Harold that she'd been unable to see back then. All the while, Kate had been right—something complicated drove Harold. What grown man lies to his own mother to somehow impress her?

That entire story about being a bombardier originated in his miserable, sick soul. Addie stamped her foot. "Of course he wouldn't write that lie to me. He knew Berthea wouldn't know the difference, but that Kate would read it and call him out."

In a way, his strict religiosity carried out the same kind of duplicity—Halberton folks thought of him as strong, reliable, and trustworthy. Poor Berthea—balancing being his mother and realizing he put on such a good act. Still, Harold must have felt desperate for her approval to write her such a bald-faced lie.

Now that the first onslaught of emotion ended, anger edged its way in. "Wasn't deceit one of the sins Harold accused me of? Oh, if only Kate were here—she could help me analyze this. She'd say, 'Oh right! Now we discover Mr. Holier-than-thou had a dishonest chink in his armor.'"

The milk cart had passed long ago. Addie breathed deep and stood up—she'd probably be late for work. But this courtyard, an oasis here in London, made the ideal spot to express her confusion and find enough peace to make it through the day.

She scanned the relentless gray sky. From somewhere in eternity, did Harold see her tears for his unhappiness, his early death, and his lack of an heir? More than anything, she'd wept because he missed the fighting—no one had ever longed so desperately to be a soldier.

In life, he'd never admitted to being wrong, but now, from his new vantage point, would he? It was a Kate kind of question—but no Kate to work through to the answer.

Back in the kitchen, she wavered. Maybe she ought to stay home after all—Charles would cover for her with Mrs. Culver, and she'd have to make up some story for Mrs. T. But how could she possibly hide her up-and-down emotions all day, or explain why she decided to miss work?

Hurrying like a criminal, she brewed another pot of rationed tea. Teddy, her acquaintance from the Chicago train station, recently sent money for the children and included a packet of precious tealeaves, some coffee, and several tins of sardines.

That night, she and Mrs. T feasted. "I do believe I could become fond of sardines, though at one time I wouldn't have touched them. Even the smell bothered me. The wonders war works, turning my snooty appetite upside down."

"*The Wonders War Works*—there's a book title, don't you think? Kate and I used to keep a list of titles for future masterpieces."

"Do you remember any?"

"Not really. We chose mostly dark and mysterious ones, like *Shadows Over Halberton* or *Lingering Longings*. We were both such romantics."

"How did Kathryn's aunt respond?"

"She encouraged us. That was when we thought we might become famous authors some day."

"I daresay you still might."

"I wouldn't doubt one day Kate will pen her war memoirs."

"Or you. You certainly have the tenacity to do that, Addie."

In spite of the gloom, the robin twittered through the window while Addie's tea brewed. A forbidden second cupful fortified her, and she took a deep breath.

"No use bandying about here when I'm needed at work." Exactly what Kate would say. With a silent prayer to avoid seeing Mrs. T, Addie dressed and left for the bus stop. It seemed strange to take the packed bus rather than walking, but it was better than being late. In the aisle with passengers pressing on either side, she rubbed a plaguing pain in her temple.

Probably from crying—ah well, the onslaught clears my mind.

Passengers' conversations lulled her into such mellowness, she missed hearing her name until someone waved a hand in front of her. Red hair swept into a kerchief greeted Addie above eyes as green as emeralds.

"Addie, isn't it? American, aren't you?"

At first, she couldn't place the passenger, but then remembered. "Why, Evelyn—it's so good to see you."

Evelyn seemed eager to talk. "What has happened with you these past months?"

"Working in the office and weeding in the gardens north of town on Saturdays."

"Bully for you. Volunteering takes the edge off, I've found. Your husband?"

Addie gulped. "He—ah, died in an accident." There, she said it.

"I'm sorry to hear it."

"Thank you for asking. How is that fellow you introduced us to? Jerry, wasn't it?"

Evelyn bobbed her head. "We're going to be wed."

"How wonderful. When?"

"This coming Saturday, if we can fit the ceremony in between our jobs." Evelyn's grin showed a fine set of teeth.

"When did he ask you?"

"T'was touching, dearie. Last Sunday, right there in the mucky garage, he took my hands. I thought he'd gone daft. He held his hat over his heart and jolly well said, 'Evie, I don't want to go home at night without you. Would you be my wife?' I said yes, and that was that. So now, all that I lost, except Mum, of course—a place in this life—has returned to me. Jerry has his Mum's place, and it's a fine one. And how is Kate?"

"Kate—oh, she's—so busy. I've lost track of—"

Evelyn leaned close and whispered, "I know she's gone, dearie. If it's any consolation, I was there when she left. It's all on the sly, you know, but my nighttime tasks—let's just say, I witnessed Kate fly off."

"You did? What—"

"Oh, here's my stop." Evelyn jostled a big package down the aisle, paused on the top step and turned back. "Maybe we can meet sometime."

"That would be wonderful."

What a coincidence—Kate might not even have known a friend either drove her to the airfield or helped with the takeoff.

Jerry's admission of need was so simply stated and direct. What a lovely way to ask for someone's hand. Addie searched her memory in vain for Harold's proposal. With her slim prospects, he always assumed they would marry. The second half of her junior year revolved around him, the outstanding kicker for Halberton's football team, and one of few who would attend Iowa State in the fall.

At the time, she felt so lucky. Remembering her state of mind sent a wave of nausea through her. At least that seemed like thirty years ago instead of five. More people entered, and the driver wove through traffic as sparse as Addie's memories of good times with Harold.

Four stops later she got off. At the very moment she opened the heavy office door, the fog gave way to a sprite of sunshine, and she turned to face the sudden brightness parting the clouds.

"What is it Jane always says? Keep your eyes to the sunshine, and you won't see the shadows? Yes. I think that's how it goes."

Other last-minute arrivals climbed the stairs too, and their energy strengthened Addie. Everyone knew their destination in this building and came prepared to do their part. One of them, an extremely shy girl with usually downcast eyes, smiled at her and exchanged greetings.

This morning, she looked Addie in the eye for the first time. Mrs. Culver said she had suffered much in the bombings, but might still come out of her shell. Addie made a note to initiate a chat with her one of these days.

At one with the mass of stenographers and office girls, she leaned against the stairwell turn, knowing she had made the right decision to be out with people today. She needed landings like this—places to pull back and take stock. The chicken house provided that for her back in Iowa, with its cackling hens.

But now she had friends, even with Kathryn gone. Some of the girls here confided in her during breaks, and Mrs. Culver accepted her, too. When she walked into the office, she sensed that she belonged here. At the spacious room's far end, Charles conferred with a worker, and Mrs. Culver greeted her.

"Good morning Addie. You'll see a stack of paperwork on your desk."

"Good morning, Mrs. Culver. Thank you."

That stack offered tasks to occupy her mind. She still couldn't pinpoint her feelings, but that was all right—they could take a back seat until later.

Charles walked between her desk and Mrs. Culver's, a load of files in his hands. He sent Addie a message with his eyes: *Be good to yourself. Take all the time you need.*

Just like that, words came to her. *Love is patient—love is kind.* She took up her pen and a scrap of paper to record them.

Although I have been hurt, I can love again. I've known broken trust and sadness, but I still believe in happiness. I can move forward with confidence. I can live in hope.

All morning, the room hummed with constant action. Later, she caught sight of Charles bent over his desk—would he sense her concentration and look up? When he did, she could almost feel the touch of his fingers, and drank in the warmth of his smile.

She recalled a high school day when Kate swooned over a quote Mrs. Morfordson wrote on the board. *All I have seen teaches me to trust the Creator for all I have not seen. R. W. Emerson*

A sense of well-being washed through her, and something told her Kate was safe. Surely meeting Evelyn on the bus had been a sign—whether Kate knew it or not, a friend had seen her off.

Mrs. Culver gestured to her from the photocopy machine, so Addie slipped her paper into her pocket. As always, Kate was following her heart. And even restless, angry Harold had found rest at last. All was well.

"We have a mountain of copies to make today, Addie. Are you quite ready?"

"Yes, Ma'am, quite."

Chapter Thirty

Aman in a pressed Gendarme uniform exited the rectory as Domingo walked in, so he drew as far away as he could. Père Gaspard kept company with both sides because of his position in the community, and made it work. But that didn't mean Domingo had to do the same.

When Père spotted Domingo, he rose from his desk and led the way through a maze of stone hallways. "I've finished the work for you. Come along."

Somehow, this parish priest had managed to set up a small press in the far corner of the rectory basement, separate from the rest of the foundation. Technically, if his bishop were to visit, he explained, this room was built on a foundation separate from the rest of the building.

As dark as a bat's den, this desolate space might have been a cave out in the wilds. But from the yard or inside the rectory, nobody could hear the press. While collaborator Gendarmes made their so-called confessions in small wooden booths along the back of the sanctuary, down here in this safe fissure, the *la Résistance* carried out its work.

Père's linen robe swished back and forth along a narrow passageway. The only other sound, moisture seeping from pipe casings in the ceiling, accompanied the distinct earthy scent, like fresh-dug beets plunged into cold water. Where all the drips ended was a mystery—somewhere in the building's bowels.

An ideal setting for undercover work, but the dank walls made

Domingo long for fresh air, as he had when Kate sent her messages from Madame Chalomet's secluded cave. Père switched on a bare bulb and picked up an envelope from a lopsided table next to the press. His sideways grin always caused Domingo to wonder what he would try next, and his wiry red hair, bobbing in every direction, heightened that sense of the unexpected.

"These papers go with the card. I hope your agent can pretend well." He switched off the light and started out through another door, leaving Domingo in darkness for a second.

"Did you see that fellow on your way in?"

Domingo nodded. Père knew how he distrusted the Gendarmes.

"I know you're in a hurry to find Gabirel, but bear with me."

For the moment, Domingo disregarded his worries about Maman, Gabirel, and Kathryn to offer Père his full attention. Maybe the Allies had landed—maybe today was the day.

Minutes later, Père dipped under an archway, opened a door, and turned up some makeshift stairs. "That gendarme fakes his collaboration. He helps us out in more ways than you could guess. And he brought good news today. They've found *la Corbeille*—one less thing to worry about. I hope that lightens your heart, Domingo. It's another sign that we shall prevail."

"*Oui*. Will you check in on Maman while I'm gone?"

"If I can, but even an angel could not keep up with all the directions I travel right now." He straightened his robe and embraced Domingo. "Fear not. May God smooth your way straight to your brother."

Domingo sped homeward, his thoughts on those who waited for him and on Père's news—*la Corbeille* had fallen into the hands of *la Résistance*. Ahead on the path, a crow flew from a rooftop to the top of a dead pine, but Domingo ignored its hoarse call.

Kate stiffened when the heavy wooden door swung open admitting a man with a pack. Late afternoon sun highlighted his thick dark curls as he hesitated mid-stride. Adjusting to the sudden brightness, Kate swallowed down her fear, but Madame Ibarra lurched forward.

"Thought the Gestapo had come calling, did you?" Domingo's deep chuckle overtook the house. His mother scurried to the stove as he lowered his pack to the floor and knelt to retrieve something.

His strong arms and broad shoulders incited a hunger beyond Kate's comprehension, but she willed her hammering heart calm. Perhaps he brought news of *l'invasion*.

Domingo pulled out an envelope bathed in his scent, a soothing mix of leather, sheep's wool and homemade lavender soap. He must have stopped to wash at the pump.

"*Voila, Mademoiselle Ibarra,* your new identity card and papers."

"*Merci.* This will be my third. I may not be making vital deliveries, but I might set a record for the number of names I've claimed."

"Keep your card here with Maman's." Domingo gestured to a small crock on a shelf. His grin half-mocked her. "No self-respecting shepherdess would carry her identity card out into the fields. The dog knows who you are by now, even if the sheep go their stubborn ways."

Ink and some other indistinct smell wafted as Kate read her new information. "You and Gabirel are my brothers, and I have lived here in Lot my whole life?" She stifled a concern. The Occidental language might present a problem, although its rhythms had already become familiar.

Domingo hurried to Maman, who manhandled a skillet half her size. He carried the food to the table, and they gathered around him. Over a plate of potatoes and turnips, he explained the situation to Mrs. Ibarra, whose nods and glances toward Kate revealed her comprehension

"You have an extra daughter, Maman. Père Gaspard said if anyone asks about her, you must say she had a difficult birth and has always been slow, almost an imbecile. That way, they won't expect her to speak."

Mrs. Ibarra touched Kate's hand in acceptance, and Kate flashed Domingo a sarcastic smile. "*Merci* again."

His shrug rendered him innocent.

"Your priest made this card?"

"Père Gaspard even forges baptismal records—he's a demon for the cause." Domingo wolfed down a chunk of ham and gave Kate a smug look. "Believe me, the imbecile part was his idea."

Kate deposited her new card in the crock while Mrs. Ibarra filled the breadbasket and traced Domingo's shoulder with her knotty forefinger. Her obvious maternal love heated the backs of Kate's eyes. How many times had this woman watched him fill a canteen with hot milk and shove bread and cheese into his pack in gathering evening shadows, knowing he might not return?

After Domingo rose to go, he unashamedly immersed himself in Maman's embrace, and Kate conjectured. *What would it be like to grow up in this close home? Everyone would share familiar objects, the stove, table, baskets, plates and spices. These everyday things would spell home, like the beliefs merging with the blood in your veins.*

"I will bring Gabirel back soon." Over Maman's slight shoulders, Domingo questioned Kate with his heavy brows. *Are you ready for this responsibility?*

"We'll manage, Maman and I. The sheep will be upset with this turn of events, but I hope you find Gabirel right away."

Domingo blinked agreement and shouldered his pack. Hand on the ancient doorjamb, he twisted back and lifted his chin for Kate to follow him out. On the way to the barn, he lowered his voice so much, she strained to hear.

"*La Corbeille* has been captured."

"*Good*—I was afraid he might be that man in the village near Madame Chalomet."

"Perhaps that was him, but now he will be executed. He passed for one of the Clermont-Ferrand circuit for far too long, under the name Eugene."

Disbelief razed Kate. "Eugene? No—"

"You knew him?"

"He was our radio operator—our operator trusted him."

Domingo pulled in his upper lip. "The time for trusting is past. Take great care. Believe only Maman and Edorta while I am gone." He led the way between the barn and the sheep pen.

In the barn's north shadow out of sight from the house, and cool in spite of the growing summer heat, he touched Kate's arm. Then he drew her under the wide overhang. Eastern clouds reflected traces of sunset's glory, deep pink and lavender and gold.

"Katarin." The huskiness in his voice ignited fireworks inside her. His "*Merci*" brushed her cheek, but breathlessness halted her response.

He raised his eyes to *le Ségala* and squared his shoulders, as if summoning strength for his mission. Then, in one distinct motion, he made the sign of the Cross over her, set his jaw, and headed across the pasture.

Atop the rise, he turned with a half-salute. The acknowledgement quickened Kate's heartbeat and tiptoed shivers down her shoulders as Domingo loped away into a distant dot.

"*Allez avec Dieu.*" Her sigh echoed the benediction he bestowed on her nearly six months ago when she arrived in France. Now she knew how far he'd already traveled that winter night when he nursed her bruised ankle so patiently and carried her to the safety of that nondescript haystack.

So much had happened since then. She'd seen so many places and met so many people she'd never see again. That made her think of Eugene and brought a tremble. She'd delivered messages right into his hands. How could he possibly be a traitor?

The last time she saw him, nothing seemed amiss. All she remembered was his weariness, and attributed it to working all night. Confident he'd communicate her deliveries to London, she'd returned to town. To think he'd also shared those messages with the enemy made her cringe.

The rugged face of the Nazi soldier who accosted her that day with Celeste came to mind. Eugene cooperated with men like him, with the Gestapo. Between disbelief and fury, Kate struggled to contain these ambivalent thoughts in her head.

Rendered gray by fading light, the spring green countryside bade her linger outside. Toward the pasture, she considered the possible effects of Eugene's betrayal. How many lives did he endanger? An all-too familiar helpless feeling descended over her.

The sheepfold lay quiet, the animals' distinct odor drifting her way on an evening breeze. She circled back, and the Ibarra's hand-laid stone house, along with its inhabitants, captured her thoughts again.

A vast ache crept under her collarbone. Domingo's family nurtured him here. Every niche and cranny, every inch of pastureland meant home to him. No matter where he went, this place awaited his return.

With the first rising star, Kate considered afresh how close she held him. Before she passed under the archway into the house, she sought a view of the distant heights, and her prayer curved back to her in the growing darkness. Praying was all she could do, but oddly, it seemed enough.

"Keep him safe—oh please do bring him back."

Chapter Thirty-one

"**D**o you hear anything from your husband?"

Mrs. T's inquiry sent Addie on a mental search of her recent behavior. She'd tried to act normal since hearing about Harold, but tonight at a fundraiser, she got teary-eyed. She'd have been fine if someone hadn't recited *In Flanders Fields*.

> *In Flanders fields the poppies blow*
> *Between the crosses, row on row,*
> *That mark our place; and in the sky*
> *The larks, still bravely singing, fly*
> *Scarce heard amid the guns below.*

The next two verses were lost on her. The poem's cadence and the forlorn image it created drew Addie into contemplation. No white cross for Harold, and no poppies—and most signifant to him, no revenge or glory.

Mrs. T must have noticed. But, dignified British woman that she was, she only clutched her hankie tighter. Somehow, Addie made it through the rest of the evening, and now they walked home together.

Almost two weeks had passed since Charles broke the news of Harold's death, and Addie's shock had turned to quiet acceptance interspersed with relief. No more worrying or wondering what Harold would do next, but how to explain that to Mrs. T?

"No. You know our marriage wasn't happy, right?"

"Yes, but I—" Mrs. T glanced toward the other side of the street,

where a constable checked office doors for the night. "That poem has always touched me too."

Addie couldn't help but smile to herself. Mrs. T had good intentions of a heart-to-heart talk, but her discomfort led her to change the subject.

If only she could tell her about Harold's accident, but that was impossible. Still, there must be a way to communicate the way she felt. After a period of quiet, interspersed with the roving RAF strobe that lighted their path every few minutes, Adide plunged in.

"I have a feeling Harold—" She started again. "Have you ever had a premonition, ma'am?"

"Why I—once, I believe I did. The last time I expected a baby, a terrible sensation overcame me one day, as if I knew. I felt guilty even *thinking* the worst—but I knew the truth. Our child's heart had stopped beating. The Colonel scorned my mention of this. He would have none of it—grew quite agitated with me, in fact. But the doctor confirmed my suspicion."

"That's exactly what I mean. I've had some similar feelings about Harold."

"Oh, my. Just yesterday one of my bandage ladies said she'd heard rumors of accidents during the preparations here. I suppose with all these thousands of soldiers mixed together on our little island, such things are bound to occur."

"I'm sure there have been many. But you see, my relationship with Harold has been so strained, he didn't even list me as his next of kin. He's written me only once since he deployed, and that was to make demands. We never were—close, to be honest. I'm sure that sounds strange, but it's true."

"Strange? Oh no, my dear. Every marriage has its challenges, and I've friends who for all practical purposes only put on a show of being married." Her pause led her close to more disclosure.

"With all his absences, the Colonel and I—" They turned onto her street, and Mrs. T shrugged. "It's all in the past now. I guess I can say we did the best we could."

"I can say that, too. And at least the experience taught me to stand up for myself. As a good friend back home told me one day, 'No one can do that for you.'"

"Halt!" A figure in a World War I uniform darted into their pathway. "Out on a jaunt, ladies? Haven't you heard the warnings?"

"Archibald Kramer, is that you?"

"Indeed it is, Mrs. Tenney. Sorry to startle you, but they're all set to go across down at the coast, so we've been put on high alert."

He gestured to a patch of stars peeking above the clouds. "See there? The weather's breakin' up. In a few hours they'll be shipping out. My cousin sent word—he cooks for 'em down there, and they've got orders to feed the boys a good breakfast 'fore they take off. The Huns won't take this lightly, so you'll be out patrolling for incendiaries the next few nights, I warrant."

"You mean—you mean the—" Mrs. T poked her head toward him and whispered, "The invasion has begun?"

He tightened his lips, but failed to stifle an excited chuckle. "That's it, ma'am. Tomorrow's the day. This time it's for certain— we're ringin' in the end of this blighter war. Well then, a good night to you."

When they entered the house, Mrs. T yawned. "I'm going right up to bed, in case he's right and we get called out in a few hours."

"You don't believe Mr. Kramer?"

"I do, but with reservations. He told me this same story once before."

Weariness stalked Addie but not as much as restlessness. She changed into her nightgown and robe and wandered back down-stairs. Meandering through the rooms did little to satisfy her, so she slipped out into the courtyard.

A heady honeysuckle scent wafted the cool night air, and she fingered the soft blossoms. What a gift this space was, a smidgeon of her Iowa yard in the middle of this huge city. But the honeysuckle took her straight back home. Walking around the farmyard, even when the temperature turned bitterly cold, had always brought her serenity.

She hadn't spent any time out here since the day Charles broke the news about Harold, and she needed to. Over there in the corner, maybe she could pull out that weathered trellis and find some bright pansies to plant, and halfway up the other side, perhaps she might fill a large pot with petunias for the summer months.

Being out here helped her breathe more easily, even though the mesmerizing effect of *Flanders Fields* still lingered. Memorizing the poem in Mrs. Morfordson's senior English class had been simple—she and Kate recited it to each other several times the evening before and discussed its meaning. But back then, they had no idea how the sentiments it evoked might one day affect them.

With Harold no longer here, her new sense of peacefulness increased day by day. Before, she'd never have come out here like this in the dark of night. Just as she gave thanks, footsteps sounded on the walk outside the courtyard. No need to panic now, she told herself. Probably that home guard making his rounds.

But then the gate creaked open, and she recognized Charles coming her way. He took off his hat. "I thought I might find you out here, garden girl."

"I'm too restless to sleep. One of the home guard told us the invasion is underway. Have you heard?"

"That's what I came to tell you. I can't sleep either and thought a long walk would do me good. We're in good company, though—half the city is awake." Charles paused. "Would you mind if I sat down?"

"Oh, no, please do. I guess I know only enough about the invasion to make me nervous."

"Um—I know what you mean. I know way too much. Everyone agrees the Allies must invade, and now the decision's been made. We've given General Eisenhower responsibility, so there's no use second-guessing."

"But I imagine with your background, you still wonder?"

"Exactly."

"And you'd like to take part in the invasion?"

"Absolutely. However, I've had time to reconcile myself to the facts. Isn't that what a great deal of life comes down to, accepting things as they are, not as one wishes they might be?"

Charles quieted when someone came up the street and walked on. Once again, Addie relaxed in his friendly companionship. The steps receded, and he patted her hand. "Well then, I ought to be going, or neither of us will get any sleep at all this night."

"I'm glad you came. Now I think I'll be able to drift off. Talking with you always helps."

They walked to the back door, and Charles gave her a salute. "See you in the morning, Addie Bledsoe."

She half-opened the door to watch him go. Then, a few steps away, he turned back, his forehead a maze of wrinkles. "I came because I wanted you to know about the invasion, but I must admit, my primary motive was to see you."

She reached for his hands and he wrapped his arms around her. The strobe lights passed over, reflecting fiery emotion in his eyes.

"It seemed important to share this pivotal event with you." He drew her closer and whispered in her ear. "I want to share every event with you, dear. Every single event for the rest of our lives."

She pulled back to see his eyes misting. Her voice failed her, but she stood on tiptoe, and his lips met hers. Such tenderness ran through her, she swayed, but his promise fortified her.

"Whatever lies ahead, dear girl, we shall face it together."

Purple and lavender violets, tiny white, daisy-like blossoms, wild periwinkle iris, and some yellow flower buttons sprinkled the expanse. Kate bent to pick a few. If Addie were here, she would uproot some to nurture in the clay soil of Mrs. Tenney's courtyard.

It seemed strange to consider that far-away city world now, in the midst of such pressing danger. But if Kate let her imagination go, she could visualize Waffen SS troops closing in, so she focused on memories, following her training instructor's advice.

Lead your thoughts instead of letting them lead you. If this vagabond life taught her nothing else, she'd become less prone to monitor events into acceptable mental bins to ruminate over during the night.

Over on the road, a lorry passed. Weeks ago, Domingo told her about the Nazi's constant requisitions. "Every week, we place our share by the roadside for a lorry to gather—meat, milk, and produce. But local Maquisards are loath to feed the enemy.

Often, they lock up the driver, pick up the Figeac grain merchant's employee and deliver the supplies to the *Résistance*. Later they return, free the Vichy driver and the merchant reports the loss to the gendarmes as a burglary."

That day, Domingo had stood arms-akimbo, eyes sparkling, black waves swarming his ears. "We fight back however we can."

She allowed a moment to contemplate his image, then gave herself to her book until a figure approached from the opposite direction—the same man who came earlier and led the sheep away. *Le Chien* read his hand signals and complied. Now, two hours later, the flock re-entered its normal pasture just as Madame Ibarra hurried from the house, basket in hand.

"You must be hungry."

"*Merci.* Why did that man take the flock away earlier today?"

Mrs. Ibarra lifted her shoulders. "I ask no questions. He watches out for us when Domingo is gone." Her smile caught Kate off-guard. "He treated you like one of us?"

"I think so, yes."

She headed back, so under a chestnut sapling, Kate munched the basket's contents—a small loaf of dark bread, a cheese chunk, dried apples, and water. Along with the food, she chewed Madame Ibarra's comment.

... like one of us. With Alexandre, Aunt Alvira, her baby, and Monsieur Le Blanc passed from this world, could she claim oneness with anyone on earth? Addie, yes. Addie—her dearest friend, her adopted sister.

Wispy clouds floated above, and Kate spent the afternoon exploring cave-like indentations in a rock formation at the far

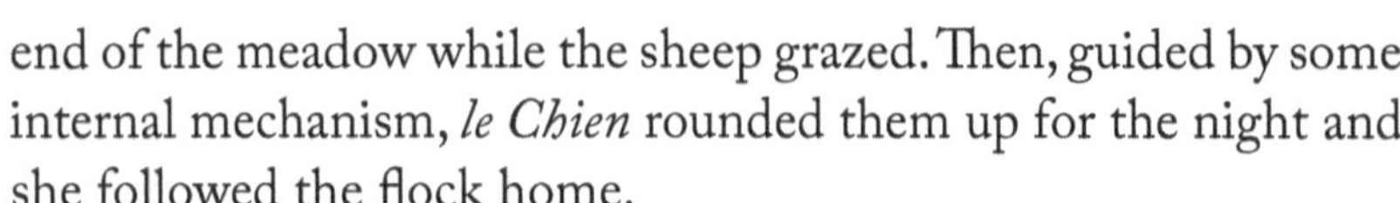

end of the meadow while the sheep grazed. Then, guided by some internal mechanism, *le Chien* rounded them up for the night and she followed the flock home.

Inundated by the dusty grain scent inside the heavy barn door under massive rafters fitted into thick stonework, a gentle, wordless sensation enveloped her like Aunt Alvina's country church liturgy so long ago. Even with the Gestapo so near and *l'Invasion* at hand, this sudden feeling of safety caressed her and remained throughout the evening.

In the night when she rose to feed the fire, a muffled voice sounded outside. She wrapped her blanket over her nightgown, unbarred the door, and peered out. Even in this world of black eyes, she would know these anywhere. They claimed her imagination as a younger version of Domingo whisked in and hurried toward Madame Ibarra's bedroom.

Behind him, Domingo brought night's freshness mingled with the old leather smell of his pack. Kate stepped back as he stooped to drop it on the wooden floor.

"You found him?"

"*Oui.*" The syllable drifted as Domingo lighted the lantern and set it on the table. His presence filled the small space, like a wild animal abruptly enclosed.

Madame Ibarra and Gabirel came forth arm in arm from the back of the house, and she set to work at the stove. Nothing but fresh hot porridge would do for this celebration. She seasoned the concoction with sweet spices and dried grapes from last fall's harvest. Heads together, the four of them ate, with Kate following the conversation as best she could.

"Finally, *l'Invasion* is upon us." Unable to mask his weariness, the fervor in Domingo's tone lessened into a sigh.

"You knew this on the trail, but kept it from me?" Gabirel's tone produced no response from Domingo.

"Things will change fast now. All the more reason to remain steadfast here."

His eyes took Kate in, communicating he had more to say, but not here, not now. Madame Ibarra broke into a pronouncement in Euskara that muffled Gabirel's outburst and reddened his already ruddy cheeks. Tense silence filled the room as everyone ate.

Then Domingo shifted in his chair. "I will do the chores." Kate finished her porridge and pulled on her milking trousers as Domingo took his mother's hands.

"Tonight I must leave again, Maman."

"Ah. Then before you go, we feast. Why let others enjoy all of our *cochons*?"

Domingo nursed his chin stubble while Kate buckled her chore boots. Clearly, everyone waited on his word, but he directed his words to his brother.

"Take your rest today, Gabirel." Not needing to be told twice, Gabirel retreated to the loft.

Madame Ibarra cleared the dishes as, with a lift of his chin, Domingo beckoned Kate outside. He waited for her on the stoop, and she fell in step.

"An operator radioed your location to London and received word back." He handed her a folded paper.

"You know what it says?"

He nodded.

"Tell me."

"The Gabaudet organizer visited the *Résistance* camp, so I spoke with him. He sent you a present." He waved behind him with a sideways grin. "A transmitter. Now you have a full-time job."

A hair of light brightened the east as he continued. "Danger is high, with the Gestapo on alert, and the heightened transmissions during *l'Invasion*. The organizer says you must move often."

"And you?"

"Missions every night." He dropped his voice to a whisper. "Decazeville for one."

"Isn't that where the *Maquis* scares Gestapo agents away? That's a day from here!"

"They gave me a motorbike." Domingo clicked his tongue for a cow to come. "And now, we must hide the transmitter."

"Here? Your mother was so brave when the Germans came, but—" His face blanched. "They were here?"

"Yesterday."

Domingo's cheek muscle went into a spasm, and Kate's eyes stung. He'd so longed for his ancestral home to avoid the worst of the war, but even that hope was being dashed.

He started filling a pail with milk, so Kate tied a nanny goat to a stall divider and set to work. In the early-morning stillness, they each might have milked alone, yet Kate had plenty to consider. A radio—now she could make a contribution. And she'd regained contact with London. Headquarters must wonder about her, but maybe she'd ended up in the right place to make a difference, after all.

The cow's oily, warm scent rose when Domingo ruffed its back on the way out. Birds stirred and twittered as he approached the house. Kate followed, carefully toting her pail. Then he halted in the yard and surprised her with more information.

"On the twenty-fourth, the *Résistance* attacked the Bussy plant, the twenty-fifth, Tarbes, and the twenty-sixth, a hydroelectric station. We can expect severe reprisals until the Allies work this far south."

He relayed this information in a low whisper. Then, within hearing of the iron kettle's burbles from the cook stove, he stooped toward her and tightened his tone even more.

"Keep a sharp eye for danger. His jaw moved with emotion. "You must not be found." He rubbed his fingers with his thumb, and Kate's breathing went shallow at the grim certainty lacing his words.

"For us, the war has only begun." His slight pressure on her shoulder ignited lightning all the way to Kate's toes.

"There is so much I must say to you, yet everything must wait, Katarin, for the cause. You understand?"

"I think so. Yes."

"Today you will meet Père Gaspard, who will help us locate safe places for your transmissions while I am gone." Domingo's eyes glinted with seriousness. "I would trust this man with my life."

The full meaning of her new position as a radio operator opened up to Kate—she was becoming exactly what Mr. Tenney warned her not to. But as Domingo said, no sacrifice was too much at this point.

"Maman wants to slaughter a pig and feast today, but we must be about our business. I will tell her now."

He took her pail inside as Kate shed her chore clothes and washed her hands. Strange, this war. Overnight, an imbecile milkmaid evolved into a highly trained worker. But Mr. Tenney's warning rang in her ears.

Avoid becoming a wireless operator if you can. The Gestapo continually upgrades their detection devices, and once they locate an operator, there's little hope of escape.

"Sorry, Mr. T, but I have no choice."

Kate raised her eyes to the highlands, aware of so many risking their lives at this very moment. Whatever danger she might encounter paled in comparison to what the *Résistance* saboteurs, including Domingo, faced.

A sense of purpose fueled her, as it did him and countless others. Hemmed in by history, confronting that danger had become their only alternative.

About the Author

Words have always been comfort food for Gail Kittleson. After instructing expository writing and English as a Second Language, she began writing seriously. Intrigued by the World War II era, Gail creates historical fiction from her northern Iowa home and also facilitates writing workshops/retreats.

She and her husband, a retired Army chaplain, enjoy grandchildren and in winter, Arizona's Mogollon Rim Country. You can count on Gail's protagonists to ask honest questions, act with integrity, grow in faith, and face hardships with spunk.

Visit Gail online at: GailKittleson.com

Also available from

WordCrafts Press

The Pruning
  by Jan Cline

Angela's Treasures
  by Marian Rizzo

Plague
  by Marian Rizzo

Not By Sight
  by Elizabeth Jacobson

Grace Extended
  by Paula K. Parker

www.WordCrafts.net